MIKE STARED AT HER, WEIGHING THE ODDS, MENTALLY CALCULATING DISTANCES. . . .

Mary shook her head. "No, don't. Don't even think about trying it. It only works on television, and on television the bullets aren't real, and the baddies can't shoot straight." She waved the gun. "These are real. And I've had lots of practice."

He gave her a contemptuous smile. "So you're a very dangerous lady. I've got nothing to say."

"You will have. First, who the hell are you? Who are you working for?"

She stepped forward, extending the hand that held the gun until the muzzle was a yard from his groin.

"Come on, Mary," he said hoarsely. "You can't shoot me. Not me."

Her extraordinary eyes burned back into his, unblinking. Another second passed before she spoke.

"Try me, Michael." Her voice was a diamond-edged whisper.

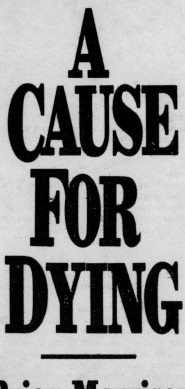

A CAUSE FOR DYING

Brian Morrison

HarperPaperbacks
A Division of HarperCollinsPublishers

This is a work of fiction. The characters, incidents, and dialogues are products of the author's imagination and are not to be construed as real. Any resemblance to actual events or persons, living or dead, is entirely coincidental.

HarperPaperbacks *A Division of* HarperCollins*Publishers*
10 East 53rd Street, New York, N.Y. 10022

A hardcover edition of this book was published in 1991 in Great Britain by HarperCollins*Publishers*.

Cover illustration by Jeffrey Terreson

First HarperPaperbacks printing: November 1992

Printed in the United States of America

HarperPaperbacks and colophon are trademarks of HarperCollins*Publishers*

10 9 8 7 6 5 4 3 2 1

CURVING BANDS OF SLEET SWEPT THE STREET, DRIVEN ON the cutting wind. Shoppers hurried on, heads down, murmuring to themselves at the filthy weather. A group of football supporters advanced along the pavement. They came arm-in-arm, their heads thrown back, bawling a song. Their parkas hung open over tee-shirts bearing the name of their club across the chest, and their short hair stood in dishevelled spikes. The only other people who seemed oblivious to the freezing rain were a woman in her thirties and the small boy whose hand she held.

The boy skipped along beside the woman, laughing as he stamped tiny green wellingtons gleefully in the dirty puddles. Their clothes, brightly colored ski-gear, contrasted with the muddy shades of grey and khaki of the anoraks and raincoats around them. The woman laughed down at the boy. Her blonde hair, darkened by the rain to the color of old pine, whipped at her face, but she made no attempt to control it, giving all her attention to her son. Tugging him close to her to avoid the group of louts, she turned into a narrow side-street. Laughing out loud at something the boy said, she gave him a mock clip on the side of the head and ushered him, still skipping, into a poorly-lit shop.

At the end of the street the pylons with their banks of floodlights stood out against the slate sky. The lights would not be switched on for almost two hours. There was plenty of time for the fans to do a lot more drinking. On the corner three more supporters stood in the shelter of a pub doorway, drinking and talking. As they talked they kept their eyes on the street, as though on the look-out for trouble.

The traffic on the main road rolled slowly through curb-deep puddles and filthy water lapped across the wide pavements, adding to the slimy mulch of litter beneath the feet of the shoppers. In the narrowed side-streets, cars moved at walking pace as shoppers and supporters competed for parking slots. Forty yards down, almost opposite the first turnstile, a red Ford Escort rolled to a halt, blocking the traffic behind it. A young man sprang from the rear seat and ran to a battered Jaguar parked at the roadside. He unlocked it with keys he held ready and slipped into the driving-seat. It took him half a dozen maneuvers to get the big car out of the tight space. As he drove away the Escort slotted into the empty space. It was two or three minutes before three men got out of the car and began walking briskly away toward the corner.

There was a sudden quickening of interest from the three supporters in the pub entrance. One of them spoke softly to his companions. They exchanged looks, consternation on their faces. One of the men glanced quickly at his watch and shook his head, as if he were having difficulty believing something; the one who had spoken was looking up and down the street, searching for something and not finding it.

The three men from the Ford were within twenty-five yards of the corner. They, too, were examining the street as they went, casting nervous looks all around them as they hurried toward the junction. The oldest of the men, who walked slightly ahead of the others, swept a glance over the three in the pub doorway. His eyes met those of one of the group. There was a brief, almost imperceptible moment during which their eyes held each other, then both groups were fumbling frantically in their clothes.

The boy came bursting from the doorway of the little shop. The blonde woman came after him, laughing as she struggled to hold under one arm a small antique table, made awkward to carry by a protective wrapping of polythene, while trying to open an umbrella with the other hand. A sudden squall of wind turned the umbrella inside out.

"Tom!" she called from the doorway. "Come here and help Mummy. Hold the table for me."

The boy turned and began to run eagerly back to her, but lost his footing on the wet pavement and fell full-length. With a cry, the woman rushed forward and crouched beside him. Still holding the table she helped him to his feet. His lip quivered, on the verge of tears. She lifted his chin and spoke, smiling. His lip trembled for a moment longer and then he burst into laughter. She laughed with him, too distracted to hear the single, sharp warning shout. The crash of gunfire drowned any further sound. The shooting lasted no more than twenty seconds. When it was over the three men from the Escort lay twisted on the pavement. One of those in the doorway had slid to a sitting position, slumped against the dark green tiled wall. He clutched at his stomach. His companions shouted into the mouthpieces of walkie-talkies.

The blonde woman lay stretched on the wet pavement between them. A rivulet of her blood already reached into the gutter, staining the stream of dirty rain-water that poured into the drain. The boy squatted beside her. His eerie wail rose high over the screams of the horrified shoppers.

CHAPTER

1

MIKE SCANLON STEPPED DOWN FROM THE TRAILER, HIS pale blue eyes screwed up against the blinding light. He was naked except for the unlaced tennis shoes he wore against the stones and the scorpions. He raised the towel he carried in his right hand and rubbed perfunctorily at the scrubby pepper-and-salt hair on his thick chest. A band of slightly raised flesh as wide as a man's finger ran from front to back six inches below his right armpit. A half-dozen smaller puckered marks clustered high on his chest, between the collar bone and the nipple, half concealed by hair. They were old scars, a faintly paler brown beneath his tan. He tossed the towel behind him into the open door of the trailer. There was no need to dry himself properly. The western Egyptian sun would take care of that.

Singing the first couple of lines, all he could remember, of a song that had been a big hit around 1960, he walked easily across the stony ground to another trailer. Beyond it he could see the drooping rotors of a parked helicopter. It had come in with their routine weekly delivery while he had been in the shower. He climbed the steps into the air-conditioned chill of the trailer.

A group of men wearing only shorts or nothing at all, like Mike, crowded around a table, pretending to squabble over a heap of letters and parcels. The helicopter pilot, a tall, lean, darkly tanned man with sunbleached blond hair, stood slightly apart from the group, looking on with detached curiosity, like a man who had just thrown meat into a shark pool. He was naked except for an old grey sock which he wore over his genitals.

"Hi, Hans." Mike greeted the helicopter pilot with a grin, rolling his eyes in pantomime horror at the noisy group at the table. He showed no surprise at Han's attire. It was his usual working gear. What it protected was about the only thing the pilots seemed to give a shit about. He picked up a beer—somebody else's—took a long swig, and stood back to wait as one of the men tore open a package the size of a pillow.

It held a wad of newspapers. Several of the men made a grab for them. One of them, a softly smiling Pakistani, picked up a bundle of *Guardians*.

"Here, Mike." He tossed the papers across. "Your papers. My beer. How about getting one of your own?"

Mike grinned, nodded, surrendered the can, and walked over to the big refrigerator. He took a beer, and carried it over to the steps. Behind him, a wiry, sunscorched man with a stud in one ear and a pronounced Birmingham accent was opening copies of the *Sun* at page three and laying them out on the table. Several others jostled at his shoulder making obscene observations.

"Bunch of fucking animals," Mike called, laughing, as he sorted his papers into date order and settled down to read.

The others were still crowded over the pin-ups when they were silenced by a ghastly noise, a deep-throated bellow of anguish. They fell abruptly silent and turned to where Mike sat on the steps of the trailer. The paper he had been reading had fallen to the ground. His face was contorted, and he stared sightlessly at the strewn pages. With a look at the others the Pakistani walked quickly across the trailer. He crouched beside Mike, and put a hand on his shoulder. His face was close to Mike's.

"What is it, Mike? What the hell's happened? What's wrong?"

Mike pawed at the air, vaguely indicating the paper. He made a noise in his throat, still unable to speak. The other man pushed past him, jumped lightly down to the ground and picked the paper out of the dust. Most of the front page was taken up with a report of an IRA attempt to plant a car-bomb outside a football ground. He looked at Mike, frowning.

"I don't understand, Mike. What is it?" He spoke very gently.

Mike's face worked as he tried to speak. His cheeks were wet with tears. He batted a hand at an inset box on the front page. The Pakistani looked at it more closely.

"Oh, God." His gaze returned to Mike's face. "You knew her?"

Mike stared at him, as though the question amazed him. "It's Allix." He said it flatly, as though he expected it to mean something without any further explanation. The other man went on looking at him. "Allix," Mike repeated, more emphatically. He blinked at the man. "You don't understand, Saïd—Allix. She's my fiancée." His shoulders heaved as fresh tears came. "Oh, Christ! *Was* my fiancée! We were going to be married in a couple of months."

"Oh." The other man sank on to the steps next to Mike. He put an arm around his shoulders. "Oh, my good God." He was almost whispering.

Mike's head had dropped into his hands. Tears ran

between the knuckly fingers and fell into the dust. "The fuckers! The bastards! The fucking brainless, useless murderous bastards!"

Saïd glanced behind him at the other men, who stood frozen around the table, watching silently. He nodded to one of them to bring a drink. The man grabbed a brandy bottle from on top of the refrigerator, slopped a couple of inches into a glass and rushed across to them. The Pakistani snatched it and pushed it under Mike's face.

"Here. Drink this. It'll help."

Mike looked blankly from the glass to the face of the other man, as though in his grief he did not recognize either of them. Tears spilled in an unbroken stream down his battered, boxer's face. "You don't understand, Saïd. We were going to get married. She was *pregnant*. She was going to have my child!"

"Another fifteen minutes, Mike, we'll be there." As he shouted over the din of the rotor, Hans glanced across at the seat beside him. Mike sat staring through the windscreen at the tan haze ahead that told them they were approaching Cairo. He nursed a canvas hold-all on his knees. He lifted a brandy bottle to his lips and tilted it, then took it away and stared at it uncomprehendingly. It seemed to dawn on him only slowly that it was empty. The pilot tried again. "What are you going to do?"

Mike looked around abruptly, stared at Hans for a moment and then shrugged. "First, get to a phone. Call Allix's parents. Talk to Tom, if they'll let me." He fell silent again.

A few minutes later the helicopter dropped on to the pad amid a cluster of dilapidated prefabricated buildings on the dusty fringe of Cairo airport. Mike stepped stiffly down on to the tarmac. He was not sure if he was drunk or sober. He had a curious, unreal feeling, as though he were seeing the world from behind glass.

Hans came around the front of the machine carrying Mike's jacket. He handed it to him. Mike pulled it on automatically and slung the flight bag over his shoulder.

"You okay? Anything you want me to do? Want a ride to the office?"

Mike looked at him and shook his head. "Fine. Thanks, Hans. There's no point going to the office. If you can just drop me off at the main building, I can phone from there."

The other man shrugged and smiled and put a hand on Mike's shoulder. "Sure. Whatever you want. Just let me get some clothes on." He pulled off the sock and dragged a pair of filthy shorts from behind the seats. Putting a hand back on Mike's shoulder he began moving toward a dirty Land Rover. "Come on. I'll have you there in five minutes."

Like everything else in Cairo, the airport was thronged with people. Hans propelled Mike roughly through the mêlée toward the telephone office, both of them a head taller than the crowd. He pushed Mike up to the counter.

"Got the number?" Mike looked vague. "Her parents. The people you want to call."

Mike shook his head like a boxer shaking off a punch. His eyes came into focus. "Ah, yeah. Sure." He reached into an inside pocket and pulled out the scuffed notebook that had served him as a wallet for the last fifteen years or so. Several old visiting cards fell to the floor. Hans stooped and collected them and pushed them into Mike's pocket as he thumbed through the book. "Here." He scrawled a number on to a form the desk clerk proffered. The clerk mumbled something and waved an arm generously toward a row of seats. They were all full. People sat on suitcases and on bundles. Some lay on the floor, apparently asleep. Mike and Hans found a corner and wedged themselves between two figures dozing with their heads on their chests; they looked as though they had been there for a long time. Hans grimaced at Mike, who managed a faint smile.

"Want a drink?" asked Hans.

Mike nodded. Hans looked around and caught the eye of a fat-faced man in a badly fitting lightweight suit and scuffed basketwork shoes who hovered by the door. The man hurried over, already smiling ingratiatingly. Hans raised one hip and pulled some money from his back pocket. He counted out a few notes and handed them to the Egyptian. "A bottle of Remy Martin." He raised an eyebrow to Mike as he spoke. Mike nodded. The man flexed his knees in something like a curtsy and hurried away. Through the office window they saw him weave his way among the crowd to the passenger-arrivals door. With a nod to the policeman barring the way, he slipped out of sight into the customs area.

He was back in less than ten minutes. As he passed through the barrier his hand brushed the policeman's. The policeman smiled and pocketed the tip without looking down. Hans paid off the runner, opened the bottle and passed it silently to Mike.

The bottle was two-thirds empty before the counter clerk called Mike's name and pointed to a booth. Watched by Hans he entered the booth, walking with the slightly exaggerated purposefulness of a man consciously holding his liquor.

"Hello?"

The voice was amazingly clear. The shrill, condescending voice with its bogus vowels could have been coming from the next room.

"Mrs. Lorimer?"

"Er, yes. This is the Lorimer household. Who's speaking, please?"

Even in his dazed state of mind he had to choke back a snort. The "Lorimer household!" A piece of speculative building in Kingston-upon-Thames! Detached, though, as they never failed to remind you. Separated from its identical neighbor by a gap hardly wide enough for a cat to squeeze through.

"Mrs. Lorimer, it's me, Mike. Mike Scanlon."

There was a pause. "Oh, yes. Mr. Scanlon. Er, Mike." The vowels had grown as brittle as icicles. He raised an eyebrow. There had always been an unspoken mutual loathing between them, but some extra embarrassment was making her flounder. "Er, How are you?" She did not wait to learn. "I'll get my husband," she said, hurriedly, and left him hanging.

Over the humming of the line he could hear faint sounds of muffled conversation. He waited for several seconds, trying to keep his irritation in check. She was a stupid, snobbish little woman with no friends, who had devoted her life to finding additional grounds for believing herself superior. Her husband was her enthusiastic ally. He had worked in a bank all his life. Out of kindness they had made him manager of one of their most dead-beat branches just before he retired. The idea had been to help him to a decent pension. He had acted ever since as though he had been the head of the Bundesbank. He came on the line, using the voice he had developed for refusing people loans.

"Michael?"

"Yeah, Mr. Lorimer. I'm calling from Cairo airport. I've only just found out the news. How are you? How's Mrs. Lorimer taking things?"

"It's very hard, Michael, very hard. We're bearing it as best we can."

Mike shook his head and grimaced. The man still sounded as if he were turning Mike down for a mortgage. "And Tom?" Tom was the only one of the three who really interested him. "How is he? Is he okay? I mean, well, is he, well, shit, is he *all right*?" He felt stupid. How all right could a six-year-old feel when he had just seen his mother shot?

"Well, of course, it's hit Tom hard, Michael. But he's a very brave lad. He's bearing up. Mrs. Lorimer has been wonderful."

Mike bit back his anger. He knew well enough there were no words adequate for the situation, but this man sounded as though he were reading mottoes from Christmas crackers. "Look, Mr. Lorimer, as I told you, I'm in Cairo. At the airport. I'll get the first plane back. When's, ah, when's Allix, er—" Grief flooded up in him, choking off his words. He palmed a tear off his cheekbone. "Mr. Lorimer, when's the funeral?"

There was a pause. It grew longer. He could almost hear the man writhe. Anger and grief knotted in his chest. He knew what the man was going to say.

"Er, our daughter was buried yesterday, Michael. We thought it was best for Tom. We . . ."

Hans scrambled to his feet and rushed toward Mike as he walked blindly from the booth. He grabbed Mike's arm hard with one hand and threw his other arm, still holding the bottle, around his shoulders. As the booth door swung closed he heard the faint sound of a voice still speaking from the receiver that hung twisting at the end of its wire.

"Jesus Christ, Mike! What's happened now? You're as white as a fucking sheet."

Mike strode on through the crowd, almost dragging Hans along. Hans broke away to throw some money at the protesting desk clerk and hurried to rejoin him. He moved in front of him, forcing him to stop. "For Christ's sake, what's going fucking on?" Like a lot of Dutchmen who spoke virtually perfect English, Hans sometimes got his swearing slightly misplaced. "Tell me. Can I help?"

Mike stared at him, his eyes focusing only slowly. When he spoke his voice was a rasp. "Her parents.

Those two vicious little shits. They didn't wait for me, didn't even try to get in touch with me. They've gone ahead and buried her."

Hans stared back at him. He let out his breath in a long sound just under a whistle. Finally he held out the bottle. "Want this?"

Mike nodded and drank off a long swallow.

"What are you going to do?"

Mike shook his head. "I don't know. Get out of here, back to Europe. The first plane out of here. I need to think."

"Oh, shit!" Mike's voice was muffled. He lay with his face buried deep in a pillow. With an effort he turned his head. Sun streamed into the room, making him wince. He shut his eyes again. It was hot as hell. With another groan he rolled over and pushed back the bedclothes. He was fully dressed except for one shoe. His mouth felt as though it were coated with lint. He pushed himself up from the bed and crossed unsteadily to a mirror over the dressing-table. His appearance jolted him. His clothes were filthy, and a four-day growth covered his throat and jaw. A graze on his forehead was caked in congealed blood. He looked as though he had been sleeping rough for a week. Or maybe not sleeping at all.

He started throwing off clothes and moved to the bathroom. His other shoe lay in the middle of the floor. He made to take off his watch. He was not wearing one. Before he finished undressing he was sick twice. He turned on the shower at its fullest power and as hot as he could bear it, and let himself slide down the wall to a squatting position. He stayed like that for more than a quarter of an hour, trying to get some order back into his thoughts. It did not help much. His mind was a blank from the time he had said goodbye to Hans and boarded the plane. He knew nothing about the intervening period, except that it had not even begun to dull the pain and rage that burned inside him.

He walked back into the bedroom and pulled the curtain aside. He thought he recognized the view. He turned back to the room, sat down on the bed, and picked up an embossed book of matches from the floor where he must have knocked it. He examined it briefly and grunted agreement with himself. He was in Athens, the Hilton hotel. He glanced at the clock set into the bedside table. It showed three o'clock. Another question needed answering. He called reception.

"What day is it?"

"Sir?"

"What day. Of the week?"

"Thursday, sir."

"Fucking hell!"

"Sir?"

"When did I check in?"

"This morning, sir." There was a pause. "At four-thirty."

Mike looked around the room. There was no sign of the hold-all. "Didn't I have any baggage?"

Another pause. Mike heard muffled conversation. "No, sir."

"And you let me in? In my state?"

"My colleague knew you, Mr. Scanlon."

"Thank him for me. He's very understanding."

"Our pleasure, Mr. Scanlon. You had your credit cards. He had you sign a slip."

Mike smiled wryly at the man's deadpan courtesy, automatically patting a pocket to check that he really did still have the old notebook which held his credit cards. "Get a boy to bring me up some shaving-gear, toothpaste and a toothbrush, will you." His eyes fell on the clothes on the floor. "Oh, and a shirt. Forty-two collar."

* * *

An hour later, shaved and clean, his suit still faintly damp from the pressing and sponging it had had from the hotel valet service, Mike walked out of the front doors. He set off in the direction of the center of the city, walking fast. He needed the exercise to clear his head and get his thoughts back into order. As he walked images of Allix formed pell-mell in his mind.

It was almost a year since he had met her. In London, between contracts, he had run into someone he had known as a teenager in Birmingham. Mike had been buying some Bulgarian red in the wine section of the Cromwell Road Sainsbury's. The other man had been filling a trolley with champagne. He had acquired a new accent to match his new tastes, a braying impersonation of an upper-class drawl. He had invited Mike to a party.

The flat turned out to be in one of the squares where the Earls Court Road is becoming Kensington. The old acquaintance had made money as some kind of dealer in a merchant bank, and the other guests had either made it or were waiting to inherit it. They all spoke in the same accent and at the same volume. It never crossed their minds that what they had to say might not be of interest to everybody else within earshot. Mike had felt out of place and almost instantly bored. His crumpled suit was conspicuous among the wide-shouldered jackets with the cuffs turned back. Not that it bothered him. None of the men had made any effort to speak to him; one look told them he could not do them any good. Two or three of the women had tried a speculative approach, apparently attracted to the beat-up look. Each time it had taken only seconds for his heart to start sinking.

He had been there less than half an hour and was putting down his third champagne glass, preparing to leave, when a new group of three people, two women and a man, entered. A posse of guests set upon them in a gale of bogus endearments. Amid the kissing one of the women, tall and slender with honey-colored hair, hung back at the rear of the group. She let a succession of people plant kisses on her cheeks without losing the hint of reserve she carried about her. As yet another woman swept forward to embrace her she caught Mike's eye. Almost without realizing he was doing it he had picked up another drink and decided to stay a little longer.

It had taken her perhaps five minutes to disentangle herself and make her way over to him. She held out a hand: "Allix de Salobert."

"Mike Scanlon." They shook hands. Mike smiled. "Did I get that name correctly? French aristocracy?"

"You did. De Salobert. It was my husband's family name. Very *minor* aristocracy." She smiled. "Although his parents would turn in their grave to hear me say it. Mine would turn in their his'n'hers Dralon armchairs. To them Philippe was almost a pretender to the French throne."

"Was?" He felt his throat constrict as he said it.

"Uh-huh. Was. He died four years ago. In France. A car accident. A truck ran across the road and hit him head-on."

Mike grimaced. "A drunk?"

She shook her head and gave a quick, bitter smile. "Not by French standards. A bottle of red wine with his lunch. Not what a French truck driver calls a drink. That would be three Pernods, then the wine, and a few brandies as a *digestif*. They regard the wine as *food*." She smiled again, more warmly, and shrugged. "Philippe died instantly. And I'm over it." She cast a quick glance around the room. "Do you know anyone here?"

"Only Patrick. And I only knew him way back when he was just Pat. Am I missing anything?"

She looked at him mischievously and shook her head. "Are you hungry?"

He turned and glanced at the buffet behind him.

"For food. Not for little square things with olives on them."

"Shall we go and eat somewhere?"

He was already putting down his drink. He took her gently by the elbow and began steering her toward the door.

They had walked the few hundred yards to an Italian restaurant in the Brompton Road. By the time they left, with the yawning headwaiter locking the door behind them, they both knew their lives had changed irrevocably. At thirty-seven Mike had only ever known two women he would have felt able to spend his life with. In the last three hours he had discovered one he could no longer live without.

They stopped on the pavement outside the restaurant. He turned to Allix. In the headlong ease of their conversation he had not had to resort to asking her where she lived.

"What now?"

She smiled. "We go home."

"Where's that?"

"For me, Battersea. You?"

"Fulham."

"Where's your car?"

"I don't have a car. I came on the Underground. I was planning to get a cab back."

She raised her hands in mock horror. "Am I falling in love with an environment freak?" She dropped her hands, smiling, and grabbed one of his. "Come on, I'll give you a lift. My car's back at the Square."

They walked slowly back to her car, a tiny Fiat. She climbed briskly into the driving-seat and opened the door for him to fold himself into the seat beside her. It took only a few minutes to reach Mike's house and draw into a space a few yards from his door. She settled back in her seat and turned to him, but she did not switch off the motor, thus answering the question he had been asking himself since they had finished eating. She leaned toward him and kissed him lightly on the mouth.

"Sorry. There's a baby sitter."

He returned her kiss, putting a hand lightly on her shoulder, then sat back against the door, looking at her. "Are you busy tomorrow?"

"With Tom. Are you free in the day? Why don't you come over and meet him?"

He nodded. "What time's breakfast?"

Tom and he had taken to each other from the first moment. He was a bright, lively boy with dark hair and intense dark eyes that Mike guessed were inherited from his father. As soon as breakfast was over he had monopolized Mike. While Allix worked in the kitchen, making occasional comments through the open door, Tom enlisted Mike in a hectic series of jigsaw puzzles, model car races and sessions in which Mike expressed extravagant admiration for Tom's collection of "treasure"—a few foreign coins and some oddly shaped stones. In the late morning the two of them had gone to Battersea Park while Allix went shopping, and Tom had appointed Mike goalkeeper to his center-forward. When Allix opened the door on their return to the flat she had been unable to contain her laughter at Mike, who stood looking ruefully down at his trousers. The tan cord at his knees was caked with mud and grass.

By the time Tom had been put to bed at eight o'clock he and Mike were close friends. Two hours later, with dinner still unfinished on the table, Allix and Mike were lovers.

For three weeks they were together every day. Allix worked in the mornings for a Kensington estate agent. He met her each day at the office and they either returned to one of their homes to make love, or took in an exhibition or a film until it was time to pick up Tom from school. The hours until Tom's bedtime the three of them spent together. At the end of the three weeks, when the time came for Mike to leave again for the Middle East, Tom had been the most inconsolable of the three. In those weeks he had come to love and trust Mike as he would have loved and trusted his own father.

The four months of the contract had been almost intolerable. On his three-day breaks from the desert he had flown from Abu Dhabi to London to spend two days and a night with them before flying straight back again for another stretch of unbearable loneliness. But the spells in the desert camps had offered one advantage: they had given him time to contemplate his good fortune. Mike was an only child. In some families that would have meant being smothered in love. In his own it just seemed like an oversight. His father was too selfish and too often drunk, his mother too cowed and exhausted to have any love to offer. The exhilaration and joy that informed his every waking moment since encountering Allix, the depth of pleasure he took in Tom's trust in him, were quite simply something he had never known before. It was as though she had ignited some unsuspected inner flame in him that was bathing his whole world in a new light.

It was on one of those brief visits that they had decided to try to have a baby. Talking about it late into the night, their only fear had been for Tom's reaction, but when told about it the next day he had leapt at the idea—a new brother or sister *and* Mike as a new father. He liked the idea as much as they did.

The other major decision made that night was that as soon as Allix did get pregnant Mike would find another way to earn a living, a way that would not take him away from home. It was only two weeks ago last Sunday that he had spoken to Allix and found out this contract would be his last. For two joyous, euphoric weeks he had known that she was going to have his baby. And for one week of that time she had been dead.

The thought struck him as a fresh blow, wrenching an involuntary choking noise from his throat. A couple of passersby turned sharply. Their stares brought him abruptly back to the present. The lights of the cafés had come on; evening had fallen without his being conscious of it, and there were more people on the streets now. He became aware that many of them were shooting him strange, guarded glances. He wondered why, though not really caring much. He entered the glass enclosure of a café terrace, sat down in the first empty chair and ordered a brandy. The waiter, too, gave him a strange look. Mechanically, he ran a hand over his face; it came away wet with tears.

He wandered from bar to bar, scarcely aware of the thickening crowd as Athens emerged for its nightly celebration of life. His drinking was no celebration at all. Although he downed a steady stream of Greek brandies he did not get drunk. His thoughts remained focused on the situation ahead of him.

He had no close family; there were still a few cousins around the Birmingham area, but none of them meant a thing to him. He had seen nothing of them since representing his mother at a funeral six or seven years earlier. He had a few close friends, but all of them had families of their own. Nobody, anywhere, needed him. Except Tom. In the few months he had known the boy he had come to see him as his own son. In just a few more weeks Allix and he would have been married. Tom would have *been* his son. And now?

Legally, Allix's parents would be responsible for him. The thought made him exclaim aloud with anger. Images of his times with Tom flooded his mind: their football games; the boy's concentration as he struggled with a jigsaw puzzle; his screams of delight when Mike carried him aloft on his shoulders; a thousand tiny, insignificant things. He felt his throat constrict as he again came close to tears. Under his mother's influence the boy had been full of fun, eager to play and to learn, naturally polite. In the hands of his grandparents it was hard to see how all that would survive. They were a narrow, sanctimonious, dull pair of petty snobs, no substitute for the smart, open, tough, funny, happy woman Allix was. He gulped hard—that Allix *had been*. He put down his glass, only half-emptied, went out into the warm night, and walked quickly to his hotel.

By the time he arrived the sky held the first hint of dawn. His mind was made up—he would return to London and see Allix's parents. He would talk to them, try to find an arrangement that would take account of their daughter's own intentions, an arrangement that would enable him to stay close to Tom, as though he and Allix had been able to marry.

CHAPTER
2

THE TAXI DRIVER LEANED BACK AND SPOKE OVER HIS shoulder.

"Sitwell Gardens, guv'nor. This it?"

Mike was sitting well forward in his seat, holding the grab handle. "Yeah. Number twenty-eight. After the blue Ford." It was a pleasant, leafy street, lined with brick villas; elaborate, faultlessly groomed front gardens separated the houses from the wide pavements. "Right here."

The taxi rolled to a stop. The house opposite stood behind a low brick wall backed by a rhododendron hedge. The double wrought-iron gates bore the words "The Cedars" fashioned in copper-plate script from more wrought-iron. No number. The postman had to work it out for himself. The gates gave on to a sloping concrete drive. The company Cavalier that Allix's father had kept into retirement stood in the open garage, still wet from its twice-weekly shampoo.

Mike stepped out of the taxi. A lace curtain fell two inches back into place. The face at the gap had been unmistakably Mrs. Lorimer's. He smiled to himself; she could have seen him quite well through the curtain, but a born peeper like Mrs. Lorimer needed the extra detail. The cab pulled away, leaving him standing in the middle of the empty road. He paused, facing the house. He was not looking forward to the next hour. It was almost a week since he had returned to London, and it had taken until now, phoning every day, for them to run out of excuses not to see him. He gave a lop-sided grimace and set off for the far pavement.

He was about to ring for a third time when he heard a movement behind the door. It opened about six inches, as though the person behind feared an attacker. The ruddy, wide, rather handsome face of Mr. Lorimer appeared in the gap. Low on his nose he wore the half-moon glasses that he felt fitted his distinguished persona.

"Oh, Michael. It's you." He remembered to smile. He pulled the door wider, half-sheltering behind it. "Come in. It's nice of you to come over."

Mike nodded and gave him a big, friendly smile. The man sounded as if Mike had come to repossess his car. "We'll use the front lounge, Michael, if you don't mind." He indicated a door to Mike's right. "Mrs. Lorimer, er, Muriel, er, sends her love. She hopes you won't mind her not joining us. She's a little under the weather."

Mike shrugged and entered the room. It was only the second time he had been in there since Allix had brought him home and spoiled her parents' retirement by telling them she was getting married. Nothing had changed. There was still a lot of furniture whose only purpose was to get dusted. Every flat surface carried framed photographs. In pride of place, dead center of the mantelpiece, above the realistic coal-effect electric fire, stood the big wedding picture of Allix and Philippe. Alongside it, more wedding photographs featured both sets of parents. Ranged on the upright piano were studio shots of Allix, Philippe and Tom. The one of Philippe showed him with his chin cupped in his hand, showing off the signet ring with the family crest.

Mr. Lorimer opened a cabinet. "Er, not too early for a drink, Michael?"

Mike looked around from contemplating the picture of Allix. "Scotch, please." It had not been too early for a drink since he had seen the newspaper back in the camp.

Mr. Lorimer poured with the heavy-handedness of people who hardly ever drink. He handed Mike his glass and poured himself a port. He raised his drink with a jerky movement. "Well, Michael, here's to, er, to the future," he said limply, as if he was not confident the future would happen.

Mike tilted his own glass. "M'mm." He took a swallow of the whisky. "In fact, Mr. Lor— Reg, the future's what I wanted to talk to you about."

Mr. Lorimer shifted his weight and shot a glance past Mike toward the door. "M'mm, so Muriel mentioned." He flapped a hand toward the sofa. "Let's have a seat, shall we?" Mike sat down and leaned back against the cushions. He could almost see the man wince as the Dralon crumpled. Mr. Lorimer sat on one of the matching armchairs, keeping to the edge. "Er, fire away," he said with an uneasy attempt at heartiness.

"Look, Reg, mostly it's about Tom. You know Allix and I were going to get married. I know you and Muriel had your reservations about that, but—"

"Oh, now, come on, Mike," Mr. Lorimer began to protest.

Mike held up a hand. "It doesn't matter. I respect your feelings. Anyway, that doesn't really count any more, does it. The point is, Allix wanted it. And above all *Tom* wanted it. I don't know if you realize how I feel about Tom, how I think he feels about me." He paused, looking at the other man, searching for the words he needed. Mr. Lorimer's wide face was a deep crimson. "I love that boy, Reg. As if he were my own son." He paused. When he continued, his voice was hoarse with emotion. "Well, you know, a few more weeks and he would have *been* my son."

He paused again, watching the other man's face. Mr. Lorimer was looking intently at the bottom of his glass, his cheeks still burning. He took a hurried swig of the port and coughed. He still did not look directly at Mike. "You're driving at something, aren't you?" he said, unpleasantly. "You'd better tell me what it is. Clear the air."

Mike leaned forward on to the edge of his seat. Lorimer was looking truculently back at him, ready to manufacture anger. He wiped a hand over his face before he spoke. "Look, Reg, it's . . . I came here to ask you to let Tom live with me. I'm asking you to let me have custody."

For three seconds the silence was total; then Reg Lorimer sprang to his feet. He slammed his glass down on the piano, spilling port on to the gleaming lacquer. "Custody?" His voice was an incredulous whisper. "You? We're his guardians, Muriel and I!" He flapped a hand at the picture of Philippe. "His father was a *baron*! Do you realize that? Tom's a baron now. He's got a title. And you think we'd hand his upbringing over to some . . . someone like *you*?"

Mike stayed in his seat. He looked at the purplish, congested face above him. "I'm an engineer, Reg, not a drifter." He stood up and put his own glass down on the mantelpiece. His voice was very gentle. "It was the way your daughter wanted it, Reg. She wanted me to be a father to Tom."

"*She* wanted?" He was almost shrieking, carried along by his own outrage. "And how long had she known you? Five minutes! The boy hardly knows you! *We* hardly know you. And you expect us to hand his future over to you, just like that?" He paused, panting with rage. "For all we know, you might be a . . . a criminal. You could be a child molester." He broke off, blinking over his glasses at his own audacity.

Mike's fists clenched. His nostrils flared. He took a step closer to the man. Reg Lorimer gave ground. The backs of his knees caught against the edge of the armchair. He teetered foolishly, struggling to remain upright. Mike stood for several seconds staring with gritted teeth into Lorimer's big, red, complacent face. At length he let his breath escape with a soft hiss through his nose, opened his fists and shook the tension from his arms and shoulders. He turned to face the photograph of Allix. "I'm so sorry," he murmured, almost inaudibly.

Without another word, he spun away from Allix's father and walked out of the room. He strode from the house, slamming the door so hard he had the fleeting satisfaction of hearing a pane of glass tinkle to the ground behind him. He walked down the immaculate drive without looking back, not seeing the lace curtain twitch as the two faces behind it pressed close to the glass, watching him go.

In the following days he hardly ate. He got up late, walked the streets until the pubs opened, drank into the afternoon, walked some more, and then drank again until they closed. Half a dozen times he called the Lorimers' number. Each time they had rung off the moment they realized it was him. Once, he had felt an almost unbearable pang at hearing Tom's voice quite clearly in the background, asking who it was.

On the fifth afternoon he was sitting on a bench in Sloane Square. With his five days' stubble and crumpled clothes, only his morose silence distinguished him from the cluster of raucous alcoholics that lounged a few yards away, passing around a cider bottle. Empty-eyed, he watched the crowd that spilled from the underground station and filled the pavement in front of W. H. Smith, intent on the shopping possibilities of the King's Road. Turning, he let his gaze fall on the entrance to the Peter Jones department store. He sat with his hands pushed into his jacket pockets, watching without any interest the carefully dressed women who passed through the doors.

A woman emerged, talking over her shoulder. Behind her, a small boy ran from the store. He grabbed her hand in both his, and, laughing up at his mother, swung himself around in front of her. Mike felt his chest contract. The boy was blond, the mother dark. They looked nothing whatever like Allix and Tom. And yet, there was something in the way the boy had swung on his mother, something in her laughing response, that was an aching reminder of them. Mike stood up. For several seconds he stood staring after the pair as they crossed the road and disappeared toward Cadogan Square, then strode abruptly to the edge of the pavement and hailed a taxi. He gave the driver the address of a small private school in Putney. Tom's school.

He paid off the taxi a few minutes' walk from the school. There was a good quarter of an hour before lessons finished. It took him half that time to buy disposable razors and a can of shaving foam and have a quick cold-water shave in the men's room of a hamburger bar. He ran his fingers through his scrubby hair, clamped his handkerchief to his face to staunch the blood from half a dozen tiny cuts and hurried out on to the street. Seven minutes later he was approaching the gates.

He looked again at his watch—it was almost time. His heart pounded at the thought of seeing the boy. Ahead of him a cluster of parents, mostly women, waited at the gates. A dozen cars stood at the curb with people at the wheel. He took a last look at the handkerchief; the bleeding had slowed, leaving only pin-points of red. He stuffed it into his pocket and moved forward to stand a pace behind the group of parents. A girl of about six emerged, bursting exuberantly out of the door and down the short path into the arms of her waiting mother, laughing aloud. Other children came after her, running or skipping the few paces to the gate. Some joined their parents, some made for the waiting cars.

Tom was perhaps the tenth one out. He was running alongside another boy, laughing as he came. The sheer grace of his movements made Mike draw a sharp breath. The mother of the other boy spoke to Tom, making him grin. Then, his face suddenly earnest, he turned and began examining the row of cars. Mike followed his eye as it traveled along the row and fell on the familiar Cavalier. Tom broke into a smile and began skipping away toward the car. Mike stood motionless among the thinning group, watching silently. His heart was hammering. A woman passed him holding her little girl by the hand. She went on for a few paces and then stopped and turned. She stood staring warily at Mike, but he did not notice her. His attention was entirely on Tom. The boy was three yards from the car.

"Tom!" Mike stepped a pace forward, breaking through the few remaining mothers. He held his hands low in front of him. His face glistened.

Tom stopped in his tracks and spun around. Several other heads turned to look. Tom paused for half a second, frowning as he sought the source of the voice. Then his face lit up and he began running back to where Mike stood. Mike swept the boy off his feet, raising him high above his head. He gazed up into the tiny, beautiful face as Tom whooped with laughter. Mike whirled around twice. Tom's laughter almost became a shriek. Laughing himself, Mike lowered him gently to the ground. He remained squatting in front of him, their faces on a level.

"Hello, Tom. How are you?"

The boy laughed. "I'm all right. It was really good

in school today. We did dinosaurs." His face grew suddenly grave. "Mike, are you crying?"

Mike blinked and pursed his lips, trying to smile. He was still trying to find his voice when somebody shoved him violently on the shoulder. Caught off balance, he fell back, reaching behind him awkwardly. With his weight on one hip and a hand he looked up, a flash of belligerence in his eyes. Mrs. Lorimer was turning away from him and grabbing for Tom's hand. "Come on, Tommy. You come home with me now."

Tom eluded her and ran close to Mike. "Grandma, it's Mike. I want to play with him."

She turned and made another grab for Tom, catching him by the shoulder. She secured his hand firmly in hers. "No. We're going home." Her eyes flashed venomously at Mike, who was still pushing himself slowly upright. "Mr. Scanlon's got no business coming here bothering people."

Mike took a step towards her. "Mrs. Lorimer, I just wanted to *see* Tom, that's all."

She looked at him with pursed lips, taking in the bad shave and the crumpled shirt. "I can smell the beer on your breath," she said, abruptly triumphant. She turned toward the car, yanking at Tom's arm. "Come on. Grandpa's waiting. He's got something nice for you," she added, in a tone of vacant desperation. She was at her car when she twisted to look back. "I'll see my husband gets the law on you!" she shouted across the intervening twenty yards.

Mike stood silent in the same spot, oblivious to the stares of disgust and pursed-lipped disapproval of the other parents. He watched as she pushed the boy into the car. Tom hung back, craning around to see Mike. His little face was contorted with crying. His grandmother slammed the back door and hurried around to the driving-seat, her head held stiffly on her shoulders. Her jaw jutted with the effort of controlling her indignation. Mike did not move until the Cavalier was almost out of sight. Then, he simply raised a hand in salute to Tom, hoping he was looking back, turned on his heel, and walked away, ignoring the stares of the last scattering of parents.

Mike pulled the bedclothes down and stared around him. Only slowly did he realize it was the telephone that had woken him. He rolled to the side and groped the telephone from the table. As he took it up, his hand caught a glass with half an inch of stale whisky in it, knocking it to the floor.

"Hello?" He massaged the bridge of his nose as he spoke.

"Mike?"

"Yeah. Maggie!" He pushed himself into a sitting position, suddenly fully awake. "I was hoping you'd be back today. What's the news?"

"Not very good. I spoke to the Lorimers' solicitors this morning."

"And?"

"No deal. I'm sorry, Mike. They won't let you near the boy."

He bit his lip. "How about the courts? Can't I *ask* for custody, or at least access?"

"Yeah. You can ask. As a solicitor I might take your money. As a friend I'd have to tell you not to bother."

"But surely I must have *some* rights. Allix and I would've been married by now."

The woman at the other end paused for a moment. "Look, Mike, I'm sorry. As I said, you can try. But who says you and Allix were going to get married? Is there any evidence of it? For heaven's sake, you only told *me* four days ago! What have you got for a court? Your word? The Lorimers are denying it. They swear you hadn't seen Allix more than a couple of dozen times. 'Casual boyfriend' are the exact words they use."

Mike shook his head under the impact of the words. "But how about Tom?" he said, his voice cracking. "He knows how it was. He could hardly wait. Won't his word carry any weight?"

He heard her make a soft sound with her tongue against her teeth. "It might, Mike. It might get us into play. But it'll get very tough. They're already saying you tried to molest Tom while drunk. Is it true?"

He groaned, an angry, tortured sound, deep in his chest. "Oh, God, no, of course it's not. I just wanted to see him, that's all. I couldn't stand it any longer."

"But were you drunk?"

He grimaced. "No. I'd had a few drinks, a while earlier. I was sober enough."

"They seem to have a bunch of people ready to swear you weren't." She paused again. "Look, Mike, I'm really sorry. You can ignore my advice if you like, but I don't think you have a hope. To the court, you're someone off the street. Allix's parents are a respectable couple who can take good care of the lad."

"They're a pair of hung-up little shits, Maggie."

"That's a definition the court won't take much notice of. They're respectable people, who obviously dote on the boy."

He took a deep breath. "What if I decide to go ahead and fight?"

"They'll fight back. Right up to the High Court, if necessary. Apart from anything else, it would cost a fortune."

"I don't give a shit about the cost."

"All right. But think about it. It'll be long and ugly. There would have to be welfare reports, hearings, the High Court, all the nasty business of injunctions, Ward of Court proceedings. Think about the effect of all that on the boy. You do give a shit about him!"

There were several seconds of silence. Maggie

spoke again, very softly. "Drop it, Mike. Please. For the boy's sake."

For almost an hour after Maggie rang off he sat in the same position, his knees drawn up under the crumpled quilt, his head thrown back to rest against the wall. The telephone rang twice, insistently. He ignored it. Finally, he pushed himself off the bed and walked naked to the bathroom. He leaned on the washbasin and examined himself in the mirror.

The white-flecked stubble at his throat was a quarter of an inch long. A graze on his cheek, probably the result of stumbling against a wall in some drunken stupor, had hardened and scabbed over. He drew back his lips. His teeth were rimmed with white deposits against the gums.

His gaze went to the cluster of scars at his shoulder. He raised his left hand and touched them with his fingertips. They had been put there many years before, by "security" men working for a diamond-mining company. Mike had been fresh out of England, on his first contract in Zaire. On a free weekend he had taken a Land Rover out into the bush. He had been wakened in the middle of the night by three Belgians, security men from a nearby mine. They were looking for links in a chain they thought was getting diamonds out of the mine. They decided Mike was one of them. The scars at his shoulder and armpit were from the lighted cigarettes and a machete they had used to try to get him to agree with them. Disappointed, they had burned his Land Rover.

Mike had walked the forty kilometers back to the nearest settlement. He had spent a couple of days in the local fleapit of a hospital, returned to camp to work out his contract, and then gone looking for the men. He had caught up with them in a bar in a dump called Bukavu, on the river frontier with Rwanda, one of the staging posts of the stolen diamond racket. None of the three had ever been fit enough to return to his job—and Mike had never returned to Zaire.

He looked again at his reflection. He saw again the grief and anger, and for the first time, he saw the self-pity. The shock made him stagger. He saw with absolute, blinding clarity what he had been doing. He had been directing his anger at his loss toward Allix's parents. Being angry at them for being narrow and stupid, for their reaction to a situation they had done nothing to create, instead of at the people who had been at the root of his devastation; the people responsible for Allix's death.

He continued staring at the mirror for several seconds more. In those seconds the idea that had been born as he put down the phone grew to fill his existence. He knew with absolute certainty what he was going to do next. Just what he had done with the men who had invaded his life almost two decades earlier, in Zaire; he would track down the people who had stolen Allix and Tom from him. And he would destroy them.

Two weeks after coming to his decision Mike pulled the door of the house closed behind him and locked the three locks carefully. He dropped the keys into an envelope, already stamped and addressed, sealed it, and pushed it into an inside pocket of his cheap brown suit. For several seconds he remained in the shelter of the porch, looking up and down the street. Even though it was not yet six-thirty there was always the risk that a neighbor might be out walking the dog, or, even more likely in this part of London, jogging. He was in no frame of mind to try explaining the clothes—shabby suit, broken black shoes, grubby shirt buttoned to the neck, no tie.

Satisfied he was unobserved, he set off toward Fulham Broadway. In his left hand he carried a chafed, mud-colored suitcase held closed with a worn leather belt, in the other he held a bulging plastic bag. Even the plastic bag was not new. He rode the Underground to Paddington. Emerging from the station he began walking briskly northward, past the precarious businesses with their hand-painted shopfronts toward the seedy, multiple-occupancy villas of Kilburn. He deviated once, crossing the road to drop the envelope into a mailbox. The envelope held three things: the keys, a note to an old friend asking him to take care of them until Mike's return from "overseas," and a sealed copy of his will. The will was a simple one, written on a standard form bought from a stationer's for the purpose. It left all his estate to the trust he had set up for Tom; cash and shares worth together about sixty-five thousand pounds, the last time he had checked out the stock market, and the house. He had had it witnessed by two strangers in a pub. Their services had cost him two pints of lager. The rest of his estate was in his pocket; four thousand pounds in fifty-pound notes, and his passport.

He turned into Brondesbury Villas and began stopping in front of the "hotels," squinting at them as if trying to gauge from the state of their façades the prices that none of them displayed. He selected one with averagely peeling paint and pressed the bell.

He was about to turn away when the door opened. The man standing in the doorway was unshaven, disheveled and unhealthy-looking. His shoulders rounded in a stoop. His body was thin except where it erupted into a beer-belly low down under the singlet.

"Yeah?"

"I'm looking for a room."

The man stared back at him, a look of shrewd mistrust in his face. "We don't do overnight," he informed Mike truculently. He belched loudly, with no change in his expression.

Mike smiled, not flinching as the acrid fumes of

digestive fluids and alcohol drifted past his head. "I was looking for something for a bit longer."

"How long?"

Mike shrugged. "Few weeks. A few months, maybe. Depends if there's any work about."

"On the dole? It's two weeks in advance."

"Between jobs. Can I see the room?"

The man turned and walked back inside, jerking his head at Mike to follow. Mike stepped in and closed the door. A meaty smell pervaded the place. At the top of the stairs the man threw open a door and stood back to let Mike see inside. The room would once have been nobly proportioned, but a thin, jerry-built partition had been installed across it, cutting the ceiling cornice and falling arbitrarily a third of the way across one of the sash windows. The resulting space was higher than it was wide, so that although it was not unduly small, it had the oppressive feel of a cubicle rather than a room. Mike looked it over. The decor was cheap and unpleasant, with the unmatched wallpapers testifying to a remnant sale in a DIY store, but it was not noticeably dirty.

"How much?"

"Sixty-five."

Mike raised his eyebrows.

"A week," the man added sullenly.

"Okay. How about getting a bath?"

Wordlessly, the man led him along the landing and threw open another door—the bathroom, and it *was* dirty. A greasy tidemark ringed the stained enamel of the bath. An ancient gas heater with a meter hanging conspicuously beside it offered a grudging promise of hot water.

"Does the sixty-five include breakfast?"

The man looked at him for a moment as if he were about to weep and then led him back to the room. He walked over to a chipped formica-topped cabinet and flipped back its hinged lid. Beneath it was a greasy gas ring.

"Do your own. You can suit yourself about the hours." He looked at Mike smugly, as if he expected to be complimented on the unexpected luxury of the facilities. "D'you want the room?" He sounded disappointed already.

Mike nodded. He took a roll of crumpled ten and five pound notes from his pocket and laboriously counted off a hundred and thirty pounds. The man's eyes stayed on the money left on the roll for a fraction of a second after Mike had stopped counting. He seemed to be trying to calculate how long it would be before Mike's money ran out and he would have to go to the trouble of changing the sheets again. Mike let him see there was no more than sixty pounds or so left, pushed the fortnight's rent into his grasp and shut the door on him.

The moment he was alone he began a detailed examination of the room. He started with the furniture: a sink, a sagging divan covered with a threadbare, cigarette-scarred bedspread, a wooden dining-table with swollen, carved legs, two mismatched kitchen chairs, the cabinet holding the gas ring and a few pieces of dilapidated crockery, and a clothes cupboard made of PVC over a frame of plastic-coated wire that closed with a zip. Nowhere to hide anything bigger than a train ticket.

Working silently, he moved the furniture to the middle of the room. Dropping to his knees, he dragged back the musty-smelling carpet from the skirting board. It took him a few minutes to find what he was looking for. A short length of floorboard had been renewed, close to a wall. He opened his suitcase and took out a canvas pouch, then knelt down again, spreading the pouch beside him. He took a short screwdriver from the pouch and began carefully prising up the board. Placing it to one side he unfastened his belt and slid from it the leatherette wallet that had been nestling at the small of his back. He took four fifty-pound notes from the wad inside, fastened the wallet and placed it in the cavity. He maneuvered the board back into place, ensuring that the points of the nails went back into their original holes. He put the heel of his hand on the board and leaned hard on it, pushing the nails back into place.

A few minutes later, with the furniture back in place, he stood listening. There was no sound from outside the room. Nobody's curiosity would have been aroused. It was important that his war chest be safe. From that morning he had severed all links with his former existence; no credit cards, no checkbook to tell the story of his life to an inquisitive searcher. He could, of course, always go personally to his own bank and draw out money. But if somebody stole his four grand and he simply replaced it without actually getting a job he was going to look like a very strange kind of building laborer. He reckoned that with the rent he was paying, food and booze, the money should last him five or six months. For the duration of that time he had enlisted in the cash economy.

He looked at the cheap watch he had bought to replace the one lost in Athens. Nine-thirty. Knowing how long he had been up made him hungry. He left the room, locking the door and trying the handle as he went. As he crossed the landing the open door of the bathroom caught his eye. He stepped inside, bolted the door, and turned both bath taps full on. The gas boiler knocked and rattled as water gushed loudly into the bath, but there was no steam. The previous user had been careful to get the full benefit of his coin. It did not matter; he was not there for a bath. He knelt and took a small Swiss army knife from his pocket. Quickly, he unscrewed the panel from the side of the bath. It came away easily, revealing the rubble-littered space beneath the tub. Satisfied, he replaced the panel, turned off the taps, flushed the toilet and walked out, toweling his hands on his handkerchief. A broken-down man in a dressing-gown waited outside. His attempt to respond to Mike's nodded greeting foundered in a fit of coughing. It was a quiet, apologetic kind of cough that followed Mike down the stairs. He had heard it often before, in the days when he travelled upstairs on buses. People seemed to die of it.

Forty minutes later he had finished a heavy-duty breakfast in a greasy spoon in Kilburn High Road. It seemed like the right start to the day for a man planning to enlist in the Irish Republican Army.

He got off the underground at Colindale. It was a part of London he had heard the name of, but he had never known where it was until a couple of days previously. As he left the station he saw why: the wind howled along the charmless street, driving a stinging cold rain with it; buses kicked malicious spumes of spray at the legs of the rare pedestrians. An inquiry for directions drew a silent jerk of the head from a newsvendor. Following the direction of the nod Mike crossed the road and made for the warehouse-like building opposite. A few minutes later he had completed the few formalities and been issued a slip of paper pronouncing him a reader at the Newspaper Section of the British Library.

The British Library held in its archives every edition of every newspaper published in Britain, and many published overseas, going back to before the modern IRA had been formed in the early part of the century. Mike found a seat among the silent, studious researchers, parked his jacket on it by way of staking his claim, and walked over to the shelves holding the rows of massive index books. He stood in thought for several seconds and then took down the index of the "Times" for 1970. Twenty-odd years of the history of the Republican movement ought to give him as much information as he could handle.

By mid-afternoon he was beginning to understand the magnitude of the task he had set himself. The indexes listed all the occasions when a subject had been referred to in the paper. They gave the date, page and column and indicated if there was a photograph. There were pages upon pages of references to the movement. The spiral-bound notebook he had brought with him was already a third filled with details of the editions he would want to see; their dates, page numbers and columns. He made a special note of the items listed as having photographs, completed a first request for material and handed it over at the desk. Twenty minutes later an attendant appeared, wheeling a trolley loaded with the bulky, bound volumes which he abandoned by Mike's chair. Taking up the first one, Mike began searching for the place he had noted.

It was after six when he returned to the hotel. Smells of cooking and the sounds of television sets filled the narrow hall. At the end of the passageway the door to the landlord's lair opened silently and the unshaven face stared out, looking with frank curiosity at the plastic bag Mike was holding under his jacket, protecting it from the rain. With a nod to the man Mike hurried up the stairs to his room.

He sat at the table to study the photocopies he had brought back with him, absorbing the information they held about personalities and events in the IRA. By a little after eight he was ready to call it a day. He stowed the documents in the space beneath the floorboard, took a bath, cleaning the worst of the filth from it first, and went out. He ate in the same dismal café where he had eaten breakfast and set out on the second part of the job he had set himself. Trawling the pubs.

* * *

In Valletta, Malta, the evening was still. It was warm enough for the men to be in shirtsleeves, the women in cotton dresses with thin cardigans over their shoulders. At the terraces of the cafés and ice-cream parlors overlooking Grand Harbor family groups and clusters of friends sat talking animatedly. At a few tables groups of taller, older, more angular people, English expatriates eking out their pensions, were more restrained, exchanging discreet boasts about the size of their swimming pools or their childrens' distinguished careers. At a corner table of one of the less popular cafés a man sat alone.

He was in his late fifties, slender, with short grey hair which still bore traces of the redness of his youth. He was dressed in an unobtrusive tweed sports jacket and grey slacks. His glasses were thick-framed, tinted, almost as dark as sunglasses. On a chair by his side lay a pair of good binoculars and a notebook. He put some money on the table, gathered up his things and left.

The waiter cleared the table, nodding to himself at the size of the tip. He had become used to the man's generosity. It was about three months ago that the man had first come in. As today, he had come early in the morning, and then again at the end of the afternoon. Since then he had returned every three weeks, each time following the same routine. On his last couple of visits he had taken up sketching and begun making notes in the notebook. The sketches were terrible, more like maps than pictures. Another British pensioner escaping from the climate. It was surprising how many of them, after a lifetime of stifling service to a provincial bank, went the whole hog and decided they were Gauguin. They never seemed to realize that when Gauguin left France he had talent to go with the change in the weather. But at least this one did not share the usual English taste for diluting small tonics with large gins and complaining about how England was going to the dogs;

this one only ever drank tea or coffee, and he hardly spoke at all.

As the man left the café terrace the thought struck the waiter that perhaps he was connected with the cruise liners. It would explain why he was there only when one of them was in port. He caught the sound of children's voices drifting up to the terrace and glanced down. Below him, in the center of the huge harbor, the ferry had almost finished disgorging its cargo of children back on to the cruise ship that lay at anchor, dwarfing the dirty freighters, brightly painted fishing boats and launches that busied themselves around it.

Squeals and laughter drifted upwards. The waiter turned back to wiping the table, smiling wryly to himself. He had a family of his own; still, he was glad that this time the children from the cruise ship had not chosen *his* café to invade. These groups of English schoolchildren always seemed to behave like animals; they bought Cola and drank Southern Comfort from bottles, until half of them were being sick in the toilets while the other half insulted him. He had seen it during his brief attempt at working in England. English kids seemed to be brought up to think of waiters as some kind of underbeings, only there to be sworn at and abused. All in all, he preferred the reserved, older types like the gentleman who had just left. Quiet and courteous, they left tips that showed they appreciated the service you provided. He looked in the direction the man had gone. Thirty yards away he had stopped, and was now leaning on a low wall, watching the ship through his powerful binoculars.

CHAPTER

3

IT WAS AFTER ELEVEN WHEN MIKE RETURNED TO THE HOTEL. He was dispirited and bloated with beer. He had not realized what a long evening a Monday night in the pubs of Kilburn could be. He had tried a dozen or more places; all of them had shared the same desolate atmosphere, scarred floors and sparse custom. Most of their clients had blown their money during the weekend, and the ones who could still afford a drink were standing alone, hunched protectively over glasses of stout. Almost all of them were men. The only progress he had made with any of them was getting them to accept a drink. His attempts to talk had all foundered on a reef of indifference or morose incoherence.

He drifted into sleep to the sound of snoring from beyond the thin partition, and with thoughts of Allix filling his head.

He fell quickly into a routine. Each day he ate breakfast in the same café before heading for Colindale. Each day his file of photocopies of newspaper items grew bigger.

Each day his knowledge of the IRA grew as he accumulated more facts; events, names, and especially photographs of everyone who had counted in the organization in the last twenty years. Each evening from six to eight he spent arranging his material, going over what he had unearthed that day, fixing facts and faces in his mind. Each night he spent dragging himself from one depressing pub to another. Every evening for more than three weeks he had drawn a blank.

He looked at his watch and sighed. It was coming up to eight o'clock. He carefully replaced the sheaves of paper in their ordered places, stashed the file into its hiding place and pushed the table back into position. He pulled off the shirt he had been wearing for the last few days. As he put on a clean one he plucked at the flesh at his waist. The beer was giving him a gut. He had already considered doing some exercise, but had let it go—a beer-belly would do more for his credibility than ridges of iron-hard abdominal muscle.

He had covered every Irish pub in the Kilburn and Kentish Town area, so in the last few days he had widened his area of operation. For the second night running he got off the tube at Hammersmith, risked his life among the traffic of Hammersmith Broadway and set off on foot for the dark stretches north of King Street.

The third place he tried seemed to offer some kind of promise; a handwritten poster in the window advertised country music every Friday and Kelly and Curtis on Tuesdays. They were Britain's leading country and western artistes, it said. He pushed into the bar. Until the music hit him he had forgotten it was Tuesday.

Britain's leading country duo was performing on a low stage. Half of it was a middle-aged woman with flagrantly dyed red hair and a silver dress, singing a broken-hearted ballad of a lady being done wrong. She sang better than she looked. Her partner was a grey-faced man with three-inch sideburns, who played piano one-handed while he bent to manipulate the controls of an intractable drum machine with the other.

There were quite a few people in the place, and Mike had some trouble finding a space at the bar. Many of the drinkers were the standard loners, men from building sites who had probably been waiting in front of the door for the opening of the evening session, to avoid going through the strain of sobering up after lunch. Sad men, living in desolate bedsitters, for whom beer played the role of family. As the place filled, a different type of customer came in, younger and happier.

A group of youngish men pushed their way to the bar. Their conversation was lively and funny, and Mike laughed along at one of their jokes. A little later they laughed at one of his. He bought them drinks and by ten they were friends. At eleven they left, promising to be back on Friday. In the meanwhile they had given him the names of several other pubs where there was music, and where there might be girls. He returned to his room in a better frame of mind than at any time in the last three weeks. Despite the heavy drinking his role forced him into, he was completely sober.

On the following Friday Mike was at the bar early, waiting for the group to show up. In the intervening days he had been to every one of the other pubs they had mentioned. The Wednesday night had brought him one stroke of luck. He had come across one of the group and been invited to join him and the friends he was with. One of the men had made a harmless jibe about Mike's English accent. Mike had been ready for something like it, hoping for it, even. He seized the chance, turning on the man with a force that surprised them all. His lips tight with fury, nostrils flaring, he had treated the man to a venomous outburst, about how he could not help his accent, and how he might *sound* like a Brit, but he damned well did not *feel* like one of the bastards!

Seething with anger at the grievous insult, he had turned on his heel and started to stalk toward the door. The acquaintance of the previous evening had come after him. Mike had let himself be talked into returning to the bar. There had been some surly apologies, a few drinks were bought, and the incident had been allowed to rest. But for the remaining half-hour of drinking time Mike had been conscious of a new wariness, a respect in the way they addressed him. On the bus back to his lodging he had let himself smile about it. He knew he had played the scene well, letting them have an insight into his feelings without overdoing it. With luck, word would start to get around.

The country singer was in full voice by the time the Tuesday night group turned up. They had been drinking for a while when one of them made a joking, but pointed, reference to Mike's outburst. Mike snatched at the chance, immediately steering the conversation to politics. His views were strong, simple and loud.

"The fucking Brits ought to get out now, and take their fucking stooges, the RUC and all the rest, with them."

"There doesn't seem to be anyone in the British government wants to take you up on that suggestion, Michael," one of the group said softly.

"I know that. The bastards think they can shoot the resistance out of us. This lot think if they shoot enough of our people down we'll wind up by calling it a day. Well, if they think that's how it's going to work, they'd better take a look at Ireland's history!"

One of the men laughed outright. "Ireland's history," he mimicked. "The way I heard it, you're a Brit yourself."

Mike spun to face the speaker. He leaned close, his face only inches from the other man's. He spoke very quietly. "Listen, you stupid fucking Paddy git. I might have been born over here. It doesn't make me one of the bastards. My mother and dad came over here from Donegal. Dad was an active Republican since he was a kid. Before you were even born. The fucking Brits did him in for it! So you'd better get this into your thick Paddy head, anyone who takes the piss out of me's taking the piss out of him! You want to try again?" As he asked the question his fists clenched.

The soft-spoken man stepped in and put an arm on Mike's shoulder, smiling affably. "Take it easy, Michael. He was only kidding with you. You being English and talking like you do. He didn't mean any harm."

Mike shook his head and sighed, letting the tension flow out of him. "Okay. Sorry. It just pisses me off, that's all." He drank off the last of his beer. "See you around."

In a corner of the bar, a small barrel-chested man in a grey anorak sat alone at a table. Throughout the scene he had not taken his eyes off Mike. His drinks, a pint of bitter and a whisky, had stood untouched on the table in front of him. He continued to watch the door for some seconds after Mike had left. Then, with an almost imperceptible lifting of his eyebrows, he raised the whisky slowly to his lips.

By seven-thirty the following Friday evening Mike already had a drink in front of him. He stood at the bar and watched the customers coming through the door. There were a lot of couples, and several family groups spanning two or three generations. They were livelier and better dressed than the crowds in the cavernous dumps of Kilburn. At eight the music started, and it was not long before the singer was getting help from the audience with the better-known songs.

Mike scarcely took any notice of the thickset man in the grey anorak who entered alone, bought a drink and found a seat at a corner table. Two young men and their girlfriends made as though to sit at the empty places beside him. The man spoke softly to them, taking his eyes off Mike for a fraction of a second to let them have an icy smile of warning. One of the young men began to argue. His friend took him by the upper arm and pulled him away, murmuring into his ear. The first man's eyes widened perceptibly as he listened. He went on staring at the man in the anorak but let himself be pulled away, making no more attempt to protest.

One of Mike's new friends came up to the bar. He accepted the drink Mike offered and they started talking, shouting to compete with the music. Within a few minutes, and without appearing to strain at it, Mike had again led the conversation to politics. While he spoke the man in the anorak was joined by two others, who sat each side of him, in positions where they had a view of the bar, and of the door. The three of them began talking in low, earnest tones, their heads bent over the table toward each other.

Mike was on his fourth beer when a group of skinheads, six men and two girls, pushed noisily into the bar. The youths wore Union Jack tee-shirts under open parkas and military-style denims pushed into high-laced boots. As they shoved past Mike on their way to the bar it was obvious from their voices that they had already been drinking. One of the men shouted at the barmaid for service. His accent was not Irish. It was a harsh, nasal cockney, the voice of London's louts. They got their drinks and stayed at the bar, sneeringly contemptuous at other customers' efforts to reach the counter. Mike and his group gave a little ground. The newcomers expanded to fill the space they left, smirking aggressively around them. Other customers avoided their eyes, anxious to keep out of trouble. One of the skinheads made a sniggering remark about the singer, just as another of them was in the act of drinking off three inches of beer. He snorted with laughter, and a gout of beer erupted from his mouth. It splattered on to the front of the dress of a girl standing three feet away. She recoiled in disgust, as the skinheads bayed in raucous amusement. The girl's boyfriend, a frail-looking young man in a cheap tweed jacket and a woolen tie, turned angrily to face the grinning group.

"Hey, can't you be a bit more careful? Look what you've done." His anger made his voice reedy.

One of the men leered at the girl. "Want me to lick it off for you, darling." He grinned around at his group and put out his tongue, letting it dangle obscenely from his mouth.

The young man's face turned scarlet with fury and embarrassment. His rage made him brave. "Shut your mouth, you ignorant bastard. Don't talk to her like that."

The skinhead grinned at the young man, cleared his throat with a loud rasping noise, and spat very deliberately into his face. The young man recoiled, pawing at the disgusting gob of saliva that hung on his cheek. The skinhead laughed at the shock and shame in the young man's face. "Now fuck off," he said contemptuously, turning back to his grinning friends.

"No. You fuck off. All of you." Mike spoke very softly.

The skinhead looked over his shoulder at Mike, still smirking. "Talking to me, prickface?"

Mike's fist slammed against the man's cheekbone. The skinhead staggered and fell against the bar, his back toward Mike. Before Mike could move in to hit him again, the others had started throwing punches. Mike was not acting a part now. He was too angry even to consider the odds. He snatched a handful of the cloth of the nearest skinhead's jacket, dragged him forward and up and rammed his head into the expression of stupid surprise on the man's face. He dropped the man's jacket, letting him fall back clutching both hands to his damaged nose.

A fist hit Mike full on the mouth. He roared with pain and rage and aimed a punch at the young man who had thrown it. One of the girls grabbed his arm, impeding him. The blow landed without any force. He hurled the girl from him. Before he could get set again two of the youths and the girls were swarming over him, raining kicks and punches. Mike was a big man. He freed one arm and jabbed stiffened fingers into the abdomen of one of the youths; he folded silently, his face contorted. Mike hit out again, driving his fist upward against the jaw of a snarling face that appeared a foot from his own. Again, somebody clung to his arm, sapping the force of the blow. With a bellow of pure rage, he tore himself free of the hands that tried to restrain him and took a step backward, giving himself a little space. He threw another punch, felt it land with a sharp crack high on the face of one of the men, and then buckled as something crashed on to the back of his head. He doubled over, his vision blurred. A boot smashed into his groin. His knees started to give way. Through the pain he heard women screaming.

Something in the screams set off some primitive alarm in him. He blinked away the pain and looked up. The skinhead who had spat at the young man had recovered himself and turned from the bar to face Mike. One hand was held low in front of him. Mike had sunk to one knee, so that the man's hand was on a level with his face. The screwdriver it held was a foot from his eyes. He caught the glint of bright metal where the tip had been filed to a deadly point. He tried to scramble away, desperately mustering his reactions, preparing to throw himself out of reach of the weapon. He was aware of the weight of the man's friends crowding him, trying to confine him to the spot. He looked up into the face above him. It was contorted in a fixed, madman's grin.

The man drew the weapon back level with his hip. Mike tested his balance. To his right the bar hemmed him in. He prepared to hurl himself up and to his left, hoping to avoid the weapon and get to his feet. At that instant a knee slammed down on to his left shoulder and stayed jammed against his neck. He saw the knees of the man in front of him flex as he shifted his weight, preparing to ram the weapon home.

"Drop that, you fucker." The words were spoken very softly, as though it were almost too much trouble for the speaker. Nevertheless the voice cut through the shrieking of the women, silencing the whole room. The skinhead's eyes flickered to a point behind Mike. Fear swept the triumphant leer from his face. He froze, his weight still poised to strike the blow.

"I'll kill you." The voice was still soft, but the threat was quite unmistakable. The screwdriver clattered to the floor. "And you."

The pressure of the knee was withdrawn from Mike's neck and the skinhead responsible stumbled forward, pitching heavily to the floor, as though somebody had shoved him from behind. Warily, still on one knee and keeping close to the bar, Mike turned. The speaker was one of the men from the corner table. The shapeless fawn raincoat he wore hung unbuttoned. His hands were through the pocket slits, so that from behind it would appear as though he had his hands in his pockets. Only from in front, where Mike and the skinheads and a handful of dumbstruck bystanders stood, could the huge revolver he held be seen.

The man with the gun murmured to the two companions who stood at his shoulder. They stepped forward. The one in the anorak moved to within a few inches of the would-be killer. He clenched a big, knuckly fist. In a neat, economical movement, with all his weight behind it, he drove it into the stomach of the skinhead. The youth made a noise between a retch and a sob and pitched forward. The two men grabbed an arm each as he began to fall and half-marched, half-dragged him backward behind the bar and through a door into a back room. The door closed softly behind them.

The gunman turned to the other skinheads, who stood in a sullen group, gaping witlessly. "Piss off, all of you." There was just a moment when it looked as though they might argue. "You want to join your pal?" He jerked his head in the direction of the back room. As he did so the beginning of a scream sounded from the room, quickly tailing off into a stifled gurgle. The gunman made a quick gesture to the singer and the music started up again, the woman resuming her country classic. Gulping, the one who seemed to be the leader, a rawboned youth with an ugly, lumpy face which was tattooed on both cheeks, turned and led his friends shambling from the pub.

The man gave a quick contemptuous grin at their backs, then turned to Mike and smiled. "You all right? That bastard really walloped you. Show us your head." Mike obligingly bowed his head. The man probed it with his fingers. They came away bloody. "You'll be all right. Don't seem to be nothing broken." He nodded at the floor. Pieces of a glass ashtray lay there. "Lucky, though. He might have killed you. What'll you have to drink? Bitter? A drop of whisky?" He turned to the barman without waiting for an answer. "Pat, bring us three doubles and a pint of best, will you."

He led Mike to the corner table, buttoning the raincoat as he went. As they sat down Mike saw the door behind the bar open. The two men emerged holding the skinhead between them. He was grey-faced, and one of his legs dragged uselessly. It was plainly broken. His face contorted as the leg caught on a raised edge of the worn carpet. His teeth sank deep into his lower lip, yet despite the obvious agony he did not call out. A look at the man's face told Mike it was not courage that kept him silent, but rank fear. The men who held him had instructed him to make no noise. The brief period he had spent in the room with them had been time enough for the lesson to be unforgettably learned. When these men told you to do something you obeyed as though your life depended on it. Because it did.

By the time the barman hurried over with the drinks the two men who had escorted out the injured skinhead had returned to the table. In answer to a questioning look from the man in the raincoat they nodded.

"In the taxi. He'll be put down south of the river. Clapham. We took a driving license off him. Got his address. The little prick's shitting himself."

"Good. Meet . . ." He turned to Mike, smiling. "Who? What *is* your name?"

"Mike. Mike Scanlon."

The man in the raincoat shook his hand. "John. This is Terry, and Liam." The other men shook his hand in turn.

"You did nicely there. Lucky not to have been very badly hurt, though. Bit silly, really." The man called Terry smiled as he spoke, a slightly mocking smile.

Mike shrugged and gave a bitter little laugh. He touched a hand to his head wound and winced. "You're telling me. That little bastard would've killed me if it hadn't been for you fellers. Thanks." He flashed a look of genuine anger to where the group he had been with still stood at the bar, talking and shooting glances across at the table. "I thought those bastards would have stepped in, instead of watching me get knifed."

Terry shrugged. "Not everybody likes to get mixed up in fights. Some of these skinheads have a reputation for being very nasty."

"Yeah? Maybe I've been away too much. I didn't know enough to be scared. It just made me so fucking angry. I just hate trash like that. Coming in here looking for trouble. British trash at that," he added bitterly.

The gunman, John, shot a look at the others.

"Yeah, well, we get a lot of that around here. It's something most of us have had to learn to live with." He pointed to Mike's glass. "Another?"

They talked through the evening, but kept the conversation very general. They did not seem particularly interested in politics, though they never interrupted if Mike brought it up. They simply listened, leading him on with the gentlest probing, never committing themselves. The drinks never stopped coming, and each time he tried to buy a round he was good-naturedly laughed back into his seat and encouraged by their gentle, friendly questions to go on talking about himself. He was trying to order pints of bitter, but they were buying him pints and whiskies each time. They drank only whiskies. Mike's years abroad had taught him to hold a lot of liquor; nevertheless, by the eighth or ninth round he could feel it getting to him. He excused himself and went to the toilets.

There was only one man inside. He stood facing the porcelain-lined wall. His arm was raised against the wall and his head rested on it. His eyes were tight shut as he cursed the world in an unbroken stream of repetitive filth. Mike passed behind him to the two cubicles. The locks of both doors were broken. He walked into the less fouled one, treading carefully in the wash of unspeakable fluids that covered the floor. He pushed the door shut behind him, bent low over the bowl, and forced two fingers down his throat. He gagged painfully, then tried again. His diaphragm wrenched and he coughed. At the third try he managed to make himself vomit a stream of undigested booze. He straightened and flushed the toilet. He made saliva and swilled it around his mouth to rinse away the taste. He gave a single shudder of revulsion, settled his jacket on his shoulders and walked out of the cubicle. The man had slumped to the floor, snoring. One hand trailed in the channel of the urinal. Mike stepped past him without a glance and pushed through the two doors into the bar.

He settled back at the table. The three men welcomed his return with a fresh drink. Outwardly, they were still affable. Something in their manner, though, made him glad he had taken the precaution of getting no drunker. There was an indefinable change, something in the way they positioned themselves that was more businesslike than a few minutes previously. It was as though in his absence they had been discussing him and come to some kind of decision. John smiled.

"Michael," he said softly, "why don't you tell us a little more about yourself? Tell us about your family." The man's gentle tone had cords of steel in it. He was not just making a suggestion.

Mike felt a flash of excitement. What they were asking was something he had gone over a thousand times in the solitude of his miserable hotel room. He had rehearsed for this very question every day on the Underground. He had woken in the mornings repeating the story until he had it word-perfect in his mind. There was a wry edge to his feelings. It was the first time in Mike's entire life that his father had been any use to him. He smiled back at John, spreading the smile around to include the others, then turned it into a doubtful laugh, as if he were afraid they were mocking him.

"Sure, if you like. But what d'you all want to hear about my family for?"

John shook his head. He was not smiling now. "Never mind that, Michael. Just let's say we're fascinated. Tell us about your parents, for example."

Mike looked from one to the other, letting them know he sensed the change of mood, then raised his shoulders in a small shrug.

"Okay, if you really want to hear it. Dad was Irish, a Sligo man. He was born and brought up in Tobbercurry. Know it?" He looked at each of the men. Only John nodded. "Never been there myself. Anyway, dad stayed there till he was about eighteen, then he came over here to England, looking for work. Sometime just before the war, it must have been. He ended up living in Birmingham. He had cousins there."

The one calling himself Liam laughed. "Haven't we all."

Mike laughed along with him. The others frowned. "Well, anyway, he met my mother in Birmingham, apparently. She was from Sligo, too. He'd known her before he left Ireland."

"Any other children, apart from yourself?" John asked.

"No." He smiled fondly. "Dad was too good a Marxist to be a good Catholic." He let a sudden flash of anger show in his face. "That's what got him killed."

John raised an eyebrow and exchanged glances with his companions. "He got killed? For being a Marxist? Half the British upper classes called themselves Marxists in the thirties and forties."

"Yeah! Called themselves. Dad was the real thing. Republican more than Marxist, I suppose. That's what they killed him for, not for his Marxism."

John's frown deepened. "Michael, just a minute. *Who* killed your father?"

Mike leaned toward him, putting down his beer glass. "The fucking Brits. The police. Or Special Branch, probably. They took him in and did him in while he was in custody."

Terry and John looked hard at each other. Terry spoke, his voice hardly louder than a breath. "Michael, when was this?"

"Nineteen sixty-nine. September. The fourteenth of September."

"What did you say your dad's name was?"

"Scanlon. Pat Scanlon. Patsy, everyone called him."

"Patsy Scanlon." John was smiling now, a strange, distant smile. "So you're Patsy Scanlon's boy! Well, well." He turned to Liam. "This calls for another drink. You want to get them?"

While keeping his face set in the expression of someone who could not believe he was not boring them to death, Mike had been watching them like a hawk, alive to every slight change in their eyes. Now, within himself, he was jubilant. These were not young men, newcomers to their cause. None of them was under fifty. The name of his father had struck a chord in them. Everything he had told them was the simple truth. The facts could all be checked. What he had not told them was the story as he and his mother had actually lived it.

His father had come to Birmingham in the late thirties. He had stayed there until he died in police custody, getting more Irish by the year. By the time of his death he was indeed a Marxist, and a full-blown Republican. But only in the pub on a Friday and Saturday night. At home he was a wife-beating ignoramus who had a drink problem and was proud of it, leading his wife and son a dog's life. In the mornings, sober, he was surly and taciturn. In the evenings, drunk, he was loud and vicious.

His death had fitted his life. He had been arrested one Saturday night after the pubs had closed, not so much for the anti-British diatribe he was bawling; the police were used to that. They had arrested him, as they had done so often before, for relieving himself in the middle of the road. It was routine, as much a part of their Saturday night as his. The next morning he had been found dead in his cell, asphyxiated. The police claimed he had choked on his own vomit. Mike's mother had known the policeman who had found him. She believed him totally. It was not difficult—she had several times saved her husband from dying the same way as he lay drunk next to her in bed.

"I remember your father's death well, Michael. The

papers played it up a lot, didn't they?" John may have felt like celebrating Mike's parentage, but he was still watching for every nuance in Mike's reaction.

Mike shrugged. "Some of them tried. The fucking police just covered it all up. The papers never got anywhere. You know how the law is. Stick together like glue." He took a swallow of beer, slamming his glass down to show his disgust.

Once again, the facts stood up. Anybody could check the old newspaper articles. It was the end of the sixties; Grosvenor Square, the peace movement, Vietnam. The papers were big on civil rights cases, and an Irishman dying in police custody was a natural for them. Reporters and do-gooding lawyers had made his mother's life a misery for most of a year, trying to cajole her into taking action against the police. All the poor woman had wanted was to be left alone to enjoy her newfound peace. She was glad to see the back of the old bastard.

Mike sighed, as if the thought of his dear old dad was about to bring tears to his eyes. "He was a lovely feller. But bitter. He just couldn't get it out of his system, fretting about what the Brits had done to Ireland. Hardly a day went by that he didn't want to talk about it. I swear, he'd sit me on his knee and tell me about it when I was only that high. It took me years before I even understood what the old bugger was on about." The others grinned. Mike smiled fondly. "Other kids had Peter Rabbit. I had the Black and Tans for bedtime stories."

Liam arrived back at the table with the fresh drinks clutched awkwardly in his spread fingers. They each took theirs. John raised his glass. "Here's to your father." They drank. John leaned an inch or two closer to Mike. His soft voice fell further until it was little more than a murmur. "Don't you ever feel bitter yourself, for what the Brits did to your dad? Don't you ever feel you want to, well, get back at the bastards?"

Mike felt his senses reeling. The tone of the man's voice was absolutely unmistakable; it was the approach he had been trawling for. He had expected to wait months for it. He raised his fresh beer and drank off a long gulp, giving himself time to consider his response. Lowering the glass and looking quickly around him, as though checking nobody would overhear, he hunched closer to John: "I want that so bad it chokes me."

John kept his eyes on Mike's for a second or two. Then, as if deciding something, he simply nodded and changed the subject, asking Mike an anodyne question about life in the Middle East.

They continued talking and drinking steadily until long after midnight. The band packed up and left, and the crowd went with them, leaving the small group at the table alone in the bar. Mike stayed dead sober through the drinking, treating every casual, sidelong enquiry as though it were a live grenade. John's question had unsettled him. It still seemed to hang in the air above their heads.

At length, John seemed to reach some sort of conclusion. He stood up abruptly, turning to Mike. "Fancy something to eat?"

He led the way outside and to a nearby fish and chip shop. A knot of boisterous teenagers and three or four defeated single men queued at the counter. John did not speak until they were out of the shop.

"You living near here?" he asked through a mouthful of fish.

"Kilburn."

"How're you getting home? Got a car?"

Mike shook his head. "The Underground."

John looked at his watch. "You've had it. They're never still running at this time."

"I'll get an all-night bus, then, or walk. Do me good after all the booze."

The man laughed. "Don't be silly. After that crack on the head? I'll give you a lift." As he spoke he stepped into the road and hailed a taxi. He asked Mike the address, repeated it to the driver and climbed in, urging Mike to follow him. They were almost at Brondesbury Villas before John spoke again. "Got anything planned for next Friday night?"

"No. Go out for a beer, I expect. Why?"

"There's a party, if you fancy it. There'd be people you'd get on with. They'd like you."

Mike grinned. "Sounds right up my street. Where is it?"

John scribbled an address on a scrap of paper and handed it over. Mike glanced at it and pushed it into a pocket. "Great. I'm always game for a party. Be any women there?"

John shrugged. "Probably. There's usually a few."

Mike nodded and smiled. He made to pull some money from his pocket. "Here. Let me share the taxi."

John pushed his hand away. "Forget it. It's a pleasure after what you did tonight."

Mike protested half-heartedly and then put the money away. "Okay, thanks. Goodnight. Maybe see you on Friday." He opened the cab door.

"Goodnight, Michael." In the semi-darkness John held out a hand. Mike took it. John shook his hand very briefly but very hard, like someone trying to show how strong he was. "As you say. Maybe I'll see you Friday."

At the front door Mike made a deliberate show of having trouble finding the keyhole. He pushed the door open a fraction too hard, slammed it behind him and walked slowly up the stairs to his room. By the time he locked the door of the room it was maybe a minute and a half since he had got out of the cab. He went to the window and peered around the thin curtain, taking care not to move it. The cab was still in the street below. He withdrew into the room, walked back to the door, switched on the light and stood listening. The sound of the cab drawing away came clearly to him.

CHAPTER

4

T HE CURTAINS TWITCHED BRIEFLY ASIDE. A MAN'S FACE
stared out, examining the street of shabby terraced
houses in a part of Windsor well off the tourist track.
The pavements were deserted, still in Sunday morning
torpor, and rain fell steadily. Except for the drone of an
aircraft overhead nothing disturbed the silence apart
from the Transit van that cruised to a stop twenty-five
yards down the street. The thick net of the curtain fell
back into place. Behind it, the watcher remained in the
bay window, his eyes fixed on the van. Nobody got out
of the vehicle. The driver spread a newspaper and sat
reading.

The watcher turned to look through the smudged
window on the other side of the bay, biting his lip as he
studied the street in the other direction. Some way off a
man had appeared walking an alsatian dog, moving leisurely in the direction of the house. Another man, a jogger in a loose tracksuit, turned the corner and began
overhauling the man with the dog. The watcher turned
quickly back to look at the van. At the moment the

jogger had appeared the van driver had folded his newspaper and laid it on top of the dashboard with the title in full view. The watcher spun away from the window, shouting.

"It's the fucking SAS!"

The other two men in the room dropped their mugs of coffee on to the carpet and dived for the weapons that lay to hand on a low table. They were still in the narrow passage leading to the rear when the front door was kicked in. The sound of gunfire filled the cramped house.

It was twenty-four hours later, reading his newspaper on the Underground on the Monday morning on his way up to Colindale, that Mike learned of the raid. It was on the front page. Another IRA bomb factory. Two IRA men killed. One escaped, killing a policeman. A Photo-fit picture of the escaper, supposedly put together from neighbors' descriptions, accompanied the story. According to the report, the police were on the track of a man believed to have been involved in a series of armed robberies, and the raid had been aimed solely at this man. The reporter duly recounted the police's statement, issued after the raid. They had been as surprised as anybody at their luck when the robber turned out to be a Provo activist and the house proved to be a bomb factory.

That was the story. To Mike, immersed day in and day out in IRA affairs, it read differently. For "police" he assumed he could safely substitute "SAS," and for "luck," laborious intelligence work. It was the seventh incident in the past twelve months where the police had been similarly "lucky."

To the general public the story would sound plausible, but to someone taking the kind of interest he was taking it added up to something else. The security services were obtaining very high grade intelligence. The stories that made the newspapers were designed to minimize that fact, making it appear that the successes were all the result of accident and ordinary police work.

He smiled. It was an old enough intelligence ploy, using selected truths to conceal your sources. Probably one of the dead men *had* been carrying out robberies. It was public knowledge that a recent crackdown by European governments on the movement of money had made it harder for the IRA to transfer funds. Active service units were having to become self-financing, and they were not doing it by running whist drives. If the IRA command knew that, then it was possible that the newspaper story might be true. They would not actually *believe* it, but it all helped in the war of mutual confusion that paralleled the war of grenade attacks and gunfire.

The man in the ticket booth turned his newspaper inside out at the British football results and started checking his pools coupon. Like most Maltese men he was football crazy, as expert on the performance of English league sides as he was on the Italian league. He had never seen a live match in either.

A few people stood in a loose group waiting to be ushered aboard the boat. An agile young Maltese leaped ashore, too cool to use the gangplank, and began shepherding them aboard. Boarding was almost completed when a shadow fell over the ticket-seller's newspaper. His eyes stayed on the paper for another three seconds before he looked up at the newcomer with a desolate expression. They were the three seconds he had needed to learn he would not be rich for at least another week. He raised an eyebrow at the man in front of him.

"Is this the harbor tour?"

The vendor let the eyebrow fall again and nodded. "You're just in time. One?"

The man adjusted his heavy, dark-tinted glasses, nodded and handed over his money. He was last on the boat. He chose a seat well apart from the sprinkling of other people, mostly elderly tourists on cheap out-of-season trips, killing time perhaps between looking over retirement possibilities. It was cold on the water. Most of the tourists retreated to the shelter of the plexiglass cover that protected the rear of the boat. The man was quite alone. He took a chart from the blue plastic hold-all he held on his knees. As the boat cruised the immense harbor he took out a felt pen and began making notes on the chart. He took a special interest in the flag-bedecked liner anchored in the middle of the harbor, and a grim smile of satisfaction touched his lips as he noted the exact position of the vessel on the soiled, heavily creased chart. It was incredible. Every time, since he had begun his reconnaissance many weeks before—the same spot, the same attitude to the shore, the same daily routine.

He took out a pair of binoculars and focused on the white-painted ship. He swung them until the name of the vessel came into view; the *Maribella*. A nice name, full of the promise of blue skies and calm, untroubled seas. He watched for another second or two and then lowered the glasses, still smiling. Since conceiving the scheme, a few days after the oil company announcement, his watching had told him that there were three vessels that regularly did the run. He had had them all investigated. Two were modern vessels, sound, well-built and well-run. The third, the one now sailing under the name *Maribella*, the one that at that moment lay a few hundred yards from him, gleaming white beneath a fresh layer of paint, had been built many years before. She had begun her career with a Norwegian cruise company. At the end of her useful life the Norwegians had sold her to a Greek operator, and in the ensuing years she had changed hands on several more occasions, each time passing to less reputable companies, until her true ownership was lost in an impenetrable jungle of paper companies that were little more than box numbers in the capitals of seldom-visited republics. By the time she had been re-named and superficially smartened up to serve for these cruises she was scarcely more than a rusty shell. And she was the one scheduled for the oil company's promotional public relations trip.

He put away the binoculars and the chart and reclined with one arm along the seat-back next to him. He crossed his legs and began to hum softly. For once, everything seemed to be conspiring in favor of a project.

Mike approached the five-storey house with unobtrusive caution, moving slowly along the far side of the road, counting the numbers. Several times people with bottles under their arms had crossed the pavement in front of him and climbed the steps into other houses where parties were in full swing. Friday night in bed-sitter land.

He stopped in the shadow of an overgrown hedge, and stood for a moment watching the house. All the curtains were drawn, but tiny chinks of brightness told him that there were lights on on all the main floors. The basement and the top floor seemed to be in darkness.

He crossed and strode up the half-dozen broken steps and rang the bell. The door was opened immediately by a young woman. He caught himself being surprised to see that she was attractive, even slinky, in a clinging jersey dress. He realized, with a touch of shame, that he had been expecting a lumpy girl in a cardigan. She took the bottle of cheap Scotch he held out to her with a mock curtsey and directed him into the room where the main party was going on.

As Mike moved across the wide hallway toward the room he noticed a man sitting upright in a hard chair, positioned out of sight of anyone standing at the open door. On a low table next to him stood a glass of flat beer and a crumpled brown bag. The mouth of the bag was open, and the man's hand lay idly on the table two inches from it. He responded to Mike's bright smile with an almost imperceptible nod. He did not look as if he were enjoying the party. It seemed unlikely that the bag he kept so handy contained peanuts.

Mike liked the party the moment he entered the room. There was something in the choice of music, the sheer unyouthfulness of the crowd—even the young ones—the slightly old-fashioned clothes. People were gathered in groups, talking and laughing. The music was not so loud they had to shout into each other's ears. Occasionally a man or woman stood alone with a drink singing along with the music. He scanned the faces. He was looking for someone he recognized, either as one of his recent drinking companions or, if his luck were really in, as one of the gallery of killers whose pictures he held in his head.

In a far corner one of the Friday night crowd stood with a group of six or seven others. The man caught sight of Mike. His face broke into a broad smile and he waved at him to join his group. Mike looked back, not immediately responding. After all, he was one of the bastards who had failed to back him up in the brawl. Finally, he collected a beer and pushed his way through to them. He had to start somewhere.

The man introduced Mike to his friends. There was a trace of embarrassment, as though he were aware of what Mike had been thinking. He tried to cover it by putting a lot of emphasis on the fight, making the most of Mike's role. Mike shook off the praise with a self-deprecating smile. It was no use; a pretty, dark-haired woman of about his age had already decided he was a hero. She propelled him with tipsy insistence into a dance.

Mike grew more and more morose. The last time he had danced was with Allix, alone in her flat, and the memory threatened to overwhelm him. For twenty minutes the woman refused with playful obstinacy to let him off the dance floor. As he became more despondent she grew more flirtatious, believing she was not doing well enough. She snaked her arms around his neck and clasped her fingers behind his head. Her own head dropped against his chest. She let her weight press against the hard contours of his body. Her breasts and pelvis ground into him. Through his grief he could feel himself beginning to be aroused. At length, unable to stand the strain any more, he broke away, almost angrily, on the pretext of needing another drink. He was still trying to get away from her, made angrier with himself by the perplexed and hurt look in her eyes, when he caught sight of Terry, the thickset man from the pub, slipping into the room. He took up a place to one side of the door and began scanning the crowd, frowning. As he spotted Mike the frown lifted. He gave him a quick smile of recognition that was hardly more than a twitch of the lips and signaled him, with just the faintest jerk of his head, to come and join him.

Mike turned back to the woman, glad of a genuine excuse to leave her. Gently, he prised her clasped hands over his head. He touched two fingers to her lips, forestalling the start of a pout, and quelled any further protest with a promise to be back shortly. He made a show of not forgetting his drink, and wove his way across to the door. Terry was waiting in the hall. Mike greeted him cheerfully, taking a mouthful of beer as he spoke.

"Get you a drink? It's in there."

Terry shook his head, not smiling. "No thanks, Michael. I've got someone wants to meet you." He nodded at Mike's drink. "Leave that." He waited, not hiding his impatience as Mike gulped it down. "Come on, through here."

Mike followed him, making a jokey quizzical face at the girl and the man behind the door as he went. They looked back blankly, as if looking right through him. It was as though being in the company of Terry had made him invisible. Terry walked quickly through the house, past a group of women who stood in the kitchen buttering currant bread, and out of the back door. The women stared furtively at Mike's back, their eyes flicking to the patch on his scalp where the hair was still matted over his wound. A faint admiring murmur mixed with the girlish giggles as Mike pulled the door closed behind him.

In the yard Terry turned and spoke. "Mind how you go. There's some steps."

They felt their way down the steps into the pitch blackness of the basement area. In the brief flood of light as Terry ushered him through a door at the bottom Mike caught sight of a seated figure well back in the deepest shadow of the sunken area. The figure was muffled in a quilted jacket and a balaclava helmet that left only his eyes visible. In the momentary glow from the open door Mike caught the dull glint of the gun the man held across his thighs.

They were in the kitchen of the basement flat. A gas fire hissed unhappily in the yellow-tiled hearth. Strong odors of closed rooms and bachelor cooking reminded Mike of the hotel. The wallpaper was discolored with damp. A frying pan stood on the stove; it held a quarter of an inch of congealed fat. A fried sardine lay beached in it, staring up at them. The broken remains of another lay next to it, showing it how lucky it had been. A garish portrait of the Virgin Mary looked down from the opposite wall. She wore a distressed expression that was all eyes and open mouth. Like the sardine.

"Sit down a minute," Terry waved Mike to one of the unmatched chairs. "I'll go and fetch him." He walked out into the passageway.

Mike's mouth was bone dry. He was excited and afraid. For the first time he felt certain he was moving close to the core of the organization, close to the people who had destroyed Allix, destroyed their child. The people who had destroyed all the meaning his life had briefly held, and would, if they doubted his sincerity for a single moment, call on the armed thugs who sat at every exit to destroy him, too.

Terry came back into the room. Another man followed him. He wore a pair of blood-stained brown corduroy trousers and grey socks. Above the waist he was naked, except for the heavy bandages that swathed his right arm. Mike rose to his feet in a reaction of surprise he saw no point in concealing. The face he was looking into was unmistakable. It was the one that had stared out at ten million newspaper readers the previous Monday morning, the face of the man who had escaped from the bomb factory. If the police had put the picture together from descriptions they had done a remarkable job. Terry waved a hand vaguely from Mike to the injured man. His eyes were on Mike's face, watching for his reaction. Seeing the open surprise there, he smiled, as though he had just performed a successful trick.

"Michael, I'd like you to meet Brendan." The injured man nodded and smiled as though smiling hurt him. He made no effort to shake hands. "Maybe you recognize him?"

Mike looked slowly from Brendan to Terry. He did not need to *act* impressed. The man was sought by every police and security man in the country. "Half the country would recognize him. The picture in the paper. The house in Windsor. It was you that shot the policeman."

Terry was beaming. "Right! Surprised?"

Mike shrugged. "Surprised? Yeah, I guess I am." He gestured to the ceiling. Music throbbed from above them. "But here? With all that going on? All the people in and out?"

Brendan and Terry shared a derisive laugh. Brendan sat down opposite Mike. "What would you expect? We'd hole up in some semi out in the suburbs where the whole street's deserted from morning till night? Where nobody goes in or out without being sussed by some nosey cow of a neighbor with a photographic memory for anything that's other people's business!" He jerked a thumb at the ceiling. "Up there they have parties every fucking night! They'd need an army of old bags to keep track." He gestured to a chair and dropped his voice. "Sit down, will you. There's something Terry and I want to talk to you about."

They all sat around the table. Brendan's voice was just above a whisper. "They tell me you're carrying a bit of a grievance against the British, Michael. That right?" The voice was educated, with only a trace of an Ulster accent.

Mike nodded. "Yeah, you could put it like that. A grievance."

"Their police killed your dad?"

"Killed him and got away with it, the fuckers. They covered it up so nicely, not one of the bastards ever answered for it!" His voice had risen, full of angry sarcasm.

Brendan made a patting motion in the air with his good hand. "Don't worry about all that now. There's time enough," he said, his voice so low Mike had to strain to catch his words. "Look, Michael, Terry here tells me you seem to be a good man. A bit impulsive maybe, but you've got your heart in the right place. That right?" His eyes burned into Mike's. There was a faint trace of mockery in them.

"Impulsive? If you're talking about the other night, then yeah. I can't stand there and see somebody getting hurt. I never could. Especially not by a bunch of vicious scum like that."

Brendan made a slight pursing movement with his lips. "Hurting people is our business, Michael." He was still looking straight into Mike's eyes.

"That's different. It's like war. Anyway, there's nothing impulsive about me when I've got a job to do.

Fifteen years handling oilfield explosives saw to that. Nobody fucks around with that stuff."

Brendan and Terry glanced at each other. "Right. Terry told me about that. Maybe we'll talk some more about it. Some other time. Like a drink?"

Mike nodded.

"Whisky do you?"

"Fine."

Brendan went to the kitchen cabinet and produced a bottle. He trapped it under his bandaged arm, and with his free hand lifted some glasses from the sink. He shook out the remainder of whatever was in them, not bothering to wash them, and carried them back to the table. He poured three big drinks and pushed two of them across.

"Cheers." He said it flatly, without a sign of conviviality. Something about the man put a chill on a room. "Terry here, and John, seem to have got the impression you wouldn't mind a chance to settle a bit of your score with the Brits. They seem to think from what you were saying you might be ready to do something to get back at them?"

Mike threw a long look at Terry. He had thought a lot about John's question of the previous Friday. It had been a test, a bait being dangled. He could have rejected the idea out of hand, and they would probably never have contacted him again. He had not done that. And he had come to the party. No sensible person would have come there unless he wanted to pursue the contact. It was obvious to all of them—if he had not been ready to say yes he would have stayed away.

Mike made a wry face. "Maybe. The bastards have got a lot to answer for."

"Only maybe?" Brendan held Mike's gaze and waited for an answer.

Mike shook his head. "Maybe only maybe. It depends. I've thought a lot about what John was saying. I wouldn't be here tonight if I hadn't. I'm not stupid. But I'd need to know more. I'd want to know what it was you wanted me to do before I committed myself."

Brendan extended a finger, pointing over Mike's shoulder. "Don't you think you committed yourself when you walked through that door?"

Mike shrugged. He kept his eyes on Brendan's. "No."

Brendan looked at Terry and laughed. "No, he says. He walked in here past a man with a gun that would blow him in half, and he doesn't feel he's committed himself." He turned back to Mike. "They said you were brave. Now I see what they mean. Come on. Listen to what I've got to say. If you don't like it we'll shake hands and you'll be free to leave."

Brendan and Terry looked at each other. A message seemed to pass between them. Brendan pulled his chair closer to the table, and leaned forward so that his face was no more than a foot from Mike's.

"Look, Mike, we've got somewhat of a, ah, a problem." He raised his injured arm. "As you see, last Sunday's left me in a bit of trouble. I'm going to be a little, er, indisposed for a while. Also, you've seen the papers. You said it yourself, half the country knows my face. So you'll appreciate, it's difficult for me to be out on the streets for a bit." He grinned and looked at Mike with his penetrating stare. Mike did not know if he was required to smile back. He made a grimace that might have been one. "Now, there was something I was supposed to do, be involved in, in a few days from now. I'm not going to be able to do it. We'd been thinking we'd have to call it off. Then, as I say, Terry told me about you, how you feel about the British." He paused, his eyes staring into Mike's. Mike's mouth was absolutely dry. "We wondered if you might like a chance to get involved."

Mike nodded. He forced saliva into his mouth. "I might. Tell me more."

Brendan leaned two inches closer. Mike could see the pulse throb in his temple. "Good. Before we go any further, though, there's something you should be clear about. You know who we are, don't you?"

Mike shrugged and laughed. "Well, if you're not the IRA then I'm going to be feeling pretty stupid."

"Provisionals."

"Right, sure."

"So you understand who you're getting involved with. We're serious people. We won't have anybody fucking us around. Do you understand what I'm telling you? If you don't want to hear any more say so now. We'll say goodbye, and, as I promised you, you can walk out of here. We'll never trouble you again." He said the last words as if he enjoyed the taste of them. His eyes never left Mike's.

Mike was fighting to control his reactions. Until now the risk he had been taking was a limited one, the risk maybe of a beating for being too inquisitive, at worst a smashed knee-cap. A "yes" now would change all that. To betray these people, after once agreeing to their proposal, would lead to only one thing. A bullet in the back of the head. He stared back at Brendan. As he met the man's chilling gaze he forced himself to concentrate not on where he was, or the dangers that lay in store, but on the loss of Allix; on the destruction of the unborn child; on the way his own future had been destroyed with their deaths.

"Tell me about it."

Brendan smiled his first real smile. He leaned across the stained Formica table-top and stretched out his good hand. "You're a good man, Michael. Nice to have you on our side."

It took them only a few minutes to outline to Mike what they wanted of him. Details were sparse. They told him only that he would be going along as company for somebody else, to take the "bare look" off the person, as they called it. He would be collected at the rendez-vous point they gave him. From then on all he had to do was listen to his operator and do as he was told. There would be no heroics, no guns, no danger.

"It's just a little reconnaissance job. Boring, really, isn't it?" Brendan grinned.

Mike made a dubious face. "The way you tell it, yeah. When is it going to be?"

"A few days. You got the phone number of your digs?"

He wrote down the number. Terry pocketed it. "Good. We'll phone you. D'you want to go back up-stairs? You seemed to be making out all right."

Mike shook his head. "Thanks. I think I've had all the excitement I can handle for tonight."

"Okay. Come on. I'll let you out."

Terry led the way to the front door. He tapped on it twice before opening it. Mike climbed the steps out of the darkened area. As he turned to say goodnight to Terry he was aware of a darker shape against the black-ness. Terry stayed in the doorway, watching Mike climb the steps. Seeing him glance back he raised a hand in a final goodnight and closed the door. He rejoined Brendan in the kitchen. "Well?"

Brendan shrugged. "We'll see. After this job."

"D'you like the look of him?"

Brendan's deadpan expression did not change. "He seems like a good man. Doesn't talk too much."

"But do you get the feeling we can trust him?"

Brendan looked at him for a long time before he answered. "We've got no fucking choice. After the last few months we've hardly got a decent man left opera-tional on the mainland. That's more than coincidence, Terry. Personally, the way things are just now, I'd as soon trust him as those idiots in Dublin." He stood up, dropping his voice almost to a sigh. "You think he might be a plant?"

Terry spread his hands. "I *always* think that. On principle. But if he is, then he took an awful chance in the pub. Another second and that little bastard with the screwdriver would have killed him."

"Unless *he* was a stooge, too."

Terry shook his head, smiling grimly. "No chance. I was in the back room with him. He was just a little hooligan tanked up and out for trouble. You can take my word for that."

Brendan made for the door. "All right, then. We can all sleep soundly in our beds. I'm going to, anyway. Ask them to turn the music down a little, will you?"

CHAPTER
5

Mike stopped at the kiosk. He bought the *Daily Mirror* and a packet of Senior Service. It was the first packet of cigarettes he had bought in his life, and maybe the third *Daily Mirror*. As he walked out of the station he threw a couple of pound coins into the hat of an accordion player. Another first.

"God bless you, sir. Merry Christmas."

He gave the man a lop-sided smile of acknowledgement. Neither of the man's good wishes seemed likely to apply.

The call had come at seven that morning. A voice he did not recognize had given him the name of the pub. It was a place Mike knew well, in a mews off Wigmore Street. The voice had added a time and instructed him to buy the cigarettes and the paper. The caller had been very insistent about *which* cigarettes and paper, but he had given Mike no clue as to what to expect when he got to the pub, only strict instructions about what to carry, what to wear and how to behave. Somebody was going to be able to recognize him. Somebody in the anonymity of the crowd would know that he was on a mission for the IRA. He would not know them. It was a strange, vulnerable sensation that made his spine tingle with unease. Several times he found excuses to loiter and casually examine the street. Nobody seemed to be interested in him, no furtive figures flicked into doorways as he turned.

He strode the last few blocks along Wigmore Street and into the mews. It was twenty past twelve, ten minutes before the time he had been given. The place was already full. Refugees from the shopping crowds of Oxford Street jammed the bar. He got a drink and a packet of peanuts. It was several minutes before he was able to find a seat near the door, as he had been instructed. He had to snatch it from under the nose of an outraged lady in a silver fox coat with a clear prior claim. He wedged himself into the narrow space on the red upholstery and set his beer down on the tiny, wet wrought-iron table. He made space for his newspaper beside it, put the cigarettes and the nuts on top of the paper, and settled down to wait, pointedly ignoring the inflamed look of the lady in the fox fur.

By one o'clock the place was solid. Mike watched the door as new arrivals, encumbered with bags and packages, forced their way good-naturedly through the crowd. Many of them craned to see around the bar, obviously looking for friends. The woman in the fox fur left, still in a huff. Nobody else's gaze lingered on him.

A young woman of around twenty-eight or nine turned into the mews, walking briskly. She wore a beige quilted jacket that hid everything about her figure except that she was slender. A blue woolen hat pulled close around her face concealed most of her hair, leaving visible only a few stray wisps of dark brown at her neck. One hand gripped the strap of a capacious leather shoulder-bag. In the other she carried a glossy paper carrier-bag from a fashion-store. She quickened her pace. A

group of men and women some years younger than herself had entered the mews a few seconds before her.
They were headed by a tall man in a dark suit who was
talking in a loud bray about somebody called Dominic.
His companions, three men and four women, laughed
approvingly at what he was saying, and seemed to agree
that Dominic was an aggressive little shit. They were a
few steps from the door of the pub. The woman drew
level with them at the moment the tall man pushed open
the door.

They moved inside as a group. The tall man shoved
his way with casual belligerence toward the bar, still
giving them his opinion of Dominic as he went. The
woman laughed along with the others, moving in their
wake and looking as though she did not think much of
Dominic either. As she moved she kept a hand firmly on
the big shoulder-bag at her side, like a timorous provincial, up in the big city for the day, who had heard a lot
about bag-snatchers. She kept close to the group, all the
time smiling with them at the tall man's banter. While
he bellowed at the others, collecting their orders, she
quietly bought herself a glass of white wine. She paid
using loose change from a pocket of her jacket. Her free
arm stayed tightly around the bag.

She picked up the drink and sipped it, turning casually away from the bar. Above her glass, her eyes
roamed over the faces in the room. It was a slow,
methodical look that gave her time to take in each face
without letting her gaze rest long enough on anybody to
make eye contact. The door opened as somebody left.
She let her eyes go to the door, as if vaguely attracted by
the movement there. As she did so her gaze floated over
Mike's face. She watched absently as the door swung
closed, and turned back to the bar. She stood with her
back to the room, sipping the wine and frequently
checking the time, as though somebody was keeping her
waiting. With a last glance at her watch, she turned and

began easing her way through the crush, nursing the remains of her drink.

Mike looked at his own watch for the fiftieth time. It was close to one-thirty. He was jumpy, tense and depressed. His drink stood untouched in front of him. He was certain his contact was not going to show. From all he knew of them, their taste for military jargon and military-type hierarchies, he had expected a taste for military precision. For them to be this late seemed like a piece of amateurishness. He was surprised to find himself faintly disappointed. His edginess turned to annoyance when a drably dressed woman planted herself in front of his table, blocking his view of the room. He looked up at her, scowling, and his annoyance gave way to the first flutter of excitement. The woman had paused to open a map of the Underground system. She studied it for a moment before folding it, inside out, and placing it on top of his paper and cigarettes. The doubt and disappointment fled. His first, almost idle, speculation erupted into an exultant certainty. The woman finished her drink without a glance down at Mike, picked up the map, and left the bar. He had to force himself to let thirty seconds go by, as he had been instructed. Then he was on his feet and heading for the door, mumbling apologies over his shoulder as he jostled people roughly aside.

The woman was already out of sight. He almost ran to the end of the mews. She was heading purposefully west along Wigmore Street. It took fifty yards of very fast walking to come alongside her.

"They didn't tell me it would be a woman."

She shrugged and gave him a quick, aggressive look, not slowing. "And so you're surprised! Heaven save me from chauvinist Paddies!" She shook her head, her lips pursed in an exasperated smile. No amusement showed in her eyes, and although she turned to him as she spoke her glance was never on him, but flicked constantly around her, checking the movements of cars and people. Mike recognized the mannerism. He had seen it in policemen; the habit of being alert for the fractionally unusual, the person on the street without apparent purpose, the car that dawdled. "Does it make any difference to you?"

Mike shook his head and laughed. "No."

"Good, because you're here to do exactly what I tell you to, woman or not. Okay?"

He dipped his head in acknowledgement. "That's fine. It's what I was told."

She checked the street again, ensuring nobody was within earshot. "Good. We're a couple. Christmas shopping, all right? Be natural, but just remember that's all we'll talk about. Nothing else. Is that understood?" She paused for his assent. "Good. My name's Jane. Yours, for today, is Tom."

He nodded ceremoniously. She may have been late but her briskness impressed him. Maybe she had been late for reasons of her own. Maybe, for example, they had been watching the pub, making sure he was alone. "Hi, Jane, nice to meet you. Just do one thing for me, will you?"

She frowned. "What?"

"Don't buy me socks. Not this year, again."

She smiled in spite of herself. "I just asked you to act naturally, not like a complete dick-head."

"How do you know that wouldn't be natural?"

She pursed her lips. "Okay. Now just shut up and follow me."

A few seconds later they hit the packed pavement of Oxford Street and she turned into the flow of people. They went with the crowd, silent among the chattering, excited shoppers. After fifty yards she snatched his arm and dragged him into a store. She thrust through the press of people until they were lost among the racks of clothes before turning abruptly to watch the entrance.

Mike moved close to her side, his heart pounding. "What the hell is it?" he murmured, following her gaze.

She shrugged, not taking her eyes from the people entering the store. "Nothing. Just a routine check. Do what I do. Watch the people. You're looking for anyone who comes in hurrying and then hesitates. Watch to see if they look at the merchandise or the faces."

"Why?" He was already doing as she said, scrutinizing the people passing through the triple glass doors.

"In case they're looking for us," she muttered, baring her teeth grimly.

He could feel ice in his stomach. "You think somebody is?"

She looked away from the door, apparently satisfied, and turned to him, checking nobody stood too close. She gave him a pitying look. "Somebody *always* is. This is Oxford Street. It's nearly Christmas. Any face in the crowd could be a copper in plain clothes. Bear it in mind. They'll have been drafting every able-bodied policeman in to mingle with the crowd for weeks past. We've been here before. Remember?" She turned to lead the way out of the store.

He nodded. It was true. The crowd would be full of policemen on the look-out for a known IRA face. He hoped Jane did not qualify. Over the years this part of Oxford Street, with its busy department stores, had been a regular IRA bomb target, almost always in the period before Christmas when the shops were thronged. A lot of innocent people had been maimed. A few had been killed.

He hurried to draw alongside her. "Yeah, I remember. It's an institution. Like the Queen Mother, or the Cup Final."

A bitter edge had found its way into his voice. Her head snapped around to look at him. He could almost feel the intense blue-green eyes burn into his face as she stared at him with a sharp, strange look. She hesitated, as though she were about to speak, and then spun away again. "Come on. We've got a job to do."

He followed her out on to the street, violently angry with himself for letting his guard drop.

Twice more she led him through the same routine. Between the detours into shops they drifted through the carpet of litter, pausing at display windows to discuss theoretical Christmas gifts for imaginary relatives. A uniformed policeman stood at an intersection controlling the traffic and the crowd. Mike could feel his heart pounding as they stood waiting to be signaled to cross. The traffic stopped. They were carried forward by the press, toward the ornate bulk of Selfridge's. On the opposite pavement a street photographer worked the crowd. He had in tow a haggard-looking Santa Claus in a mid-calf robe and damaged brown brogues. The Santa was sidling up to unsuspecting shoppers and coiling an arm around their shoulders. The photographer snapped them quickly, before they could recoil from Santa's breath, and thrust cards into their hands as they fought free.

Jane hung on to his arm, smiling as she made him stop to watch the photographer. Mike grinned as another panicky shopper shied at discovering Santa's seamed face attempting a jovial leer inches from her own. The photographer pushed a card at the startled woman. Then, with a professional's instinct for a sale, he aimed the camera at Mike and Jane. Mike's grin fell to pieces. He threw up an arm in protest and turned to Jane, just in time to see a slightly built man on the far side of her disengage himself from her other arm. The man slipped off back across the road, dodging around cars as the solid mass of traffic surged forward again. Instinctively, Mike tried to turn to follow the man. Jane's weight on his arm impeded him.

"Come on. In here," she said.

He shook his arm free. "Who was that? What the fuck was he up to?"

She pulled at his sleeve. "Forget it. Don't make a scene. Just do as I tell you. Let's get to work."

He continued straining to see the man, but it was useless. Two buses passed, nose to tail. By the time they had swung into Oxford Street, clearing Mike's line of vision, the man had disappeared, swallowed up in the dense crush. Jane had taken Mike by the hand and was dragging him across the pavement, toward Selfridge's. He followed her into the store, still craning angrily after the man. As they entered he noticed that the photographer, too, had melted away. The flea-bitten Santa was standing aimlessly in the middle of the throng, his pinched, down-and-out's face staring vacantly around him.

Mike turned angrily to Jane and grabbed her by the shoulder, yanking her around to face him. "Look, I want to know what the fuck's going on! Who was that?" A few shoppers stared covertly around at them. Mike's voice was low and controlled but an intensity in his tone aroused their curiosity.

Jane gave them a sweet, quick smile and laid a restraining hand on Mike's arm. "An old friend of my family," she said sweetly. "I don't think you know him." As the bystanders lost interest, disappointed at her conversational tone, she jerked hard on his arm. "Remember we're here for a purpose," she said in a gritty voice hardly louder than a murmur, "and that I'm running things. You just do whatever the hell I tell you and stop screwing around trying to second-guess me. Okay?"

"Okay. And just what the fuck *is* the purpose?"

"Yours is to do what you're told. Come on."

Jane led him through the store, roaming from counter to counter and department to department, an ideal couple in search of the ideal gift. She was looking at her watch with increasing frequency. Mechanically, not knowing why, Mike checked his. It was coming up to two o'clock. She led him to the escalators.

The toy department was on the third floor. A large sign indicated where they could get a sleigh ride and a children's choir sang through loudspeakers, competing with the babble of young voices. The place was crammed with excited children dragging their parents around the animated displays. Robots spoke in metallic voices; overhead, tiny trains sped around an elaborate aerial railway system. Mike was looking up at it when he felt her weight against his side. She began propelling him toward the lifts, from one of which excited children were pouring, hauling smiling parents in their wake. Parents and children laden with packages began cramming in. Jane held back until the lift was nearly full, then she ploughed roughly among the last few people and shoved Mike inside. She stepped close up against him, her mouth an inch from his ear.

"We split here. See you back at the pub. Go straight there. We've got four minutes."

The doors were already sliding together when she stepped back, shoved him hard in the chest and turned away. Off-balance, he watched her back disappear as the doors swished closed. She no longer carried the shoulder bag.

For a moment Mike stared dumbly at the closed doors. In the instant before the lift began to move the realization of what was about to happen hit him like a blow to the head. Nausea wrenched at his stomach, making him gag. He fought it down and leaped for the panel of buttons, fighting to get through the tight wedge of passengers, oblivious to their angry protests.

The lift gathered momentum. Shouting incoherently, Mike redoubled his efforts, pushing parents and children roughly aside. He had already missed one floor. He stabbed a finger at the first-floor button. Images of the children whirled in his mind. He *had* to get out of the thing, find a fire alarm, get back up to the toy department and warn them, anything. In his desperation he was moaning and yelling unintelligibly, impervious to the alarmed looks of the other passengers.

Abruptly, the lift stopped. They were plunged into total, inky darkness. Some of the women had already begun to scream when the emergency light flickered on, bathing them in a watery blue glow. Mike waited for an instant, then pressed close to the doors, hoping they might open. Nothing happened. He glanced up at the panel above his head. The floor indicator light was out.

The crowd pressed further to the back of the lift as Mike shouted, his voice a choking sob. "No! Not a power cut! Not now! Please, not now!"

With a bellow of pure rage he began clawing at the doors, scrambling futilely to insert his fingertips between them and drag them open. It was useless. He began beating on the doors, nearly crying in sick frustration. A man, almost as big as Mike, pushed through the cowering crowd. He put a hand gently on Mike's arm.

"Easy now, mate, don't panic. It's just the power gone, that's all. They'll soon have us out. It's only a bit of claustrophobia. Shut your eyes, take deep breaths, you'll be okay."

He recoiled as Mike shook him off, snarling. "Leave me alone. It's the kids. Up there."

Under the man's uncomprehending gaze he reached up to claw at the panel set in the ceiling. Without any kind of tool, he could make no impression on it. He abandoned it and turned back to the doors, hammering and shouting in an absolute frenzy. He was almost mad with desperation. The four minutes she had mentioned must be very nearly gone. He tried again to prise the doors apart, tearing at the steel with his fingernails. The other passengers were pressed back against the walls, staring at him as though he were a madman. The children clung to their parents' legs, crying. Their wails mingled with his shouts in a mind-jangling din.

The power had been off for more than two minutes and he was still beating at the steel doors when the lift shifted, as though the air in the shaft had compressed. Simultaneously, they felt as much as heard a distant, muffled crump. Mike slid to the floor, crying bitterly. He sat hunched against the door, his face buried in his hands. The other passengers watched him silently, frightened or smirking. He had been there for several minutes before the lift jerked to life and began descending with the erratic, irregular movement that signaled that somebody was winding it down manually. In another thirty seconds he was looking up into the face of a fireman. The fireman looked at the expression on Mike's face and grinned knowingly at the rest of the passengers.

"It's all right, mate. You're out now. It's all over. Come on."

The other passengers flooded from the lift, shepherding their children well clear of Mike. They cast curious glances back at him as they hurried toward the exits. Mike stood motionless by the lift entrance, staring unbelievingly at the fireman. He shook his head, confused and incredulous at the man's cheerfulness.

"What about the kids?" His voice was a rasp.

The fireman had already turned his attention to another lift. He looked over his shoulder, puzzled. "Kids? What kids?" His eyes followed the direction of Mike's gesture as he pointed toward the ceiling. "Oh! The third floor!" He laughed. "We had them all out of there before *that* one went off. A couple of staff people hurt a bit, otherwise, no problem. We'd got the whole place half empty by then, after the first one. Mad bastards!"

Mike frowned. "The *first* one? There were *two* bombs?"

The fireman laughed sourly. "That's right. The first one was over in the men's gear. An incendiary in the bleeding sheep-skin coats. Can you imagine that? Animal Rights nutters, probably. Never thought we'd all have reason to be grateful to them bastards, did you?"

A shout from a colleague took the fireman's attention. Another lift had reached the ground floor. "You all right? Need an ambulance?" Mike shook his head. "Well, there's ambulances and first aid out on Oxford Street." The man turned and hurried across to help his colleague, leaving Mike staring dumbly after him. He stood there for a few moments more, trying to bring order to the tumult of his thoughts and emotions. At length, he turned and walked slowly toward the street.

Outside was chaos. Fire engines, ambulances and police cars stood parked at all angles across Oxford Street, and more were arriving, their sirens sawing the air. Police and firemen conferred in groups. As Mike emerged a stretcher was pushed into an ambulance which screamed away from the curb, lights and siren on. Gawpers stood in dense crowds at the police barricades. The front rows watched in fascinated silence as he sat down at the curb, his feet in the gutter, and was violently sick.

Mike awoke with a terrible hangover. It was nearly nine o'clock. He eased himself gingerly out of bed, threw a couple of heaped spoons of Maxwell House into a mug and half-filled it with hot water. He drank it off black, pulled on yesterday's underpants and made his way to the bathroom. A long bath did not improve things much. He returned to his room, pulled on the rest of his clothes and went out to buy a copy of every one of the Sunday papers. Back in his room, he made a jug of coffee and sat down to go through them.

The papers were having a field day. Three-inch headlines screamed from the front pages of the tabloids above shots of a bleeding figure on a stretcher. He pushed them to one side and began searching for the facts. The first thing he looked for was the number of casualties. It turned out the fireman had been right; two people had been injured, both men. One of them was reported as being in a serious condition. He read it carefully in several papers. They all agreed on the phrase—the man's condition was "serious." He laughed with relief, but the laughter was very near to tears. Nobody was going to die; when they were going to die the press invariably used the word "critical." However bad their injuries might be, they were not going to be fatal. "Thank God for that." His relief was so great he said it aloud.

He read through the whole story in each of the papers, turning over every detail in his mind. Just before two o'clock an incendiary bomb had gone off among a rack of sheepskin coats in the men's clothing department on the ground floor. It had been a big device and the resulting fire had caused considerable damage. Much space was given over to congratulating the store on its evacuation procedures. This was natural—it gave the readers a warm sense of being prudent themselves, of having somehow collectively outwitted the terrorists.

It was no doubt true that the years of being a prime target for the IRA, and every other bunch of cranks in the country, had been an incentive to devise an efficient plan and to make damned sure the staff practiced it regularly. By the time the second bomb, the IRA bomb, had exploded in the toy department the top two floors had been virtually empty. The injured men had been staff who had been supervising the evacuation of the toy floor. First inquiries seemed to indicate that this second bomb consisted of a relatively small amount of explosive packed around with short nails. There was even a photograph of the type of nail used; galvanized clout nails, an inch long, sharply pointed and with a wide, flat head. The sight of them actually made him shudder. But for the accident of the first bomb alert going off a few minutes earlier and upsetting the IRA's plan, the nails would have ripped into the packed crowd of parents and children. Picturing to himself the horror that would have resulted made him shudder again, as if to shake himself free of the image. He pulled on his jacket and went out.

For a long time he simply walked the almost empty streets, incapable of coherent thought, not even noticing the fine sleet that clung like dew to the rough material of his jacket and frosted his hair and eyebrows. Gradually, the walking calmed him, and his mind slowly began ordering his tumbling thoughts.

At one moment, he felt a chill at the pit of his stomach at the thought of himself as having come within moments of being a mass child-killer. The next, he was telling himself that, had the ALF firebomb not cut the power, he would have raised the alarm, even though it would have meant the end of the task he had set himself. He tried to put aside the horrors that might have been and force himself to concentrate on the facts.

As he did so, it became clear that the episode had been intended as a test for him. Not a test of whether he was ready to plant the bomb—she had not even let him know about it until after it was in place. The reasoning was plain to see. If he had known beforehand he could not only have prevented the bombing, he could have turned her in to the authorities. As she had arranged it, he *could* have raised the alarm, but only after she had melted into the crowd. The realization of his luck struck him with the force of a blow. Nowhere in the newspapers was there a mention of the ALF firebomb having cut the power, and no reference was made to the lifts having been stopped. As far as the girl and her organization knew he had had ample time to raise the alarm, yet he had not done it. For them, he had passed his test. He had been a willing participant in what would have been one of their foulest escapades. He had proved that from now on he was trustworthy.

The horror of it made his stomach churn. He tried telling himself that the bombing was planned to happen with or without him, that Brendan could have been replaced by any of the anonymous gunmen who silently guarded the doors behind which they planned their outrages. It did not work. The sickening thought refused to be suppressed; they could trust him to kill children.

A burst of shouting broke into his thoughts. He looked up. A football match was going on, and the noise was from a group of people under umbrellas bunched on the sideline. He had been too preoccupied even to notice that he had entered Regent's Park. He headed south, toward Portland Place. By the time he reached the gate leading to Park Square he had managed to put the idea aside long enough to get his mind around his options.

Essentially, he had just two choices. The first was to get out now, leave England and take up the threads of his previous life. Doing it, he could give the police some scraps; the address of the house where the party had been, descriptions of John and his friends and the girl, all of which might lead the police nowhere. There was every chance Brendan would no longer be at the house. The others were at best middle-level people, talent scouts doing the legwork for others he had not yet come close to. The structure would remain intact. The beast would be wounded but very far from dead.

The other choice was to go on and finish what he had started: to capitalize on the new confidence they would have in him, to continue until he had penetrated the darkness at the very heart of the organization, until the war he had declared had been won.

He crossed into Park Crescent, dodging the sparse traffic. A woman with beautifully groomed white hair descended the steps of one of the elegant town houses, preceded by a setter on a retractable leash. She smiled and wished Mike good morning. He walked blindly past her, not even aware she had spoken. She stared balefully after him, offended at the waste of a democratic impulse. He turned into Portland Place. To continue his subterfuge might, almost certainly would, mean he would be asked to participate in other bombings, with the likelihood of more innocent deaths. He struggled with the idea. The implications were almost overwhelming; he would be forced to play at being God, to stand back and allow bystanders to die in the pursuit of a greater goal. It was an attitude that went against the grain of the way he had tried to live his whole life. But, if he turned his back on it, if he returned to the desert somewhere, kept his own hands clean, would there be a single death less? They would simply go about their murderous business without him.

His father's death, and the test he had passed, put him in a unique situation. It could take the security forces years to get an infiltrator into the position he was in. If he could only bide his time, keep his own nature in check, he had a reasonable chance of penetrating deeply enough to identify the High Command, the handful of fanatically motivated hard men he held ultimately responsible for Allix's death. And if he could do that, if he could once have the chance to come close to the head of the monster, he would destroy it. They would pay for all the lives they had taken. Most of all, they would pay for taking Allix away, and for denying life to his unborn child. The beast would be slain. He looked around him. He was on Regent Street, almost at Oxford Circus. Knots of tourists in brightly colored waterproofs braved the rain. He called a taxi and gave the address of the pub off King Street.

By the time he returned to his room it was late afternoon. The few beers he had drunk seemed to have dispelled his hangover. He had seen no familiar faces at the pub. He had been relieved at this, since he had been in no mood for lunchtime banter; his object had been only to show himself. He wanted to let them know, following his failure to appear at the rendezvous after the bombing, that he was back in circulation. He locked the door, leaving the key in the lock. The keyhole was big enough to give the landlord a fair view of the table area. He prised up the board and lifted the bulging file from its hiding place.

Sitting at the bare table he wrote the fullest description he could of the girl. It was not much; the bulky clothes had effectively disguised her outline and the hat had hidden her hair and forehead. He had not realized until then how much he relied on the hair to describe a woman's appearance. Only the vivid blue-green eyes, wide-set and large, offered any kind of hold on her. The description finished, he began trying to sketch her. He was no artist, but he had developed a technique over the last few weeks which served him reasonably well. First he drew the best approximation he could of the general shape of the face; then he gradually refined it by concentrating on each feature in turn, relying on purely physical matters such as the distance between the eyes, the length of the nose. An hour later he had a passable likeness.

It resembled none of the grainy photographs already imprinted in his memory, and yet somehow fitted among them. He was looking at yet another of the apparently ordinary young women who, over the years, had proved to be some of the IRA's best operators. He found himself reflecting briefly on the underlying appeal of the Republican cause that enabled it to continue attracting these young people, who knew full well they were running a high risk of being shot. He immediately pushed the thought to the back of his mind. He was not at war with Republicanism. His fight was with the

Provos and their deadly methods. For all he knew Jane might be a loving, dutiful daughter, a loyal and attentive elder sister. But she was still ready to go out at the Provos' bidding and slaughter children.

CHAPTER
6

MIKE WALKED OUT OF THE POST OFFICE. IT WAS A DARK, grey day; a raw wind gnawed at the faces of the shoppers and a little earlier it had tried to snow. Mike's stride and his closed expression were a stark contrast with the pre-Christmas bustle and determined cheerfulness of the people around him. He had just sent a Christmas present to Tom. He was disappointed with himself that the gift was two fifty-pound notes. He would have preferred to send the boy something chosen, something personal. But a pervading wariness, the fear of being observed, had kept him out of toy stores. Now, the act of posting it had brought a surge of loneliness. Amid the expectant children and the laden shoppers the renewed sense of desolation and loss was overpowering.

He strode through the dense crowd that eddied around the identikit façades of the high-street chains. The sheer relentless power of the decorated windows and the low-fi caroling from the Chamber of Commerce loudspeakers deepened his depression.

He had enclosed a letter with the money, saying

that he had found a job on an exploration crew in Indonesia. It was a long letter, a dozen or more pages crammed with the kind of minute detail he knew Tom loved to hear. He had included everything he had ever heard from colleagues in the oil business who had spent time there. In addition, he invented a lot. It was all stuff any boy would enjoy; deadly snakes, impenetrable jungle, helicopter transport, weekend leaves spent snorkeling around gorgeous coral reefs. Sharks. The stone-age way of life of the outlying tribes. He had ended by joking that the Indonesian post office still maintained stone-age methods, too, which explained the lack of exotic stamps for Tom's collection and the London postmark; he had given the letter to a crew member to post as he passed through London on leave.

His lips formed a brief, bitter smile as he thought of the Lorimers' relief. Thinking he was a few thousand miles away might make it easier for them to deal with the hundred pounds. He wondered how they would react to the money, hoping they would give Tom his head to choose something for himself. They would probably use it to buy him a few shares in a unit trust, keeping the tainted money out of his grasp until he was old enough to cope with the stigma of its origins.

He turned into the Underground and bought a ticket to Colindale. Apart from his usual researches there was another matter that needed more urgent investigation. It had been triggered by an incident the previous evening. It was four days since the bombing and the third evening Mike had spent in the pub. It was the last full week before Christmas, and the place had been packed solid every night. Among the hundreds of faces Mike had not seen a soul from among the limited group he knew. Despite that, he had been getting a strong sense, from the behavior of the barmen and the other drinkers, that they were treating him with a new respect. It might just have been that word of his role in the fight had got around. Or it might be that word was out that he was now a Provo soldier, a man to be treated with deference. Then, last night, there had been an incident that had worried him deeply.

For the first time since the bombing he had seen a familiar face. Its owner was a big, florid, stupid individual who hung around the fringes of the group Mike had come to know, ingratiating himself with an unpleasant line in dirty jokes. He was a man who would have drunk with a mass child-molester as long as the other man was buying. But he had not wanted anything to do with Mike. By feigning drunken insistence Mike had virtually forced the man to let him buy him a drink, but he did not get much for his money. The few words the man spoke as they waited for the drinks were said in a strange, jerky rush. He looked around him constantly. He was afraid of something. And it was something connected with Mike. The man downed his whisky at a gulp and slammed his glass on to the bar. With a nervous nod and a grunted acknowledgement, he backed away, turned and hurried out of the pub.

Mike had left the place soon afterward and taken a taxi home, instructing the driver to stop two blocks from the hotel. He had approached on foot, watching very carefully for anything unusual, and did not relax until he was safely in his room with the door locked. As an afterthought, he had jammed a chair under the door knob.

He had lain awake deep into the night going over the man's strange behavior in his mind. Normally, the idiot would have been even happier than usual to take a drink, knowing it was bought by an active member of the Provos—it would have swelled his own ego. But it seemed he had heard, or thought he had, something which made Mike's status less of a racing certainty. And once there was a question mark over anybody you steered clear, just in case, so as not to be standing too close if there happened to be any shooting.

Mike went over every move he had made since the beginning. He could see no reason for them to think he had failed his initiation—unless they knew about the lift incident. But even if they knew, they could not blame him for that. It would have meant they needed to test him again, nothing more. The more he thought about it, the more he came back to worrying about the one glaring inconsistency in his story, the one point that did not yet stand up. For hours he had lain in bed wrestling with the problem. It had been nearly five o'clock when he had suddenly snapped upright in his bed. A possible solution had emerged from the depths of his memory. He had fallen asleep jubilant, determined to spend the next day plugging the gap.

The train stopped at Colindale. The jubilation of the previous night had ebbed. With the dank greyness of the dawn the weakness in his story loomed larger, the chances of his being able to eliminate it less sure. He strode from the station, nodding brusquely in response to the newsvendor's greeting, and crossed the busy road to the Newspaper Library. He did not even know if they kept what he needed, or even whether it qualified as a newspaper.

What he was looking for was not in the main indexes. It took him some time to track down the English language newspapers of the Arabian Gulf. There were several of them. Mostly they carried heavily edited wire service copy or re-hashed items from the British and American press. The overall effect was to give them a curious stale flavor, like the "European" edition of the *Herald Tribune;* right up-to-date on the price of pork belly futures and two days late with the news. He had a pretty accurate idea of the date of the event he was looking for. It had happened sometime in the late spring, while he had been taking a short break in Bahrain, one of the more attractive places in the area for oilfield men to take their short leaves. He found the item in less than ten minutes.

The *Gulf Courier* was a thin tabloid that mostly carried three types of story. The front page invariably covered "political" news, like the verbatim text of a speech by one of the local rulers as he opened yet another already obsolete petrochemical complex. The rest was padded out with a lot of stuff promoting the spurious, fabricated "events" of Gulf life. Except for the "society" page. In his years in the Gulf area Mike had never been able to decide if this page was *meant* to be parody. Mostly, it consisted of captioned pictures of young male members of the ruling families taking part in "sports" that required very little skill and huge amounts of money.

Anything resembling a piece of genuine news that happened locally was an irresistible windfall for them. The editor had been so excited by the item that lay spread in front of Mike that he had devoted a whole page to it. Better still, he had accompanied it with a six-by-four photo.

So close to Christmas there were very few readers in the Library, and it had not been difficult to find a chair where he could be unobserved. He slid the old-fashioned double-edged razor blade he had brought for the purpose from its wrapping and quickly sliced the page from its binder, folded it and slipped it into his pocket. He closed the binder, confident the missing page would not be discovered for forty years or so, and strolled out into the street.

Mike was hardly through the entrance of the hotel when the door at the end of the passage opened abruptly. He recoiled against the wall, his knees flexed, his hands up in front of his face, ready for trouble. The landlord slid from the shadows. He gave Mike a cock-eyed look and handed him a torn corner of the TV Times. A number was clumsily scrawled in thick pencil in the margin.

"You're s'posed to call this number." The landlord glanced at his watch. "At five. He said it was important. If you can't ring at five then you've got to do it at six. Or seven. On the hour, he said."

Mike nodded, examining the number. "Did he leave a name?"

"No. Just said you'd know." The landlord sidled closer, detecting the heady scent of mystery. "Who is he?"

Mike looked at him distractedly. "My psychiatrist!" he murmured confidentially. He turned away and walked up the stairs, leaving the man staring nervously after him, as if he were trying to guess the extent of the psychiatric disorder that lurked above his head.

At five o'clock they met again in the hall. The landlord had some urgent idling to do within earshot of the phone. Mike called the number. It was answered before he had even heard it ring.

"Hello. This is Mike Scanlon."

"Yeah, right." Mike did not recognize the coarse voice. "You're wanted for a meeting. There's some people want to see you. Tomorrow."

"Where? What time?" He glanced up to find himself looking the landlord right in the eye. He held the man's stare. The landlord sniffed and shuffled a couple of reluctant paces backward in the direction of his lair.

"Get the District Line at Whitechapel tomorrow. The first Upminster train after two o'clock. Third carriage. You got a decent watch? Check it by the BBC time signal. Get on by the door in the middle of the carriage. Don't sit down. You'll be met. Got it?"

"Yeah. Who should I look out for?"

"Don't worry about it. They'll look out for you." The man rang off.

Mike stood biting his lip for a few seconds before

slowly replacing the phone. The landlord was closing in again. He gave him the tight smile of a man fighting to keep insanity in check and took the stairs two at a time.

Mike scanned the scattering of people on the platform. None looked the part, whatever the part might be. Most of them were ill-dressed white people with the pale faces and pinched mouths of those who somehow seemed not to have heard about the prosperity sweeping the nation. There was a sprinkling of Asians, a black youth with dreadlocks swagged inside a bright woollen cap, and three foul-mouthed teenaged girls whose short skirts offered little protection from the rawness of the wind that sliced across the open platform. If what he had been reading in the Sunday papers about yuppies flocking into the East End were true, they did not seem to be doing it by the District Line. While listening incredulously to the filthy conversation of the three girls he was keeping an eye on his watch. Two o'clock ticked by. He waited another twelve minutes in the biting wind before a train rattled to a stop.

He boarded, remained standing just inside the door and made a quick survey of the other passengers. Nobody among the sparse crowd in the carriage appeared to be taking any notice of him at all. He stayed by the door. At each stop the tension within him rose, subsiding again as the doors slid closed with no approach made. The only person who got on or off near him was a thickset middle-aged woman with a headscarf knotted tightly over her hair, grappling with a laden shopping trolley. The train re-emerged from the tunnel into the above-ground dereliction of the East End stations. The doors opened again. Nobody moved on or off the train. A gust of wind blasted through the open door. The sudden chill on his back made Mike aware for the first time that his shirt was soaked with sweat.

He watched the platform through the windows.

There was not a soul there. The doors jerked and began to close. The gap between them was down to two feet when the thick-set woman shoved out an arm. The doors slammed against her elbow and her cupped palm, leaving a space a foot or so wide.

"Your stop, Mr. Scanlon. Quick!"

He looked at her in momentary surprise. She reached forward, grabbed his jacket and hustled him toward the gap. Recovering himself, he ducked under her arm and squeezed out on to the platform. He felt a firm shove in his back and the doors slammed shut. Under the impact of the push his shoe caught an unevenness in the concrete and made him stumble. By the time he recovered his balance the train was already pulling out, and he was alone on the deserted platform. It had been nicely done. The woman looked like a housewife but she had the timing of a real pro. If he had brought anyone along to keep him company they would have been on their way to the next station. He spun at the sound of a voice calling his name. A man in corduroy jeans and an army-surplus combat jacket appeared from behind a low building that had housed toilets until the vandals and glue-sniffers had forced the station management to padlock it.

The man strode off along the platform, nodding to Mike to follow. He led him to a waiting Ford Escort, parked so close to the car behind that as they approached it from the rear the number plate was hidden. It might have been like that by accident. The man drove in silence to where a row of dilapidated houses awaited demolition in a landscape of abandoned factories. Some of the houses were boarded up, others still had tattered fronds of thin curtain blowing from empty windows. They were coated with spray-can graffiti, even at first-floor level, the only place a spray-can vandal with any integrity could still find the virgin space his art demanded.

The car stopped outside the one house that still had a few of its windows intact. The driver grunted to Mike to get out and escorted him across the pavement, where tough-looking city grass heaved at the asphalt, through the gap where a front gate had once hung and up to the front door. It was opened before they reached it by a thin, sandy-haired young man of around twenty, surprisingly dressed in a cheap blue suit with the neatly ironed points of a folded handkerchief peeping from the breast pocket. He looked like a clerk dressed up for an interview for a new job. Except for his face; it was a narrow, active face, with flickering, excited eyes. His gaze darted past Mike to twitch up and down the deserted street, then nodded and pressed himself aside to let Mike pass. As he brushed past the man Mike noticed the bitten-down fingernails. And the scratched metal of the pistol he held hidden from the view of anyone in the street. Behind Mike, the driver returned to the car and sat in it, his eyes twitching constantly from the street in front of him to his rearview mirror.

The gunman turned Mike to the wall and silently and roughly searched him. Over his shoulder Mike tried a joke. The man's face was only inches from his own, and the nervous eyes drilled back into his. Mike shrugged; not everybody had a sense of humor. Straightening, the man urged Mike down the narrow passage ahead of him. It led into a meanly proportioned room, made dingy by the tattered curtains drawn across the windows. In the middle of the floor stood a makeshift table made from a door ripped from its hinges and placed across two up-ended crates. Another crate stood on its end on his side of the table. Three men sat facing him on the other side. One of them, a man of around fifty with the permanent red-brown tan, ingrained grime and split fingernails of a lifelong outdoor worker, motioned to the armed man to withdraw, then smiled and waved Mike to sit opposite them. Mike nodded and sat carefully on the upturned crate.

"Nice of you to come, Michael."

Mike turned slightly to look at the speaker. He was a man of about twenty-eight. He had a narrow, handsome face with a well-kept blond moustache. The leather elbow-patches on his tweed jacket were just for effect—the jacket was new. His voice was cultured and cool; this and his rather fussy, pedantic politeness seemed to indicate a man who would enjoy sitting on committees, a man who would know a point of order when he saw one.

"My name's Eddie. This is Tommy," he gestured to the older man, "and this is Kevin."

Mike nodded and smiled briefly at each of the men in turn, openly studying them. He had to work hard not to let his gaze stay longer on Kevin. The man was about forty-five. Under an expensive leather jacket he had the wide-shouldered, compact trunk of a gymnast. A gold Rolex showed below the cuff of the jacket. On the other wrist he wore a heavy gold bracelet with a broad name tag set in it. The tag was blank. He had the hard, closed face of a slum landlord, and as Mike looked at it he felt a thrill of excitement run through him, excitement mixed with the chill of real fear. He knew this man! The same face looked out from a couple of dozen photographs in the file that lay beneath the floorboards of his room. This was a different breed of animal from the low-level recruiters he had been dealing with so far. This man was a convicted killer, on the run from prison in Ulster. He was somebody very close to the top.

"Nice place," Mike said affably, waving a hand at the streamers of wallpaper dangling from the wall.

Eddie smiled thinly, letting Mike know nobody was in the mood for jokes. "Don't worry yourself about the soft furnishings. We never use the same place twice, anyway. We've made the mistake before."

"Yeah, so I've heard." He smiled. Ever since the phone call he had been calculating that smile. It was vital to hit the right note with these people, to let them know he was not intimidated by their reputations, that he was confident. Not brash, not cocky; just sure of what he had to offer them. "From what I've been reading in the papers these last few months there've been a few other mistakes made." He dropped his voice, making his tone somber. "The way things seem to be going lately those SAS bastards are well on the way to closing you down completely. Every time I pick up a paper I seem to read about another fuck-up."

He studied them as they exchanged a quick look. Only the older one gave a clue to his reactions. His lips pursed and the flesh around his eyes tightened in a hint of a rueful smile. The faces of the others stayed absolutely closed. Eddie spoke again in a voice that crackled with contained anger.

"We didn't ask you to come here to seek your advice. We get plenty of that from over the water."

Mike smiled inwardly. So they did have nerves, and he had just struck one.

The older man, Tommy, spoke next. "Look, Michael, why don't you start by telling us a bit about yourself?"

He smiled and shrugged. "What d'you want to know?"

"Everything." It was Kevin who replied. His voice was harsh, with a permanent sneer not quite concealed within it. "Start at the beginning. Where you were born, for instance. Who your parents were. Where did they come from? Just tell us everything that comes into your head."

Kevin's eyes drilled into his. Mike held his stare for a moment and then looked negligently away, as if the man's tough pose bored him. He started telling his story. He had been rehearsing it for weeks past and every minute detail was absolutely clear in his mind. He could have recited every event, every date, every name, exactly in its place. That was not the way he had prepared it. Instead, he told a story full of the leaps, hesitations, revisions, groping for dates and sudden recollections of someone who had not thought coherently about his past until that moment.

His parents had come over from Ireland some years before he was born and settled in Birmingham. His father worked, when his health was up to it, in the building trade. His mother kept house. Mike had been their only child. He had left his Catholic-run school at sixteen, and had gone to work in an engineering company, taking evening classes toward a diploma in electrical engineering. He had never finished it. It was during this period that his father had been killed. His voice grew harsher at the mention of it. Eddie made a motion with his hand, calming him.

"We'll come back to that. Just get on with your story."

Mike flashed the young man an angry look, hesitated, as though he were struggling to control his emotions, and then went on with his story. His mother had suffered from severe asthma attacks that prevented her working. After his father's death it had fallen to him to support her, and a factory wage did not go far, so he had gravitated to contract work in the oil industry. It was well paid, gave him a chance to save, and West Africa or the Libyan desert did not seem so bad if you were comparing them to Lozells Road.

Up to the point where he left Birmingham anything he told them as a concrete fact would stand up to investigation. He stuck strictly to the truth. In areas less amenable to checking, such as his attitude to his father, he used more imagination. He did as he had done the night of the skirmish with the skinheads; he transformed his father effortlessly from the shiftless, limited, bullying drunk of real life into good old Patsy Scanlon, lovable Republican philosopher. They had no way of knowing the truth. Mike's mother was dead. It was not quite the moment to tell them about his father's enchanting habit of vomiting in the bedroom.

The story from the moment he left Birmingham posed a more delicate problem. The truth was that he had left to go into the oil industry, and had joined a company specializing in seismic work. They had sent him first to Zaire, then Angola and then on to Libya. He had stayed there for three years before joining an oil company and moving to Saudi Arabia and the Gulf. He had filled the empty evenings in remote camps by studying, taking correspondence courses in electronics that had brought him a degree. Far from being the drifter he needed them to believe, he had been an industrious and resourceful hand.

That was where the problem lay. If he told them the truth about his professional life it would be completely at odds with what he now claimed to be, and it would be comparatively easy for them to locate people he had worked with. Apart from showing up his adopted persona as a fabrication, not one of those people would ever have heard Mike Scanlon utter a single word of support for what the Provos were doing. And anyone who had heard him talk of his father would not have recognized the lovable rascal Mike was now describing. The harder he could make it for them to get a handle on his past the safer he would feel.

The story he had rehearsed was not altogether untrue. He simply blurred the edges a little. Instead of listing the steps in a creditable career, he claimed to have been drifting from country to country, working short contracts, going wherever the chance of a job had taken him. Between contracts he claimed to have hung around Africa and the Middle East until his money ran out, forcing him back to work. He owned up to making desultory efforts to keep up his electronics studies through correspondence courses, but without ever finishing. It was plausible, close enough to the truth for him to be able to support it with a rich supply of anecdote, and it was very difficult to check.

They sat poker-faced through his narrative. For a long time, none of them made any comment at all. Only when he talked about his time on seismic crews did they ask any questions, concentrating on his experience with explosives. When he had brought them up to the point of the fight in the pub and the conversation with John and his friends he sat back and looked at each of them. "I guess you know the rest as well as I do."

Eddie nodded. "M'mm. How about languages? We hear you speak Arabic."

Mike laughed and gave a modest shrug. "A bit, you know."

Kevin shook his head. The sneer had not left his voice. "No, we don't know. We'd like to. A little bit or a big bit? Do you speak it or don't you?"

Mike smiled, still modest. The truth was, he had spent a year at Kuwait University studying the language, sponsored by his oil company. That was something else he definitely did not have it in mind to tell them. It would have been at odds with the picture of himself as oilfield trash, one of the itinerant workers of the industry.

"Aw, I don't know. A fair amount, I guess. I've spent quite a bit of time hanging around out there. The only thing you might call serious learning was one time I had a boat for a few months, me and an Egyptian friend of mine. We spent the time bumming around up and down the Gulf. He used to try to teach me." He laughed fondly at the memory. The boat was real, the Egyptian was pure imagination.

"You like them? Arabs, I mean." Kevin pulled at the cuffs of his blouson. He was scowling as he spoke.

The tone and the expression made his own position clear.

Mike grinned. "*Like them?* I don't know. I guess I always got along with them okay. Mind you, speaking some Arabic helped. And treating them like people. Most of the people in the oil business seem to treat Arabs like shit, unless they happen to be working in a ministry handing out licenses."

"Yeah, well," Kevin said sulkily, settling his jacket around his shoulders, "maybe the people in the oil game are not far wrong." Abruptly, he leaned closer to Mike. His forearms lay flat on the table, and his powerful shoulders hunched beneath the jacket. His voice was hard and low. "Look, friend, you know a little bit about us or you wouldn't be here. You know the kind of people we are. You know what we're trying to achieve. And you must know about our politics. You know we're Marxists, I mean." He glanced contemptuously at the older man. "Or some of us are." He leaned still closer across the table. His voice had dropped to a venomous hiss. "And how about you? What are *you?* A Marxist? In the oil industry?" His lip curled. "Don't make me laugh! And a Brit into the bargain." The sneer faded, leaving a look of pure hostility on his face. He leaned back and pointed a thick finger at Mike's face. "I think you'd better do a little more talking, don't you?"

This sudden flaring of open hostility knocked Mike momentarily off-balance. His eyes flicked to the other two. They sat silently, giving nothing away, letting Kevin have his head. Mike turned back to Kevin. The man's eyes glittered with venomous mistrust. Mike's stare locked on to his. He paused for the briefest instant. Until the man's snarling question he had felt he had the initiative, but now it was being wrested from him. When he began to speak his voice was as low as Kevin's had been.

"Look," he said, almost spitting the words, "let's

get one thing straight right away." Almost imperceptibly, his voice gathered force. "I'm not a Marxist. I never
have been. Frankly, I know fuck-all about Marx. But,
from what little I do know, it's all a lot of balls. You
must be mad to still be taking it seriously! For Christ's
sake, even the *Russians* don't believe in all that stuff any
more." His voice had filled with contempt. "What d'you
think? That the IRA, the Chinese and the Red Army
Faction are the only ones in the entire world that have
got things right?" He snorted, looking mockingly at the
man in the blouson. "You must be out of your fucking
mind, pal."

Kevin's face worked angrily. He began to push himself to his feet. Eddie reached out quickly and took hold
of the leather of his sleeve, yanking him back down. "Sit
down, Kevin. And control yourself. We're not here to
start brawling." Kevin let himself be pulled slowly back
into his seat, still breathing heavily. The younger man
turned to Mike. "And you. Keep a civil tongue in your
head. This isn't a bar. We didn't ask you to come here to
start a fight."

Mike turned to look at the young man, shaking his
head. "Ah, what's the use? It's a thing that's always
pissed me off about you people. Worrying about the politics instead of getting on with the job you've got to do.
Like a bunch of fucking students. Dad was the same,
when it came right down to it. You would have got on
well with him. Talking about it till the cows come home
instead of getting out and doing something. And in the
meantime what are the bastards on the other side doing?
Shooting you on sight. Sending the SAS into your homes
to shoot you down in front of your families. They're
taking you apart. Because they *never* forget who their
enemy is." He swung back to face Kevin, his nostrils
again flaring angrily. "As for me being English, some of
the best people you've had in the organization were
born over here. I'm a Brit. I'm not a Marxist. And, while

we're at it, I don't get up and do 'Danny Boy' of a Saturday night, either. I just want to see the fucking Brits out
of Ireland, that's all."

He sat back, staring into their faces, breathing
heavily. The emotion was not feigned; the need to convince them was real enough to make him sweat. He did
not know the whole purpose of the interview, but he
knew for certain what would happen if he failed it. The
three men would leave the house. He would stay there—
with a bullet in the back of his head.

Tommy smiled at Mike and gave him a wink, unseen by the others. "Give it a rest, Kevin. It's right what
he says. Some good fellers have been British. With the
people we've had killed in the last few months we can
hardly put an active service unit together right now. You
know that as well as I do. If Mike's ready to join us I say
let's take him. He's proved himself. And the SAS won't
have his photo pinned up in their mess-rooms." He gave
them all a gloomy smile. "Which is more than you can
say for any of the rest of us."

He looked around at the other two, looking for
their agreement. Mike watched them, the traces of anger
slowly draining from his face.

While the older man had been speaking Kevin's
eyes had not left Mike. Now he gave a tight little sideways smile, acknowledging the older man's words. Then
he spoke himself.

"How old are you, Mike? Thirty-seven?"

Mike's mouth dried out. He could see where the
question would lead. The place he most feared it might
go. "Thirty-eight."

Kevin nodded, still smiling the same grim smile.
"Look at us, Mike." He pronounced Mike's name with
a faintly exaggerated emphasis, as though he was hint-
ing it might be a false one. He nodded to the older man
on his left. "Tommy here's over fifty years old. He's been
active in the movement, one way or another, for more

than thirty years. And Eddie. He's only twenty-seven. He was with us before he was even out of school. He'd killed men for us before he ever had a job. Myself, I was in the Maze for my eighteenth birthday. Now tell me something that's been bothering me ever since we first heard about you. What took you so fucking long?"

Mike forced saliva back into his mouth. All their eyes were on him. The older man, Tommy, no longer wore the encouraging smile. He was not as hostile as Kevin, but he had not survived so long in the movement, hunted day in and day out by the security forces, by being a bad listener to the answers to that kind of question.

"I told you about dad, what they did to him. The bastards—"

Kevin cut him off with an impatient movement of his hand. "Sure. We know all about Patsy Scanlon. Big-time Republican. Bigger-time drunk. We know he died at the hands of the British police. We also know it happened *twenty years ago*. The question I want you to answer for me, friend, is why have you come to us now? Why not then? What makes a man who's not even been in England, let alone Ireland, for most of his adult life suddenly so concerned with what we're trying to do?"

"What's the fact I've been overseas got to do with anything? Half your funding and weapons come from America, don't they? There are people in Boston doing twenty-year raps for it who could hardly place Ireland on a map. Do you ask them to explain?"

Kevin made a wagging motion with one raised finger. "Nice try," he said, with an ugly smile. "We're not talking about them. We're talking about *you*. They just send us stuff. You're trying to get right in."

Mike reared back from the table and got to his feet. Kevin's hand moved to his chest. His fingers nestled inside the zip of his blouson.

Mike took a step backward, moving closer to the

door. *"Trying* to get *in?"* It was his turn to sneer now. "What the fuck are you talking about? I've not been trying anything. Remember one thing, you bunch of dick-heads, it was *you* seemed to want *me!* It was John and his pals made the running, not me. If that's how you feel, fuck you. I'll leave right now."

Eddie sat quite still. His right hand was out of sight beneath the table. He shook his head. "No, you won't. Sorry, Michael, but it's too late for that." He sounded genuinely sorry. Mike did not move. Kevin's hand slid further inside his jacket. Mike saw the leather bulge as his hand made a fist, gripping something. "Come back and sit down," Eddie said, quietly reasonable, nodding at his seat.

Mike stood looking down at them, panting. Gradually, his breathing eased. He moved back to his place and sat down.

"That's a good man, Michael. Thank you." Eddie took his hand from beneath the table. Slowly, his heart not in it, Kevin let his hand slide from his jacket and back into view. Eddie spoke again, still in the same measured, calm tone. "Now, answer Kevin's question. Please. We'd all like to hear it. Why the sudden conversion?"

Mike sat silently for several seconds. When he finally spoke his voice was reluctant, as though they were dragging from him something painful. "Okay, look. As I told you, when dad died I was nineteen years old. Practically a kid. Mum didn't have the money or the energy to take on the police. They told us he'd choked, that it was an accident. She accepted it. What else could she do, a woman in her situation?"

"There was enough of a fuss about it at the time. There must have been lawyers ready to help." Kevin's eyes drilled into his.

Mike laughed. "Lawyers? Sure. It was the end of the sixties. The civil rights marches, Bernadette Devlin, anti-Vietnam demos, Grosvenor Square. It seemed like half the lawyers in the country were falling over themselves to offer their services. And you know what? Every one of the bastards was out to make a point! None of them really wanted to help mum. All they wanted to do was use us to attack the police. Mum didn't want that. She *respected* the police, for Christ's sake. They told her he'd choked, she believed them."

"Did *you* believe them?" asked Kevin.

Mike straightened and met his look. "You said it yourself; dad liked a drink. He'd have choked on his own vomit more than once in his own bed if mum hadn't been there to save him. I had no good reason *not* to believe them. He was a lovely man, but he couldn't hold his drink." He shook his head regretfully. "At the time it was all too plausible."

"So?" Kevin was not yet satisfied.

"So I found out I was wrong." Mike's voice had dropped almost to a whisper. "The coppers throttled him. And they covered it up. Everyone. The police, their doctors, the lot of them." He paused, his voice choked off by suppressed emotion.

Eddie spoke. "You say you found out. How was that?"

"And when?" Kevin asked, aggressively.

"Last year. I met someone, in Bahrain. Here." As he spoke he groped deep into an inside pocket of his jacket. He dragged out a tattered newspaper cutting. Very carefully, he spread it on the table in front of them. The clipping was falling into several pieces at the seams, worn from many unfoldings. The cutting was the one Mike had taken only the day before from the Library. He had spent an hour in his room laboriously folding and unfolding it, handling it, working grime into the paper. It looked as though he had been carrying it in his pocket for months. He pointed out the story and sat in silence while they read it through, their heads hunched together.

It referred to something that had happened in Bahrain. The body of an Englishman, a security man from a hotel, had been recovered from the sea at the Sheikh's beach. Mike knew the spot well. It was one of the few available beaches in Bahrain, on a property belonging to the ruler. He allowed foreigners to use it. The opinion locally was that it was his way of getting to see the expatriate wives in swimming costumes. The body had been hauled out of the sea by the Yemeni mercenaries of the Sheikh's bodyguard. An investigation by the local police had concluded that the man had drowned, probably while drunk. It had not needed an ace sleuth to reach such a conclusion—an empty whisky bottle had been found next to his clothes.

Eddie looked up from the cutting first. "What's this got to do with anything?"

"I knew him. I used to drink with him whenever I was in Bahrain on leave. He'd gone out there after he retired." He paused for a fraction of a second. "He used to be a copper. In Birmingham." There was a moment of total silence.

Eddie broke it. "He was there?"

Mike shook his head. "No. Not that night. But he worked at the same nick. They'd done a good job of hushing it up. Apparently, it took months before rumors started to circulate, even inside the police station itself. Then, finally, this feller," he pointed to the cutting, "was having a drink one night with an old police friend, another one who'd retired, and suddenly this other copper just blurted it out."

All three of them were watching his lips in total silence, hanging on every word.

He gestured to the cutting again. "He told me the whole story one night, after he'd had a good drink. He was actually proud of it. Thought his mates had been dead clever about it, the way they'd covered it all up, fooled everyone. Police solidarity. How they'd been able to stitch up the bastard of a doctor." He paused. He was breathing heavily again now, his anger swelling as he relived the moment. "That bastard hardly examined the body. He virtually took their word for everything."

"So what did you do when you found all this out?" Eddie's voice was loud in the room.

Mike looked at him, wide-eyed, as if surprised not to be alone. "I decided to get my own back."

Mike's story seemed to convince them that he could be trusted for the rest of the interview lasted less than half an hour. Their questions were brief, his answers briefer. He was sure of his ground. They could take their time checking out their story. The newspaper cutting was genuine. The stiff really had been a policeman, and had actually worked at the station where Mike's father had died, and at the Bahrain hotel. The truth was, though, that Mike had never met him. That would stay a secret between him and the dead man.

The fact was, Mike had been in Bahrain when the man drowned, and in the very small world of Bahrain's expatriates his death had been a very big story. Despite that, Mike would have paid it no attention at all if the name had not struck a familiar chord. However little he had cared about his father, the names from that time so many years ago were indelibly imprinted on his mind. Out of curiosity he had begun to take a closer interest.

The local radio and television, astonished to have a genuine home-grown news story, had given it blanket coverage. An interview with the dead man's wife, broadcast late one night, had confirmed Mike's supposition. She mentioned that her husband had served at the same Birmingham police station where Mike's father had died. The man's age tallied. He had been a detective inspector at the time and had done a lot of the fielding of press questions.

Mike had left Bahrain two days later to return to the desert and the incident had passed completely from his mind. Until that moment, only the other night, when he had dredged it from his memory, realizing it would provide the final underpinning for his story. Once again, he was able to rely on factual events that would stand up to scrutiny.

Mike stood up, and the three men rose with him. Eddie was smiling. "Have you got a passport?" he asked.

He had one—but it would tell them a lot of things he did not need them to know. "I did have. I lost it, in Athens. I did a bit of celebrating coming back last time. Had to get the Consulate out there to do me a travel document."

Eddie handed him a small notepad and a pen. "Give us your details, we'll get you one."

Mike bent to the table to write. "Wouldn't it be easier if I just applied for a replacement?"

Eddie shook his head. "You've been away too long. The passport office needs three months to deal with an application." He smiled, a smile of genuine amusement. "We can do you a real British passport much quicker than that."

He guided Mike up the passage. While the armed man opened the door and checked the street Eddie reached into a pocket and drew out an envelope. He handed it to Mike. As Mike made as though to open the envelope Eddie made a clicking noise with his tongue. "Not now. Have a look at it later, when you get back to your place. When you've got a bit of time." Smiling, he extended a hand. "Welcome to the Provos. We'll be in touch. Until you hear from us stay out of trouble and away from booze."

"I'll try."

"Don't try, Michael. Do it. You're on active service now. It's an order."

CHAPTER

7

MIKE AWOKE BEFORE SEVEN TO THE SOUND OF RAIN HITting the windows. It had been falling almost without a break for the three days since New Year. He was bored and restless. Since the interview he had heard nothing. Taking Eddie at his word, he had not been to any of the usual pubs since leaving the derelict house. Once only, on New Year's Eve, he had gone out, to a jazz pub on the south-west fringe of London, far from any of the areas where there was a risk of being recognized. Far, too, from the tidal wave of sentimentality that would be breaking over Kilburn and Hammersmith as midnight approached. Even there, he had lasted only two drinks and six or seven tunes. By that time the atmosphere of celebration, the knots of people getting happily drunk on alcohol and counterfeit goodwill, had made the emptiness and grief inside him so acute he could not stand it. He had returned to his own room with a couple of bottles of wine under his arm. By the time New Year struck he had been deeply asleep for half an hour, the two wine bottles lying empty under the bed. It had taken that to dim the image of Allix long enough to let him sleep.

His only other break from the tedious routine of waiting had been an attempt to see Tom. The desire to see the boy had become overwhelming. He had rented a car, driven to Kingston-upon-Thames and parked close to the corner of Sitwell Gardens, sixty or seventy yards from the Lorimers' house. Finally, after several patient hours' waiting, Allix's mother had appeared, over-dressed in a cheap fur coat and the kind of hat she thought set her a cut above the neighbors. Tom trotted at her side, clutching her hand. They had begun walking toward him.

His throat constricted at the sight of the boy, co-cooned in the bright clothes he and Allix had helped him choose. Abruptly, Tom let go his grandmother's hand and sprang away from her to stamp gleefully, two-footed, in a puddle. Mrs. Lorimer recoiled as drops splashed on to her legs. She spoke sharply to Tom, snatching his hand back and yanking hard at his arm in admonishment. She twisted her heel outward and pee-vishly examined the stains at her ankle. She swung her head in an angry flounce, gripped Tom's hand harder and continued walking, faster than before. The laughter dropped from Tom's face as he fell glumly back into step at her side.

Mike had been half out of the car when he felt the sudden coolness of the air on his chest. He glanced down at himself. Tears were tumbling from his chin. A wet patch the size of a plate had formed on the front of his shirt. He wiped a hand ineffectually over his face and looked up again. Tom and his grandmother were still forty yards from him, on the opposite pavement. Nei-ther of them had seen him. He remained with one foot on the pavement, his hand gripping the door-pillar. For perhaps three seconds he was unable to take his eyes from Tom. Finally, he looked from the boy and stared, bereft, at the wetness on his shirt. Abruptly, he made a noise that was a suppressed cry and dropped back into his seat. He hesitated a moment longer, looking once more from the tearstain to Tom. Then he threw the car into reverse, skidded untidily back around the corner, hauled the wheel around and drove hard across the street entrance and away from them.

Rubbing his eyes, he forced himself out of bed and made some coffee. The stale smell of the half-finished glass of whisky that stood abandoned by the gas ring made him grimace. He carried his cup to the table and pushed aside the cheap briefcase that stood where he had left it the previous evening. It contained his files, which had outgrown the original envelope. He had been spending his enforced confinement going over the material, cross-indexing, studying the faces. Using a felt-tipped pen and a piece of transparent plastic, he had overlaid the photographs with every variety of beards, glasses and hats. He felt sure that, short of their having undergone plastic surgery, he would know on sight any member of the Provos whose picture had appeared in the press in the last ten years.

One in particular he recognized very well. It was the third face that smiled out at him, next to himself and Jane, from the photograph that stood propped against the marmalade jar. The photograph that had been in the envelope that Eddie had handed to him. It must have been taken by the street photographer with the Santa Claus stooge. It showed Mike and Jane arm-in-arm. Linked to Jane's other arm, for all the world one of their group, was another smiling figure. The man wore a scarf wound loosely around his neck in such a way that if he pulled in his chin his face would be half concealed. Mike could see why. The face belonged to one of the most notorious killers in the movement. It was the figure whose back Mike had fleetingly glimpsed as he slipped away from them, the man Jane had prevented him from pursuing. Behind them, the animated display of Sel-fridge's window was unmistakable.

From the moment Mike had opened the envelope he had understood. They had taken away from him the option of going to the authorities. The picture branded him, a willing participant in the attempted outrage. A bomber. They had him by the balls. At the first sign of treachery the photograph would be sent to the police.

Jane and the other man in the picture would have the resources of the movement available to them; escape routes, safe houses, the network of sympathizes, English and Irish, prepared to give them shelter for months at a time, would all be at their disposal. He would be alone, tracked both by the Provos and by the British security forces. Their treatment of suspects was the one thing the two groups had in common. They shot them.

A sudden noise made him stiffen. It was the faint sound of a door being closed with great care. It was the care that alarmed him; in the hotel nobody *ever* shut a door quietly. He sat absolutely still, his head cocked, listening intently. There was no further sound. Shrug-ging, he was about to take another gulp of coffee when there was a single sharp tap at his door.

He placed the cup soundlessly on the table and rose quickly but silently to his feet. He looked hastily around the room. His eyes alighted on a cheap kitchen knife that lay by the sink. He took it up in one hand. In the other he took a dish towel. He moved toward the door, placing his weight carefully, testing the floorboards un-derfoot at each step. As he went he bundled the dish towel into a ball. He reached the door without any of the boards betraying his movements. Taking shallow breaths, he waited, pressed against the wall, listening intently. There was another rap on the door, then the handle moved as somebody tried it. It was pointless, he knew, to try to turn the key silently; the person outside would certainly hear it. Keeping his body hard against the wall he reached out the hand holding the dish towel and unlocked the door. It flew open.

As it swung wide Mike hurled the towel into the opening, aiming it at the level of a person's eyes. It was an old but infallible street-fighting trick. To throw something, anything, at the eyes of an assailant would always make him blink, giving you a split-second opening. He swung into the doorway, his knife hand arcing upward toward the intruder.

He froze in mid-movement.

Jane stared in at him. She was pulling the towel from her face with one hand, and with the other she was supporting herself on the door frame. Her hair clung flat to her scalp, a drop of rainwater hung at her chin, and she was panting hard. As she opened her mouth to speak, a pulse of pain contorted her face, preventing the words from forming.

"Jesus Christ!" Mike opened the door wider and yanked her into the room, almost pulling her off her feet. She stumbled inside. When he turned from locking the door to face into the room she was slumped face down, her head and torso on the crumpled divan, her legs trailing on the ratty carpet. He stared down at the prostrate figure. "How the hell did you get in here? I didn't hear the bell. Did someone let you in? The landlord see you?"

Still lying flat she turned her head to the side so that he could see her face. Smiling feebly, she worked her hand into the tight-stretched back pocket of her jeans, pulled out a broken credit card and waved it weakly. "Don't worry. I let myself in. With this. A door like that's child's play. Nobody saw me." She caught his nervous glance toward the door and gave a soft, breathy laugh. "And the SAS aren't about to burst in here after me. Can you help with this?"

As she spoke she glanced down at her leg. Following her gaze, he saw for the first time that the rain-soaked jeans were wet with a darker color below the left knee. Fumbling, he unzipped the jeans. As he loosened the waist a scratched automatic pistol fell from beneath the material of her sweatshirt on to the divan. He looked at it for a moment, and then picked it up and laid it gently on the floor. He slid the jeans down and dragged them off her.

"Christ! Does it hurt?"

She gave him a look that told him it was a stupid question. "Like hell," she said, conversationally.

He lifted her legs on to the divan. There was a gouge in her calf as deep as a finger. Blood soaked her sock and had run into her shoe. The flimsy canvas pump was saturated. Fresh stains on the threadbare carpet marked her progress from the door. With an exclamation Mike snatched up the dish towel, ran some cold water into a plastic bowl and rushed from the room, pulling the door shut behind him.

Working furiously, it took him several minutes to clean the stains that led from the front door to his room, minutes in which he hardly dared breathe for fear of the landlord emerging like some underwater creature from his dim lair. He surveyed the work. The wet patches showed dark on the carpet, leaving a tell-tale trail to his door. He thought for a moment and then stooped and continued along the landing. He carried on rubbing at every second or third stair up to the next floor. He left one last damp patch in the middle of the landing above and crept back down to his room; if there were any stains on the pavement he would rely on the rain to deal with them. It would not allay the landlord's curiosity, but it just might deflect it. He would probably conclude that an inmate had come home drunk and for once had cleaned up his own vomit, and would be pleased that standards were rising at last.

The girl was still sprawled on the divan, exactly as he had left her. Although her wound was no longer bleeding the sheet beneath her was already a hopeless mess. Mike found another dish towel. Kneeling beside her, he pushed a cushion beneath her leg and began cleaning the wound. Until he touched the flesh she lay so still he had thought she was unconscious. A sharp intake of breath as he began probing with the wadded tea-cloth told him she was not. She cursed once, very softly but very bitterly. It was the only sound she allowed herself. After that, she lay with her head raised awkwardly, watching in total silence as he worked, her teeth pressed ferociously hard into her lower lip.

It was some minutes before he could staunch the new bleeding provoked by his attentions. He examined the injury. It was a clean, straight gouge that ran on a downward slope from back to front on the side of the calf. The raw, scarlet flesh at the sides of the wound twitched and quivered.

"You were lucky."

She looked up at him from under lowered eyelids. "Oh, sure. It's really lucky getting shot."

"I'm serious." He pointed to the wound. "That looks as if it was done by a big bullet. What was it?"

She shrugged feebly. "How the fuck would I know? I didn't stop to ask the bastard who did it to show me his gun. Some sort of pistol. Why? Are you some kind of firearms expert, too?"

He laughed and shook his head. "No. I've never held a gun in my life, not even a shotgun. A funny thing, though, a lot of the guys on the crews used to be gun nuts. Something about the work seems to attract them. They'd drive you crazy talking about them. It's amazing what you pick up sitting in a trailer in the evenings." He nodded toward the wound. "The reason I say you're lucky is that the bullet missed the bone. Apparently, when a big bugger like that strikes bone it brings you down, no matter what part of the skeleton it hits. Another half an inch and you would have been a dead lady."

"Don't be stupid. It would have hurt like hell. Broken my leg. It wouldn't have killed me."

He looked at her in disbelief. Finally, he laughed and shook his head. "Hell. And you're supposed to be the seasoned pro. Haven't you been reading the papers lately? If you'd gone down the next one would have been in your head, not your leg. Those security service bastards are not taking prisoners."

A startled look flickered in her eyes, as though the thought had only just struck her.

He chuckled and patted her arm. "Don't worry. You won't die now. Stay still while I get something to keep it clean."

He foraged in the cheap wardrobe and brought out a clean shirt and a handkerchief. He tore the shirt carefully into strips and dressed the wound, using the handkerchief as wadding. Getting to his feet, he smiled wryly down at the girl. She lay on her back now, staring up at him through half-closed eyes. He shrugged.

"Well, it'll hurt, I imagine, but you'll have to put up with that. Anyway, that's the best I can do until the shops open, then I'll go out and get some TCP or something." He glanced at the window. "Now, how about telling me how the hell you got here."

"I drove."

He was startled. "What! Where's the car? Where'd you leave it?"

She laughed. "Relax. Far enough from here. And I've parked it legally, in a car park, like a good girl. It'll sit there for weeks before anyone notices." She looked at her watch. "Got a radio? I'd like to hear the half-past-seven news bulletin."

He hauled the radio from where it stood, half-hidden among the bloodstained bedclothes that hung to the floor, and flipped the switch.

The news was freshly in. Another success for the police in the anti-terrorist struggle. Listening to the report, it was plain to Mike that the police had not yet released the full story. What they had given the media so far was that another bomb factory had been unearthed, this time in West London. In the raid, by what were described as the "security forces," which meant SAS men in jeans and combat jackets, one terrorist had been shot dead. A second bomber, believed to be a woman, had escaped. It was thought she might have been wounded. An artist's impression of the woman would be released later in the day.

With a frowning glance at the girl, Mike went quickly to the window. He pulled the thin curtain back an inch and studied the street. It was still dark. Passersby hurried head down against the rain, or fought with umbrellas in the gusty wind. He could see no sign of anybody loitering, but that did not mean much. There were enough dark porches and shadowy front gardens to conceal a hundred watchers. But at least there were no street cleaners sweeping with give-away slowness, no closed vans parked where they had a clear view of the house. He turned back to the girl.

"How do you know you weren't followed? They obviously had your *place* sussed out. How come they weren't watching your car, as well? I would, if I was doing their job. Wouldn't you?" He stared down at her.

She shook her head pityingly. She had seen the pinpoint of mistrust that danced in his stare. "Yes, I would. Except that the car I came in wasn't *ours,* you smart bastard." He looked blankly back down at her. "I *stole* it."

She laughed again as he continued to stare. "What's up? Are you shocked? You don't think that's a nice thing for a girl to do? You think I should have had a man around to do that kind of thing for me?" She gave a derisive laugh. "I bet you don't swear in front of women, either, right? Because at heart, for all your traveling, you're still a good Catholic boy from a nice working-class conservative family. With your head still full of all the hang-ups the priests at your school stuffed into it, huh?"

She struggled up to support herself on her elbows, raised one hand and pointed an index finger at him. Her eyes narrowed to slits. "Well, look, here's something for you to get straight, guilt-ridden Brit. I'm not a misty-eyed colleen from a sweet little picture-postcard village in Killarney or somewhere, who joined up to try and meet a man. I'm just your average girl from the Belfast slums and I'm doing this because I believe in it. I stole my first car when I was eleven years old. And probably one a week ever since. Joy riding was about the only entertainment we had, except for throwing stones at the soldiers." Her tone had grown strident.

He ignored the mockery in her voice, not taking the trouble to be provoked. "Keep your voice down," he said, matter-of-factly, keeping his own voice very low. "And just start explaining something to me. What the hell's going on?"

"What do you mean?"

He spoke very softly, standing close over her. "You know damned well what I mean. Just exactly what happened this morning?"

She struggled into a sitting position, pushing the two thin pillows behind her. "You heard the news. We'd had the house over in Brentford for eighteen months or so. Used it on and off, as a safe house. We only started using it to store the stuff for the bombs a couple of weeks ago. God only knows how they found us. I was in the kitchen when they hit us. Got out through the back garden. Nearly made it clean away, too. Got this just as I was going over the wall."

He smiled down at her. "And with that leg you had time to steal a car before they came over after you?"

The room was quite silent. She shook her head. Her hand trailed on the floor. Without warning, her fingers closed around the gun. He recoiled as she swung it up to point at him. She laughed, opening her mouth wide.

"Relax. I had this, remember. I got off a shot at the bastard who hit me. He wasn't about to come diving over the wall after me. By the time he'd organized a couple more of them to spread the risk, I'd gone. I can be into a Cavalier and away in under thirty seconds." She put the gun down and indicated her sweatshirt. "Mind if I take this off?"

As she spoke she plucked at the cloth at her chest. It was wringing wet. Without waiting for him to answer she crossed her arms and pulled the sweatshirt awkwardly over her head; she wore nothing underneath it. Mike did not even try to read the strange expression in her face. Silently he handed her a towel. While she dried off he searched in the bottom of the hanging closet and emerged with a clean shirt. It was his last one. He tossed it on to the bed.

"Okay, so that's this morning. But that wasn't exactly all I meant. I meant, what's going on all over? The British are ripping us apart. This is the third time in almost as many weeks. You said yourself, we've had that place for eighteen months with no trouble. Then, the moment we start using it as a bomb factory, the SAS bust the joint. How the hell are they doing it?" Listening to himself, he was pleased to notice how easily and naturally the "we" came off his tongue.

She dropped her head. The ambiguous expression left her face. Suddenly she looked exhausted. "Yeah, I know what you mean. It's as if they had some sort of direct line to our plans. They seem to know in advance, almost." She looked up at him in sudden frank appeal. "It's why I decided to come here. To you. None of the old places seem safe any more. Do you mind?"

He stared down into the amazing blue-green eyes.

They gazed frankly back into his. Just a hint of a plea entered her face as he watched it. The beginning of a smile nudged her lips. It was full of the promise to become a full-blown smile of gratitude, if only he would say the word. He found himself admiring her. She was a good-looking woman and she was clearly accustomed to using her looks to get what she needed. He could read every move in her attempt to manipulate him, and still she was damn near to succeeding.

Smiling faintly himself, he let his eyes move off hers. It was like turning off a light. He allowed himself to look her over, not hiding it. Her body was very pale, without any of the ghostly imprint of bikini marks that betrayed a faded tan. It was as though she had never been in the sun. Despite the pallor, her body exuded health. It was as taut and slender as a boy's. Even though she was lying on her back the small breasts did not flatten. The chill of the damp sweatshirt had made her nipples harden.

He swallowed. "So you think here really is okay?" He smiled a lop-sided smile. "You think *I'm* okay?"

She laughed wryly. "Well, it was Brendan briefed me about you. He gave me the address. There's only a handful of people even know you exist. You've hardly been with us five minutes. If the Brits are on to you then we're *really* in trouble. Then they're on to all of us."

He looked straight into her eyes. "That's not what I meant, Jane. I wasn't asking whether you think the security forces are on to me. I meant do you trust me? Me. The new boy?"

She returned his gaze, puzzled. "Trust you? My God, you did the job in the store didn't you?"

"Did I? How do you know I didn't raise the alarm?"

She laughed, relaxing. "How do I know? Who do you think you're dealing with? We're pros at this game. We had people watching for that. The other bomb was a shitty piece of luck, that's all. But we saw how they got the kids off the third floor. No panic. Very relaxed. It was a routine evacuation. Believe me, if they'd known about our bomb they'd have been in a lot more of a hurry. As it was, at least we got a couple of the staff people." She smiled up at him. A hand reached out and touched his own, very lightly. "Don't worry about it. These things happen. You couldn't know the Animal Lib bunch would be setting a bomb, could you? You're okay. We all know you're in the clear."

He turned to the stove as she spoke, keeping his face hidden from her. He had not fully trusted himself to hide the triumph that surged in him.

"Coffee?"

"Please. Milk, no sugar."

Mike busied himself at the stove. She had confirmed what he most wanted to know; they were not aware of his being trapped in the lift. They had deliberately given him time to give a warning. He had not done it, so he was a good man, a man they could trust. With the filthiest work they could devise. He glanced over his shoulder at her. "Want a drink? There's Scotch."

"Aagh, no thanks. Not at this hour. I'd love to eat something, though. Escaping must sharpen the appetite."

"It's probably the loss of blood. There's nothing here. I usually eat in a café round the corner. I'll go and get us something. Here." As he turned to her with the coffee he caught her gaze flickering over the room. He saw it linger for a split second on the briefcase and the turned-back portion of carpet. He handed her the cup, giving no sign he had noticed her look.

He pulled on a stained raincoat and made for the door. As though on a second thought, he knelt by the loose board and began carefully replacing it. His back was to her. Shielding the movement from her view, he slipped the money pouch into an inner pocket of the raincoat. Standing, he kicked the carpet roughly back into place and turned to her, smiling.

"As long as you're here I guess I can leave the radio out. With the people that live in this place I don't normally leave so much as a half-eaten banana lying around. You don't mind if I lock you in, do you? Nothing personal. I keep it locked all the time. That shifty bastard of a landlord."

As he spoke he drifted to the table where the briefcase stood, crammed with documents. He picked it up, being very careful *how* he did it. The case probably weighed eight or ten pounds, but he swung it easily toward him, as though it were empty. He blew her a travesty of a kiss, gave a last look around the room and closed the door.

In twenty minutes he was back. At that hour there was a lot of movement in the hotel. He waited only a couple of minutes before somebody left, then slipped in silently through the open door and mounted the stairs, treading softly. Instead of going directly to his room he entered the bathroom and shut himself in. He turned on all the taps and crouched by the bath. It took him under three minutes to remove the side panel.

Shaking out the plastic bag full of groceries on to the floor, he transferred the documents from the briefcase to the bag and stowed it under the bath. He hesitated for a moment before pulling the money pouch from his pocket. He slid several notes from it and tossed it in beside the bag, replaced the panel, shoved the groceries into the case, turned off the taps and walked silently back down the stairs. He opened the front door, slammed it carelessly, and mounted to his room.

He breezed in, humming. Jane lay on her side on the divan, breathing in a deep, slow rhythm. At the sound of the door closing she started and jerked herself into a sitting position. Her hand came out from a fold in the sheet holding the gun. Mike froze, his hand still on the doorknob. She stared at him for a moment with an expression of vacant terror, as though she did not know him. Slowly, as she came to herself, the light came back into her eyes. She smiled wanly, sinking back on to the mattress.

"God, you frightened me." She rubbed a hand over her face, pressing her fingertips to her eyes. "I was so deeply asleep, I didn't know where I was."

He returned her smile, glancing wryly around the room. "Well, you knew you weren't at Claridge's. I got some stuff to do that leg." He turned his back on her to rummage in the briefcase.

She was good. Every tiny gesture was judged to absolute perfection. She was every inch the invalid, woken from the deep sleep that would naturally follow what she had been through, the shooting, the desperate flight, the loss of blood. Her behavior was exactly consistent with her plight—except that she had carefully searched the room. Since the night John had brought Mike home in the taxi and learned where he lived Mike had forced himself into the habit of laying small traps, minute things that even the most professional of searchers would overlook. A dozen of them had been sprung. The sock he had left half pushed into a shoe had been disturbed, obscuring the motif that he had left visible. There were slight displacements of the clothes that lay around. The zipper of the cheap clothes cupboard was open an inch further than when he had left, and a ruck in the loose corner of the carpet had been smoothed out.

"I hope you got some food, too."

He turned to face her again. "Sure I did." He brandished a bottle of antiseptic. "But first, the leg."

He cleaned the wound with the antiseptic and dressed it decently with lint and sticking plaster. He got to his feet and stood looking down appraisingly at his work. Beneath the shirt he had given her, her legs were exposed from mid-thigh. They were like her body, slen-

der and pale and muscular. A rush of recognition made
his head pound. The anatomical definition, like a runner's, the narrow feet and straight toes, all seemed to
touch a trigger in him. The woman's body had exactly
the trim, tightly contoured look that had been one of the
things that he had loved about Allix. In the weeks since
Allix's death he had not thought once about a woman.
Now, Jane's attractiveness seemed to spring at him,
catching him off-balance. With a conscious effort of
will, he fought down the idea. With sudden gruffness he
reached down and took her arm and helped her roughly
to the table.

He boiled eggs and made more coffee while she sat
awkwardly in one of the hard chairs buttering bread. He
scooped the eggs on to a plate and carried them over to
the table, and handed her the plastic spice-jar cap that
served as his only eggcup.

"Sorry. I didn't know I was going to be entertain-
ing. I would've collected the silverware from the bank."
He sat down. "So, tell me a bit more about what happened back there." His voice was casual, just making
conversation.

She looked at him over her coffee mug. "What
more is there to tell? We were in the house. I'd just gone
out to the kitchen to make some tea when I heard a bit
of a scuffle at the front door."

"A *scuffle*? You mean they didn't just kick it in?"

"No. There wasn't much noise at all. As if they
might have had a key, or something. Just more or less
walked in."

"Who was it? Police? SAS?"

She shrugged, sucking in her cheeks. "Look, it's as I
told you. I didn't hang around to check their credentials.
I was halfway down the garden by the time they reached
the kitchen. I would've been over the wall if we hadn't
had so many locks on the bloody door," she went on,
ruefully. "All I know is I looked back and saw a big

black shape in the doorway. I managed to get a shot at him but I wasn't set for it. The next thing, I heard plopping noises and then my leg was on fire."

"Didn't you go down?"

"I don't know. The next thing I remember I was falling off the wall on to the pavement. I just got up and ran."

"It took them that long to get over the wall after you?"

"I don't know how long it was. Not more than a few seconds, probably. I could hear them calling and whistling to each other. I was dead lucky they didn't have dogs."

He nodded. "You sure were. Damned lucky to outrun them, too, with that." He gestured toward her leg.

She looked at him with a flash of impatience. "Yeah, well, it wasn't just luck. We don't choose houses on the basis of their avocado bathroom suites! We chose it because it was among other houses with plenty of space around them. Remember, it was pitch dark." She smiled mischievously at him. "Don't forget, I really *am* an ace car thief. I doubt if there's a car made I would need more than two minutes to steal. It was a nice middle-class neighborhood. Plenty of company Cavaliers standing around in driveways. Thirty seconds was plenty."

His eyes were fixed on her face. "Well, whoever it was, police or the army, it's nice to know the people we're up against are stupid."

His remark seemed to hang for a moment in the air. A faint light of unease showed behind her eyes. "How's that?"

"They didn't bother to cover the back door."

She gave a little snort of dismissive laughter. "They didn't think they needed to. It was six in the morning. They must have thought we'd still be in bed." She looked suddenly grave, as though a thought had just struck her. "That explains the plopping noises. The silencers." Horror made her voice a rasp. She reached out and put a hand on his arm. "Oh, my God. The filthy shits! Don't you see what they had planned? They were going to come in, wipe us out while we were still in bed, and be gone again without even waking the neighbors." Anger had driven the horror from her face. "The murdering bastards!"

Her hand had closed over the back of his and he could feel her breath on his face as she leaned close to him across the table. Her eyes moistened as she thought of how close she had come to being executed. Her fingers tightened their grip.

Roughly, he withdrew his hand. "Yeah, maybe," he said harshly. He leaned back in his seat, putting a little more distance between them. "It's policy nowadays. Since Gibraltar. They don't want any more embarrassments like Guildford and Birmingham. So instead of putting us in prison, they shoot us. Dead people can't complain there's been a mistake, can they." He snorted. "Anyway, the important thing is, you got away. Want some more coffee?"

They went on eating and drank off several more mugs of coffee, talking away the awkwardness that had threatened to set in. As they talked Mike gently probed for information about her career in the movement. His probing was delicate and unobtrusive, the sort of questions that came naturally from their situation. Her responses were equally gentle, equally discreet evasions. They were long, good-humored, witty, and completely devoid of the smallest speck of information that could be useful to an enemy of the movement. She could make bomb circuits, pick locks, hot-wire cars, take pain, and, above all, keep her mouth shut. In short, he was dealing with a pro, a very dangerous one, who, however well she trusted him, would tell him no more than she thought he absolutely needed to know.

"How about other matters?"

He thought for a moment before grabbing his raincoat again. "Stick around!"

He went out. As he left the building the landlord's pale face watched him from the shadows of his den, like a deep-water fish that spent its life below the reach of daylight.

Forty minutes later Mike bellied his way back into the room, a bulging paper sack in each arm. Stuffed plastic bags from a supermarket dangled awkwardly from his fingers. Mary watched from the divan, half-smiling as he struggled to set everything down on the table. He picked up one of the plastic bags, and with a flourish tore it away to reveal a plastic bucket with a close-fitting lid. He set it down and rummaged in another bag until he found a boxed roll of bin liners. He tore one off and lined the bucket, set it on the floor in the corner and placed a packet of toilet rolls next to it. From the other bags he unpacked a heap of groceries and stacked them neatly at the back of the table. He turned to Mary, gesturing at the bucket and the food.

"How about that. All our bodily needs for the next few days entirely catered for. Yours, anyway," he added, cheerfully. "No need to leave the room at all."

Mary eyed the bucket balefully. She turned the same look on him. "You're not serious?"

Suddenly he was. He spoke just above a whisper. "Very serious. Let me make a few things clear, Mary. You shouldn't have come here. You shouldn't have, but you're here, and you can stay. But there's something you'd better know. I'm involved with something big that's brewing. Something very big. I don't even know myself what it is. But I do know the people across the water don't want it blown." He took the few paces across the room until he was standing right over her. He lowered his voice even further, until it could not have been heard six feet away. "Now, I know I'm new and you've probably been around this organization for a long time, but let me tell you how I see things. To my mind, what's been happening lately, all the things that seem to be going wrong all of a sudden, including what happened to you this morning, all that can only mean one thing. The British are getting some damned good intelligence—much better than they've ever had in the past. Right?"

He paused long enough for her to nod.

"Okay. There are just two ways they could be getting it, then. One, they've got some kind of fancy electronic bugging system going. Maybe they've got some of the top people wired and they don't even know about it."

"Is that possible? To put a mike on someone so they wouldn't know it was there?" She sounded skeptical.

He grinned. "Listen, electronics has been a hobby with me as well as my job. Believe me, they've got stuff so small they could sew it into your underwear and you'd never know it was there."

"Maybe I'd better stop wearing any?"

He brushed aside the hint of mischief in her voice. "I'm not kidding, Mary. Even if MI5's still run by the kind of nutty incompetent that used to be in charge you shouldn't underestimate their technical capacities. They've come a long way since "Spycatcher.""

"So you really think that's how they've been getting on to us? You think they really have got *people* bugged?"

He shook his head. "We'd better hope so," he said grimly. "Because the second possibility is that we've got an informer somewhere very close to the top." He paused to let her digest the idea.

"You don't think it's me, by any chance?" She smiled up at him with no humor at all.

He made a small movement with his shoulders. "Are you that close to the top?" He let her think about it for a moment. "Anyway, that's a chance I've no choice but to take, short of throttling you right now." There was something chilling in his voice, and her eyes dulled momentarily as a shadow of real fear drifted over them. That fear gave him a brief glimmer of satisfaction —it was the confirmation that he was playing his part well. "What I *do* know is that I want to achieve something, not get wiped out for nothing like some of the other poor bastards have recently. Dying on active service would be one thing, getting blown away by the SAS before I've even had a chance to serve would really piss me off." He crouched in front of her, his face softening as he did so. "So, all I want is to give myself the best chance. That means not giving that little rat downstairs any grounds for suspicion. And it means you don't leave this room, for any reason whatsoever, until you leave for good, all right? No phone calls, no visits from your boyfriend, no baths. And if you using that bucket instead of the bathroom helps keep me out of trouble, that's what you'll do. Do you understand me?"

She made a little salute. "You're a pro already," she said, trying for a touch of sardonic humor.

The day passed slowly. They listened to the radio, talked in careful whispers and drank cup after cup of the fresh-ground coffee he had bought. Mary slept a lot, genuinely exhausted from the events of the early morning and from her injury, and by ten o'clock she had fallen asleep for the night. Mike bedded down on the scuffed carpet, using a single thin blanket and his raincoat for bedclothes.

He got up before six, too cold and uncomfortable for further sleep. He dressed, fumbled the key from beneath the cushion that had served him as a pillow and let himself out, locking the door quietly behind him.

When he returned a quarter of an hour later with a sheaf of newspapers and magazines, the aroma of coffee was mingling with the other smells on the stairs, and grew stronger as he approached the landing. He entered the room. Mary had drawn a chair over from the table and was sitting by the stove coaxing water through a coffee filter. She waited for him to close the door before reaching down at her side and picking up the bucket. She handed it to him, smiling wryly.

"Welcome back to the Maze. I'm afraid it's your turn to slop out."

By the time he returned from the bathroom she had already hauled herself to the table, where cups of fresh coffee stood beside the pile of papers. She had the *Daily Telegraph* open in front of her, and had finished the front-page coverage and was scanning the editorial, a slight smile on her lips. Mike put on the radio, loud enough to drown soft conversation, sat down opposite her and took up a paper.

The hours they had spent together the previous day had removed much of the awkwardness from their attitudes to each other. They read aloud snatches of the newspaper accounts of the previous morning's events, finding it easy to laugh together at the obvious hand of the security services in the published versions.

There was a lot of coverage, but not many facts. The basic story was the same in every paper, a rehash, no doubt, of the Home Office handout. The skeletal version of the actual event was heavily padded out with paragraphs in which the Home Office congratulated itself on its progress in defeating terrorism. There was a lot about the need for continued vigilance. Conspicuously absent from all the stories was any information or clue as to what had led the authorities to the bomb factory in the first place. There were reproductions of an artist's impression of the person, believed to be a woman, who had slipped away. The pictures made them laugh outright—they looked as much like Mike as Mary.

For the remainder of the morning they read the rest of the news in the papers and the magazines. When they had been through them all from cover to cover Mike picked up the *Guardian* and started on the crossword.

"Want some more coffee?" asked Mary.

Mike looked up quickly. "Let me do it. Your leg must hurt like hell." He made to get up.

She put a hand on his shoulder. "It does. But I'd prefer to give it some exercise, otherwise it just stiffens up. So sit down."

He returned to his crossword, and remained intent on it while Mary stood at the stove waiting for the battered kettle to boil. He stormed through nine or ten clues and then came to a dead stop; none of the others made any sense to him at all. It just was not a good day for it. He sat tapping his teeth with the cheap pen with its dusty blob of ink on the end. A mug of coffee landed on the table beside him. There was a short pause. He could feel her supporting herself on the back of his chair.

"Staged."

He looked up at her. "Huh?"

" 'Staged'—seven down. 'Put on a deer by an editor.' "

He frowned down at the paper on the table, and was still reluctantly penning in the word when she spoke again.

" 'Marshal.' " He looked sourly up at her again. "Nineteen across."

He squinted at the clue—"Official spoils young Henry." He shook his head; of course. He wrote it in.

She gave him three more answers, including completing the quotation from Shakespeare, a line from *As You Like It*. Far from being able to quote from the play, Mike had never even read it. He had spent a lot of time in joyless places with little else to do but crosswords, and knew he was reasonably well attuned to the things. But she was better.

"For a car thief who spent half her time playing truant, you've got a hell of a vocabulary."

He looked up in surprise as he felt her rear away from the back of his chair. Her face was flushed with anger.

"Fuck you! What do you think I'm supposed to be? A piece of crumpet?" Her voice was heavy with sarcasm. "A witless piece of meat seated admiringly at the feet of my rescuer? Is that what you'd prefer a woman to act like?" She looked into his startled face, angry and contemptuous. "God, you might talk like a Brit but you're Irish all right!" Her voice had risen, driven on by her flaring anger.

"Stop it! Shut up! For Christ's sake!" Mike sprang to his feet, turning. He grabbed her upper arm and shook her violently. His other hand was raised, ready to slap her. "Keep your voice down!" His own was a vicious hiss as he nodded toward the thin partition. He watched her give a long sigh, letting the anger subside, before he spoke again. "I'm sorry. Jesus, it was just a joke, it wasn't meant to be an insult."

She rolled her shoulders and sighed again. "Yeah, sure. I'm sorry. I overreacted. It comes from living among all those chauvinist bastards in Belfast. It makes you sensitive." She smiled. "Let's stop the puzzles, can we? I'm still dog-tired after yesterday. Maybe that's what's making me edgy."

For the rest of the afternoon, they talked and laughed, keeping their voices just above the level of a whisper. The whole time they played the radio, as loud as they thought the neighbors on the other side of the partition would tolerate. As the afternoon wore on Mike found himself laughing aloud at her stories of life in the dismal backstreets of Belfast. She turned out to have a cool eye for the absurdities of life in the torn city, dividing her scathing comments about equally between the lunatic posturing of the Loyalists and the outer limits of Republican foolishness.

After several weeks of joyless solitude the company of almost any woman would have been a welcome change. But this one was something far more, and more complicated than that. Facially, and with the short, glossy brown hair and lively aquamarine eyes, she looked nothing like Allix. And yet, the physical resemblance, the way she moved and laughed, the brightness of her manner, were constant, overwhelming reminders of what he had lost. Instead of succumbing to the pleasure of her company he found himself struggling between two extremes of emotion. On the one hand, the constant reminder of Allix fueled his hatred of everything she represented. On the other, he was lonely and vulnerable and found her genuinely attractive. It was a very dangerous combination. The lust that crowded at the edges of his awareness, like a caged animal demanding to be let loose, increased the danger, distracting him from the need to be alert to every nuance and word.

In her easy, laid back, humorous way she was littering the conversation with traps for him. Completely naturally, without in any way seeming to probe, she led him into talking about his early life. Each time she spoke of herself was an invitation to Mike to do the same. She was very skillful; dozens of times she related something about herself, usually regarding one of the host of jobs she had held in Belfast. Then, making it no more than politeness, she would pause, leaving a space for him to fill. If he hesitated, unwilling to offer anything in return, she always took up the conversation again, not letting the pause grow long enough to be embarrassing. And then, a little later, she would try again.

She was vivacious, amusing, and unbelievably persistent. What she was doing, in that sweet, fond, bright-eyed way was interrogating him expertly. Many times, as she back-tracked apparently innocently over details of his past, he had reason to be grateful so much of his story was essentially true. Had it not been so he doubted he would have got through the day without her catching him in some discrepancy, some loose connection that would have been enough to arouse this very smart lady's suspicions. And which could prove fatal.

Evening fell. He had been out of her company for only a few minutes in the course of the afternoon, when he had gone out to obtain a supply of coins for the gas fire. Despite all his anxiety, despite the strain of having to suppress the hatred that the constant images of Allix engendered, he was having to admit to himself that he actually liked her. He was quite sure he could kill her if the time came, but there would be a note of regret in it. He was equally certain that she intended to try to seduce him.

He made dinner. In his previous life the circumstances would have dictated careful cooking, a candlelit table and some terrific wine. The person he was now supposed to be settled for scrambled eggs and bacon. The wine he pulled out of the greasy cupboard had the supermarket price sticker still on it. He left it there—with the Bulgarian label, the damage was done.

She leaned heavily on him as he helped her to the table, laughing and cursing the pain. They spent longer over eggs and bacon than would be considered normal, and laughed more than could have been expected over Mike's efforts to liberate a chunk of New Zealand cheddar from its impregnable polythene with one of the blunt kitchen knives.

Throughout the meal she had missed no opportunity to touch his fingers or to reach out and take hold of his arm as she leaned her head back to laugh. In a calm and detached corner of his mind he could almost laugh at her obviousness. Part of the task she had set herself was to find out as much about him as possible, and clearly she had decided that sleeping with him would help her get closer, to breach any last defenses.

They were most of the way through a second bottle of wine; a few broken fragments of cheese lay on their plates. Mike said something which made her laugh again. Her fingers were already on his, and she tightened her grip. Slowly, she stopped laughing. She looked him in the eyes with only a lop-sided remnant of a smile on her face. Her fingers were still twined in his.

He looked back at the slightly twisted smile. To refuse what she offered would be out of character. He was a free-wheeler, a single man, without ties or family. Her eyes went to where her fingers were on his and then back to his face. Her smile widened tentatively. At best, his refusal would offend her; at worst, it would feed any lingering suspicion. He decided to let the animal out of its cage. Without letting go of her hand he got up from the table, lifted her bodily from her chair and carried her the three steps to the bed.

At first their lovemaking had a strange flavor to it. Not that he needed to feign desire. That was real enough, the pent-up result of the weeks of solitude. But there were other ingredients, a fierce undercurrent of vengefulness that gave his actions a barely suppressed edge of violence, and a faint unease somewhere in him, a spark that would not become a flame, that was somehow connected to her outburst over the crosswords.

Mary's response, too, although instant and willing, had an edge of restraint in it, a faintly mechanical enthusiasm, as though she were discharging some kind of obligation. Gradually, as he eased the shirt from her shoulders to expose the resilient flesh of her neat breasts and the narrow, muscular hips, as his lips caressed and probed the recesses of her slender body, whatever troubled each of them seemed to shrink away, submerged by desire. Doubts, suspicions, loyalties, all of them were consumed as their bodies and their minds fused in the frenzy of their embraces. It was as though there were a tacit understanding between them that each was haunted by something, something that needed to be blotted out in their lovemaking.

Throughout the next day Mike went out only once, to get the papers. The rest of the time they read, ate and made love. By the end of the day his mind was in utter turmoil. He *had* to hate this woman. He needed to hate her. And yet each hour that passed was making it harder to keep a grip on the crucial, fundamental truth; that this woman was one of those responsible for Allix's death, a warped killer ready to bomb innocent children in the service of the Provos.

"You have to leave."

She stood naked at the cooker, her back to him. She turned to stare uncomprehendingly.

"Huh?"

"You have to go." She opened her mouth to respond. He shook his head. "It's too dangerous—everything we're doing. Your being here at all. You've got to go."

She looked at her watch. It was eight o'clock in the evening. "Now?" There was no argument in her voice. It was as though she had been ready to voice the same thought.

"Tomorrow. Early, before that shit-head of a landlord's around. Your leg's good enough now. You can walk far enough to get a taxi. Got any money?"

She nodded. She was biting her lip. "You might find it hard to believe, but it wasn't money that was bothering me."

CHAPTER

8

MIKE LET HIMSELF OUT OF THE HOTEL AND BEGAN STRIDing toward the corner. Mary's departure had left him depressed and off-balance. For the three days since she had gone he had been trying to tell himself he had only made love to her as part of the role he was playing. He was having a lot of trouble getting himself to believe it. He walked fast and breathed deeply, trying to clear his head. He had drunk himself to sleep again, but that was not working either—the idea that he had betrayed Allix was still there. It slept coiled in his brain like a viper; every morning it woke up at the same time he did and started hissing.

The Pakistani newsagent's window had been smashed the previous Saturday afternoon by a mob of drunken louts. He had boarded up the damage and become friendlier than ever, and Mike winced imperceptibly at the man's enthusiastic response to his nod. It was a little rich for his stomach at seven-thirty in the morning. He gave the newsagent the money and a noncommittal smile and walked out, leaving the man determinedly encouraging him to enjoy his day.

The moment the door closed on Mike the newsagent turned his attention back to the man he had been watching attentively for the last ten minutes. For all that time the man had been browsing vacantly among the greetings cards, and each time a customer had come in he had raised his head to study them. It was the certain mark of a shoplifter. They always watched the people—shoppers looked at the merchandise. The man replaced the card he had been holding and strode from the store without a word. The shopkeeper craned over his counter, staring with mournful desperation at the back of the man's thick donkey jacket and wishing he had X-ray vision.

The man let the shop door slam behind him, looked quickly up and down the street and half-ran to fall into step alongside Mike.

"Fancy a cup of coffee, Michael?"

Mike took a fast half-step to the side and turned to the man. His fists had bunched, his elbows were in at his sides. The man laughed and shook his head. He spread his hands in a show of harmlessness. "No, no. There's no need for that. I've got something for you, that's all." The accent was unmistakably Ulster.

Mike let the man lead him across the street to a café, and studied him as he went to the counter. It was a face he definitely did not know; the over-sized ears alone were too conspicuous to forget. The man was youngish, around thirty, tall and slender, with huge hands to match the ears. He wore working clothes, plaster-smeared jeans and the standard building-site laborer's blue felt donkey jacket with a scuffed leather insert across the shoulders. He returned with two grey-tinged drinks he said were coffee. Mike shoved the remains of several breakfasts to one side, making room for the man to put them down.

The man frowned at the sticky mess on the table, gave it a wipe with the cloth of his sleeve and pulled out a sealed brown envelope. He laid it in front of Mike.

"The travel agency sent this over." He grinned knowingly.

Mike raised an eyebrow and picked up the envelope. "What is it?"

The man cast an eye quickly over the room. They were alone except for two men at separate tables across the café who sat with their mouths nine inches above their plates wolfing forkfuls of sausage that trailed skeins of egg yolk.

"Have a look for yourself." He looked pleased with himself.

Mike ripped open the envelope and looked inside. It held an airline ticket and a passport. He drew out the passport.

The man signaled to him to keep it out of sight below the table-top. "Good, eh?" He was smirking across at Mike. "Have a good look."

Mike thumbed through the passport. It looked perfect. The date of issue was shown as three years previously, and there were several visa stamps inside, some for Middle Eastern countries. The binding was slightly worn, the edges of the pages soiled; the whole passport carried the scars of three years of hard use by a travelling man. It looked almost exactly like his own, the one he had claimed at the interview in West Ham to have lost in Athens. He nodded in admiring acknowledgement. The ticket was a single to Dublin. The booking was for that same morning at eleven-thirty.

"Take the passport with you."

"To Dublin? I didn't think I needed one."

The man smiled slyly. "Maybe you'll be going on somewhere from there."

"What about my room? The rent?"

"You're to pay up for this month and next. Have you got enough cash?"

Mike nodded. "Yeah. How about clothes and stuff? How long am I going to be away for? And where? What kind of clothes am I supposed to take?"

"Don't worry about it. I've got a bag of junk for you in the car. Toilet gear, a few bits and pieces. You won't need any of it but you don't want to be travelling with nothing at all. Empty-handed travellers stand out like sore thumbs. Specially on the Dublin run." The man gave him a wink that contorted the entire side of his face. "Half the people hanging around the check-in'll be Special Branch on the look-out for anyone who might be heading back to the old country in a hurry." He laughed softly at the implications of the idea. "You'll be given everything you need when you get there." He stood up. "Come on. Let's go."

Mike looked surprised. "Let's go? Are you coming too?"

"Only as far as the airport. I'm running you out there. The car's round the corner. We'll go by your hotel on the way, so you can settle up." He was already heading for the door.

Mike shrugged, drank off the last of the filthy coffee, and followed him.

When they reached the hotel, the man stopped the car and turned to Mike. "I'll come in with you. Just pay the rent and let's be off, quick. The traffic can be murder at this time of morning." As he spoke, he climbed out of the car, and followed Mike up the path and into the hallway. "Go ahead. I'll wait for you here."

Mike ran up the stairs. He had to wait several minutes before the bathroom was free, then he shut himself inside, unfolded the screwdriver on his pocket-knife, removed the bath panel and pulled out the pouch. He considered for a moment how much to take. Finally, he slipped three hundred pounds into his pocket, peeled off the money for the rent and, after a moment's hesitation, pushed the rest back into the cache.

He replaced the panel with even more care than usual and levered himself to his feet. He stood for several seconds, hesitating. His notes were in there with the money. He could retrieve them and try to leave them in a left-luggage locker at the airport, except he did not think they even had lockers at the airport any more. Too many people had been leaving bombs in them—people like the IRA. The alternative was to leave them where they were. From the dirt in the cavity he guessed the panel had not been removed in twenty years, and the chances of the landlord becoming a hygiene freak at this point in his career were small. The stuff was safer where it was than travelling with him.

He bounded down the stairs. The landlord's pasty ferret-face peered suspiciously from the shadows, eyeing the stranger who loitered in the hall, near the telephone. Mike pushed into the landlord's narrow lair and counted out eight weeks' rent. He laid it in the man's palm.

"I've got to go away for a while. Got some work, up north."

The man stared at the money as though he thought it might not be genuine. Mike pressed another ten-pound note into his hand.

"Keep an eye on things for me, will you?" he said, in a confidential voice calculated to show the man there was no one in the world he would rather trust. "All my stuff's up there. I'm not sure when I'll be back. Maybe a few weeks. Maybe a couple of days." He added the last phrase as an afterthought, the idea being to sow enough uncertainty to discourage the landlord from renting his room out by the night to truck drivers while he was away.

As Mike re-entered the hallway the driver shrugged

himself away from the wall where he had been lounging and strode ahead of him out of the building.

The traffic was already packed, promising to make the journey to Heathrow long and tedious. The sudden detours the man used to establish whether they were being followed made it longer still. They included one heart-stopping dash the wrong way down a one-way street that left Mike surprised to be alive. The driver hardly said two words all the way. At the airport he insisted on parking the car and staying with Mike to the entrance to the departure lounge, brushing aside his protests that he knew how to get on a plane. As Mike made to pass through for departure the man took him by the arm and pulled him abruptly aside, out of the flow of people.

"No phone calls, okay?" The smile he wore for the benefit of passersby was belied by the threat in his voice.

Mike shoved the man's hand away. "Okay. Get your paw off. Who would I want to call?"

The man shook his head. "I don't know. I don't care. Just don't use a phone. That's an order."

Mike smiled ironically and turned away. The man laid a hand back on his arm. He was not smiling.

"You're being watched—remember that."

Mike walked through into the lounge. The flight had already been called, and he strode straight through to the departure gate without even a glance around to see if anyone was taking an interest in him. In the crowded lounge it would have been futile, and it made no difference, anyway.

At first, the man's mistrustful manner, the wariness about his trying to phone, had scared him, but by the time he was settled into his seat he had stopped worrying about it. The man's instruction not to use the phone would be routine to anyone new in the organization; the security services probably had a permanent tap on them. If they really did not trust him they would have killed him in Kilburn and saved the cost of a plane ticket. The way things had been going for them lately they had probably simply given up trusting, as a matter of principle.

"Jamie Pike. Debbie Thomas." The Headmaster smiled broadly as he called the names. There was a stir among the assembled school, and he could see the swirl of movement around the two children whose names had been called as others craned around to look at them. "Debbie, Jamie. Would you like to come up here, please."

The two children made their way out of the close-packed rows and moved toward the stage from which the Head conducted the morning assembly. Debbie carried herself coolly, with the calm assurance of a fourteen-year-old girl aware of her approaching womanhood. The boy, Jamie, although a year older, walked with the awkward, faintly swaggering gait of an adolescent boy thrust into the limelight. They mounted the few steps to the stage and took up places beside the Headmaster, Jamie shuffling and grinning at friends in the audience, Debbie looking out at the hall with cool, chin-up composure.

The Head beamed down at them. The school was in one of Liverpool's most run-down suburbs, and if he had an announcement to make at the end of an assembly, more often than not it was news of a new piece of vandalism, or announcements of rearranged classes due to staff shortages. It was a rare pleasure for him to have some good news for the school. He raised the letter he held in his hand, as though he expected the whole school somehow to read it from thirty yards away. With one more proprietorial glance at the two children, he began speaking.

"This letter I'm holding here is from the, ah, Chieftain Oil Company. I'll, ah, read it out for you, I think."

He cleared his throat and gave one last look at the children. " 'Dear Mr. Walgrave,' " he coughed modestly at the mention of his own name. " 'We have great pleasure in informing you that following careful assessment of the results of our national essay competition, 'Energy and the Environment in the year 2000,' the essays of two students from your school have been selected as among the four hundred most original and meritorious entries submitted. We are therefore delighted to confirm that Debbie Thomas and Jamie Pike are invited to join the other national winners of our competition on the educational cruise organized by ourselves aboard the MV *Maribella*, departing from Southampton on January 29. Please be kind enough to confirm that your students will be able to take up the offered places. Yours sincerely, Burt D. Ingram, Vice President for Public Affairs.' "

The Headmaster's grin was growing wider by the second.

"I think they deserve a big round of applause. School?"

Even the few catcalls from boys who thought it was cooler to be disparaging were muted. From the rest of the school the applause and the cheers were loud and sincere. They were two genuinely popular children, both from fairly poor homes. They were clever, modest and ambitious, with a lot of friends. Jamie waved and grinned to his cheering cronies; Debbie blushed and examined her shoes. The Head beamed at the school's reaction. It was a great boost to morale in a school where such events were rare. For a pair of kids from their background, three weeks cruising the Mediterranean on a liner was genuinely something to dream about. He would not have minded doing it himself, for that matter.

He made a tactfully short speech congratulating the two of them, careful not to be appearing to steal the children's thunder. Their English teacher, a harassed-looking man whose premature hair-loss added ten years to his age, was called up to take a bow. He, too, was manifestly basking. The Head kept the two children up on the stage with him as the school dispersed to begin lessons. A photographer and a reporter from the *Liverpool Echo* were waiting in his study. In his three years at the school it was the first time he could remember dismissing an assembly with such awareness of a sense of well-being in the hall.

Burt D. Ingram stood at his office window and surveyed Hyde Park. It was a big window—it was an astonishingly big office, far bigger than anything he would need, or anything he had ever had before. He turned and sat on one of the three large sofas, relishing the comfort. This morning, he knew, his letters were being read out in a couple of hundred schools. He smiled. It was all bullshit, but it was classy bullshit.

A couple of months earlier Chieftain Oil had suffered badly from some avoidable accidents. In the first a North Sea rig had blown out due to lousy procedures, and had spewed oil into the sea for weeks before they had capped it. Oil-caked seabirds had been dying nightly on the nine o'clock news. As if that were not enough, a week after the blow-out, one of their tankers had been holed in a collision in the Channel, dumping its load of crude on to Cornish beaches. The authorities were out to hang a negligence charge on the company.

Burt Ingram was a good-looking, intelligent American in his mid-fifties, who had gone about as far as he could go in the company, given his preference for remaining in London and not returning to the States. He had been shunted into a senior but not very demanding position in the personnel department. There for a couple of years he had shared an office with another man with whom he often played squash, and had been coasting contentedly toward his pension.

Two days after the Channel collision he had been astonished to find himself facing a hostile press conference as the hurriedly created Vice President for Public Affairs. One of the Vice President's first tasks had been to put something together to restore Chieftain's image, something public-spirited that could be put in place fast.

The essay competition had been his idea. The company's public relations machine had made certain it received national prominence, and every school in the country had been invited to take part. The best of the essays were to be printed in the national Sunday newspaper in which Chieftain had a twenty-eight percent stake. The cruise was to be the climax of the operation. Several hundred of the best of the nation's young men and women would be escorted around the Mediterranean on a luxury liner. They would take lessons on board, attend lectures on the cultures and glorious pasts of the cities they visited, and be generally force-fed on culture; dragooned into museums, paraded before great pictures.

His personal view was that they would return without having added much to their knowledge, apart from the serious discrepancy between the price of alcoholic drinks in Britain and the Mediterranean countries, but that was not his problem. The President liked the idea, and the newspaper's color supplement was eager to do a three-week story on the trip. It would feature the cream of Britain's youth assembled on a gleaming white, flag-decked MV *Maribella*. Four hundred clean-cut achievers without a glue sniffer among them, being introduced to the finer things of life by Chieftain Oil. He smiled to himself. The color supplement journalists knew who paid their wages; they would omit the drunken rampages and aghast café owners in every port of call.

There is no passport control at Dublin for flights from London. A solitary official who might have been a customs officer scanned the arriving passengers with no show of interest. If the Irish Special Branch were watching they were doing it discreetly, perhaps on the monitors carrying pictures from the cameras that hung overhead. Nobody appeared to give Mike a second glance as he strolled out on to the concourse.

He hesitated, looking around him at the sea of unfamiliar faces. A young woman detached herself from the waiting crowd and moved to his side. She pecked him on the cheek, laughing and fussing at him, as though he were a member of her family back from a long stay in Britain. Chattering animatedly, she guided him out of the building to a waiting car, ushered him into the rear seat and climbed in next to the driver, a very dark man with a bar of eyebrow as thick as a finger in a straight line across his forehead. Another man sat next to Mike. He was older, fleshy, with heavy jowls and strands of hair brushed unconvincingly across the bald expanse of his crown. A button had gone where his shirt strained above his belt. Both men greeted Mike with restrained friendliness and then said nothing more as they drove out of the airport. All their attention was on the road; the driver kept a constant watch on his mirror, and the fat one screwed painfully around in his seat to stare through the rear window.

The moment they were clear of the airport the girl turned to Mike. "Here. Put these on." She handed him a pair of wraparound dark glasses. As soon as he put them on, a chill of unease ran through him—the glasses were totally opaque.

Abruptly, the car swung wildly, sending him lurching against the fat man, then bucked and jarred, as though they had run across an obstacle. He fell against the man again.

"Steady." The man was laughing. "You'd better hold tight for a few minutes, just while Joe makes sure we're not followed."

Mike guessed that they had just done a U-turn on the dual carriageway, driving across the grassy central strip. They drove on, swinging through several more evasive maneuvers, for what Mike judged to be about twenty minutes. The last part of the journey was slower, with frequent turns, as though they were in side streets. They drew to a stop. There was a grinding of gears that made Mike wince, they reversed briefly, and then the engine died.

The fat man helped Mike out of the car and up a few steps, as though he were blind. He could hear the sound of children playing close by. A door closed behind him. The glasses were taken off. The fat man stood in front of him, grinning. They were in the hallway of a house.

"Sorry about that. Sure you'll understand though, the way things are."

Mike nodded and laughed through his nose. "Sure. I know how it is. Pity everyone doesn't have the same attitude. It's because security's so terrible things are in the state they are."

The man looked grave. "You're right, my friend. It's been a terrible time these last months. I've never known a spell like it, the men we've lost. Women, too. It's going to take years to rebuild after the losses we've taken. Fucking years!"

Mike nodded, and thought, *you haven't seen anything yet.* "Don't worry," he said cheerfully. "They seem to be getting it together now."

The fat man nodded dubiously and led the way up the stairs. As they passed a telephone in the hall, Mike noticed it had a lock on the dial and the number had been obliterated from the face of it. Maybe they were learning.

The room into which he was shown contained a bed, a low table, a worn armchair and a television set. A handful of books lay on the table, and alongside them stood a plate of corned beef sandwiches and a six-pack of Guinness. The unlined curtain at the window was drawn. He picked up a sandwich and took a bite.

"Make yourself at home. The bathroom's next door. Shout if you want anything, I'll be downstairs. You're supposed to stay up here. Okay?"

Mike waved the sandwich and smiled, indicating the table. "Okay. You've thought of everything. What's your name?"

"Sean."

"Right. How long am I going to be kept cooped up here, Sean?"

"Dunno. I'm just the doorkeeper, nobody tells me anything."

Mike smiled quietly at the pent up rancor in the man's voice. "Seems as if we're both in the same boat." He steered the man gently toward the door. "I'll give you a call if I need anything." He plucked expressively at the cloth of his shirt. "After that journey the first thing I want is a bath."

As soon as Sean had descended the stairs Mike drew back the curtains. The room gave on to a paved yard, and beyond that was the blank wall of a warehouse or factory. He examined the window. Several nails driven through the frame sealed it shut.

The bathroom window was secured in the same way. While the bath was running he crossed the landing and tried the doors of the other two bedrooms. Both were locked. He listened for a moment at the top of the stairs. No sound came from below. However, he could see that the door of the front room, opposite the foot of the stairs, stood open. Sean would not miss his call. He would not miss a footfall on the stairs, either. Mike took a quick bath and retreated to his room to wait, uncertain if he was a guest or a prisoner.

CHAPTER

9

MIKE WAS WOKEN BY LIGHT. HE GATHERED HIS SENSES instantly, and was already swinging his legs out of the bed when he caught sight of Sean's broad face grinning at him from the doorway; his hand was still on the light switch.

"Startle you? Sorry," he said, cheerfully. "I brought you a cup of tea. You're leaving in a few minutes."

Mike stooped to pick up his watch from where it lay by the bed. As he slipped it on he glanced automatically at it; it was six fifteen. Taking the cup of tea Sean held out he crossed the room and pulled aside a curtain. It was still pitch dark. The room was freezing. He turned to Sean with a shudder.

"Right. Have I got time for a quick bath?"

Sean looked at him as if the idea of taking a bath before you had a chance to get dirty was slightly suspect. "If you like. Just hurry it up, they'll be here in ten minutes. The people you're seeing won't stand for indiscipline."

Mike gave him a satirical salute. "I bet. See you downstairs in a few minutes."

Sean waved a finger from side to side and made a clucking sound with his tongue. "No. Just get dressed and wait here. You'll be called when you're wanted."

By the time Mike had finished the tea the taps had dribbled a reluctant two inches of water into the scaled tub. He took the best bath he could in the tepid puddle, shaved and dressed quickly. As he finished he heard the street door open and close softly, and a murmur of conversation wafted up the stairwell. Sean sang out his name from the foot of the stairs. Swilling down the last dregs of the over-sweetened tea, he went down to the hallway. The girl and the driver, Joe, waited just inside the front door. She handed Mike the dark glasses, and with a word to Sean they led him down the steps and installed him in the back of a car.

They drove for what must have been half an hour. From the frequent turns he guessed they were zigzagging through backstreets, winding and doubling back to flush out any pursuit. When hands reached in to help him from the car they could as easily have been five doors as five miles from where they had started.

The hands on his elbows led him into a house. The quality of the air, the way their steps sounded, told him they were passing along a narrow passage. The smell of frying bacon brought a sudden pang of hunger that almost made him laugh aloud—it was absurd that a man being led blindfold to meet a group of organized killers could feel hungry.

The pressure on his arms brought him to a stop. A pair of hands gripped his biceps from behind and turned him to the left. They started down some wooden stairs. Even wearing the dark glasses Mike could picture the layout of the house. It was the typical terraced construction he had known through his childhood. They had walked from the street door along a narrow passage, jinking once as they avoided the staircase. Straight ahead would be the door to the kitchen, and the door they had just turned through would be under the main stairs, giving access to the cellar. A coolness in the air as they descended told him he was right.

"Undress." It was a new voice, male, harsh and rough-edged, without a hint of friendliness.

"Huh?"

"Take your clothes off." The voice was impatient. A hand started to pull his jacket from his shoulders.

"Hey!" He shook himself free with an angry movement, and one of his hands went up to the glasses.

"Leave them on. Get your clothes off, like he tells you." This was another new voice. It was softer and more educated than the first, and had a quiet venom the other did not have. His hand dropped away from his face. Reluctantly, he began to undress. A hand took each garment from him as he removed it. He stripped to his underwear.

"And them."

Resigned, he stepped out of the shorts and handed them over. There was a metallic sound, then a pause, punctuated by shuffling and intermittent brief bleeps. A sudden coldness on his back made him flinch, then the chill faded as an object began moving slowly over his skin. It covered every inch of him, from hair to toes. He called out in protest as a helper dragged his buttocks apart roughly, to facilitate the probing. The second voice told him sharply to shut his mouth. He had a sense that they were enjoying putting him through such humiliation. The probe left his skin.

"He's clean." The operator sounded surly, as if he were disappointed.

"You can take the glasses off now, Michael."

Astonishment mingled with the anger in his face as he tore off the glasses—the last voice had been Mary's. He stood blinking in the light, focusing on the scene that confronted him, and was immediately glad of Mary's presence. It provided a pretext for the surprise and recognition that no amount of self-control could have kept from his eyes.

Across the table, in a line next to Mary, sat three men. He recognized each one of them as a member of the Provo High Command; each of them, on his own admission, was a multiple killer. Two were on the run from prison, one from Ulster, the other from Walton on the mainland. The third was wanted in the Republic for the murder of two members of the Garda. A Provo squad running for cover after killing two soldiers outside Portadown had been caught in a joint ambush set up by the British and Irish police. Two of them had been taken alive and spirited back over the border. The police thought they had this man, too, until he produced what was reported to be an Israeli-made Scorpion machine gun from under his jacket and blasted his way out.

This event had created a major stir. It was the first time this firearm, especially favored by Middle East terrorists, had been seen in Ulster. The British authorities were worried sick that the Provos might have received a major shipment of this particularly dangerous weapon. The Irish were more concerned about the two dead Gardai; they were not interested in which weapon the killer had used.

Mike forced himself to keep his eyes on Mary, hardly even glancing at the others. His head was pounding, the hate coursing through him like a lava flow. He was standing four feet away from the people believed to be the very heartbeat of the organization.

He raised a hand and waggled his fingers jokily at Mary. "Well! Surprise, surprise." He gestured negligently around the room. "What's a nice girl like you doing in a place like this?" He heard his own voice as though it were somebody else's. Cool and flippant, and without a trace of the turbulent cocktail of hate and exultation that boiled inside him.

"You can put your clothes on again now," said Mary.

Mike dressed hurriedly.

"Sit down." The man in the center, the Garda killer, pointed to a wooden chair.

Mike sat, looking around the room in a casual appraisal. The scene confirmed his blindfold impression. They were in a cellar, a low-ceilinged place, without windows. The walls were lined with strips of glass-fiber insulating material, roughly held in place by wooden staves jammed into the angle of the wall and ceiling. It was a very temporary arrangement. The wooden steps they had come down were behind him. Two men sat near them, one of them holding a device like an airport security metal detector across his lap. His companion held an automatic rifle.

The atmosphere had the distinctive fungal smell of damp earth, but despite that, he guessed the insulation was not for warmth. These did not look like people with an excessive concern for personal comfort. But they would have plenty of concern about the possibility of directional microphones, and with good reason. Mounted on a roof such a microphone could pinpoint the origin of a sniper's bullet; directed at a building, it could pick up a conversation through a nine-inch brick wall. The body search he had just undergone would have been for transmitters implanted under his skin. The catastrophic events of the past few months had finally started to teach the bastards something.

The four people opposite began firing questions. They worked as a practiced team, and never once did he have an instant to think between answers. Frequently, one of them would backtrack over ground already covered by another, slanting a question slightly differently.

Mike was shaken and there was no point in hiding

it. They seemed to know every detail of everything he had said since the beginning. Every opinion, every observation or comment dropped in a conversation in a pub seemed to have found its way to them, reported word for word.

The questions were not too difficult to field. Once in a while, when one of them became too insistent over ground they had already covered, Mike let his temper flare. He used these occasions to try to seize back some measure of control, showing a cutting contempt for their lack of achievement.

Gradually, their probing narrowed from general inquiries about his past and his motives and focused on his command of Arabic, his experience with the Arabs, and his knowledge of explosives. Mike had already begun to recover his balance after the uneasy moments brought on by the realization that his every word had been relayed back to this house. Now, he was on his firmest ground. Nothing needed to be invented, even if a lot had to be left out.

He talked in a soft, level voice, without a trace of false modesty. The man on the extreme left, the one who had broken out of Walton, produced a piece of paper with some phrases written on it. He was a soft-looking man with sagging jowls and a frieze of wispy grey hair skirting a freckled expanse of scalp. With the manner of a cat about to pounce on a wounded mouse, he laboriously read out the first phrase.

Mike fired the translation back at him without an instant's hesitation, emphasizing the gutturals for maximum effect. The man pursed his lips, staring at his paper, and went on to the next phrase. Once again, Mike responded without a pause. They continued like that for a couple more phrases and responses. At each of Mike's replies, the questioner squinted at his paper, trying desperately to match the flood of sounds to the crude phonetic renderings he had in front of him. After Mike's fourth response he snorted and threw the paper on to the table and away from him. He looked from one to the other of his companions and then turned back to Mike.

"Fucked if I can make head or tail of it, to tell you the truth."

Mike smiled helpfully and shrugged.

The one who had killed the Gardai looked at the bald man from under lowered eyelids. He shook his head, and turned to Mike. "Look," he said, patiently, "according to what you told our people back over the water, you speak 'a bit' of Arabic. I'm no linguist, especially not in Arabic. So is it really 'a bit' or do you speak the bloody language? Properly, I mean."

Mike nodded, sharing the man's disdain for the bald man's efforts. "I speak it."

"Perfectly? Or just to order yourself a meal in whatever passes for a restaurant out there?"

"Somewhere between the two. I can say whatever I need to say. And they have some pretty good restaurants."

The bald man scowled. "How do we fucking know he's telling the truth?" He frowned, tapping his fingers edgily on the table. "There's a hell of a fucking lot hanging on this."

His companion looked at him pityingly. "For Christ's sake, Dev, give it a rest. He speaks it. Better than you speak English, sometimes. He's not going to lie to us about that, are you, Michael?" He spoke the last words in a tone of sweet friendliness that dripped with threat.

Mike shook his head, smiling. "No." Their eyes locked for a moment.

"Good. That's what I thought. Now, let's get on with it."

For most of the remainder of the interview Mary hardly spoke. She sat with a tiny hint of a smile, her eyes staring unfocused past Mike's shoulder. He had the impression she was mentally checking every detail of what was said with what he had told her during the stay in his room, checking everything about him for consistency with what she had learned. At a little after eleven the Garda killer, who seemed to be emerging as their leader, called for a break. The two men who had been seated at the back of the room escorted Mike up the stairs to the cramped kitchen. As he turned from the door at the top of the stairs and into the kitchen he caught a glimpse of two more men lounging by the street door. Both cradled rifles in their arms.

The girl who had accompanied Mike to the house sat at the oilcloth-covered table presiding over a tray of teacups and a heap of cold bacon sandwiches. She served the three of them and took the rest down to the cellar. Mike sat watching the taciturn minders. The one with the rifle kept a light grip on the barrel as he ate. His companion grabbed a sandwich two-handed and ploughed his face into it. As he moved the ugly, unmistakable outline of a big handgun showed through the cloth of his jacket.

Mike drank his way through three cups of the strong tea before the girl reappeared in the kitchen.

"They want you back down there." She jerked her head at the door.

The two gunmen followed him silently down the stairs. The four interrogators were in the same seats, their faces like stone. The leader stared up into Mike's face for several seconds as though he were expecting treachery to be written there.

"We've been discussing what you've told us this morning, Michael." The tone was utterly expressionless.

Mike felt sweat gather and skid down his spine. Behind him he heard the soft movement of cloth as the two minders shifted their weight. He wondered if the people at the table were armed. They almost certainly were. The whole setup was built for trouble. He half-turned his head, trying to gauge the positions of the two men behind him. He had left them standing one slightly behind and to one side of the other, blocking the stairs. They had not looked bright, but they had looked rough; taking a gun off one of them was strictly for people in books. His chance of making a break for it was nil. The leader stood up slowly, his eyes never leaving Mike's face. He leaned slightly forward, his palms flat on the table.

"Welcome to the general staff of the Provisional IRA." The man reached out a hand.

Mike's laugh sounded almost like a sob. The four of them were smiling at him. He looked around. The two gunmen were grinning. He shook hands with each of the four, and as an afterthought, with the gunmen as well. Mary held his hand just a fraction longer than the others. The leader called them all to order.

"All right, now. Sit down, Michael." He looked at the two minders. "That's all for now, lads. You can leave us alone."

He waited until he heard the door at the top of the stairs close firmly before drawing his chair closer to the table and addressing Mike.

"Sorry if we gave you a grilling. By the time I've finished what I've got to say you'll see why." Mike made a movement with his hands that told the man there was nothing to apologize for. The man went on without acknowledging the gesture. "We've a job we need you to do for us. It's an unusual one, and it's important. I can't exaggerate how important." He glanced around at the others as though looking for corroboration of his words. "You read the classy newspapers, so I don't have to tell you that we've had a lot of help from the Libyans over the years. Never a week goes by one or another of the British papers doesn't give it an airing. Usually, their reports are garbage, as far as the detailed facts are concerned, but they've had the gist of it right. The Libyans have been helping us out one way or another since back in the sixties."

Mike's mouth twitched in a smile. "Yeah. It's another of the secrets that's not been very well kept."

The man returned his smile with an acid one of his own. "No. But here's something that has been. They're giving us a lot of trouble. It's not exactly new, they've been getting harder to deal with for the last couple of years, but in the last two weeks it's come to a head. They're being *very* difficult, about supplies."

"What kind of supplies?"

The man dropped his voice further. "Semtex, mostly." He paused, letting the word sink in, and smiled grimly. "You're familiar with that?"

"I know what it is, anyway. Who doesn't? I've never handled it."

"You will soon, I hope. Look, I don't have to tell you, Libya's where we've always got our explosives. It used to be other stuff, for quite a few years now it's been Semtex. Not that we're insisting on that, right now. Any plastic explosive would do us. The only thing special about Semtex is it doesn't have a smell. And frankly, at the moment we wouldn't give a fuck if the stuff they gave us stank like pigshit. Semtex just happens to be the one the Libyans have—or did have. That's our problem. The bastards are refusing to let us have any more."

"Why the hell not? It's never been a gift, has it? I mean we've always paid for it, haven't we?"

"We always have in the past, eventually."

"Eventually?"

"Look, this is the Provos you've joined, not the fucking Prudential Assurance Company. Our money comes in in chunks, not in nice regular weekly amounts."

"Like from bank jobs?"

The man gave him a sharp look. "Never mind that. We've got a lot of sources. But they're irregular. It's okay for the regular outgoings, rents, travel, subsistence for the active service people. It's the big items that pose a problem. Arms shipments, for instance. Semtex."

"And our suppliers naturally like to feel they'll be paid."

Anger flashed in the man's eyes. "We pay our way. That was never a problem. They understood our situation. We have to take opportunities as they arise. If we could get a shipment in we took it. If there was a boat available to make the run, they shipped and waited for their money. We had an account, if you like. They never pressed us too much." He held up a hand to stop Mike interjecting. "Don't bother getting wrong ideas. Like I told you, we pay our bills. We don't owe them a single dollar. Anyway, the point is, in the past they were glad to help. Nobody wanted to see the color of our money first. It was a very civilized arrangement."

"As you say, very civilized. And now they've stopped it?"

"That's right. It's that mad bastard Ghaddafi. That last effort, where the other bugger, Jamal, had his men try to shoot Ghaddafi's plane down, seems to have finally unraveled him, sent him even further off his rocker. He's gone completely round the bend, completely unpredictable. The excuse they're giving us is that the Czechs won't supply them any more. Ever since they slung out the Communists."

"Well, isn't it true? The Czechs have said it themselves."

"Sure they have. They've also said enough was shipped to Libya in the last few years of the Communist regime to last five hundred fucking years." He shook his head angrily. "No, it's Ghaddafi's the problem. Loony sod."

"Could be he's just got other things on his mind, or maybe he's heard about the way things are going here and he's just given up on us. Incidentally, the Czechs still make the stuff, don't they? Wouldn't it make sense for us to try some other channels?"

The man was looking at him sharply. "You press your luck, friend," he said in a low growl. "As for other channels, we're working on that. There are a few countries around the world, Central America and what have you. We've got a man out scouting. You got any experience with the South Americans?"

Mike shook his head.

"Well, we have. It'll take time. They're getting a lot of aggravation from the Yanks over the stuff. None of these tin-pot Presidents wants to make the move that'll give Bush the chance to do what he did to Noriega. They've all got their snouts too deep in the drug money trough to go out on a limb for us."

"How about Lebanon? There must be tons of that kind of shit for sale out there."

The man showed another flash of impatience. "We're working on that, too. Those fuckers are worse than the Libyans. We need the stuff *now*. So just concentrate on Libya, like we're asking you to. That's where we know there's stuff, and it's available, if only they'd hand it over."

Mike laughed, ignoring the man's aggressiveness. "So what's the big hurry? Why don't we raise the money first? I don't know Latin America but I sure know the Arabs. There's nothing they understand like a cash transaction."

The man glanced first up at the stairs, reassuring himself that there was nobody there, and then at his companions, as if seeking their approval for what he was about to say. He lowered his voice even further.

"I'll tell you why. We've taken a lot of bad blows lately. The Brits have been hitting us hard. You know that as well as I do. In fact, you've been mouthing off about it all over London."

Mike inclined his head in mocking acknowledgement, not speaking.

The man continued. "Well, it's worse than you know. Over the water we've had a dozen good men shot dead." He seemed to feel Mary's eyes on him. "And women," he added, grudgingly. "Anyway, most of our mainland units. There was no need to shoot them. They could have been arrested. But the Brits aren't interested in arrests. They've changed the rules. All they want to do now is put in the fucking SAS and wipe us out." He jabbed a finger angrily at Mary. "You saw Mary's wound? She came within a couple of feet of being shot in the back. The man who was in the house with her had eleven bullets in him. Handgun bullets. He was butchered as he lay there. You know what else? Three weeks ago three of our people were found dead in bed right here, in *Dublin*. The three of them were shot in the head. You know who did it? The fucking RUC. E4A. Their 'special' squad. Well, that's what they're special for! Shooting people while they're asleep in their beds!" The man paused, surprisingly affected by anger and grief at the memory.

Mike used the space. "So the Brits are shooting our people. Why does that make us in a hurry? Seems to me more like a time to cool down. Take stock. Try and figure out what's happening."

"No! That's what they're hoping, that we'll lose heart. Well, we won't! We've had enough of it, Michael. We're going to hit back at the bastards—hard. The British government think they've got us on the run. They've got the courts, the papers, everyone stitched up, on the mainland as well as in Ulster. They don't even have to admit to the stuff they're doing, let alone answer for it. The only thing that'll make them change their minds is British public opinion."

Mike's laugh was genuine. "Oh, sure. The British government's very concerned about public opinion!" He stopped laughing, and the sarcasm left his voice. "You still haven't told me why the hurry. Just what have we got in mind?"

The man again looked quickly around at the other three, then said in a voice hardly more than a whisper. "There's not one of us in this room knows that. All we know is we've been told the stuff's got to be available in seven days from now. Maybe they'll tell you when you get to Tripoli. We just do as we're told."

Mike had thought he had himself completely under control, set for any shock. Still, he could not keep the flicker of surprise out of his eyes. The man's last words, spoken with a hint of bitterness, slashed at his senses. Until that very moment he had imagined himself to be facing the ultimate authority, the war council of the Provos. According to everything he had read these were the policy makers, the people who chose the targets, decided whether to shoot a soldier in Hanover or bomb a pub full of innocent bystanders in Coventry. In those few words the man had told him he was wrong. Somebody, somewhere, was giving *them* instructions. Instructions that the man's tone told him they dare not disobey. Somewhere there was a further layer of command, an authority that had never been hinted at, never reported in the press, whose existence the security services themselves had probably never even suspected.

He kept his voice matter-of-fact. "Tripoli. My favorite place! I need a rest from the booze! What would I be supposed to do when I get there?"

"You're going to get that Semtex, Michael. You're going out there. You're going to talk to them. Our feller there will give you all the help he can but it'll be up to you. You're going to get that stuff. You're going to use all that Arabic and you're going to make quite certain that we have it. We've got just a few days. That's to say, *you've* got just a few days."

The emphasis told him quite explicitly the answer

to the question he was about to ask—what would happen if he failed. These people had killed with their own hands. They had organized the deaths of perhaps hundreds of people, many of them innocent civilians. Some, he thought, with another blinding flash of bitter anger that he had to fight to quell, unborn. They had never hesitated to kill their own people when they had no further use for them. For them, in the war they saw themselves as fighting, assassination was routine. In firms he had worked for they had operated incentive schemes— you reached your target and won a week in Spain. The Provos operated one, too—you did your job or you got your knees drilled.

"When do I leave?"

"Tomorrow."

They were fifteen minutes from the house before the girl removed Mike's dark glasses. For the first time, she smiled. From the traffic he guessed that they were in the center of Dublin. The car drew up outside a store with an old fashioned wooden façade. In the window a dummy in expensive waxed waterproofs threatened a decoy duck with a shotgun. They entered the shop, and after speaking to a salesman who looked as though his employers had been keeping him in the dark about pension rights for ten years or so, the girl led Mike up the wide wooden staircase to the third floor. In a deserted corner they found a couple of racks of tropical clothes. Under the courteous eye of another soft-spoken, heart-rendingly subservient veteran of the gentlemen's outfitting trade, Mike tried on the only thing that looked likely to fit. It was a beige safari suit of the type in which he would be discovering new pockets for several years to come. It made him feel like a correspondent for the nine o'clock news. The girl paid.

Downstairs, he chose a pair of suede ankle boots to complete the dashing journalist look. On the way out he surprised the girl by stopping to buy a couple of good sweaters. She was another of those who learned their geography from the covers of tour companies' brochures. Her notion of North Africa was an unbroken series of sun-kissed days and balmy nights. He spoiled the image for her; Libya in winter could be miserable, squally and wet, and the desert at night was downright cold.

At three o'clock the girl helped Mike, a blind man again, with the outfitter's paper sack in his hand, back up the steps to where Sean waited at the front door. She left Mike to mount the stairs and ushered Sean into the front room.

Mike had been upstairs a few minutes when Sean appeared in the doorway carrying a tray bearing tea and a plate piled with sandwiches. He winked at Mike as he cleared a space and set down the tray.

"Back to England, then, is it?"

Mike looked surprised. "Huh?"

Sean winked again, and dropped his voice dramatically. "They shipping you back over? For the big one they've got coming off?"

Mike frowned and stepped closer to Sean. He kept his voice conversational. "Big one? In England? Me?" He laughed. "It's news to me. What's that, then?"

"Nothing!" It was the girl's voice. She stood in the doorway, glaring at Sean. "Keep your mouth shut, you old fart. That's nothing to do with him. Get back downstairs, and stay there."

Sean recoiled under her venom. Looking as though he had been slapped, he backed out of the door and slouched down the stairs. The girl gave Mike a quick smile.

"Don't worry about Sean, he's past it. Talks too much about things he doesn't understand." She withdrew into the doorway and waggled a key at him. "Sorry. Instructions. Seems you've become a very hot potato. I'll be here for you tomorrow morning, at half-past-six. Be ready."

He stood watching the door as the key scraped in the lock.

CHAPTER
10

THE YOUNG MAN STIRRED, GRIMACED WITH DISCOMFORT and twisted bad-temperedly on to his left side. He dragged the blanket closer around him, pulling it tight over his head in an effort to cocoon himself from the noise in the aircraft. He had been lucky. The moment the seat belt signs had gone off, minutes after taking off from Boston, he had been on his feet, prowling the tourist section of the 747. He had discovered three empty seats together in the rear. Immediately, he had snatched his rucksack from the overhead locker and moved to claim them. He had confirmed his tenancy of the seats by arranging the rucksack as a pillow and stretching himself across all three, covering himself with an airline blanket, and settling down to try to sleep.

He had straightened when the drinks trolley came by before dinner. He had taken two Scotches, and with the meal he drank another Scotch and four beers. The drinks had done the trick and calmed the insistent fluttering in his stomach, enough for him to get to sleep. He had hardly stirred in the hours since. Now, the voice of the First Officer coming over the speakers was forcing him into a gritty-eyed, hung-over wakefulness. He dragged the blanket off his face and lay for a few moments, his long hair tangled, frowning resentfully as he tried to collect his wits. He wondered irritably what the announcement had been about. Slowly, he became aware of a stir of conversation running through the cabin. He pushed himself on to an elbow; other passengers were looking around at each other, the seeds of panic in their faces. People who had spent six hours side by side without uttering a word began murmuring to each other in voices tinged with fear. The speakers crackled once more as the First Officer prepared to speak again.

"Just to repeat my message, ladies and gentlemen." The voice was a reassuring deep drawl. "We're having to interrupt our flight to Rome. We're just approaching Heathrow airport, London, England, where we'll be making an unscheduled stop. Let me reassure you, there's no problem at all. We have no technical problem whatever. The aircraft is performing beautifully. We'll just be making a very short stop in London and then we'll be on our way to Rome. We apologize for the inconvenience, ladies and gentlemen. At the moment we're a little ahead of schedule so we hope we'll be able to make up some more time after our stop. We should still be getting you all into Rome about on time. Thank you."

Grumbling, the young man struggled upright and threw the blanket aside. He fastened the belt which he had loosened on going to sleep and ran his fingers through his matted hair. A crease from the pressure of his makeshift pillow ran like a scar from his temple to his jawline, giving his spoiled adolescent face a temporary tough-guy look.

A stewardess offered him breakfast. He peered at the plate of warmed omelette and settled for an orange juice and some coffee. The woman handed it over with a big, white-toothed Pan-American smile. Despite the sulky expression he was a good looking young man, tall and muscular. His hair was tangled but it was an attractive light brown color with the fairer streaks that came from a lot of time at the beach.

He had hardly finished his coffee when he felt the pressure pop his ears and the girl came by to deliver another smile and collect the trays. She and her colleagues were moving with a kind of accelerated calm, designed to be reassuring, which had brought some passengers close to hysteria. The young man was watching the elderly woman in the window seat to his left. In profile he could almost lip read the prayer she was repeating to herself as her fingers twitched over a rosary. He knew it by heart. Like every other kid in his part of Boston he had heard it a thousand times from the lips of his own mother.

Several passengers screamed as the plane hit the runway and bounced once. Then they were down. The aircraft slowed and stopped. He craned to look out of the window past the old lady, but could see only an occasional light. A thought seemed to strike the young man. He started and grunted to himself, and his frown deepened. He pushed himself up from his seat and, moving across the aisle, leaned close to the window, peering into the darkness. There was no sign of the lights of emergency vehicles, only the white headlights of a half-dozen cars whose glare, reflected in the wet tarmac, effectively masked whatever was happening behind them. There was a change in the air which told him that up ahead the door of the plane had been opened.

There followed an interval of about a minute before a steward with a moustache as thick and glossy as a small animal emerged from the first-class section ahead of four dour-looking men in civilian clothes. The steward stood aside and the men eased past him and began moving down the aisle. As they went they opened the overhead lockers and pulled out bags. They leaned over the passengers, holding out the bags and asking questions. The passengers stared back from blank, fatigue-puffed faces, nodding or shaking their heads. Four more men appeared in the right-hand aisle and began the same process.

The two teams moved unhurriedly toward the back of the aircraft, occasionally smiling a wry response to a passenger who mustered some kind of enquiry, but never once speaking, beyond asking the same laconic question. The young man watched them approach for a while before shrugging and dropping back easily in his seat. He gave the old lady a smile that said he was as glad as she was to be safely down and just as mystified by events. He took a guide to doing things cheaply in Italy from his rucksack, shoved the bag out of his way under the seat in front of him and began reading. He was thoroughly engrossed in learning how to save money in Florence when one of the men reached down and touched his arm.

"Sir. Are you Mister Carl Denham?"

The young man looked up at them, nodding. "That's . . . er . . . yes. Why?" His voice was strained. His face had lost the outdoor flush. Flesh twitched at the corner of one eye.

"And is this your bag, sir?" The man's eyes went to the rucksack.

Again the young man nodded.

"Is it all you have, sir?"

His Adam's apple bobbed as he nodded again. "Right. Just some clothes and a few books. Who's asking?" On the last words he tried to put some outrage into his voice. It came out as a whine.

The man ignored his question. "Would you come with us, please, Mister Denham."

As he went, escorted by two of the men, the others

continued checking the ownership of every last piece of hand baggage.

Four men stood around the windowless room, looking down at the young man. Another, sitting across from him, threw the last of the slim wads of dollar bills on to the heap in front of him. The pile took up the space of a couple of shoeboxes. Each of the slender packages, bound with a narrow sleeve of plastic, contained twenty thousand dollars. They had been packed into the bottom of the rucksack that lay empty next to a few tangled clothes on the floor beside them.

The man at the table murmured to the others and then turned to the young man, who had sat pale and silent throughout the counting. He reached out a hand and lifted a few of the wads, then let them fall negligently back on to the heap. He leaned back in his chair, and spoke in a gentle voice.

"Now why don't you tell us, in your own words, Mister Denham, to save us all a lot of wasted time. There's almost two million dollars here. Whose is it?"

It was six-thirty in the morning when Mike heard the front door open and low voices in the hall. Sean called up the stairs. Mike had been up since four-thirty, unable to sleep. For the intervening two hours he had been trying to read the books in the room and listlessly watching the television. It was the first time in his life that he had tuned in to early morning TV. By the time he heard Sean's voice he knew it would not happen again. He flipped off the set and strode down the stairs carrying the hold-all with his few clothes. The girl was waiting for him at the foot of the stairs.

"You ready?"

Mike nodded.

"Good. Let's go. The plane's at eight." She turned and headed for the door.

Mike followed her, waving a cursory salute to Sean, who stood watching him blankly from the doorway of the front room. She handed him the dark glasses, waited until he had put them on, and led him out of the house.

They had been driving for three or four minutes, enough to be well clear of the house, before she spoke. "You can take those off now."

He pulled off the glasses. They were in a broad main road. She reached into her bag wedged between the seats and handed him a ticket and a sheaf of money. He flipped through the notes—three hundred American dollars. He pursed his lips. From his memory of Libya it would be enough to buy him two good dinners, except that nowadays they would be two terrible dinners. He opened the ticket, then turned to look sharply at the girl.

"I thought I was supposed to be going to Tripoli."

"Uh-huh. You are."

He held up the ticket. "What the hell's this, then? It's an Amsterdam-Kuwait."

"Sure it is. What did you expect? A direct to Tripoli? You'd have every Special Branch man in Dublin, and probably a few from London, giving up his weekend to rush out to the airport to talk to you. You're an oil man, aren't you? On your way to Kuwait to take up a contract." She turned to give him a quick glance. "You collect your Tripoli ticket at the transit desk in Amsterdam. Keep that Kuwait coupon, by the way. We'll get a refund."

Mike had already started to laugh when he realized she was not joking. The Provos had their accountants, like any other organization.

"How about the money?" he asked sarcastically. "D'you want me to sign a chit for it?"

She looked at him without a hint of humor. "No. Just hand it over when you get to Tripoli. You won't need to spend any money there. It's just part of your oil man image."

He shook his head. "Jesus. By the way, there's one little thing I haven't been told. What happens when I get there? What do I do?"

"Nothing. Go through customs like everyone else. You'll be met." The car had drawn up in front of the low airport building. "One other thing. You'll have a few hours to kill in Amsterdam. Don't use it to phone a friend. Get your ticket and go and sit down and wait for your flight."

"What will you do if I don't?"

She flashed him a short, sweet smile. "*I* won't do anything. The people that'll be watching you might jump to some wrong conclusions, though." She leaned across him and opened the door on his side. "Have a nice trip."

"Yeah. Say a mass for me."

The car was moving before his door had swung fully closed.

Check-in for the Amsterdam flight had already begun. Mike walked easily to the desk. To the left, twenty feet from the queue, a man in a dark suit sat with a flight bag on the bench beside him and a folded newspaper on his lap. He looked for all the world a businessman awaiting his flight. Only his eyes gave him away; every few seconds he raised them from his newspaper. Instead of looking around idly or watching the women, he fixed his attention on the faces of the passengers as they checked in. As Mike joined the queue the man got up, pushed his paper into the bag and walked away. He exchanged an almost imperceptible nod with the fiftyish woman in cardigan and flat shoes who happened along at that precise moment and took his place. It was just seven-fifteen. Mike smiled to himself; the Special Branch might have been expected to show more imagination than to synchronize their fifteen-minute stints with the clock.

The security check of hand luggage was thorough.

Even the priest a few places ahead of Mike found his toilet gear being turned out on to the bench. He used expensive aftershave.

Mike started for the gate on the first call for the KLM flight to Tripoli. He had waited in Schipol airport for almost five totally uneventful hours. He had read the *Times* and the *Guardian;* by the time he had started on the *Independent* the news had begun to seem awfully familiar. He had eaten, read most of a paperback book, drunk coffee and been to the toilet three times. Every once in a while he had risen to his feet and strolled around the airport lounge, browsing among the duty-free boutiques. The stuff they sold had long been a source of wonder to him. It seemed to cater to no need except the need to relieve tedium by parting with some money.

One of the sudden, unpredictable memories of Allix assailed him. The merchandise reminded him of times they had laughed over the junk mail that seemed to come in every post. The flimsy mail-order catalogues that offered electronic devices for the man who has everything—except an independently functioning brain. Digital, do-it-yourself blood pressure gauges, exercise machines on which go-getting executives were pictured insouciantly shedding pounds. Until the second week, when they put them in the cupboard under the stairs for the next twenty years or so and got on with ordering an electronic tie-knotting aid, using their gold card.

Moving around the lounge he tried hard to check if anybody was observing him, but not once in the five hours had he surprised anybody taking the slightest interest. Probably there was nobody. On the other hand, in the constant movement and hurry of one of Europe's busiest airports, a dozen watchers could have gone unseen. Twenty yards from the departure gate he took a seat in one of a row of moulded plastic armchairs and settled down to watch.

He studied the faces of the passengers as they eddied around the desk. It was the mix he had learned to expect for a flight to an oil-producing country: oil-field personnel in badly matched casual clothes; continental businessmen in good suits or very smart sports clothes, their English counterparts in brown suits and ties that looked like part of a special consignment from Albania; Arabs in western suits, silk ties and two-ounce gold rings; Arab families with beautiful dark-eyed children and smooth-skinned, broad-hipped mothers. There were no non-Arab women at all.

It was getting very close to departure time, and Mike was getting to his feet when the sight of a figure striding toward the desk brought him up short. He dropped back into his seat and watched, motionless, as the newcomer presented his boarding pass. He sat, keeping his excitement in check, waiting for the profile view that would enable him to be sure. His blood raced as he examined the man. In the dozens of pictures the nose was badly broken. Now, remodelled by a comprehensive nose-job it was straight, thin and characterless. His gold-rimmed glasses and clipped mustache were also absent from the press photos, his face was fuller, his waistline thicker than they had shown. All of this, combined with the well-cut clothes and big-name designer briefcase made him almost unrecognizable as the rough-hewn character in the ten-year-old photographs. Yet Mike was absolutely certain of his man.

On so many of the evenings spent alone in his room memorizing faces, this one had looked back at him from the page. Always it had been in a photograph with somebody else, someone of more interest. For this man, Jack Randall, who stood twenty yards from Mike, had been of no interest at all. Because Jack Randall was dead.

A sometime history teacher at a Belfast school, Randall had been acknowledged for many years as the Provos' quartermaster. He had been the most brilliant fund-raiser and organizer of weapons supplies they had, one of the three most wanted men in the British Isles, right up to his death. It was a historical fact. Every newspaper in the country had confirmed it. Jack Randall had died in an IRA own goal.

Two men had stopped in a car outside a Belfast cinema, intending to plant a bomb. It had gone off prematurely. The occupants of the car had been unrecognizable. Some shreds of a driving license and the heavy signet ring that he was known to wear had been taken by the British authorities as irrefutable proof that one of the dead men was Randall. At the time they had been cock-a-hoop. Well, they had been wrong.

Mike moved forward to join the queue at the desk. Jack Randall was standing ten feet from him, carrying a fancy briefcase and looking every inch the prosperous businessman. The ring on his left little finger was a modest gold band with a small stone. And the queue he had just joined was for a flight to Libya, the IRA's principal arms supplier.

CHAPTER

11

It was several years since Mike had been in Libya. It was still brown. The plane broke through the thin film of cloud to reveal the newly built suburbs of Tripoli stretching beneath them. Villas stood in their own walled patches of parched garden. From the air, even the thick-leaved succulents and occasional eucalyptus looked a tan color. Amid the villas, neat low-rise apartment blocks stood on patches of newly excavated earth, deeper, red-brown scars amid the surrounding tan. Even before you got there the country exuded a serious lack of charm, but there was one thing in the country's favor that struck Mike forcibly. Nowhere around Tripoli was there any sign of the squalid shanty-towns that encircled most cities of North Africa and everywhere else in the developing world.

They were only a few hundred feet above the parched ground. Mike felt a sudden twang of misgiving as he saw the runways and buildings of what he recognized as Tripoli airport slide past, far off to his right. He recovered himself quickly. He had forgotten that the civilian airport had been out of use since the American bombings several years earlier. Even by the leisurely standards of the area the intervening years would have provided enough time to fill in a few bomb craters, but the government had made a deliberate decision to go on using the old American Air Force Wheelus base. It was further from town. If ever anybody attacked again—and the country had a gift for making enemies—there would be less chance of civilian casualties.

They dropped smoothly on to the concrete of the runway. There was a brief stir of interest as the passengers caught sight of the tanks and anti-aircraft guns standing conspicuously among the dilapidated buildings. Mike gathered up his bag and prepared to file off the plane. He had seen Randall only once during the flight, when he had walked back through the plane to the toilet. Randall had been sitting reading a Dutch newspaper and smoking a small cigar from a flat tin that lay in front of him, and had shown no sign of recognizing Mike.

There was no transport from the plane to the buildings, and the passengers walked the two hundred yards to the low customs shed in a loose gaggle. Their way was clearly marked by a line of sullen young conscripts cradling dangerous-looking submachine-guns. There were six makeshift passport control booths; only one of them was manned. It was almost half an hour before Mike's turn came. The booth was wooden with a window at the front. A semi-circle was cut out of the bottom of the glass at waist level, forcing the passenger to stoop in order to hear the passport officer's questions.

Mike smiled to himself. To listen to what the immigration man was saying or to answer his questions a passenger was obliged to bend from the waist, to grovel, almost. Airports all over the third world had developed the same system. It was a reaction to their colonial pasts. It seemed intended as a warning to citizens of ex-colonial powers, a foretaste of the humiliations that could be inflicted by anybody in a uniform once that barrier was passed. So start behaving yourself right now!

The officer scrutinized Mike's passport as though it were a counterfeit banknote. After a pause of thirty seconds or so he made an almost imperceptible movement of his head. A man in civilian clothes lurking in a nearby doorway returned the nod, and walked across to Mike. He greeted him by name and steered him into an office with whitewashed windows.

Randall was already there. Another Libyan civilian had him enveloped in an embrace. The Libyan's chin was on Randall's shoulder and his arms were thrown round his chest. He was beating Randall on the back with a flapping motion of one hand. Randall was tentatively returning the embrace. His eyes met Mike's over the man's shoulder, but he did not smile or make any show of greeting. His face was almost blank, except for a film of distaste.

The Libyan drew back, beaming. "Ah, my dear Mr. Jack. You're back with us. So happy to see you. You have baggages?" Randall nodded. "Then let us take it." He peered around the door. "It will be here now."

As an afterthought, he turned to Mike. "And you are Mr. Scanlon?"

Mike gave him a lopsided smile and a nod.

"You have bags, too?"

Mike shook his head. "Uh-huh." He held up his bag. "Just this."

"Good. Please come with Mr. Jack and myself." He led the way from the office as an open pick-up truck roared and swayed to a halt by a new-looking baggage carousel that snaked around the hall. Two men leaped from the cab and began hurling bags enthusiastically on to the carousel. It did not move. The passengers who had managed to persuade the immigration man to let

them in clustered around the growing pile of luggage
like hyenas around an ailing antelope. Every once in a
while one of them would dart forward, flinching under
the hail of bags, and grapple a suitcase from the heap.

Randall stepped smartly forward, his face still expressionless, and ducked back again, pulling a grey Sam-
sonite suitcase from the heap. The civilian immediately
dashed to his side and wrenched it from him, brushing
aside Randall's protests. He led them past the low
counters where the other passengers were resignedly
watching the harsh-eyed customs men ransack their luggage. None of the customs officers gave the three men a
glance.

The Libyan talked in a constant stream all the way
to the car, mostly at Randall. By way of reply, Randall
let him have two or three monosyllables. His taciturnity
had no effect on the man's determined good humor. In
the moment of silence when Randall and Mike were installed in the back seat and the Libyan was busily loading their bags in the boot Randall turned to Mike. He
held out a hand.

"Jack Randall." He kept his eyes on Mike's as he
spoke the name, looking for a reaction.

"Mike Scanlon." Mike shook the offered hand. He
paused for a brief moment and then let himself frown.
He glanced behind him. The Libyan was locked in an
embrace with a man with a quarter-inch of grey stubble
and one eye out of true. They probably had not seen
each other since yesterday. It would take them another
five minutes to say hello. "Randall? Didn't somebody of
that name get it a few years back? Wasn't there a
bomb?"

The other man smirked. "There was a bomb, yeh.
A couple of people died. That was the name they gave
one of them. Poor bastard, eh?"

Mike kept looking at the man. Slowly, as though he
were only now understanding, he put some admiration

in his face. Finally he inclined his head. "Jesus!" He shook his head, openly impressed now. "Jesus. That *was* nice work. There's never been a whisper."

The man's eyes went cold above his smirk. "Let's keep it that way." He jerked a thumb over his shoulder. "The clown back there, Hamid, thinks my name's Randolph, okay? Jack Randolph. Hamid is our contact man with the Libyans," he said, unenthusiastically. "He's okay but we *strictly* don't talk business in front of him, except when we have something specific we want transmitted to the government here. Clear?"

Mike nodded, glancing around at the figure of Hamid. He was laughing with the disreputable old man, holding one of the old boy's hands in both his. "Okay." He kept his voice very low. "Is there any special reason why we don't trust him?"

Randall gave Mike a long look, as if he suddenly suspected they had sent him an imbecile to work with. "He's a Libyan," he said, as if no reasonable person would need to ask any further questions.

Mike had several, but before he could put them he was cut short by Hamid climbing into the driving-seat, already talking in a flood.

The sun was going down over the Lisbon waterfront, making the colorwashed houses glow with a gentle pastel light. High up on one of the wrought-iron balconies a grey-haired man sat looking down at the panoramic view of the harbor. He was thoroughly relaxed in the late sun; his heels rested on the parapet, his ornate dark wood chair tilted backward. He carved a bite-sized piece from the cheese that stood on the low table next to him and chewed it with slow relish. Sighing, he poured mineral water from a condensation-frosted bottle into a cut-crystal glass, sipped at it and replaced the glass on the table. Reaching down to the blue plastic hold-all beside his chair he took up a big pair of naval binoculars, removed his heavy, dark-tinted glasses and lifted the binoculars to his eyes.

The sight made him draw in his breath. She looked superb, finer even than he remembered her the last time he had seen her, in the harbor at Valetta. The setting sun reflecting off the white paint made her appear edged with flame. He swiveled the binoculars, taking in the full length of the deck. Hardly a soul stirred. He glanced at his watch and then swung to focus on the dock gate. A bus sped into view and swept through; another followed, then another, until there were more than a dozen of them, drawn up alongside the ship. He smiled as the bus doors opened and the children spilled out. His smile grew wider as the children formed into orderly ranks by their buses, each group shepherded by a young man or woman. These young adults were wearing identical clothes, immaculate uniforms of dark red blazers, white trousers or skirts, and white shoes. They looked faintly ridiculous, something between navy personnel and the chorus in an atrocious musical. He laughed audibly to himself as the sound of catcalls and whistles from the dockers drifted up to him as the children, many of the girls in miniskirts, began filing up the ship's gangway.

On the dockside, in the midst of the children from the third bus, Jamie Pike and Debbie Thomas talked excitedly with the others around them, exchanging impressions of the day's excursion. In the few days since the cruise began back in Southampton they had progressed from acquaintances to close friends. Debbie clutched a fistful of postcards. Jamie was laughing gently at her; she had bought Portuguese stamps—her next chance to post the cards would be in Naples.

The sun dropped below the horizon in a last dying riot of color. The man continued sitting in the same posture, oblivious to the distinct bite that had crept into the air with the departure of the sun. Keeping the binoculars to his eyes he watched the ship come to life as the crew prepared to leave port. It was almost completely dark when he lowered the binoculars and again checked his watch. He gave an almost inaudible grunt of satisfaction; they would sail on time. He levered himself to his feet, pushed another piece of cheese into his mouth and strolled back into the flat.

A woman in late middle-age lay on the floor looking up at him. Her eyes glittered with terror and contempt. A lace-edged table cloth was bound tightly around her head as a gag, pulling her lips back in a rictus. She was dressed in an expensive-looking dark skirt of very fine wool and a black watered-silk blouse, almost the uniform of the well-off Portuguese widow. Her hair, once black, now marbled with grey, was pulled back in a tight chignon; a few locks had come loose during her brief, violent resistance. A violet bruise surrounded her left eye, and her wrists and ankles bled where the plastic-coated garden wire that bound her feet and hands had bitten into the flesh.

The material of the skirt had ridden up to her hips. She wore old-fashioned underwear, a black girdle and dark stockings. She was a handsome woman, broad-hipped and ample-breasted; the pale flesh of her thighs seemed to shine in the dimness. He paused, staring down at her. The terror in the woman's eyes mounted, and her lips moved on the gag. The attempt to scream came out as no more than a low gurgling sound. Abruptly, divining the cause of her renewed fear, the man shook his head. He squinted at his watch, turning his wrist to catch the last remaining light from the French windows. He smiled grimly at her and dipped his head in an ironic bow.

"Obrigado. Thanks for the hospitality." He turned and made for the door.

The woman's head dropped back on to the polished tiles of the floor, her eyes clenched tightly shut. Her lips moved as she tried to murmur a prayer of thanks.

The man crossed the dark, over-furnished hall and carefully opened the front door. He checked quickly up and down the narrow staircase, an ear cocked for the sound of the lift. Hearing nothing, he stepped out and headed down the stairs, leaving the door of the apartment swinging open behind him.

He walked several blocks, moving unhurried and unnoticed among the crowd out taking the air, until he reached an old-fashioned stucco-fronted post office. He strolled casually up the steps, but once inside he quickened his pace and hurried to the international phone counter. He was directed to a numbered cabin. Taking a pen and a tiny leather notepad binder from an inside pocket he began dialing the international code for Holland. The number which followed was of a top floor flat in a small block in Enschede in the east of the country. It was his own home.

He listened, relaxed and silent, as the answering machine at the other end went through a succession of callers, until a voice came on which made him hunch closer to the phone. He listened intently for a few seconds. Biting at his lip, he scribbled some figures on the little pad and pressed a finger briefly on the cradle. The muscles in his normally impassive face twitched with anticipation as he began dialing the Hamburg number he had noted. As he waited for the other end to answer he plucked the thick glasses impatiently from his nose and drummed them against his thigh, staring unfocused through the glass panel of the door. A voice on the line made him start.

"Hello?"

"Ali. Is that you?" He strained to hear the reply over the poor line. The deep furrows of his frown dissolved into a grin as he recognized the thickly accented voice that responded. "I just got your message. Did you find the subject?"

A minute later, he almost knocked a young man

down the steps as he ran from the post office, hardly able to control his excitement. The youth was still shouting insults when he threw himself into a taxi.

"The airport. Quick."

CHAPTER

12

HAMID DROVE THE WAY PEOPLE RAISED IN THE DESERT could be relied on to drive; fast and badly, with a kind of innocent faith that would have been touching if it had been less potentially fatal. The situation was not helped by half the other drivers sharing the same attitude. The dusty Mercedes and the Toyota jeeps sped without hesitation across intersections; cars and trucks catapulted without a pause out of blind turns, trusting in God and their horns in equal measure. Usually, they missed each other. Sometimes they did not. The burned-out heaps of metal that fringed the roadside were witness to the fact. To add to the excitement, whenever Hamid's incessant chatter included something that needed emphasis he would wrench around in his seat to face them, grinning into their faces until he was sure they got his point.

Mike and Randall sat in tight-lipped silence. Mike still gave some of his attention to Hamid's stream-of-consciousness jabbering. Randall, the older hand at submitting to Hamid's driving, had turned to stare sullenly out of the window the moment they had pulled out of the car park. He sat gazing stone-faced at the vehicles that skimmed past inches from their paintwork. He obviously preferred that to the strain of knowing what was happening ahead of them.

Hamid managed to slash his way through the evening traffic of the city unscathed and they came into the wider, less congested streets of the suburb of Georgian Populi. The sheer opulence of some of the villas still had the power to come as a shock to Mike. Most of the area had been constructed in the days before Ghaddafi's revolution, back in the reign of the indolent old king, Idris, a corrupt and foreign-dominated regime that the Colonel's vocal critics outside Libya seemed to have conveniently forgotten.

Hamid stamped on the brakes, throwing them sickeningly forward in their seats. They were outside one of the less pretentious villas. It was surrounded by a wall of pink-painted cinder block pierced by a wide gate. Steel plates fastened behind the original wrought ironwork effectively sealed off the interior from passing eyes. On the narrow pavement outside the gate a soldier in tiger-stripe fatigues and headcloth sprawled on a wooden kitchen chair. He held his rifle loosely by the barrel with the butt between his feet. He was rhythmically raising it and letting it drop back to the ground, killing boredom by crushing the half-inch-long ants that hurried around his boots. He looked up alertly enough at the sound of the car stopping, his hands tightening on the gun. At the sight of Hamid, he nodded, relaxed visibly, and turned his attention back to the ants.

Hamid pushed open the gate and ushered them into the paved courtyard. Before he had fully closed the gate behind them the door of the villa was thrown open. A bulky, florid-faced man, his cheeks a purple web of broken veins, came rushing out to greet them. He was big, as tall as Mike and deeper in the chest, with a thick larding of fat around his shoulders and waist. His cotton slacks creased into concertinas at the tops of the thighs and behind the knees. The buckle of his scuffed brown leather belt bit into the triangle of exposed belly below his bottom shirt button. Coils of greying ginger hair clung damply to the few inches of bare white flesh. Over the shirt he wore a thick cardigan with a hole in the elbow as big as a saucer. He grabbed Randall's hand in one of his own huge fists. With the other he took hold of Randall's upper arm and kneaded it affectionately. Randall, five inches shorter, smiled fastidiously and moved a half-step backward. He took his hand out of the other man's paw, looking as though he would have liked to wipe it on his clothes. He compromised by gesturing toward Mike.

"Mike Scanlon." He looked from Mike to the big man, leading Mike's gaze. "Pat Kelly. Pat's our permanent man here. Our ambassador."

To an attentive listener the last words resonated with open contempt. Pat grinned proudly at Mike.

"That's right. Four years I've been out here in this dump. I know these fuckers like me own mother." He made a generous gesture toward Hamid as he spoke, just to show Mike the kind of fucker he was talking about. "Pleased to meet you." He snatched Mike's hand into his meaty fist and pumped it. "Come on in the house."

They crowded through an unfurnished entrance hall into a chilly living-room. Mike recognized the furniture—standard expatriate villa issue, circa 1964. When a person in shorts got to his feet on a hot summer's day the mock leather upholstery would part from his flesh with a sound like unfastening Velcro. The floor was slabs of reconstituted marble that seemed to drink the heat from the electric fire that stood by one wall, leaving a cool edge on the atmosphere.

Mike suddenly found himself aware of Hamid's silence and looked around for him. The young Libyan was hovering a step inside the door of the living-room, shifting his weight from foot to foot. Mike's gaze seemed suddenly to remind Randall of Hamid's existence. He turned around to find Hamid's eyes on him. The appeal in them jogged his memory.

"Oh, Christ, Hamid!" He laughed insincerely. "Sorry. I clean forgot."

He set the designer briefcase down on the dining-table and twirled the combination locks. He opened it, reached in and pulled out a fistful of glossy magazines. They were stuff it was easier to buy in Holland than in England; all but two of the covers carried pictures of women bending obscenely, leering over their shoulders at the camera in a parody of enticement. The other two bore pictures of muscular young men in singlets with their jeans unzipped. They wore the same beckoning expressions as the women. Hamid grabbed the magazines and riffled their edges eagerly with his thumb. He seemed to like what he saw. He smirked happily, nodded to Randall and backed toward the door.

"Goodnight, my dears." He brandished the pornography in Randall's direction. "Thank you." He paused in the doorway. "Mr. Mike, your training is all arranged. I have fixed everything." He glanced at the other two, looking for their appreciation. "I have arranged it all. Transport will come for you tomorrow morning. At seven o'clock. Please be ready. Okay."

Surprised, Mike looked at the others for a cue. Randall nodded, moving toward Hamid.

"That's okay, Hamid. Great. Thanks. Goodnight." He placed a hand on the Libyan's arm and shepherded him firmly into the hall. The others heard the door close. A moment later Randall re-entered the room. His mouth was pursed in the expression of a man who had just stepped in something foul. He grinned sourly at Pat. "Got a drink?"

Pat bustled into the kitchen. Mike heard the sound of ice hitting glass. He turned to Randall.

"Training? I thought I was sent here as a negotiator. What the hell am I training for?"

Randall looked at him coolly for a moment. "Killing people."

Mike ignored the suspicion of mockery in the voice. "I was told my job was to get these people to hand over the Semtex. Was that right?"

Randall shrugged. "Maybe. When you need to know you'll be told. Meanwhile, you're going on a course. Enjoy it. A lot of people would jump at the chance."

Pat came into the room carrying a tray. It held a large jug of amber liquid with a thin scum of foam, a smaller brown jug, a pitcher of water, glasses and ice.

Pat raised an eyebrow. "Beer or vodka?"

Mike chose the "vodka." Pat poured two inches of colorless liquid from the brown jug. Mike glanced dubiously at it and filled the glass to the brim with ice and water. With luck it would be enough to kill the antifreeze taste of the home brew. Randall drank the "vodka" too. Pat drank both, knocking off an inch of neat spirit and half the beer chaser before Randall had finished watering his.

"Got anything for *me*?" Pat asked Randall with a huge, obscene wink.

Randall muttered a vague apology and turned to his briefcase. He rummaged inside and produced a bundle wrapped in a hotel towel. Pat opened the bundle as tenderly as if it held priceless porcelain. It was better than that—it was several jars of baby malt. Visibly contented, Pat topped up their drinks. He could afford to be more generous now that he was assured of his malt supply. It was the one essential import Tripoli's bootleg brewers needed to make passable beer.

They sat drinking long into the night. Mike

matched the two men glass for glass, saying just enough to stay in the conversation as he studied them both. Randall gave very little away. He drank as hard as Pat without once losing the stiff-backed, aloof manner that clung to him like a hang-over from his days as a teacher. Behind the studied coolness there was something else, a hint of permanent preoccupation that gave Mike the feeling he was worried about something, awaiting some kind of news.

Pat did most of the talking, and it was not hard to understand why. The man was desperately lonely, and bored out of his mind. The story his complexion told turned out to be true. Mike had seen it more often with the wives in dead-beat oil camp compounds than with the working oil men. The kind of alcoholic who loved to drink but could not hold it any more, drunk from the first glass and getting drunker fast.

The combination of an audience and the alcohol quickly unleashed the flood of his pent-up resentments. He grew louder and more bitter as the drinks went down. He was disparaging and disdainful of Arabs in general, and Libyans were a particularly contemptible strain of the species.

"Shifty bunch of fuckers. They've got ten times worse since that prick Jamal's fucked-up coup, when they nearly got Ghaddafi. Pity they didn't. The mad fucker's gone completely off his fucking head."

Mike smiled, casting a look at Randall. "I see why Jack called you our ambassador. Anything in particular gone wrong?"

Pat's face pinched. His eyes narrowed with drunken shrewdness as he struggled to identify Mike's tone. He suspected sarcasm but could not put his finger on it. He opted for getting angry.

"Anything gone wrong? Too fucking right it has. The bastards are refusing to let us have our stuff! That's all. They're trying to make us believe they can't get hold of it like they used to, trying to tell us the fucking Czechs have cut their supplies off. Personally, I think it's a load of shit. From what I hear the Czechs are still as fucked for foreign currency as ever. Worse, if anything." He took a big swallow of vodka to calm his outrage.

Mike smiled sidelong at Randall. Randall just gave a slight shrug. "Not *that* fucked, Pat. That's the trouble with people who've just re-discovered democracy. They're taking their responsibilities seriously." Mike spoke softly, with just enough for an edge of banter in his voice to keep Pat confused.

Pat stared blankly at him for a moment, then gave a snort of derisive laughter and decided on a change of subject. "Look, we *know* they've got plenty of the stuff stashed away. And they know we know it. So the next excuse is we've been slow coming up with the money. One minute they're boasting about the biggest per capita income in the whole fucking world, the next minute they're too skint to give us a couple of weeks' credit." He took another swallow of vodka. He was no longer bothering with the ice or water.

Mike took advantage of the breathing space. "Maybe they *are* broke. The Saudis are getting themselves in the same boat. Billions coming in; billions more going out." He held up a hand as Pat started to bluster. "Don't tell me, Pat. You'd like a problem like that yourself. It doesn't change the fact they'll always put their own interests first." He turned to Randall. "Can't we just raise the money and offer to pay cash on the nail? At least that would give them one excuse less."

Randall grimaced. He flicked fastidiously at his mustache with a knuckle, removing some imaginary pollution. "We intend to—a down payment, anyway. The money's due in here any time. As a matter of fact, I was expecting it in today." He glanced automatically at his watch, reassuring himself he had the date right. He flicked at his mustache again, as if it were suddenly irritating him. "Should be here tomorrow, anyway. I phoned our people in the States from the airport this morning. The courier definitely left Boston last night."

"A courier? How much money are we talking about here, for Christ's sake?"

"A couple of million." Randall spoke reluctantly, hardly audible, as though he did not want to hear himself saying it.

Mike leaned forward incredulously. "Two million *dollars*?"

Randall nodded, his mouth pinched into something like a wince.

"My God! We have that kind of money carried around by *hand*? People kill for a fraction of that. What stops the courier pissing off with it?"

"Fear. Two kinds. First, we only use people who've got somebody close to them: a child; a parent; somebody whose life's worth more to them than the money. Second, in case the temptation gets too much for them, they know there's always somebody watching them. They're nursed on to the plane by a team and they're met off it by one. These are all people from the Boston Irish community. They know who they're dealing with."

"And they never try to make a run for it, anyway? Seems to me you could get lost in somewhere like Heathrow if you really wanted to."

Randall gave him a prissy smile. "Maybe. One tried it, once. In New York."

"Did he get away with it?"

Randall's smile faded. "They fished most of him out of the East River. They're still looking for his head. We make sure the others all learn from his example. It's the only time we've had trouble."

"Until now?"

Randall shot him a nervy look of pure venom. "Shut your mouth. He'll be here."

Mike shrugged and pushed a hand at the air in a

calming motion. "Okay, sorry. I didn't mean anything personal. But, look, don't we have banks to take care of that kind of thing? There are enough of them around that don't want to know too many details. Ask General Noriega. Ask the Colombian cocaine cartels."

"We *had* banks. Not any more. This last year the accounts have all been blown. Every one of them."

"Like the bomb factories?"

Randall flinched as though Mike had slapped him. He nodded, his face grim. "Exactly. Except it could just be the American government. They're putting a lot of pressure on."

"Sure. And the bomb factories are just coincidence and good police work. Gibraltar was a lucky break, Windsor was a bunch of armed SAS men on their day off acting on intuition! Come on, Jack, face up to it. This whole organization's penetrated to the core. It has been for years."

Randall's shoulders went back, as though he were making a conscious effort to shrug off the reminders of the bad news. He leaned toward Mike, suddenly aggressive. "That's why *you're* here." His voice was icy.

Mike returned his look, searching deep into the man's eyes, trying to see past the affected confidence, seeking a trace of the doubt that had been trying to break through a few seconds earlier.

Abruptly, Randall shrugged and seemed to relax again, sinking back in his chair. "Anyway, we use couriers, and it works. We use straight young people, not even sympathizers. Kids from college who're looking to earn a little cash. I'm not even sure if some of them realize *who* they're carrying for."

Mike laughed out loud. "Sure! They think they're smuggling sacks of money around on behalf of cancer research! Those people *always* threaten to blow away the children of anyone who lets them down! Who the fucking hell would they *imagine* they're doing it for?"

Randall's eyes hardened again. "Don't get fucking smart, friend. They know it's not kosher. They just aren't told whose money it is. A lot of them think it's drug money. Anyway, there's one thing you'd better remember. You're new in this game—I'm not. We live in an electronic age. The FBI, MI5, the French, all the rest of them, are plugged right into the bank's own computers. Any money moves, they know about it. Couriers, hand to hand, is the safest way there is. It's not good, it's just the best we've got."

Mike smiled sourly. "So, here we are, trying to liberate a country, and we can't get ourselves organized as well as a bunch of South American cocaine peddlers." He paused, half smiling at the man opposite him. "Jesus, Jack, if ever an organization needed some new ideas . . ."

It was a quarter to three in the morning when the man from Lisbon pulled off the autobahn and began following the signs for the center of Hamburg. He had been lucky twice that evening, getting a flight from Lisbon to Paris and then the last connection to Frankfurt. There his luck had run out; there were no further planes to Hamburg that night. He had rented a big Mercedes and done the four hundred and some kilometers in just over two and a half hours.

He swung the car easily through the empty streets. He knew the city well; he had lived there for a couple of years, way back, when he had first been forced to leave Ireland. Slotting the car into a parking space, he put on heavy spectacles and walked quickly toward the café, glancing anxiously at his watch. Ali had said he would be able to wait until three. It was four minutes to the hour.

He stopped short inside the door, wondering for a moment if he had come to the right café. He had known it as a quiet, dingy place where old men and men old before their time came to drink coffee and play chess. Now the lights were a flashing cocktail of deep reds and blues, and mock Tiffany lamps threw pools of muted radiance on to tables set deep among polystyrene foliage. He walked further into the room, feeling conspicuously old, with his yellow-tinged grey hair. A waitress in a seven-inch-long skirt and tights that reflected the colors of the lights tried to show him to a table. He refused, smiling abstractedly, and went on into the gloom.

Ali was sitting alone at a small table at the rear of the place, trying to read a Turkish newspaper by the inadequate light of the lamp. He was a nice-looking, smooth-skinned man of about thirty, wearing cotton slacks, a polo shirt tight over the roll around his waist and a fleece-lined denim blouson. At the sight of the newcomer he thrust the paper aside and sprang to his feet. Short and dark, with a vivid, ready smile, he made a marked contrast to his dour visitor.

"How nice to see you. I was afraid you might not be coming." He gulped down the last of his coffee and tossed some money on the table. "We must go. We're very late."

They left the café and walked to the car. The Turk slid into the Mercedes, sniffing appreciatively at the leather smell of the upholstery. "M'mm. Perhaps when I buy mine, to take home, I will also have leather."

"Yeah. I bet. Which way to the hospital?"

Following Ali's directions it took them eight minutes. He parked the car, neatly and legally, in a side-street and followed Ali around the corner. The wall of the hospital ran the length of the block. Fifty yards ahead of them three concrete steps led up to the darkened porchway of a side entrance. A pale-colored Volkswagen camper stood parked nearby.

Ali led the way toward the camper. As they approached, three men climbed down and moved to meet them. Ali greeted them, shaking hands with each in turn, and spoke to them in Turkish, gesturing to the man next to him. They smiled and inclined their heads in greeting. He returned their smiles with a curt nod. Ali spoke a few more words. Two of the men turned and re-entered the camper, one climbing into the back and the other into the driving-seat. Ali turned and led the grey-haired visitor and the third Turk around the corner toward the brightly lit staff entrance to the hospital. Without a glance to right or left, Ali trotted up the steps and entered, followed by his two companions. A uniformed man seated at a desk inside the door watched listlessly as they passed, not even bothering to acknowledge Ali's cursory salute.

He led them through a lobby to a locker room. He unlocked one of a row of tall, grey-painted lockers, one of several with decals of the Turkish flag peeling from their doors, and pulled out three sets of orderly's green overalls. Looking quickly around to see they were unobserved, they each pulled one on.

Ali led the way through a series of corridors until they came to an unmarked door. He took a key from his pocket and unlocked it, stepped inside for a moment and emerged pushing a trolley laden with medication.

They strode together through the corridors. Only once did they encounter anybody, a gangling young doctor with a busy walk. The older man tensed at his approach and then relaxed again as the doctor passed by without appearing to notice that his overalls were three inches too short at the wrists and ankles.

They approached a corner. A few yards from it, Ali motioned them to stop, a finger to his lips. He was sweating. He looked nervously around him, then reached out and took the older man's lapel, pulling his head close to his own. "Just around here." He jabbed a finger at the corner. "The guard sits outside. He knows the routine. He won't be expecting any trouble."

The man nodded. He reached into a pocket and pulled out an envelope. "Do you have the stuff?"

Ali nodded. Sweat flew from his chin. "Here." He pulled a folded brown envelope from inside his overalls and handed it to the man, who opened it and glanced inside without removing the contents. "Good." He pushed his own envelope into Ali's hand. "Here. You can make a down payment on the Merc." He moved behind the trolley. "Everything else here?"

Ali nodded again. "Here." He lifted the corner of a linen napkin. "Give her these. But she will not be any trouble anyway. She never is."

The man nodded toward the other Turk. "And him? He kitted out?"

The Turk understood English. Without waiting for Ali to answer for him he grinned and raised his left arm, holding his fingers loosely curled. He straightened them, letting them see the four inches of polished wood that protruded from his sleeve to nestle against his palm.

The older man nodded. He reached out and gave Ali a pat on the arm. "You've done a nice job." He turned to the other Turk. "Let's go."

With the Turk at his side he pushed the trolley around the corner. Twenty-five yards along the corridor a uniformed policeman sat outside a door, a short machine-gun cradled across his knees. He seemed to be dozing. At their approach his chin jerked up. He looked at them blankly for a moment and then grinned, a little sheepishly. In a smooth movement, the Turk pulled the truncheon from his sleeve and swung it at the man's grin. A tooth made a snicking sound as it fell on to the metal of the gun. The policeman's head jerked back. The Turk raised the club and brought it down hard across the man's forehead. The impact made a noise like a stick breaking. He grunted and began to fall forward. The Turk caught him under the armpits. The older man opened the door and stood back as the Turk dragged the unconscious policeman into the room, then he pulled the trolley inside and closed the door.

A girl of about fourteen was sitting up in bed, staring straight ahead of her, giving no sign of being aware of their approach. The grey-haired man took up the two pills, moved quickly to the bed and pressed them into the girl's mouth. She sat quite still. He snatched up a glass of water, put it to her lips and tilted it until she coughed and swallowed. For several seconds he stood staring down at the girl. Her hair was jet black with a tendency to wave, her pale face was narrow and handsome. The family resemblance was unmistakable. The Turk, standing by the door, made an impatient sound. The other man looked quickly around at him, nodded, and pushed the girl down on to her back. She lay docilely, making no attempt to resist, not even showing signs of knowing he was there. He tucked the blankets tightly around her and bent to free the wheels of the bed. He grunted to the Turk to open the door and pushed the bed out into the corridor.

Ali waited at the far end. As soon as he was sure that they had seen him he moved away, out of sight. They pushed the bed to the corner. Again, Ali waited, and again they set off after him. They continued in this way for two or three minutes through a succession of corridors, with Ali always showing the way while staying too far ahead for any casual observer to think they were together. They turned yet another corner. Ali waited by a set of double doors with a green illuminated sign above indicating an emergency exit.

They came up to where Ali stood. His smooth face was shiny with sweat, and he flicked nervous glances all around him. Drawing close, they could see he was trembling. He shoved down on the bar that opened the door and swung it open. The second Turk ran through the narrow lobby, and they felt a rush of icy air as he opened the outer set of doors that gave on to the street.

He called softly. With cool, orderly haste the grey-haired man scooped the girl, blankets and all, into his arms and carried her out through the doors.

"Two minutes," Ali called hoarsely at his retreating back. "I have to raise the alarm in two minutes." He let the door swing closed and hurried away, leaving the abandoned bed where it stood.

In the deserted street the Turk was already at the rear of the Volkswagen camper. He rapped on the door. It was flung open immediately. The grey-haired man reached it. The two Turks took the unresisting girl from him and dragged her inside. The man stripped off the overalls, balled them up and tossed them inside. Without a further word, he turned and began striding away. Behind him, he heard the motor rev heavily once and then recede as the camper drove off.

Two and a half hours later he was at the Hertz desk at Frankfurt airport, returning the Mercedes.

CHAPTER

13

THE JEEP RACED THROUGH THE WAKING STREETS, FORCING the scattering of early traffic out of its path. The driver, a teenager with the sleeves of his paratrooper's uniform rolled tight over sinewy biceps, made Hamid's driving seem as hesitant as an elderly nun's. By the time they skidded to a halt in front of the sentries at the Al-Azziziyah barracks Mike was looking forward to some training as a terrorist as a chance to relax.

Once inside the compound the four soldiers of his escort sprang down from the jeep and formed up around him. They set off at a run toward the camouflage-painted helicopter parked in the center of the barrack square. They seemed to be under the impression that doing things quickly was somehow more martial. Mike had never been a soldier. He ambled in their wake. The four men came back and fell in beside him, disappointed.

As he crossed the square Mike looked around him with interest. This was the very barracks where the Colonel had been sleeping on the night of the American raid that had so nearly killed him, several years earlier. According to Middle Eastern rumor, the raid had triggered a long-term change in the man's mercurial personality, making him more withdrawn and introspective than before, if no less unpredictable. Looking back as he hauled himself into the machine, Mike caught sight of a sprawled heap of building materials that lay dumped at the perimeter of the parade ground. Beyond the heap the roof of one of the buildings gaped. Another was a black skeleton of steel. It would soon be a decade since the air-raid. The repairs, it seemed, were getting the usual mature consideration.

From his seat Mike had no view of the ground below them. Only the slant of the sun through the windscreen told him they were heading south. He was not missing much. He knew it by heart; endless kilometers of arid, empty landscape. A few people had tried hard to convey their sense of wonder at these vast emptinesses. A few mad old buffers, Arabists, people like St. John Philby, had filled books raving about places just like it—which made it less surprising that he had ended up with Kim Philby for a son. To Mike it had remained obstinately unappealing, however many scorpions thought of it as home.

For the first quarter of an hour of the journey he tried talking to the soldiers who sprawled opposite him, bellowing over the clatter of the motor. His efforts petered out in the face of their blank indifference. In the end he closed his eyes and leaned back, waiting for the flight to end.

The jolt as they set down made him start. In the noisy, undemanding tedium of the flight thoughts of Allix had once again taken hold of his mind. So immersed had he been in the images of her that he had lost all awareness of time. He looked at his watch, and was surprised to find they had been aloft for over three hours.

He stepped out, squinting against the fierce light. They had come a long way south. The landing place was in a hollow, completely surrounded by dun-colored hills. A razor-wire fence stretched away to left and right, over the rim of the hollow. He looked around him, expecting the rough barrack huts of a military training camp. What he saw was a long, low, two-storey building with wide balconies at the upstairs windows. A canopy over the entrance and the carefully tended clusters of palms set in grassy beds on either side gave the place the look of a decent Californian motel.

He did not even try to hide his astonishment. The country's population numbered only three million or so, and barely a generation ago most of them had been desert nomads, tent-dwelling Bedouin. And now they not only lived in air-conditioned villas themselves, they housed their trainee terrorists in places that looked as if they were managed by the Holiday Inns Corporation. One thing you had to admit about the current regime, it made sure *everyone* shared the benefits of the oil money.

From a spot some distance away, hidden by a fold in the terrain, he heard shouts and sudden gunfire. A few seconds later a group of men in battledress, laden with packs and weapons, passed him at a run, maintaining their pace even as they entered the building.

One of the young soldiers climbed down from the helicopter and led him inside. The lobby strengthened the impression of a hotel rather than an academy for terrorists. Apart from a portrait of Colonel Ghaddafi, the pastel-blue walls were hung with framed photographs of the sort of people that the guests would regard as heroes; distinguished hijackers, eminent bombers. Mike's escort took him through a check-in routine with a lovely, solemn young woman in a uniform similar to the soldier's own, who sat alertly at a desk improbably inlaid with a mother-of-pearl motif. They spoke a desert dialect that Mike quickly gave up hope of following.

The brief proceedings over, the girl pulled open a drawer and handed over a key. The soldier led him along a carpeted corridor to a room.

It was spacious, well-furnished and chill from the noisy air-conditioner set in the wall. There were twin beds. From one of them a tangle of sheets spilled to the floor, exposing the material of the mattress cover. Mike asked his escort if he had time for a shower. The man's only response was to shrug and switch on the television set. Mike left him perched on the edge of a bed watching familiar American cartoon characters creating mayhem in Arabic.

In the white-tiled bathroom the cast-off clothes, the sweet reek of toilet water and the running tap told him more things about his roommate he would have preferred not to know.

When Mike emerged from the shower and pulled on his clothes his escort led him to a store off the lobby where he was obliged to exchange his clothes for camouflage overalls and boots. By then it was time for lunch.

He walked into the restaurant feeling like an actor, but as soon as he looked around the room the feeling passed. Everyone in the place was wearing identical brown and green striped fatigues and calf-length boots. Perhaps it was the effect of the clothes, but they all seemed to be sitting in slightly exaggerated postures, like models taking a break from a photo session for a style magazine. Mike's eyes stung from the acrid pall of cigarette smoke that filled the room. They stood in line for the food, which was being dispensed by statuesque, turbaned Sudanese men whose gentle, almost courtly manner was in odd contrast to the faintly Wild West atmosphere of the room. The meal was lousy; rice, gravy and gnarled pieces of mutton so sinewy and tough it reminded Mike of the imitation bones pet-owners give to their dogs as toys.

The place was crowded. Most of the tables were occupied by people much younger than Mike, pushing food into their mouths with their fingers. The number of women present surprised him. Mostly, they sat apart from the men. The only exceptions were at a mixed table of Europeans. Two tables were filled with black men. Mike chatted distractedly to his escort, only half-understanding the difficult accent as he tried to catch the sounds of the speech at the mixed table. It was somehow familiar but incomprehensible, a kind of Flemish, perhaps, or a German dialect. Their eyes flicked around to look at him as one of them observed him watching them. He smiled, nodded a greeting, and turned quickly back to his escort. Their faces, even from twenty feet away, had the unmistakable set of fanaticism to them.

Any feeling he might have had that it was *all* posturing was knocked out of him in the first hour after lunch. A laconic instructor pushed him to the limits of his endurance with a series of exercises that left him gasping helplessly. He was still fighting for breath when he was taken to join a group gathered in a tiered amphitheater carved out of the earth. Here the lesson was "stabbing people for beginners."

The instructor, a wide-shouldered, posturing Cuban, had each of them in turn attack him with a knife. He disposed carelessly of each assailant, throwing them or wrenching elbow joints until they screamed. Having established his credentials, he set about showing them the right way of killing somebody with a blade. He did it with the easy, competent relish of a born killer, hurting the students as he drove the clenched fist that represented the knife deep into their bodies. The victims submitted, sullenly but without complaint, hobbling silently back to their places grimacing with pain.

Mike's turn came. The man tossed him the slim commando knife with its rough, etched grip, and beckoned him to come for him. It was hard to believe it was really happening; it was the stuff of the lousy movies he had sat through so often, the low budget crap he had spent so many empty evenings watching on oil camp videos. The instructor swaggered and grinned and looked tough, knowing quite well that none of his trainees would actually take seriously the invitation to try and kill him.

Mike went along with the charade, slashing half-heartedly at the man. With contemptuous ease, the instructor swayed past the blow and caught Mike's knife arm, clamping it under his own armpit. He clasped his wrists just beneath Mike's elbow and, with a force that was totally unnecessary, he leaned back and yanked upward. Mike bellowed in pain. The man released him, smirking at his grimace. Mike rubbed his elbow with his good hand. He looked into the instructor's grinning face, shook his head ruefully, and drove his fist deep into the bulge above the man's belt buckle. The instructor gave a single retching sound and slid to the ground.

The afternoon ended with a long run, in company with a group of young recruits, that left Mike's lungs burning and his left foot badly blistered by the unfamiliar boot. After an evening meal that looked depressingly like the *same* boiled mutton and rice, he was delivered over to a Bulgarian explosives instructor, a beefy individual with a tough, ageless face framed by thick grey hair. Alone with a European, closer to his own age than the usual run of recruits, the man soon dropped his initial brusque manner in favor of a kind of conspiratorial heartiness.

Under his instruction Mike set to work making up an anti-personnel bomb. The object was to make the bomb as low-cost as possible, using a bare minimum of plastic explosive and a maximum of parts that could be found in the average tool shed. It reminded Mike of the kind of small ads that appear in the Saturday editions of the British newspapers. Make a devastating killer device in the comfort of your own home. No special skills necessary. Just a few ordinary household nails and our easy-to-follow, step-by-step instructions.

He glanced up from the wiring to the Bulgarian. "You been out here long? I didn't think Bulgaria was helping us any more."

The man laughed. "Ha! They're not. Not officially. But we've got democracy now." He laughed again. "I'm free-lancing. They can't stop me doing that, can they? Not nowadays. It's the new private enterprise culture!" He dropped his voice, unable to shake off the habit of a lifetime. "And the government still needs the foreign exchange. The bastards take thirty percent of my salary."

Mike smiled. "When did you come out, then?"

"Two months ago." He looked gloomy. "Seems like two years. And I've got sixteen more to go."

Mike gestured around him with a piece of fuse wire. "Doesn't seem that bad to me."

The man looked at him from under his coarse brows. "Do you know this country?"

Mike shrugged. "A bit. Not lately."

"Well, then, you can imagine. Back home I live in barracks in Stara Zagora and I always thought *that* was boring." He laughed again. "Can you imagine *looking forward* to a weekend in Tripoli?"

Mike grinned, threading wires to a detonator under the man's watchful eye. "It's not easy. Why did you come?"

The man gave a stagey groan. "My wife and I want our own flat."

"I always thought army people were looked after."

The man laughed again, but with an edge of bitterness. "Yes, we were. Before all the changes. We still are, for the moment. But the way things are going, who knows what's going to happen? At least, before, before all these changes in Moscow, we all knew what was going on. Now look at me." He pointed a finger at himself. "I'm over fifty years old. Another three years and I would have retired. I'd have had my flat, my pension, and some money saved up. Instead of that they're talking about confiscating army flats for families! Inflation's going to make my pension worthless. And if they do like the Poles and the East Germans and make the Lev convertible, it'll be like my wife says, my savings will just about pay the fares I'll have to spend looking for a new job!" The man guffawed, prevented by his own good nature from taking it seriously. "Of course, she's right. But I'm the one stuck down here!"

Mike laughed with him. He gestured around the room, the air conditioner, the marble floor. "There must be worse places to spend a few months."

"Eighteen. Can you think of one?"

Mike made a big show of thinking. They both broke into laughter together. He handed the bomb he had just made to the instructor for inspection. "How about the women? There must be some compensations."

The Bulgarian turned the bomb over in his hands, scrutinizing the connections. "Very nice. You have to be more careful, though. There's too much bare wire here. They could touch. Have you seen the women here?"

Mike nodded. "Only in the canteen today."

"Well, then you saw that most of them are Arabs. You know what that means?"

Mike nodded. The man demonstrated anyway, miming stretching his penis with one hand and making a chopping motion with the other.

"No, I leave them strictly alone. You'll do the same if you've got any sense. They've *all* got brothers aching to defend the family honor." He tore some wires loose and handed the bomb back to Mike. "Do those again, will you?"

"How about the European women? You don't have to worry about their relatives coming after you." Mike looked up as he spoke, and raised his eyebrows at the expression on the instructor's face. He was looking at Mike as though he had suggested leaping down a mineshaft.

"Are you kidding? Them? At least some of the Arab girls *look* all right. But that bunch? Please. I don't know what it is about what you people do, but it certainly attracts some funny-looking women. How is it they're all so thin?" he said it with the genuine bewilderment of a provincial Bulgarian, a man used to women who were short and meaty, with a center of gravity that stayed close to the ground.

It was a good question. Mike's thoughts flitted to Mary. He could visualize her nicely proportioned, compact physique, the ridges of muscle that formed a groove up her spine as she flexed her back. He surprised himself picturing her face, framed by the shiny hair, and with the big, wide-set eyes. He had a sudden twinge of unease, an uncomfortable feeling of having caught himself out in something. He shook his head, driving off the sensation. She was the exception that proved the rule. It was true that every one of the female faces he could remember from his weeks of research was inclined to be thin, the hair uncared-for. He pictured the lank-haired girls he had seen in the restaurant; some of them could have been pretty. It was as though it were some kind of obligation they imposed on themselves, almost as if they were actually keeping prettiness at bay as part of their ideology, for fear it might make them unsound.

"Give it another couple of months," he said cheerfully, passing the re-wired device back for approval, "you won't even notice."

The man examined the bomb and nodded, sniggering. "Excellent. This would do a lot of damage. If the girls are all going to be like this, then in another couple of months the camels are going to have to watch out."

Mike stood up. "At least they don't have brothers."

By ten o'clock he was in bed asleep, the light blankets drawn close under his chin against the chill of the air-conditioning, and a forearm over his ear against the rasping breath from the next bed.

CHAPTER

14

J̲ACK RANDALL WAS INSTANTLY WIDE AWAKE. IN PITCH BLACK-ness he fumbled on the bedside table, feeling for the gun which he had retrieved from its custom-made niche in the base of the white melamine wardrobe before settling to sleep. His feet were already on the floor, his hand gripping the revolver, when the voice that had woken him came again.

"Oh, shit." He groped for the switch of the bedside lamp, found it and thumbed on the light. Squinting in the sudden brightness, he pushed his glasses on to his nose and grabbed his watch. He swore again. It was still only five-twenty. He threw the gun down on the bed, grabbed a woolen dressing-gown from the floor and hurried out into the corridor, tugging the cloth of his old-fashioned pajamas from his crotch.

He hammered hard on Pat's door with his closed fist. He waited a second and then, with a groan of exas-peration, he threw open the door and put on the light. Pat lay sprawled across the bed, one calloused foot pro-truding from the tangle of sheets. He was on his belly, with only the rough mat of his hair showing above the blankets. His breath rasped and gurgled at a level just below a snore. With an expression of acute distaste, Randall strode across the room and snatched back the bedclothes. He yanked hard at Pat's shoulder. The rasping breath faltered and then resumed, like a car engine missing a beat. Grimacing, Randall took a hold of Pat's big toe between thumb and forefinger and twisted it hard. Pat bellowed and sat up, clawing at his eyes. He stared stupidly up at Randall.

"Fuck you, that hurt. What's going on?"

"Get a move on. He's here. Out there! Now!"

Pat gave a yawn that made his entire body quake. "Shit, Jack. What's the time?"

"Fuck the time. Get yourself up. Come on."

Randall yanked him to his feet and led him from the room. Two Libyan soldiers in the fatigues and cloth hoods of the desert commando regiments lounged in the hall. Ignoring them, Randall led Pat into the lounge. The room was fully lit by the harsh glare of the overhead pendant. The grey-haired man in the tinted, thick-rimmed spectacles was pacing the room. He spun to confront them, his face drawn with fatigue. His expression was black with rage. White crystals of salt glinted in his eyebrows and among the yellow tints of his hair. His dark grey suit was stained and crusted.

"Shut the door!"

Randall obeyed instantly. He turned back to face the newcomer. "What's up, Harry? You look terrible."

Harry nodded. "So would you. I haven't slept for two nights. I just brought the boat in an hour ago." As he spoke he moved to the door and jerked it open. He peered into the hall, checking that the two soldiers were not eavesdropping. Closing it gently, he turned back to the other two, and dropped his voice so that it came out as a hiss. "We've got a fucking disaster on our hands. The courier's been picked up."

Patrick stopped scratching the hard roll of fat at his waist. His face worked with dismay and angry incredulity, as if he found himself waking up into a nightmare instead of out of one. Finally he gave a short laugh of sheer disbelief.

"A fuck-up! For the love of Christ, another one. And it's me you're all going to blame if they don't let us have the stuff. I told you, though. No money, no merchandise." His voice had risen to a whine. "They've made that absolutely clear." He groaned. "What a mess. What a bunch of fucking idiots they must think we are." Abruptly, he turned on Randall. "This is your fault! You promised us this one would be okay. You checked it out from Amsterdam. It was all under control."

Randall took a step toward Pat, his jaw clenching. "I did check it. And everything *was* okay. The courier was taken to the airport. He was on the flight. Don't start telling me I don't know my business, you fucking broken-down pisshead."

"Shut your mouths."

At Harry's words Patrick winced and took a half-step backward. Randall, too, flinched and let out his breath slowly. They both turned to face Harry. He watched them both for a second, his eyes blazing with anger and contempt. He addressed Randall.

"Where's the new man the clowns in Dublin sent over? The one that's supposed to speak the wog lingo."

"Out of the way. We shipped him off to a training camp to keep him out of mischief, let him learn a few basics."

"Well, get him back here. This morning."

Mike lay in a slit trench, trying to bury his face into its rocky floor. Live bullets bit splinters out of the lip of the trench, sending sprays of stinging fragments down on his head. Grit crunched between his teeth. Abruptly, the shooting stopped. Through the echo of gunfire that still rang in his ears he heard a voice call his name. Very tentatively, he raised his head and peered over the rim of the trench. A soldier stood by a jeep beckoning him. He stood up slowly, brushing the dirt from his chest, and walked warily toward the vehicle, which had drawn up close by the firing bunker. As he reached it he saw the instructor he had hit the previous day lying behind a Cuban machine-gun with his legs splayed. As Mike passed, the man gave him an unpleasant grin.

"Shithead," Mike murmured, wishing he had known how to say it in Spanish. He turned to the waiting soldier. "I'm Mike Scanlon. You want me?"

The helicopter droned north on its way back to Tripoli. Mike was still in the soiled battledress. The driver of the jeep had given him no time to collect his stuff. He wondered why they were recalling him in such a hurry. Whatever the reason, there was nothing he could do about it for the next two hours. He looked down at his clothes and wondered about a few other things.

The camouflage clothes, the boots, made him feel like an impostor, as if he were merely playing at soldiers. He wondered if everyone felt the same way in a country where half the males seemed to be doing it. It was incredible—the country had a population hardly bigger than the Irish Republic's and yet it had the hardware of a superpower. The Libyan armories were gorged with every piece of deadly gadgetry the latest technology could provide, from chemical weapons to missile systems, and there was hardly a soul in their army who understood how to use it. So many people held rank there was hardly anyone left for them to give orders to. The whole country seemed like some appalling rich kid's toy, with make-believe versions of the things real countries had: foreign embassies, ministries, armies with complete sets of officers; a navy, entirely staffed by people who could not swim; intelligence services; official news agencies; a gigantic bureaucracy. It was some kind of mutant Toytown turned into a threat to civilization. He could not avoid the suspicion that the whole process had not been helped by the idiotic knee-jerk reactions of Western politicians, many of whom could scarcely have placed the country on a map.

He walked past the sentry and into the villa, half expecting them to laugh at his ridiculous outfit. At the sound of the door opening Randall almost ran into the hall to meet him, brushing past the loitering commandos. A single glance at Randall's face told Mike there would be no laughing for quite a while. Randall grabbed his arm and dragged him into the lounge.

"Come in. There's someone here we want you to meet."

He pushed Mike ahead of him into the room. The man in the tinted glasses stood by the fireplace, a coffee cup in his hand. He nodded curtly to Mike. "So, they finally got you here. The name's O'Keefe. Harry O'Keefe."

Mike's head spun. He was taken completely off-balance. The man across the room was ten years older than the photographs so vividly imprinted in his memory. The hair had gone from red to grey, and the thick frame and tinted lenses of his glasses concealed the green of the eyes. It made no difference—there was no mistaking the face of the one who had been seen as the top man of them all, *the* force behind the Provos. He had been regarded as the hard man of the Republican movement for decades, since long before the present round of troubles had flared up in the sixties. He had been gaoled back in the fifties for an attack on a police station, when, acting alone, he had killed three policemen with a homemade grenade. That was at a time when the Republican movement was virtually dormant, when there was no structure, nothing but his own devotion to the cause to keep him motivated.

In 1973 he had been back in gaol again, after the authorities broke up a big arms-running operation bringing in surplus weapons from Nigeria. He had been considered too dangerous to keep in Ulster and had been held in Walton prison. In 1976 he had escaped, killing a warder. From there he was thought to have gone to ground in Amsterdam, a city whose close-packed streets and freewheeling attitudes had given refuge to so many fugitives. There were good reasons to think he was the architect of the bomb attack on the Conservative government at Brighton.

What was beyond doubt was that he was a man who had always displayed an imagination and a hard-edged intelligence far out of the ordinary; until three years ago. Since then there had been no further word of him. He had disappeared totally from the scene. A rumor had gone around that he had been killed, assassinated by a faction within the Provos in a power struggle. And now he stood in front of Mike, holding out a hand for him to shake. Another one, like Randall, back from the dead.

"Mike Scanlon. Pleased to meet you, Harry. I've heard a lot about you. Like that you were dead, for instance."

O'Keefe nodded. "I heard the same thing," he said shortly, putting the subject of his past firmly out of bounds.

Randall spoke, plucking nervously at his mustache. "We've got a problem, Michael. You can help us solve it."

Mike's glance flicked from Randall to O'Keefe. There was a new note in Randall's voice, a note of discouragement. His morale seemed to have ebbed. He looked again like the teacher he had been, a teacher nearing the end of a long and not very successful career, wondering if his pension was going to be adequate. Pat sat on the edge of a chair, still in his pajamas, massaging his face with his palms. Mike addressed himself to O'Keefe.

"So what the hell is the problem? What's happening?"

O'Keefe squashed Randall's attempt to interject an answer with a dismissive wave of his hand. He spoke softly, his voice clipped and unemotional. "There's been a hold-up with the cash. It's not going to be here on time, and without it the Libyans are not about to let us have the stuff we need. Even if we'd had it, they were refusing to commit themselves."

"So? Why not wait until it gets here? Why is everybody in this outfit in such a hurry? We've fucked around for three hundred years. What's another week?"

O'Keefe's eyes burned angrily behind the glasses. Mike's tone had stung him. He was a man who had grown unused to being argued with. "Because we *can't* wait. We've got a deadline. We need the stuff, not smart-ass advice from done-nothing fuckers like you." The contempt in his voice laid across Mike like a whip.

Mike felt his gorge rise. His hatred welled dangerously close to the surface. He took a short step toward O'Keefe, his fists bunching. As he did so, he let his gaze stray over the three men in the room with him. O'Keefe's jacket creased awkwardly at the hip, pushed out of shape by what was certainly a gun. Randall, too, might very probably be armed. Alone, Pat would be a pushover. In a scrap that called for fast footwork he would be a lot of meat to have hanging around your neck. He swallowed hard, unbunched his fists and spoke again.

"Okay. So we all know they could *give* us the stuff if they wanted to. All the guff about money is just a smokescreen. It's a matter of whether they *want* us to have it. So, the first thing any of us has to worry about is who makes that decision."

Pat gave a braying laugh from behind his hands, and they all turned to him. The flesh of his jowls seemed slacker. Grey stubble grew luxuriantly almost down to his collarbone. The bloodshot eyes looked out from half-closed lids, like animals shy of the light.

"Who decides?" he said, in a slurred sneer. He looked slyly from Mike to O'Keefe and laughed again. Mike glanced around the room. Coffee cups stood empty. That explained Pat's thick speech; he had been in the kitchen out of sight of O'Keefe and Randall, making coffee, and hitting the day's first vodka. He turned aggressively back to Mike. "Who d'you think? The Colonel! The Guardian of the Revolution. The Custodian of the People's Trust!"

"Personally? You mean he keeps up with what we're doing?"

Pat's answer was truculent. This was his chance, as the man with his finger on the pulse, to talk down to Mike. "The bastard decides everything. Runs the whole fucking country as if it was his own personal property. There's nothing goes on here without he knows about it." He looked around at them expectantly, waiting to be congratulated for having the nation's political nuances at his fingertips.

"So why the hell have we been screwing around with minions like Hamid? Why don't we go straight to the top?"

"Sure! Go ahead. Just let him know you're anxious to see him. He'll drop running the country and ask you right over. Send you a government car, probably." He stood up unsteadily and moved toward Mike, pushing his face to within a foot of Mike's own. "Don't you think we've tried? That little bastard Hamid's supposed to arrange that kind of thing. That's his job, liaison between us and the government people. All we ever get to see lately is him or some other crappy little official. You bring in a few of them dirty books for *him* and he's all over you, hugging and kissing you like some fucking fairy. The minute you want him to do something for *you,* it's all 'official channels,' 'I'll pass your request to my superiors'! We've asked a dozen times, more than that, for a meeting with Ghaddafi. All we get is how the Colonel's in Tunis debating how the fucking Arabs are going to take over the world. Or he's tied up for three days with some deadbeat delegation from Albania or somewhere. Or he's gone to the desert to fucking meditate!" He said the last words with a note of incredulous anger that made Mike think he was not inventing it. He grabbed the coffee cup that stood on the low table and gulped down the inch of liquid that remained in it. "Ah, fuck 'em." He put the cup down, inaccurately. "Know what I think? Perverts. The whole fucking bunch of 'em. Walking around holding hands. Bent as three pound notes."

Mike pursed his lips in a grimace of real dislike. "Is that what you tell 'em, ambassador?" he said, very softly. He turned to look at the reaction of the other two men.

O'Keefe's eyes looked hard into his, and he jerked his head toward the door. "Come outside a minute."

"Huh?"

"Outside. We're going for a walk. I want to talk to you."

Mike felt fear prickle his spine. He glanced around at the other two. They looked as surprised as he was—whatever O'Keefe had in mind it was not something he had discussed with them. "You're the boss." He started for the door.

In the street there were few cars and no people at all; in that part of Tripoli nobody walked anywhere. O'Keefe did not speak until they were well clear of the villa. Abruptly, he stopped and spun to face Mike.

"Are you a brave man, Michael?"

The question was startling. Mike looked at him for several seconds before he answered. Finally, he shrugged. "I don't know. Depends why I'd need to be, I suppose. Why?"

O'Keefe did not answer immediately. Instead, he turned away and stared past Mike, seeming almost to have forgotten he was there. He stood motionless for several seconds, apparently deep in thought.

Mike used the time to study him. Here was someone he hated with all the hatred he was capable of and yet the man impressed him. He exuded a single-minded power of purpose that was frightening. For decades he had been at the leading edge of a struggle that he was now not an inch nearer to winning than when he began, yet still, after virtually a lifetime of fruitless striving, his dedication was undiminished. There was a hardness in O'Keefe that made the young men, the bombers and gunmen Mike had met in the course of the last weeks, seem almost childish. The same qualities put to a different purpose could have made the man a saint. Abruptly O'Keefe took off the tinted glasses and turned to look at Mike.

"Listen!" Mike felt himself impaled on the stare of the light green eyes. "Apparently you've been ready to tell us all what a bunch of amateurs we are, right? Well, I'm giving you a chance to put your big ideas into practice, show us what a pro you are. You're going to see the Colonel. And you're going to persuade him to give us what we want."

Mike looked at him. Their eyes were on a level. "Yeah, sure." He spoke lightly, with a trace of sarcasm. Inside, his blood was racing. "We don't have the money. He's sick and tired of us. He's got the Pakistanis threatening to quit helping him with his missile program, under pressure from the Yanks and the British, unless he stops helping us. And I'm supposed to walk in and see him and, with nothing to offer but my incomparable personal charm, persuade him to change his mind." He shook his head. "Sorry. I'm an oilfield technician, Harry, not a magician."

"There's not going to be any magic involved. Now, the first thing you have to do is listen to what I'm going to tell you. The second thing is, you don't breathe a word of it to anyone. Anyone. That includes those two idiots back there. Do you understand me?"

Mike nodded. He always tried to understand a man with a gun under his jacket.

"Good. Come on then, let's get some exercise."

They circled the block, O'Keefe talking in a low voice as they went. Mike listened in utter silence. They were on their second circuit before O'Keefe finished. He turned his metallic stare on Mike.

"What do you think?"

Mike returned the stare. What he had just heard had surprised him less than O'Keefe would have wished. Partly, what he had just been told did no more than confirm something that Mike had first heard years before, one of those unsubstantiated stories that thrive in the hothouse atmosphere of the expatriate communities, where wishful thinking turns into gossip that turns into irrefutable fact. One of them had just turned out to be true. O'Keefe's eyes glittered as he awaited Mike's reply.

"Even if I agree to try, he'll probably kill me."

"Refuse, Michael, and I'll *certainly* kill you." He bared his teeth in the first smile Mike had seen from him. "You've come too far, my friend. You're in too deep, you know too much. You lost the right to say no weeks ago." He put an arm around Mike's shoulders, still smiling, in a chilling parody of comradeship. His other hand was in his jacket pocket. "But it's your choice, Michael. Yours entirely."

CHAPTER
15

AN HOUR LATER, THE IMAGE OF O'KEEFE'S SMILE WAS STILL in Mike's head. It was the smile of a man so tightly in the grip of an idea he had been squeezed loose from reality. With only a slight difference in his makeup he would have been a successful businessman. He had the hardness, the single-mindedness, the direct approach to a problem that would have ensured success. Running a business, he could have fired a workforce and closed down a factory without a trace of introspection. As a terrorist, he could kill with the same dispassionate commitment, driven by his own cock-eyed logic.

The arrival of Hamid for his routine daily visit wrenched Mike out of his contemplation of O'Keefe's psyche. It was time for the first throw in the dice game he and O'Keefe had discussed.

"Sabbagh al khair."

The Libyan bridled momentarily. It was the first time since Mike's arrival that he had given Hamid the slightest hint that he knew any Arabic. Slowly, his puffy face creased in a doubting smile. *"Sabbagh al-nur,"* he said speculatively, returning Mike's greeting with the traditional phrase. *"Tala Arabi?* You speak our language?"

Mike inclined his head, returning the man's smile. He went on speaking Arabic, ignoring Hamid's reversion to English. "Would you like some tea?"

He walked into the kitchen to prepare some of the sweet mint tea without which North African society would close down. Pat was already in there, tinkering with the copper piping of the makeshift apparatus in which he distilled his vodka. He looked at Mike from under lowered brows, his expression a mixture of resentment, suspicion and truculence. Putting down the tubing he had been holding, he made for the door.

"Better get in there," he muttered, his speech slurred. "You want to keep an eye on those shifty bastards."

Mike stepped squarely in front of him and put a hand on his chest, restraining him. "No, Pat. You stay here. He'll be all right."

Angrily, Pat tried to brush Mike's arm aside. "Don't try to tell me what to do." His voice rose angrily. "I don't give a monkey's if O'Keefe does think the sun shines out of your arse. I don't care if he thinks you're an expert on the fucking Arabs, either. I know these people. Why else have I been stuck out here in this dump for years? Let one of them alone for a minute and he's got his nose in everything. Let me by or I'll fucking hang one on you."

Mike shook his head, not moving to get out of the other man's path. "You try it."

Pat's fists were bunching in a fit of drunken belligerence when O'Keefe came into the kitchen. He looked from Pat to Mike, taking in the situation. Disgust flipped briefly across his face. He put his hand on Pat's chest and propelled him backward until his rump came up against the kitchen worktop. Pat's back arched as

O'Keefe kept up the pressure, leaning his face so close to Pat's he could see every tiny bulbousness where the broken veins joined.

"For Christ's sake, Pat, I'm not going to tell you again. Until I tell you differently, you do exactly as Mike here says. D'you hear me? He's got a job to do. If you screw it up for us you're out. Understand?"

Patrick nodded, grumbling indistinctly. He understood. In O'Keefe's understated vocabulary "out" meant dead. He gave a stifled bray of protest as O'Keefe took up the still. Ignoring him, O'Keefe threw the apparatus to the floor and stamped hard on it with his heel. Turning from the wreckage, he yanked open a cupboard. Pat gave a sound that was almost a sob as O'Keefe pulled out the first of the bottles that stood there, uncorked it, and upended it over the sink. Mike walked out of the kitchen to a background of Pat's softly whining protests and the sound of running liquid.

He spent a long time talking to Hamid. He put short questions that drew long answers from the voluble Libyan, who was happy to talk all day about his family. Within minutes crumpled photographs of four beautiful, dark-eyed children lay spread on the sofa. There were three girls and a son. All of them were slim, long-legged, coltish, with beautiful grave smiles. Hamid's wife had probably once shared the same slender loveliness as the children. Now, all that remained was the beautiful smile nestling in a tumble of chins, the dark eyes pinched in folds of soft flesh. As she sat, spread across two thirds of a sofa beneath the billows of a kaftan, the lower halves of her swollen calves were visible beneath the hem. Mike studied her picture with exaggerated interest. He flattered her extravagantly as Hamid looked on, smiling his pride and pleasure.

It was not long before the conversation turned to Hamid's affection for everything English. Everybody had been so kind to him during his stay in England. He had spent a summer in Norwich, studying the language.

"It was a wonderful time for me. I enjoyed it very much. Especially the pubs, and the discos you have. I liked very much the disco." He grinned lewdly. "There were many very nice girls."

Mike nodded at the photographs. "Weren't you married?" he asked archly.

Hamid grinned again and gave him a man-to-man wink. He spread his hands. "Yes, of course, I was married here. But your girls, those English girls. They were so nice, so, well . . ." He shrugged, rendered temporarily speechless by the recollection. "They are not like the girls here in Libya. There I had many girls, many, you know." He made an unmistakable gesture.

Mike could not resist asking a mischievous question. "And here? How about with Libyan girls?"

Hamid's eyes widened with the shock. "Here girls cannot do such a thing!" He was outraged. "They would be *sharmutas,* prostitutes! Nobody would speak to such women."

Mike smiled and let it drop. Over the years he had discovered many things that it was a losing battle to discuss with people from other cultures. One of them was talking with an Arab about a woman's right to freedom of choice in her sexual behavior. It took him a while to haul Hamid's attention back from the fleshpots of East Anglia and on to the ground he wanted to cover.

It never appeared to strike Hamid as at all incongruous to be praising the English way of life to Mike, a man who was there as the guest of senior officers of the Provisional IRA. Mike steered the conversation around to the subject, trying him out. The Libyan confirmed all his suspicions. His knowledge of the Irish Republican movement's struggle for an independent, united Ireland was a little sketchy. As far as Mike could tell, he seemed to think Ireland was somewhere in England. And his notion of the IRA was of some sort of English sect, a kind of minority party. Their attempt to blow up the British government was the type of thing that any North African minority party worth its salt would regard as the give and take of politics.

It was less surprising than it sounded. Hamid was just a low-grade civil servant. Part of his job, for a few hours a week, was to keep a few Irish people quiet. He did not have to be an expert on their geography and politics, any more than they felt the need to convert to Islam before coming to demand weapons. Even so, Hamid's lack of grasp had its disadvantages when it came to putting the Provos' case to his superiors.

For another half an hour Mike spoke little, letting Hamid give full rein to his natural volubility. By the time the Libyan rose to leave, late for another appointment, they were bosom friends.

Mike carried the empty tea glasses out to the kitchen. Pat had started to sober up, a state in which he was more unpleasant than when he was getting drunk.

"What was all that then?" His voice was a childish sneer. "Didn't he want to go to your room? You not his type?"

"Shut your noise, Pat," O'Keefe said icily. He sat straight backed in a Formica kitchen chair. He turned to Mike, stone faced. "Well? How'd it go?"

Mike grinned. "He's in culture shock. His stay in England has left him with a soft spot for the British. We're included! He'll be back tonight. We're going out to eat."

"Out! With him? Jesus, it's a miracle. He normally only comes here to collect his dirty books and get a drink." Pat rubbed his fingers under his chin. "I'd better go and get a shave."

Mike looked at him as if he were a foolish child. "Not you, Pat. Just Hamid and me. You're not invited. Nobody is."

Pat sniffed loudly. "He just wants to be alone with you, eh?"

Mike shook his head; he spoke with weary impatience. "No, Pat. *I* want to be alone with *him*. He's going to lose face. The less people there are to see it the better."

"But—"

"Shut up, Pat, for Christ's sake!" O'Keefe slammed his open palm on the table. Pat flinched and closed his mouth tight. O'Keefe stood up, took Mike by the arm and led him back into the lounge. Randall, who had kept out of the way all the while Mike had been with Hamid, joined them. O'Keefe guided Mike to the sofa and sat down next to him.

"Look, Michael, the word from Dublin is that you're a good man. Tough and bright. A man we can count on." His voice was very soft. His eyes were locked on to Mike's. "Well, maybe you are. You seem like it. But, you see, Jack and I, we've been around the movement a long time. We've seen 'em come and we've seen a lot of them go. A lot of those 'good' men are dead now. Some, genuine fellers, the British killed. They murdered our people in Gibraltar. They murdered our people in the shooting at the football ground. In Windsor. They've even been down to Dublin and shot men as they slept. You were told about that?" Mike nodded silently. "Well, these were my men, Michael. People working for me. I feel responsible for them and I intend to make sure that every one of those men's lives is paid for."

Mike's anger raged inside him. He watched O'Keefe's Adam's apple bob in his throat as he calmly talked. He wanted to take it in his hands and tear it out of him, to rip the life out of the man. To leave this madman, this cool, rational, intelligent, fastidious lunatic dead at his feet. The way *his* people had left Allix.

And if he did?

A single shout would bring the commandos from

the hall. They would be on him in seconds. Even if he succeeded in destroying O'Keefe, Randall would survive, and their obscene project, whatever it was, would still be pursued. He heard O'Keefe's voice continuing, soft and insistent.

"Some of them I killed myself. Because they let us down, Michael. We won't *be* let down." He was speaking of his own murders the way only true psychopaths can, as logical, necessary steps any reasonable man would have seen the need for. "Old Pat there, he's finished. He's done us a lot of harm these last few months. It's our fault, we should have seen it coming." He shrugged. "That's a problem we'll deal with later. Right now we're relying on you to put things right. We need that plastic. Have to have it. So you do anything you need to do to get it for us. If that means sleeping with Hamid, then you'd better do it. You're going to be out there on your own. We won't know what's going on except for what you tell us, so just be clear about this. If there's the slightest whiff, so much as a hint of a double-cross, you're dead. Have you got that? I don't look like a man that would lie about a thing like that, do I?"

Mike smiled back at him, not taking his eyes from O'Keefe's. The eyes of the man he now *knew* was behind the destruction of everything he loved, the man who had denied existence to his unborn child. When he spoke his voice was very calm and even.

"Harry, you look to me like a man who'd just love to have me take you up on it." He smiled, showing them all his teeth. "So, don't worry about it. You can count on me."

"Good. I'll do that. There's no room for failure now, Michael. None at all." He grinned at Mike and half turned toward the kitchen. "Pat, would you make us all a cup of tea?"

CHAPTER

16

BEYOND THE RAILWAY BRIDGE THE LIGHTS OF EXETER'S ST. Thomas' station were almost obliterated by the clinging sleet, trying hard to turn to snow, that slashed at the empty pavements. At six o'clock in the morning they were the only promise of life in the deserted landscape of the city. Every second house in the street was a bed-and-breakfast hotel. Outside, the names on their signs evoked the rural, homely hospitality of a bygone age. Beyond the front doors, scarred carpet held the smells of decades of offhand cooking.

In one of the hotels a man descended the last flight of the staircase, made awkward by the hold-all he carried. He moved with a quietness that bordered on stealth. The proprietor was already astir. Hearing a stair creak, he emerged busily from his kitchen into the cramped hallway. Reassured to see it was the client who had settled his bill the previous evening, in anticipation of an early departure, he tried a little joke about the weather. The client murmured a surly response, not even looking around at him, and pulled open the door. The owner winced as a gust of dank, raw air blasted into the hall. He hurried to the door to ensure it was firmly shut behind the departing guest.

"Miserable Irish sod," he murmured at the door. He continued standing for a moment, trying to visualize the room the man had used. Finally, concluding the room had contained nothing the man might have stolen, he mouthed another insult and turned peevishly back to his kitchen.

Outside, the man made his way down the short path to the front gate. He walked with an awkward, leaning gait, as though the hold-all he carried contained something heavy. The man wore no raincoat. He hunched his shoulders and pulled his jacket lapels closer across his chest, and with a grimace and a muttered curse set off toward the railway bridge.

As he went, two other doors opened, widely spaced along the street. From each a man emerged, carrying a small suitcase. From the way these men walked it was plain that their bags, too, were heavy. Both of them turned and began following the man with the hold-all. Keeping their distance from each other, the three men passed under the railway bridge, negotiated the big roundabout that straddled the River Exe and where, at that hour, only an occasional car hissed by, and strode briskly toward the town center.

A few minutes' walk brought them to the central shopping precinct. They entered the pedestrian area, passing without a glance in front of the windows with their streamers announcing sale bargains. They passed the brightly lit front of Sainsbury's, where teams of cleaners were already hard at work, and mounted the broad steps that led to the top deck of the car park. The leading man pushed through the door and stood in the half-shadow of the ticket machine booth waiting while the others joined him.

The three of them stood watching for perhaps a

minute. A scattering of cars shone wetly under the lights. Not a soul moved. Leaning into the wind that swept waves of sleet over the open deck, they walked quickly to a blue Ford Granada that stood entirely alone in the far corner of the area. The first man unlocked the trunk and they heaved their bags inside. The car sank on its suspension. While the other two stood nervily scanning the deck the first man bent over the trunk and set to work. His task took him five minutes. With a word to the others he straightened and slammed the lid. The three of them crowded into the car, glad to be out of the weather.

They sat in the semi-darkness, smoking cigarettes and talking softly. As they talked they kept their eyes on the surrounding area and on the clock glowing on the dashboard. The clock ticked around to six-forty-five. The leader gave an automatic confirming glance at his watch, took a last long drag at his cigarette, threw it from the window, blew a stream of smoke out behind it, and started the car. They swung down the ramp. The lower levels were practically deserted, too. They passed the last floor and took the steep curve down to the street.

The driver stamped on the brakes, swearing. A beat-up Marina sat in their path, stalled. They saw it shudder as the driver, a woman with a shock of light hair, tried to restart it. The driver of the Granada hit the horn and held it down. The woman in front put a hand out of the window and made a gesture that said he should calm down, she was the one with the problem. The driver gave two more sharp blasts on the horn, swore, and twisted in his seat, grinding the gears as he shoved the car into reverse. He swore again, harder. Another car, swinging through the curve, managed to stop no more than a foot behind them.

"Jesus fucking Christ!" The driver began scrambling from the car, diving a hand into his clothes. The other two followed his lead. They leaped from the car, pulling guns from under their jackets.

The driver of the Marina was already out. The blond hair lay in a heap on the tarmac. The "woman" was a man in a dark overall, with a balaclava covering his face. He shouted and opened fire simultaneously. One of the men from the Granada pitched backward to the ground. Another got off several shots at the four hooded men who sprang from the car behind. He hit one of them before he, too, fell. The driver dived for the galvanized palings that topped the parapet of the ramp. He dropped the twelve feet to the ground, stumbled, picked himself up, and ran. His gun was still in his hand.

Behind him, on the ramp, the hooded men gathered around the two who lay beside the Granada, still writhing. One of the hooded ones, apparently in some authority over the others, stepped forward. He spoke sharply to the group, and they moved quickly back. The man leaned over the two men on the ground and carefully shot each of them once in the head. The two men were still.

Beneath them, the driver had stopped running. He had come up against a blank wall, relieved only by a padlocked steel roller-shutter. He stared wildly around him. The walls on three sides were too high to scale. He spun and began running back toward the entrance of the cul-de-sac. He had sprinted about a third of the seventy yards when a man strolled into the entrance ahead of him, talking into a hand-held radio. The running man checked, and threw a panicky glance back over his shoulder. Two of the men in black overalls had lowered themselves over the palings and were walking easily toward him, one on each side of the narrow roadway. He looked back toward the man with the radio, raising his gun and making as if to resume running. As he did so, a car swung in and slid to a stop between them. Four figures, also in hoods and dark overalls, sprang out.

They ran into positions across the width of the street entrance, and each dropped into a marksman's crouch. Four handguns were leveled at him.

The man spun again. The two pursuers were no longer walking. They had thrown themselves to the ground and lay propped on their elbows with their legs spread. Their guns, too, were trained at the level of his chest. With the jerky movements and panting breath of an animal at bay, he turned again to face the four guns. A voice shouted to him to surrender. His hand tightened momentarily on the gun, as though he were going to go for broke in a last desperate shootout. Then, with a movement of his shoulders, he threw the gun down. It rang on the wet asphalt and bounced away from him. He raised his hands. He was smiling a lop-sided smile. Almost immediately his smile froze. In the split second that followed he understood why the two men behind him were on the ground. The four men fired together.

In the silence that followed the shots the sirens sounded, sudden and very close. Police cars screamed to the scene. The Marina descended from the ramp and stopped close by one of the police cars. The driver, no longer hooded, wound down his window. Smiling, he addressed a policeman who had remained in the back of the car.

"All yours, Superintendent. Better be quick. Their weapons are still there. We don't want souvenir hunters taking them home." The two men exchanged a laugh.

A few seconds later, the bodies were screened off. Another minute later, as the first gawpers were beginning to gather, there were only policemen and police cars to be seen.

Kevin pulled up the cuff of his leather jacket and looked again at the bulky Rolex. He swore under his breath. He was already over twenty minutes late for the meeting. Exasperated, he shoved some money through the gap in the partition and jumped from the taxi. He slammed the door hard enough to draw a laconic insult from the driver and strode off along Fulham Road, moving much faster than the solidly jammed traffic.

By the time he rang, three short and one long, third from the bottom of the column of bellpushes, his back was damp with sweat. The door was opened by Tommy, the oldest of the men who had interviewed Mike at the house in West Ham. His broad, affable boxer's face was pinched with worry. Without a word he led Kevin up to a cramped bed-sitting-room. The third man who had been present at the interview, Eddie, was already there. He sat in an old brocade armchair worrying at a thumbnail with his teeth. Almost before Tommy had shut the door Kevin started talking. He was too angry to sit down.

"The whole fucking organization's falling to pieces! They were practically the last lads we had left with any training. And they walked right into it. Those fucking soldiers *knew* every detail. They were just sitting there waiting for them! Waiting to execute the poor sods. Christ, it wasn't even execution. They exterminated them, like vermin!"

"Sit down, Kevin. And keep your voice down." Eddie sounded tired. "We all know all that. As of now that's history. The only question now is *how* the damned SAS knew—who the hell's telling them."

Kevin snorted angrily. "Well, we know it's none of us three. We didn't even know where it was going to be. *Nobody* over here was supposed to know, except the lads themselves. And they all got shot in the head, so I doubt if any of them was working for the Army."

Tommy looked at him ironically. "Good thinking, Kevin. So who d'you think it *is* that told them? One of the Dublin crowd?"

Kevin shrugged. "Could've been. They sent the lad over to lead the thing. A lot of people over there might have known enough about it to set the British on to him. They could have picked him up before he even came over."

Tommy's eyes narrowed. "Are you serious? You *really* think someone over there's grassing?"

Kevin shook his head. "Not necessarily. But you both know as well as I do, the talk's looser over there. The idiots can't help feeling they're among friends all the time. They think because they've got their people in the Garda and Special Branch that keep them informed about what phone-tapping's going on, they're safe. They can't seem to get it into their heads that the *British* are down there tapping their lines. With all the changes in Eastern Europe, every time the fuckers bring a few surplus intelligence people back from Moscow they send the buggers to Dublin. The Dublin government don't want to know about it. The Brit embassy in Dublin's got more chauffeurs on its staff than Godfrey fucking Davis."

Eddie stopped chewing his nail. "Come on, Kevin. We've got to do better than that. We all know there's *something* the matter. What we need is some fresh ideas about *what*."

Kevin turned on him, nettled. "Okay! Here's one. Scanlon."

Tommy laughed incredulously. "Michael Scanlon? The new feller?"

"Right. Good old Mike Scanlon. Republican sympathizer for all of the last six weeks. He was in Dublin a few days ago. He could have picked something up."

Eddie scoffed. "Come on, Kevin. We know you don't like the man, but you're clutching at straws there. He's not been with us anytime at all. The problems go back a year or more."

"I'm not saying there's nobody else. But just because they already have one informer in place doesn't mean they'd give up trying to place more if they got the chance. It wouldn't make sense."

Eddie nodded, his brows drawn together. "M'mm. You're right as far as that goes. But the man's in Tripoli, so there's not much we can do about it. Not for the time being, anyway."

Kevin jabbed a finger angrily at Eddie. "Oh, yes there is. We can at least give his place up in Brondesbury a once-over."

It was five-thirty, just after dark, when the ten-year-old Cortina drew up around the corner from Brondesbury Villas, a hundred yards from Mike's hotel. The three men got out. Kevin still wore his leather jacket. He had added a woolen cap pulled low over his forehead and a big muffler loose around his throat. Eddie and Tommy wore raincoats and hats.

Kevin rang the doorbell. As they waited he pulled his muffler higher, covering the lower part of his face. The other two pulled sunglasses from their pockets, but put them on only as they heard the sound of somebody pulling back the latch. The door opened. Kevin followed it, bundling the landlord back into the passage. A jab to his pot-belly doubled him over before he could gather himself to shout. Tommy put a gun under the man's nose and dragged him, whimpering, back into his musty lair.

"Mike Scanlon. He lives here. Which room?"

The man dribbled as he spoke. "First floor. Left at the top of the stairs. Room on the right."

"Got a key?" Kevin held out his hand.

"No. Guests don't like it."

Tommy had his big paw on the man's shoulder. He shook him so hard his head whiplashed. He sniveled. "Honest, I haven't. Please, don't hurt me."

Kevin and Eddie were already on their way to the stairs, taking them two at a time. When they reached the room Kevin took a small wrecking-bar from his waist-band, jabbed it into the door jamb and yanked at it. The lock gave immediately, taking a sliver of the frame with it.

A head appeared at another door; someone was curious about the noise.

"Fuck off back inside," Kevin snarled, waving the wrecking-bar. The man came out of his room. He was in a singlet and pants, a big, beefy man with the weather-darkened hands and face and pale body of an outdoor worker. He advanced on them, belly out and big shoulders rounded, like a wrestler.

Eddie pulled his hand from his raincoat. He pointed a revolver at the man's stomach. "Don't be silly," he said reasonably.

For a moment the man looked as if he might still keep coming. Then, as the reality of the gun slowly dawned, he halted, hesitated a second, and then stepped backward into his room.

They tore Mike's place apart. Kevin worked with a kind of cold frenzy, growing angrier as he failed to turn up anything to support his theory. He shoved the table aside and yanked the carpet beneath it clear. With a grunt of triumph he dropped to his knees. The piece of floorboard came away easily in his hands. He tossed it aside and reached into the cavity, grinning up at Eddie. His hand came out empty. He swore violently and sprang to his feet.

In another three minutes they had finished their search and they started for the stairs. Kevin's face was black with anger. A toilet flushed, startling them. An old man opened the bathroom door, head down, still fumbling with his fly buttons. He shuffled past them to his room, muttering to himself, oblivious of them.

With a shout that still did not penetrate the old man's world Kevin ran into the bathroom, leaving Eddie watching the stairs. He ripped open the toilet cistern, dropping the lid into the bath. The sound of it breaking made the old man blink. He shook his head like a punch-drunk boxer shaking off a remembered blow and closed the door of his room. Kevin knelt and used the wrecking-bar to rip the panel off the bath.

Seconds later, he emerged with an ugly grin on his face, holding aloft the battered briefcase. Almost dancing with self-congratulation, he hustled Eddie down the stairs.

CHAPTER
17

Mike prowled the marble floor. Hamid was supposed to have been there at seven, and it was already eight-thirty. Pat sat at the bare dining-table playing patience with a pack of dog-eared cards. He was cheating. A tumbler of vodka from a bottle he had salvaged from Randall's outburst of moral superiority stood at his elbow. He looked up at Mike and smirked.

"Your poofter late?" He grinned around at the others for approval. They ignored him. "As fucking usual. Useless bunch of fuck-heads."

Mike gave him a sour smile and turned away. He grinned to himself, amused to find that he almost agreed with Pat about something. For all Mike's sympathy for the Islamic culture, he had never quite been able to get accustomed to the Middle Eastern conception of time. He knew it was a feeling shared by a lot of other Westerners who had dealings with the Arab world. They did not mind too much being kissed, they got used to having business acquaintances suddenly grasp them by the hand while walking along the street. They took it in their stride when a negotiating session was broken off at intervals while their business associate took time off to sink to all fours and pray. They all *hated* being kept waiting.

For all his understanding of the area he had never been able to comprehend fully how it was possible for somebody to phone you from ten kilometers across town at eight o'clock to reassure you that he was going to be on time for your seven o'clock appointment, and then turn up another two hours later. Sometimes, like Pat, he could not help feeling that fuck-heads was the only word that fitted the bill.

It was nearly nine when Hamid did finally show up. His face was creased in smiles as he offered elaborate greetings but no apologies. Being late was a concept so completely unavailable to him that he could not have apologized, he would not have known what for. He was there—that was the fact—it had no past and no future. Mike made for the door, herding Hamid in front of him.

O'Keefe dropped the book he had been reading, a cheaply made pornographic paperback, one of the three books on the otherwise empty shelves. It fell open on to the table, its back broken at one of the filthiest passages. He followed Mike into the hall.

"I hope this works, Michael."

Mike's cheek twitched in an aborted smile. "Yeah, me too, Harry. What do I do if it doesn't? Make a run for it?"

O'Keefe smiled himself, a confident, cheerful smile. "You could try. Enjoy yourself."

"Yeah. It'll be great."

They hardly saw a car until they were close to the city center. The temptations of a Tripoli night-time were easy to resist, and only an occasional car loomed alarmingly out of the darkness. Hamid was a terrible driver, but at least he put his lights on.

It was the first time Mike had really been into Tripoli in the evening since his arrival. It was even more depressing than he remembered it. Modern concrete lampposts were placed every thirty meters, erected in the days of profligate confidence in the depths of the oil reserves. Now, whether through negligence or policy he did not know, only every third or fourth lamp worked. The newly built blocks of flats and offices looked dingy in the mean light.

They skirted the red sandstone walls of the old city and swung on to the wide, palm-lined boulevard that hugged the harbor, the Sciara Adrian Pelt. Twenty years earlier, at this hour of the evening, this superb sweeping avenue would have been thick with traffic, the pavements thronged with pedestrians taking the air after the heat of the afternoon. Women and children would have crowded the ornate benches amid the palms while the men stood in groups, arguing and laughing until late into the night. Tonight there were a dozen cars and a single Mercedes bus, and no pedestrians at all. Hamid rammed his foot down with a stifled giggle of pleasure and sent the car rocketing along the empty street.

He slammed on the brakes outside an elaborate Moorish building. The plaster was scaling from the arcaded exterior in scabs the size of flagstones. From outside it looked like the abandoned palace of a desert prince; broken strands of wire protruded from the plaster over the arched entrance, testifying that there had once been a neon sign. A crude hand-painted board had taken its place, held on unequal loops of thin wire. Little dribbles of dried paint ran from the lettering to the bottom of the board. The florid script, well-spaced to the right where the signwriter had begun with a flourish, squeezed smaller as he had unexpectedly run out of room, indicated it was a hotel; the Grand Hotel.

Hamid led the way across a paved courtyard dotted with tall palms. On either hand marble basins, into which fountains had long ago ceased to play, held drifts of dried vegetation.

The reception lobby was high, spacious and cold. Three men sat behind the desk watching a portable television. Hamid greeted each of them with a complicated ritual of embraces and handshakes before proceeding to the restaurant. The room was over-lit, with huge chandeliers, and the tables were too far apart. Two out of fifteen were occupied, by tanned European types. Hamid conspired dramatically with a head waiter in an improbable dinner jacket and striped trousers, who bowed, showed them to one of the remotest tables and ostentatiously palmed Hamid's tip. Mike took a while choosing from the vast selection on the menu. When he gave his order to the simpering head waiter, the man shook his head, leaned over Mike's shoulder and pointed to a dish with his pencil.

"I recommend the lamb, sir. It's very good."

Mike felt the first icy draught of truth. He ignored it. "Thanks, but I'll have the swordfish."

The waiter shook his head. His lips were pursed in the first sign of distress. "The lamb's really good, sir. The chef recommends it."

Mike flipped his fingers at the menu. "What do you have from all this?"

He knew. He set his face not to smile; the man was uncomfortable enough.

"Lamb, sir." The head waiter writhed in embarrassment.

"Great. I'll have it." He smiled his gracious thanks.

The waiter promptly turned to Hamid and assumed the alert look of a man ready to assist in the difficult task of choosing from their extensive list of temptations. Hamid took the lamb, too.

A tall Sudanese "wine" waiter approached in slow motion and took their order for apple juice. He was gone several minutes before returning, cradling a linen napkin as though it were a baby. The foil-wrapped neck of a bottle peeked from the white folds of the cloth. Mike sat back. He might as well enjoy the spectacle. The waiter yanked the cork from the bottle, and with a ponderous flourish, poured a few drops into Hamid's glass. Hamid raised the glass and looked studiously through it, ignoring the greasy smudge on the rim. He swirled the liquid around, squinted shrewdly, and sipped it with an air of sagacity. He rolled it around his mouth for some time, making chewing movements, as if he were combating gum disease, before swallowing it with every sign of reluctance. After a cliffhanging moment while he let all the exquisite components of the flavor that apple juice is famous for implant themselves in his memory, he gave the waiter a barely perceptible nod.

The man bent almost double with the flourish of filling their glasses. They picked them up and clinked them ceremoniously. Mike took a slug of the juice. The sweetness clung around his teeth.

As they ate Hamid did most of the talking. In case Mike had not got his point earlier in the day he went over his adventures with the English girls again. They had ripened considerably during the day. Hamid did not want to cause offense, but if he were an Englishman he would not want his women to be like that; but then, perhaps Englishmen were not so good in bed as Libyans. Did Mike think that was so? Mike smiled and kept silent. Maybe fifteen years ago he would still have taken a crack at explaining.

"Hamid, we want to see the Colonel."

Hamid smiled back at him blankly. In his head he was still in a Norwich disco, grinding his thighs against a girl.

"We want to see him. Immediately. It's absolutely essential."

Hamid smiled slowly. He nodded his head. "Of course. Our leader is always happy to receive guests of our people. He would be very pleased to meet with you." He smiled through a long swig of juice. "Unfortunately, he is not in Tripoli at the present moment. He's—"

Mike held up a hand. "Immediately, Hamid. We *must* see him. We *shall* see him." He laid a hand affectionately on Hamid's forearm. "For myself, I would rather have your help. You are my friend." Hamid beamed. "But there are other people, more impatient than me, people who do not understand the ways of your people, of Islam." Hamid's smile was beginning to show signs of strain. He shifted, settling his wide rump closer to the edge of his chair. "Some of our people over there in Dublin," Mike waved an arm to his left, as though an IRA man always knew the direction of Dublin, the way a Muslim always knew the bearing for Mecca, "some of them are wild, uncontrollable people. They don't always understand the need to await the moment. They behave too hastily, in ways that may even bring trouble on their heads. Sometimes they bring trouble on the heads of their friends."

Mike was smiling as he spoke, a pained smile that spoke of the inexpressible pain it gave him to broach such distasteful matters to such a loyal friend. Hamid writhed closer to the edge of his seat.

"You know well, Hamid, our movement has contacts with groups in other countries than our own. Groups that are also struggling for their own revolutions. These people are like cousins to us, just as you are to me. They help us, just as you help us. Sometimes they call on us to help them. You understand me?"

Hamid's smile flared brighter. It was the tentative, nervous smile of a person of limited authority about to hear something he definitely will not want to know. He opened his mouth to speak. Mike waved him to silence.

"Some people have been to Dublin, to my people over there, seeking just such help. Some Palestinians; a group that's very angry with Arafat. They think he is selling out to the Zionists and the Americans, betraying them. They want arms of their own, to continue the struggle in their own way."

Hamid wet his lips. His smile had slipped. He had the look of a man who dearly wished he could go suddenly deaf. Mike continued:

"Some of our people want to help these cousins. They have been refused everywhere else, as we were, before we had the good fortune to find friends here in Tripoli. They have daring plans to hit back at the Zionists, to carry the struggle into the heart of America itself. Our people say we have arms enough to give to them." He leaned closer to Hamid and put a hand on his arm. "Thanks to your generous help."

Hamid had got the point, and was almost yelping his protest. "But these arms were given to *you*. To use against your enemies. In your own country."

Mike shook his head, burdened by an intolerable sadness. "It's not my wish, Hamid. Personally, I'm totally opposed to these people. It's the wild ones who want to do it. They say there is no danger. Even if these people were caught their arms could never be traced to our organization."

Hamid's eyes narrowed. His face was only inches from Mike's. "But to us?"

Mike leaned back in his chair and gave a slow shrug, spreading his hands. Hamid had got the message. Stripped of the bullshit it was very short—give us what we want or we'll set you up with the Americans, who will jump at a chance to come back and bomb the shit out of you again. So how about it? He watched as Hamid's face worked its way through a range of reactions. When the Libyan finally spoke it was in a tone that seemed close to tears.

"I don't even believe there is such a group."

Mike stayed well back in his chair and smiled

gently. The smile told Hamid the second installment of the bad news. Maybe there was no such group. But try explaining that to the Americans when their ambassador in Oslo or Seoul or Lagos was shot with a Libyan weapon, or when a bomb made with Libyan components brought down another Pan-Am or TWA jumbo jet.

Mike leaned forward and touched Hamid's sleeve again. "Just fix me the meeting, my friend. For very soon."

CHAPTER

18

KEVIN GRIPPED THE RAIL HARD, FIGHTING TO KEEP HIS FOOTing on the slippery deck. Spray slashed at him, and ran in sheets off the leather jacket on to the saturated corduroys. The scuffed briefcase in his left hand was dark where the porous leather had taken up sea water. He chewed his lower lip and squinted into the darkness, angry and impatient. Already, over his shoulder, dawn was threatening.

Abruptly, through the murk, he caught his first sight of the tiny boat, pitching impossibly toward him in the swell. It came alongside. One of the two men in it cajoled the outboard, bringing the dinghy as close as he dared without it being crushed beneath the looming hull of the fishing boat. The other man rose briefly to his feet and threw a line. It slapped on to the deck close to Kevin. A crewman in oilskins snatched it up and took an expert turn around a cleat.

"Away you go." Holding the rope's end in one hand, he slapped Kevin roughly on the shoulder with the other, pushing him toward the side.

Awkwardly, impeded by the briefcase which he clutched in one hand, Kevin straddled the rail and lowered himself on to the ladder. It hung loose against the ship's side, a rope affair with flat wooden rungs. Descending was sickeningly difficult. The side of the fishing boat bucked and swayed, sometimes leaning to leave him dangling in space, then rolling the other way so that he was pressed against the slope of it, his fingers crushed between the ladder and the rough paintwork.

Slowly, he made his way down. Each step brought a real risk of being shaken loose and very possibly lost in the boiling sea between the two boats. The thought did not scare him—he had no intention of missing his footing. What he was doing was simply too important to be allowed to fail through his own weakness. He groped his way down one more step, holding the briefcase aloft, high out of reach of the water. A wave smashed around his knees, almost sucking him off the ladder. A few feet from him the two men fought desperately to keep their fragile craft out from under the wildly tossing larger vessel, which suddenly plunged like a lift, dropping the ladder into the water. The freezing cold sea was up to his chest. A spume of water torn from the crest of a wave slapped him across the face.

He swore in sheer surprise and wonder. The fucking dinghy was *above* him! He found himself looking up into the face of the man who was fending off with an oar. The fishing boat righted itself, hauling Kevin up out of the sea, water cascading from the sagging corduroys. His shoulder cracked painfully against the oar, and for a frozen moment he was face to face with the man wielding it. He jumped.

"Fuck it!" He had landed full-length in the bottom of the dinghy, where four inches of water slopped around his ears. He went on swearing as he sat up and struggled to pull back the cloth of his trouser-leg. A weal across his shin, where it had caught on the gunwale, had already started to swell. He swore one last time, struggled on to the seat in the bow, and hung on tight. The fishing boat was already a grey shape in the murk, on its way back the sixty or so miles to St. Bride's Bay on the Welsh coast. They would have caught no fish that night, but the eight hundred pounds they charged for the run would compensate them.

The two men were grinning at him. The one at the tiller handed him a quarter-bottle of whisky. Kevin nodded a curt acknowledgement, took a long gulp, and turned to stare ahead. The pale line of the coast was just becoming visible. It was the long stretch between Wexford and Arklow, an almost unpeopled stretch of cliffs and sandy coves. The road that ran south from Dublin veered well inland here, so that the chance of being seen by unwelcome eyes, at dawn on a foul winter's morning, was almost nil. There was a faint chance of the coastguard picking them up. But in this part of the Republic even the coastguard thought twice before reporting odd movements of people coming off the mainland. They had wives and families at home, like everybody else.

Fifteen minutes later the man who had held the oar was at the wheel of a windowless van, bumping recklessly over a pitted lane on the way to join the main Dublin road. Kevin was shivering hard and trying to keep his seat on a toolchest in the pitch darkness of the back of the van. The blanket he held clutched around his soaking shoulders smelt strongly of dog. The briefcase lay between his feet.

At ten-twenty the van pulled up outside a house on the outskirts of Dublin, the same house in which Mike had been interviewed a few days earlier. Kevin strode inside. A young man shook his hand warmly and led him down to the basement. All those who had been at the interview with Mike were present, together with three other men, all well into middle age. Kevin slapped the briefcase on to the table.

"So, nobody wanted to listen to me!"

The people gathered in the room remained silent as Kevin recounted the events that had brought him there. When he had finished there was a long pause. Mary was the first to speak.

"He's got to be killed." She said it without passion. It was a simple matter of fact, the inescapable course of events.

Kevin nodded, his face pinched into a sour look. "We know that. The question is, how soon can we do it? And who?"

One of the older men spoke. "Randall and O'Keefe. They can just knock him off. They're on the spot, and he's not expecting trouble. It'll be a piece of cake for them to take him out."

Kevin shook his head. "They don't know."

"Well, tell 'em. Pick up the phone and tell them."

Mary turned to the man. "You're not following. What Kevin means is we can't phone. Every call we make, we have to assume it's tapped. That's one reason everything's been so fucked up."

The older man winced. He hated to hear women swear. "So what's the alternative?"

"Someone's got to go out there and either kill him or make sure Randall and O'Keefe do. Any other way and we take the risk that Scanlon gets away with it *and* those two get blown away in the process."

The man frowned. "You think the British could do that? You think they've got a presence in Libya?"

"Not themselves. Why should they, when they can get the Israelis to take care of it for them? There are enough Mossad people undercover in Libya. Christ, if the Israelis recalled their spies the Libyan economy'd grind to a halt from the labor shortage."

The man smiled grimly. "So, it's got to be one of us."

She nodded. "That's right." She stared at each of the men in turn. Her eyes alighted on Kevin. "Kevin? You want to do it? You're the one that was against trusting him. D'you want to settle the score?" Her voice was tinged with sarcasm.

He gave her a savage look. "Don't talk to me like that. Wasn't I right not to trust the bastard?" He looked around at the other faces in appeal before turning back to Mary. "You're right, though, I'd love to shoot the fucker. If he was still in the UK I'd have done it already, without even coming over here. But he's in Libya, and that lets me out. It means air travel." He shook his head and looked around the room again. "You all know we can't take the chance of me going through airports. It's ninety percent sure I'd be picked up."

"Randall does it. O'Keefe, too," Mary said flatly. Kevin scowled at her, but before he could respond, the bald man, the one called Dev, spoke up. "Forget it, Mary. Those two can get away with it. They haven't been pictured in years. Christ, Jack's supposed to be *dead*. Nobody's on the lookout for them." He waved a hand around the room. "Kevin's right. The problem is, it's the same for all of us. We're all on the big list for every security outfit in Europe. There's not an airport any of us could risk going through. It's not just a matter of one of *us* being picked up—the bastard's out there setting up Harry and Jack. We're looking at a fucking catastrophe. The stakes are too high to just be *hoping* one of us'll get through."

"So who's got a bright idea?" Mary looked around her.

"I have." They turned to look at the Garda killer. "You go."

Mary stared at him, on the brink of smiling. She laid a finger on her own chest. "Me?"

"Yeah. You're the only person here that's never been photographed. You're not on the list. You can go where you like."

She went on staring at him. "But, a *woman,* in Libya? You're kidding! I'd never get anyone in that dump to take me seriously."

Kevin spoke again. "You're going to have to. Dermot's right. You're the only one who *can* do it without the risk of being picked up."

She shook her head, exasperated. "Look, get it into your heads, I'm a woman. A woman arriving alone in Libya? They don't even let her in. They put her on the first plane back again."

Kevin grinned unpleasantly. "You sure you *want* to do it? Sure all that fucking up there in his room didn't turn your head?"

She turned on him, her eyes burning into his face. "Don't you dare talk to me like that, you bastard. I was up there on *orders.*" She paused, reining in her anger. When she spoke again her voice was once again soft and controlled. She addressed them all. "Just so nobody misunderstands me, I'd *love* to do it. I want to see that bastard dead. It's personal. It hurts, getting taken in by a British stooge." She spread her hands in a hopeless gesture. "I just don't see how I *can* do it, that's all. Apart from anything else, being the only one whose picture isn't on the locker door of every security man in Europe means I'm also the only one of us that can move openly between here and England without getting picked up, or shot by the SAS."

Dermot spoke again. "Forget it, Mary. Kevin's right. It has to be you. The rest of us can get in and out of England by boat. It takes a little longer than flying, but we can do it. As for you getting into Tripoli, the man in Holland'll fix that for us. If you've got any qualms you don't have to take him out yourself. Just fill O'Keefe in."

Kevin gave a scoffing laugh. "Yeah. Right. O'Keefe can shoot him. All you have to do's get your clothes off to distract him."

Furious, Mary spun and bent toward him. "Yeah! The way you've tried to have me distract you, often enough!" She reared away, an expression of total contempt on her face. "Don't patronize me, Kevin! I've paid the same dues as anybody else here! Sure, I've been to bed with Scanlon. The way I was told to. And now I'll shoot him, the way I'm told to. I spent a few days with the man, and I liked him. That's no secret. Most of us liked him. That doesn't mean I'm going to screw it up. O'Keefe's life, Randall's life, their whole project, are all about to go up in smoke unless we get to Scanlon damned quickly." She broke off, breathing heavily. When she spoke again her voice was a whisper. "So don't worry. If it has to be me, I'll do it. He'll get a bullet in the back of the head, and the only emotion that'll come into it is it'll give me a little bit more satisfaction than it would give anybody else here."

Dermot smiled. "Okay, Mary, relax. We all get your point. And you watch your tongue, Kevin. You're letting all that's been happening make you paranoid." He looked at Devlin. "Dev, you're the travel expert. Can we get her to Holland today?"

Devlin looked at his watch and blew out his cheeks. "There's one to Amsterdam at half-past-four."

Mary glanced at her own watch. "Come on, Dev, you're kidding. It's gone three-thirty. Isn't there anything later? I'll never make that."

Devlin smirked. "Be on your way. You'll get it all right." Mary began to protest. He waved her to silence. "I'm telling you, you'll get it." He looked around at the others with a self-congratulatory grin on his face. "It's Aer Lingus. I'll call a feller I know out at the airport. They won't take off without you."

* * *

Mary emerged from customs, changed some money, and climbed aboard the bus bound for The Hague. From the bus station she walked a few blocks into an area of tall, narrow houses whose ground floors and basements were mostly bars and cheap Indonesian and Chinese restaurants. She entered one that displayed a cracked plexiglass hotel sign above its side door, and mounted a flight of stairs, as narrow and steep as a ladder. On the first floor, in a cramped reception area that smelt of dust and old food, she found the proprietor. He was a tall, sallow man in his mid-forties with the shoulder-length, unkempt hair of a sixties beatnik. With no more than a grunt and a nod he reached behind him to a board where a dozen keys hung, each with a huge rubber keyring the size of a tennis ball. He unhooked one and flopped it into her palm. With no further word of guidance she walked straight up to the room, plainly acquainted with the layout of the twisting corridors.

After washing quickly in the cracked sink, she went out and walked without hesitation, knowing its location, to a telephone box. The phone was answered on the third ring by the familiar voice. The conversation was hurried and elliptical. She could hear the surprise in his voice. When she was sure he had correctly understood what she was asking, she gave him a time, without any mention of a place, and hung up.

The man put down the telephone, and stood for a moment staring reflectively out of the tall window at the grey expanse of the North Sea. Then he turned and strode to a doorway. A woman was seated on the bed, talking. Another woman, fleshy, with handsome, over-padded features, dressed in an enveloping silk kaftan, was emerging from a bathroom. He spoke a few brusque words across the room to the second woman. A flash of disappointment puckered her mouth. She turned to the woman on the bed and began speaking agitatedly in Arabic, pointing at the man. He made as though to respond and then, seeming to think better of it in the teeth of her tirade, he shrugged, turned on his heel, and left the apartment.

He drove the short distance to the Libyan Trade Office and parked in the reserved slot in front of it. Saluting the policeman guarding the door, he let himself into the darkened building. A few moments later a light came on on the third floor. The man appeared at the window, and stood for a second or two, his face fully lit by the bright light within the room, before pulling down the opaque blind.

Twenty minutes later, while the light still burned upstairs, a door opened in an alley behind the building. The man emerged; he locked the door carefully behind him, surveyed the street, and hurried off on foot. The dark blue Mercedes remained conspicuously in the official parking slot in front of the building. He made several sudden diversions down the many narrow alleys of the area. A number of times he abruptly turned and retraced his steps, watching the other passersby carefully. Twice he got on and then off buses at the very last moment. At last, satisfied he was not followed, he walked the kilometer to a café in the working-class district of the town.

Almost all the customers were as dark as himself. Most of them were Turkish or North African guest workers. He smiled grimly as the phrase went through his mind; a few years ago they would have been simply immigrants, then somebody had thought up the phrase "guest worker." That way nobody felt guilty when the time came to ask them to leave.

There were a few women in the place, mostly enhanced blondes, sharing tables with the men. Mary sat alone at a table against a wall, nursing a coffee and facing down the aggressive stares of the men. Her face lit up as he entered. He sat down, leaning to give her a peck on the cheek. She gave his arm a discreet squeeze.

"Did you bring it?"

He nodded and pulled an envelope from his pocket. Mary slid the typed sheet from it and looked it over; it was in Arabic. She shrugged and put it back into the envelope.

"Will it do the trick? Does it tell them enough to get them to cooperate?"

"It tells them far too much. They will give you what you need at the airport. You will have a car and an escort."

She grimaced. "I'm not sure I'm going to be wanting an escort."

He shook his head. "You won't have a choice. Not until you reach your own people. Single foreign women are escorted or they're not allowed in. You know why."

She nodded. She did know why. Single women visiting most Arab countries were suspected of being prostitutes, unless they had plenty of evidence to the contrary. Even *with* all the evidence they often turned out to be prostitutes, anyway. The pickings made it worth going to some trouble to get the right papers. The Libyans were more particular about it than some.

He spoke again. "I consider it very dangerous for you to be carrying such a document. It's dangerous for you, and if you were caught with it, it would be very bad for me."

She reached out and patted his hand. "You prefer to phone?" she asked with a mischievous pout.

He pursed his lips. "You know quite well we can't do that. The surveillance is so sophisticated now. Codes, diplomatic bags, it's all nonsense. They are finding ways to read our minds, let alone our mail." He laughed. "We have to return to the methods of our forefathers. Letters, or word of mouth, are the only ways we can trust. Still, it makes me very unhappy to have you carrying such a document as that."

She smiled, a wide flashing smile. "Me, too. But

what else can we do? I don't speak Arabic and I'm a woman. Imagine me turning up at the airport *without* this and trying to explain why they should give me a gun."

He started and stared nervously around them. "Please! Don't speak of it!" He dropped his voice very low. "Why do you even want such a thing? There is no sense to it. In Tripoli you will be among friends. You have no need of weapons there. If you need a gun why do we not arrange it here, in Holland?"

She patted his arm again and smiled proudly. "Because I need it there. I'm going along on a very big operation, a spectacular. Like a big girl. With O'Keefe and the others."

"You are leaving tomorrow?"

"Uh-huh. In the morning. KLM. Direct, so don't worry about the letter." She smiled mischievously. "I'll carry it somewhere *very* safe."

He blushed and looked away from her for a moment, then turned back, running his tongue over his lips. "And tonight? You are free?" His voice had taken on a husky note.

"As a bird." She squeezed his thigh beneath the table. "Shall we eat at the apartment?"

He coughed softly and shifted awkwardly in his seat. "Ah, you see, Mary, the apartment is a problem for me. Just these few days. My wife is here again. With her sister." He rolled his eyes in mock agony. "For some shopping. It's not possible to, er, you see, I . . ."

She laid a finger on his lips. "Is she expecting you back?"

He shook his head cheerfully. "I told her I had an important meeting with some contacts. That I might be gone all night."

She turned the aquamarine eyes on him and smiled slowly. "Let's get some food and go back to the hotel."

* * *

She led him up the narrow stairs and through the mean reception area. The owner avoided their eyes. In the room she laid the bag of sandwiches on the scratched chest of drawers. He took one of the two bottles of champagne from the plastic carrier bag full of ice cubes and began picking at the foil around the cork. Mary handed him the tooth-glass from the sink. She watched as he poured the champagne. At the same time, with a faintly ironic look in her eyes, she released the fastening of her skirt and let it slide to the floor.

He handed her the glass. Champagne ran down the sides and dripped from his fingers. His hand was trembling. She raised the glass in front of her face and smiled. He returned her smile, unable to keep his glance from flickering down to her legs. The man was listed as a Deputy Head of the Libyan Trade Delegation. Mary knew him to be their senior intelligence officer in the Benelux countries, and the main contact between Tripoli and the various factions in Ireland. This man controlled the tap through which the weapons flowed.

"Cheers."

He lifted the bottle and swigged straight from it. "Cheers, my dear lady."

She put down her glass on the chest of drawers, pulled her sweater slowly over her head and came out smiling.

CHAPTER

19

PAT WAS NERVOUS. HE PACED THE LOUNGE, SCOWLING AND pounding one fist into the palm of the other hand. Mike sat deep in one of the chairs, his feet splayed easily, smiling up at the pacing figure. Randall and O'Keefe shared the sofa.

Randall shook his head in exasperation. "For Christ's sake, Pat, will you sit down. You're giving us all the screaming shits, up and down like that."

Pat's scowl deepened. "I can't help it. That fucker's late again."

Mike looked at his watch. "Not for him," he said languidly.

Pat turned on him, about to retort, when there was a sound at the door. Hamid bustled into the room. For once his smooth face was not smiling, and his eyes looked watery, as if he was on the brink of tears. Curtly, without a trace of his usual joviality, he nodded to Mike to follow him. He and Jack Randall stood up and made for the door.

"Good luck." It was O'Keefe who spoke. He

grinned at Mike, a grin like a razor. At the same time he lifted one side of his jacket away from his body, as if he were settling it more comfortably. Hamid was already on his way out. Only Mike saw the gun that hung at his side. It looked about two feet long. He looked up from the gun to O'Keefe's face, and returned the grin with a quick, lopsided one of his own.

"Thanks, Harry. We'll try not to need it." With a nod to Pat, who stood scowling beyond O'Keefe's shoulder, he turned and followed Randall and Hamid.

A jeep took them out to the airfield, slicing through the traffic so recklessly even Hamid clung on white-knuckled. On arrival they drove to a side-gate set in the perimeter fence, far from the main buildings. After close scrutiny of Hamid's documents and some harassed discussion with the guards, the gate was opened and they were let through.

More guards appeared, muscular young men with red felt paratroop insignia at the shoulders of their short-sleeved uniforms. In teams of two they searched each of the occupants of the jeep with quick, professional thoroughness. Satisfied, they let them clamber back aboard. The jeep sped across the deserted, weed-invaded corner of the tarmac to a waiting helicopter.

Four more young Arabs, in tiger-stripe uniforms and headcloths, sat on the floor along one side of the helicopter, their feet splayed in front of them. They looked fitter, keener and better turned-out than any of the military Mike had so far seen. They carried only revolvers at their belts, and their hands were knuckly and powerful. They stared hard-eyed at the newcomers as they clambered in and sat down along the opposite wall. Mike nodded and greeted them with affable courtesy as he lowered himself into the cramped space. None of the soldiers responded. They simply continued to stare with a kind of bored hostility. Hamid made no effort to acknowledge the men, but sat down in silence and began chewing his fingernails. They flew for almost an hour before putting down. One of the young soldiers opened the door and beckoned them out.

Mike stood and stared around him, squinting in the low sun. He had been expecting some kind of encampment, a military base, maybe. Instead, they were in the middle of a vast tract of sand dunes. Presumably, the pilot had used some kind of landmark in picking his spot, but whatever it was, it was certainly not apparent to Mike's untrained eye.

A plume of smoke gradually detached itself from the haze. Gradually, as the plume grew closer, it became clear that it was not smoke at all, but a dust cloud thrown up by a moving vehicle. A few minutes later a jeep came swaying over the crest of a dune. The young soldier urged the three of them aboard, shoving them roughly between the shoulder blades to hurry them. Before they were firmly seated even, the driver rammed the jeep back into gear and roared away again, plunging across the steep escarpments of soft sand. The dunes glowed scarlet in the dying sun.

They drove for forty minutes. The driver, his head swathed in a cloth that left only a slit for his eyes, never hesitated as they sped across the featureless dunes. Mike speculated that he was a Bedouin, a member of the desert tribes that still resisted the temptations offered by the oil money to become householders. One of the Colonel's own tribe, perhaps; someone who had swapped his camel for a jeep but still felt more at home under the desert sky than in the stuccoed cement block of a house in Tripoli.

They arrived at an oasis. There was no picture-book lake surrounded by swaying palms; instead there was the tall derrick of a wind-driven pump, and close by that a cluster of low mud houses, dazzling white in the last light. For five hundred yards in every direction stretched a patchwork of tiny fields where young shoots made grey-green stripes against the red of the earth. Some distance away, well apart from the houses, was a sprawl of low Bedouin tents of striped wool. They drove up to the tents. As they approached Randall leaned close to Mike and murmured into his ear, jabbing a finger at a spot behind the tents where a collection of jeeps stood in a ragged line. Next to them, only just visible in a sharp dip, was a helicopter painted in military camouflage but with no other markings.

The jeep stopped forty yards from the tents. The driver told them to get down and walk the rest of the way, indicating the largest of the tents. Hamid's unease grew more palpable with every step closer to the tents. Sweat dripped from his chin. His whole face shone with moisture, and dark patches discolored the armpits of his jacket. He walked like somebody moving under water.

At their approach four guards stepped from the deep shadow of a kind of porch supported on poles. They searched the three visitors with the same rough vigor as the men at the airfield gate, probing deep into every fold in the quest for anything that might serve as a weapon. At length, one of the men murmured a few words to Hamid and pulled aside a woolen rug that took the place of a door. He ushered them before him into the dim interior.

Colonel Ghaddafi looked superb. He sprawled amid a low heap of cushions scattered over layer upon layer of glorious multi-colored rugs. Several men lounged in a semicircle around him. Some of them were very old, with the tough, sun-shriveled faces of true desert Bedouin. In the center of the group a hubble-bubble pipe plopped softly. The Colonel was listening with grave intensity as one of the old men spoke at great length, emphasizing his words with intricate, delicate gestures. He waited for the speaker to finish and then responded at similar length. Only when the exchange had reached its natural end did he deign to notice the newcomers standing at the entrance. He spoke softly to his audience, too softly for Mike to hear, and one by one, staring with open curiosity at the newcomers, they filed from the tent until only Mike, Randall, Hamid, and the silent guards were left. Randall rolled his shoulders in a show of awkward bravado. Hamid was actually shaking.

In a fluid, astonishingly graceful movement, the Colonel rose to his feet. Mike stood with his hands loose at his sides, studying the man. He was shorter than he had imagined. He was also far more handsome than his photographs showed. The face with its deep clefts and furrows, and the dark, alert eyes, pulsated with energy. For some seconds no one spoke. The Colonel looked them over, his eyes almost hidden as the flesh around them puckered into a squint. Quite suddenly, his face melted into a dazzling, wide grin. The semi-darkness accentuated the whiteness of his teeth.

"Ah-lan wasahalaan." He gestured to the cushions scattered in front of him. *"Fadal."* He sank back to the cushions in another cat-like action.

Mike took the lead as Randall and Hamid hesitated, Randall wary and tight-lipped, Hamid still plain scared, and sat easily among the cushions, cool and frankly amused. The others followed his example, sitting close at his shoulders, as though he had somehow become their natural protector. Randall murmured with distinct rancor as he strove to imitate Mike and cross his legs.

"Coffee?"

Mike bowed his head, accepting for all of them. To his surprise the Colonel got to his knees and began preparing it himself, manipulating a long-handled brass pot over a tiny charcoal stove. Mike smiled. It was suddenly very easy to picture the well-reported occasion at a conference when Ghaddafi had rebuked King Hassan of Morocco for offering his hand to a lackey to kiss. That would definitely not be this man's style. The Colonel handed around a brass tray with four minute, handleless cups and four glasses of water. While they sipped the coffee nobody spoke. At length the Colonel finished his coffee, took a long swig of water, mopped his lips carefully on a tiny white napkin, and began to speak.

He continued for forty-five minutes, pacing the tent as he spoke, and from time to time punctuating the speech with wide gestures. As he paced, his back was often to the guests. At those moments Randall leaned close to Mike, hissing at him to translate. Mike scowled him back into grudging silence as he himself fought to catch the unfamiliar accent.

When the speech was over Hamid attempted to respond. Within seconds he stumbled lamely to a halt, overcome with awe. Mike took up the running, launching into the speech he had been turning over in his mind, a generous homage to the Libyan Socialist People's Arab Jamahiriya. It was even harder to say it with a straight face in Arabic than in English. He praised the Revolution and its achievements, but he took care not to praise the Colonel himself. He had heard from many sources that the man refused personal praise, and even took serious offense at it. Certainly, his presence there in the simple desert encampment, and his behavior toward them so far, seemed far closer to that image of him than to the picture of a paranoid madman that the Western press persistently chose to portray.

Colonel Ghaddafi listened gravely, showing no surprise at a Western visitor on such a mission as theirs speaking Arabic. He seemed even to take it for granted. It was he, after all, who had banned the use of anything else within the administration and on public signs in Libya, confusing the hell out of a generation of visiting businessmen, who had not been able to find the airport toilets since he had come to power.

At the end of Mike's speech the Colonel bowed and

set out on another peroration of his own. Randall began to be openly restive.

"So, what the fucking hell's he saying? What are *you* saying? Are we getting the stuff or not?" His hoarse stage whisper seemed to echo around the tent.

Mike shook his head angrily, silently pleading with him to be quiet. "Search me," he murmured. "He hasn't mentioned it."

What he *was* mentioning, and at length, was the historic struggle of the Irish nation to throw off the Imperialist yoke. Mike nodded gravely, making his profound agreement clear.

Abruptly, in a characteristically mercurial change of mood, the Colonel stopped talking about the burden of British Imperialism and suggested they eat dinner with him. Mike was lucky to catch it first time. The man's tone had not changed, giving no clue to the sudden change of subject. He invited people to dinner in exactly the same voice he used to invite them to throw off oppression.

A pair of white-robed servants appeared from the shadows at the rear of the tent and laid an embroidered linen cloth on the floor between them. They began spreading dishes on the cloth. It took them some minutes to lay out the extraordinary array of rice, vegetables, fish and every conceivable cut of lamb. Randall eyed the food with thin-lipped suspicion. Following the Colonel's lead, they began to eat. Mike was first, digging with gusto at the meat. Hamid imitated him, but timidly, still in awe of the Colonel's presence. Randall watched them eat for some seconds before reaching surlily forward and taking a first tentative pinch of food. He gave it a dubious once-over before pushing it between his lips. He nibbled at it, swallowed, considered for a moment, and then gave a grunt of pleasure. He leaned briskly forward, ripped a handful of meat from the joint, kneaded it together with some rice and shoved the crumbling wad of food into his mouth.

While they ate conversation subsided to no more than an occasional desultory comment through mouthfuls of food. Randall was flagging badly when the lackeys reappeared and began removing the dishes. He sat back with a sigh, wiping the stains from his mouth with the back of his hand. Then he stared, horror-struck, as the servants returned laden with a further set of trays bearing a new selection of dishes. By the time the last of these had been cleared Randall was ready to scream. He sat behind a rampart of broken food, stuffed so full he could hardly swallow. The cross-legged posture was killing him. His left leg had gone to sleep. He had been wanting to fart for an hour. Tried beyond endurance, he finally had to do it. As the sound resonated through the near silence of the tent, the Colonel inclined his head shyly, as though accepting a particularly florid compliment.

Coffee appeared, along with a bottle of costly French toilet water for each of them and individual steaming hand towels. They sluiced their hands ceremoniously and dropped the towels into the trays held by the waiting attendants.

It had grown chilly in the tent. The Colonel, swathed in a full-length woollen robe, appeared not to notice. Randall, in a short-sleeved cotton shirt, was beginning to feel it. He crossed his arms close to his body and rubbed at his upper arms. He looked up, suddenly watchful, as Mike climbed to his feet. He gave an inward groan as he realized Mike was delivering another speech.

He began by praising the meal: he admired the tent; he spoke warmly of the life of the desert Arabs. The Colonel listened carefully and replied with frank pleasure. He was himself from the south, from the desert. He loved the life of the nomadic tribes. For a brief instant, as he spoke of his upbringing among the tribesmen, Mike caught a glimpse of what he had been looking for. It was just a hint of disillusion, of impatience with the role that had been thrust upon him. He seized the opportunity.

"Colonel, could I ask you to honor me with something?"

Ghaddafi stared, wary. "You are a guest here," he said, noncommittally.

"Would you show me the desert? Now, I mean. The night."

It was something he knew a great many Arabs, from the Gulf through North Africa, whether simple Bedouin or jet-setting sophisticates, loved to do. To go out into the desert by night and simply contemplate the immense emptiness around them, satisfying some ancient need that continued to live deep within them.

Ghaddafi stared at Mike for a moment longer, and then his face dissolved into another of his sudden, brilliant smiles. He swung himself agilely to his feet.

"Come," he said, making a sweeping gesture with his arm. "We shall go."

Gulping in surprise, Hamid scrambled to his feet. Randall, grasping the meaning of the Colonel's gesture, began cranking himself upright, grumbling as he unfurled his cramped knees. Mike stilled them both with a curt, scarcely audible word.

"No."

Randall paused only for a moment. Then, straightening painfully, he hobbled a step toward Mike. "Where the hell are you—"

Mike put a finger to his lips and then flapped his fingers in an ironic farewell. "Be good, Jack. See you later."

Leaving Hamid standing dumbly perplexed and Randall still trying to complain, he turned and strode out alone in the wake of the magnificent robed figure.

The guards at the entrance stiffened and made as though to accompany them. The Colonel dismissed them with a shake of his head. He swept on ahead of Mike and swung himself into the driving-seat of a jeep.

For several minutes they rode in silence, the Colonel driving hard, obviously enjoying himself. He appeared to have no trouble navigating the dunes by starlight. Mike glanced back. There was no sign of the oasis, no tell-tale glimmer of light to indicate the position of the tents.

Abruptly, Ghaddafi stopped the jeep and climbed out, leaving Mike to follow. He strode up the slope of a high dune, moving easily through the yielding sand. At the top he dropped into a cross-legged position, his feet on his thighs. Instantly, he was absolutely still. Mike lowered himself beside him, crossing his own legs as best he could, a long way from achieving the Colonel's athletic yoga posture. For a long time they sat in silence. Mike broke it.

"You have heard why we have come here, Colonel?"

The Colonel continued gazing at the night sky, silent.

"We need your help, Colonel. Our Revolution needs it. We *must* have it."

The other man looked around very slowly. He shook his head. "We have done so much already for what you call your Revolution. And still there *is* no Revolution. You have made no advance. Your government is beating you, killing your men, penetrating your cells. For twenty years we have given you all the assistance you asked from us, without question. And for those twenty years you have wasted it. If Jalloud and I had been such revolutionaries as you our country would still be under the heel of the old King and his cousins. They would still be taking from the people what is theirs, rotting in the cesspit of their own degradation."

In the darkness Mike almost wanted to smile. The man had certainly put his finger on the Provos' problem. "Your situation was different to ours, Colonel. You were three million people, the whole nation, united against oppression by a few of your own people. We are few, the British are many. They have the arms, the soldiers, the power. It is harder for us."

The Colonel clicked his tongue on his teeth. "Your own failings make it hard. You make it hard for those who help you." A powerful note of impatience had entered his voice. "In many ways you people and the Palestinians are the same. We provide you with the tools. You use them foolishly, on the wrong targets. Civilians die, instead of the soldiers who are your enemies. And it is we, the Libyan people, that the world reviles, our country that the Americans attack, our oil that they boycott. They cannot attack you or the Palestinians. You are not yet states. You are invisible to them. They please their voters by punishing us. You have seen their claims that we are making chemical weapons. They have filled their newspapers with such stories. They are constantly seeking excuses to strike at us again."

"The last time it was done with the help of the British, Colonel. Help us, at least one more time, to hit at the British. It will be a blow on Libya's behalf, too."

Ghaddafi shook his head very slowly. His voice had dropped to a murmur, as though he had become unbearably tired.

"No. This whole business, you people, fatigue me. We help other people. The Basques. They do not bungle. We have helped them many times and yet our relations with Spain are excellent. They are discreet! They know their enemy." He stared ahead of him as he spoke, and a faintly wistful tone crept into his voice. "Twenty years ago I was different. I was much younger and I was going to change the world. I did not care then for diplomacy or for discretion. Now, I have changed. The world no longer looks the same to me. Too many people have taken advantage of us, your people more than anybody. The oil embargo hurts our people. The American attacks hurt us. Many of our people died. I cried for our dead, for my own family."

A catch in his voice as he spoke the last few words brought Mike's head around to study him. In the faint light of the stars he saw the glistening on the other man's cheek. He *was* crying.

"I know what it's like to lose a loved one, Colonel." Mike's own voice had dropped to a whisper. The sudden feeling in it made the Colonel turn sharply, so that they stared into each other's faces. "I promise you, may God be my witness, I have also lost the one I loved. Lost her to the violence of my enemies."

He paused. Looking into the tear-streaked face opposite his own Mike felt a sudden rush of understanding for this man. From the day when he and his tiny group of fellow officers had first seized power from the old king he had been a target of hatred and derision. He had been offered the role of international bogeyman and had played it with unusual relish. And yet he remained an essentially simple man. Shrewd and charismatic, he had never wholly lost the basic naivete arising from his desert upbringing. Mike found himself liking the man.

"The American President may have to learn to feel as we do."

The Colonel's face became harder, more watchful. A change in Mike's tone had set his antennae quivering.

"He has children, too, Colonel. They may soon be in great danger. If we cannot conclude our business."

Colonel Ghaddafi did not reply. He stared at Mike. The grief had melted from his face. His expression was darkening with growing anger. Mike was scared. He looked away, staring straight ahead of him as he spoke.

"Some of our friends in the United States cannot

accept your change of heart, Colonel. They feel your decision is an unjust one."

"It is not even a question of my decision." The voice was flat and hard-edged. "You promised payment. Now you bring no money. You are all the same. You think we are all rich like the Saudis. You expect me to give away the people's money, the way the Saudi rulers do! Or like those fools in the Emirates."

"We had the money. It was on its way here, but the courier was intercepted. You must only give us a little time. More will be sent. Very soon."

"Insha 'allah! Then you will perhaps receive your material. Until then do not dare to come here with your foolish threats."

"We have to have it now, Colonel." Mike still hardly dared look at the man. He kept his eyes on the pale slope of the dune stretching in front of him and his voice on the same even, reasonable, insistent note. "Our boat is here, waiting to load. We will make no more requests of you. Our American friends are true to their word, Colonel. They pay their debts." He turned and looked into the eyes that glittered fiercely two feet from his own. "And they collect them, Colonel. They feel that your country owes us something. We have also been of help to your people. In Holland, when the consul was shot, was it not our people who provided the safe house? The American President does not yet hate your country as his predecessor did. He does not yet have a reason." Their eyes were locked now, neither of them moving. "That can change, Colonel. It makes me personally very sad. Our American friends have weapons that can be easily traced to Tripoli."

Mike could not help flinching as Colonel Ghaddafi sprang suddenly to his feet. He took several paces down the slope before whirling to face Mike.

"No!"

"You must, Colonel. My people insist on it."

The Colonel's face filled with utter contempt. "Insist! You dare to *insist*! Your cheap little organization that we have supported blindly for twenty years and which has achieved *nothing*, dares to come to me and *insist*!"

"We nearly blew up the British government, Colonel."

"Nearly? Nearly? Even that you cannot do competently. We provided all you asked for and *still* you failed! You made them *stronger*!" He snorted in disgust.

As he did so Mike reached into a pocket and pulled out an envelope, the thick, brown envelope that O'Keefe had collected in Hamburg. It was crumpled from the searches. He offered it to Ghaddafi.

"Look at this, Colonel. Please."

Frowning, he reached out reluctantly and took the envelope from Mike. He turned it over in his hands. Anger still burned in his face. He looked magnificent.

"Open it, please. Look inside."

He gave Mike a strange look, a mixture of curiosity and menace, and tore open the envelope. He pulled out an eight by ten photograph. The starlight was bright enough. Holding up the picture, he stared at it for several seconds. He gave a short, choked cry, his face twisting with emotion.

Mike rose to his feet and stood looking into the contorted face of the robed figure. He was very frightened. The man could easily be, probably was, concealing a weapon beneath the loose robe. But as well as fear a kind of fascination had hold of him, keeping the fear in check. O'Keefe, and the long-running rumor that had been floating around the Middle East for a decade, were right after all—the Colonel *did* have a handicapped daughter. Rumor had repeatedly said that there was such a girl and that she was being treated in Germany for a psychiatric disorder. Somehow, O'Keefe had done what the world's newshounds had never managed to do —he had tracked her down.

Mike stood his ground as Colonel Ghaddafi stepped closer, a rage that seemed close to madness blazing in his eyes. The Colonel thrust a hand to his hip under his robe. For a moment they stood staring into each other's faces. Mike's mind raced over his options. None of them was attractive.

"*Your* people!" Ghaddafi spat the words. Mike felt saliva speckle his face. "It is you! You that have taken her away."

Mike did not dare to take his eyes from the Colonel's. He stood stock-still, not reacting, letting the man's anger blaze around him. The Colonel's face worked and contorted with his fury. Then, very slowly, Mike saw another emotion begin to mingle with the rage. Abruptly, the Colonel stepped back a pace. Tears ran again from his eyes, and an expression of unutterable loss took possession of his face. As Mike watched, still held quite motionless by the grip of his fear, he wheeled and walked several steps away, stumbling in the soft sand. When he reached the rim of the dune he stopped, and with his back to Mike he threw back his head and began to make a weird, ululating sound in his throat.

Mike swallowed, no longer afraid but inexpressibly sad. The plaintive wailing had combined with the man's expression of inconsolable grief to touch something deep inside him. He was flooded by the memory of his own first grief, of the reasons that had brought him there, to such an astonishing scene in the starlit desert. His own eyes watered.

The sound stopped abruptly. Ghaddafi turned to face Mike. "I should shoot you and leave you here, food for the rats."

Mike blinked twice before nodding slowly. "If you refuse what I'm asking then my own people will do worse to me than that." He took a step nearer to the other man. "Help us, Colonel, and your daughter will not be harmed." He was looking deep into the man's eyes. "There can be no repercussions for your country. Our boat is waiting at Al-Bahri. There are no Israeli spies there, nobody to report the loading to the Americans so that they and their allies can track the ship. Help us just once more to hit at the British. Punish them for letting the Americans strike at you from their English bases. Let *us* hurt them for what they did to *your* family."

He had been moving closer to the Colonel as he spoke. They were almost toe to toe, their eyes unflinchingly locked.

"You give me your word that she will not be harmed? You know that if a single hair of her head should be touched, then I swear to God you and your friends will wish you had never heard of Libya."

"You have my word, Colonel. She is being well looked after. The moment our present mission is finished, not more than three days from now, she will be returned to the hospital."

Ghaddafi stood for some seconds in deep reflection, his eyes unfocused, his thoughts apparently far away. Without warning he withdrew his hand from his hip. Mike swallowed in relief at seeing it was empty.

"Come, you shall have what you want." Ghaddafi strode past Mike, heading for the jeep.

CHAPTER

20

M ARY LOOKED DOWN ON THE DARK STREET. EVEN AT SIX-
thirty in the morning The Hague was beginning to look
busy. The Libyan emerged on to the pavement below
her and began hurrying away from the hotel. A few
yards down the street he turned to look up at her window and grinned. She gave him a little wave, fingers
only. He grinned once more, waved his leather briefcase
in acknowledgement, and turned away. She gave an almost imperceptible shudder, let the thin curtain drop
into place, and turned back into the room. She picked
up her passport from where it lay open on the table, and
dabbed at the page of Arabic text with a finger. The ink,
which he had applied with a big, red, leather-backed
visa stamp, was already dry.

She shook herself again, and picked up her watch
from the floor by the dishevelled bed. There was time for
a shower. She peeled off the sweater that was the only
garment she wore and walked into the tiny, windowless
bathroom. She ran the water as hot as she could bear it
and stepped into the tub. She drew the shower curtain,

grimacing at the foot-deep border of black mould around its bottom, flipped the lever on the corroded taps and began showering. She used all of the two inches of shampoo that remained in the bottle, scrubbing at every inch of her scalp and skin as though trying to eradicate some deepseated stain on her flesh. When the shampoo was exhausted she squeezed her eyes shut and stood for several minutes letting the water flood over her, extinguishing the memory of the night. When she at last felt cleansed she stepped from the tub and rubbed herself energetically with the two paltry, smooth cotton hand-towels.

She spent several minutes cleaning her teeth. Looking at herself in the mirror, she felt faintly sorry for the man. He was impeccably clean, the most personally fastidious individual she had ever known. The only scent he gave off was of Guerlain. From the beginning, she had been under instructions to allow him to sleep with her, and on every one of the dozen or so occasions he had been kind, gentle and considerate. He was in many ways a nice man, and at least a little in love with her. She rinsed her mouth and spat the foamy water violently into the washbasin. The scrubbing and toothbrushing was less to do with him than with the powerful sense of self-loathing that such nights left in her. With a pucker of distaste, she quickly pulled on the previous day's clothes. Picking up the hold-all of ill-assorted garments that she had brought from the house in Dublin, just so as not to be empty-handed, she hurried down the dark stairs.

She dropped the key on to the reception counter. At the sound the lank-haired man stirred from where he lay on a bench behind the desk. He snatched the blanket down from his face and blinked in the stupid bafflement of someone struggling from deep sleep. She smiled, murmured a goodbye, and headed down the stairs, making no effort to settle her bill. The man, still trying to focus, plainly expected no payment.

It was seven-thirty when she arrived at Schipol airport. Already it was thronged with the morning rush of businessmen with their slender briefcases and expensive topcoats, fitting in the no-baggage, one-day business trips that were nowhere near as important as they made them feel. Before checking in for the eight-thirty KLM to Tripoli she wandered the concourse around the check-in desk, killing time at newsstands and checking for surveillance of the passengers. There was none she could see, but that did not mean much. Schipol was not a flea-ridden third-world airport; it was one of the most sophisticated and modern in the world, and very terrorist-conscious. They almost certainly had long-range cameras tucked away somewhere overhead, photographing every face that checked in for a flight to somewhere as sensitive as Tripoli. She smiled for them and presented her ticket.

The KLM girl smiled back brightly and asked for her passport. Mary handed it over and stood watching as the girl scrutinized the visa. She had the olive skin that might have been the sign of Arab origins, and might have meant she could actually read the visa. They did not get many single women travelling to Tripoli. KLM had no intention of being held to blame if the Libyans turned her right around and made them bring her back again. The girl returned the passport with another, brighter smile, as if Mary had done something especially talented, and pushed a boarding pass into her hand.

The plane was half full; Arab and Caucasian men, and only one other woman, a smiling, broad-bodied Arab mother with a dark-haired toddler and a husband who constantly grinned around at the other passengers, inviting them to appreciate fully the beauty of his child. Shortly after take-off, one of the businessmen dropped into a vacant seat next to her and attempted to start bragging about his accomplishments. On a park bench or in a bar she could have walked away; in a plane there is nowhere to go except deep into a newspaper or book. She concentrated with steely resolve on *Newsweek*. The man leaned closer, and she caught the thick stench of alcohol on his breath. A heavy paw slid on to her arm. She reached over and picked it off, replacing it fastidiously on the armrest of his seat. He laughed and invited her to have a drink. She ignored him, continuing to fix her eyes on the magazine. She endured another invitation to a drink, several jokes and an attempt to read the magazine over her shoulder before turning to him in exasperation.

He grinned triumphantly, delighted to have won her attention. Still holding the copy of *Newsweek* in front of her with one hand, she groped in the hold-all with the other and pulled out a pencil. Smiling sweetly, she leaned her face close to the man's.

"If you don't leave me alone, I'm going to scream and poke this right in your eye."

At first, he went on grinning. Gradually, the grin gave way to a smirk. Mary went on smiling with her mouth. Her eyes drilled into his face. The man shrank away from her, hunching toward the aisle. He tried another grin. It failed as his eyes flicked to the sharpened point of the pencil. With a sick look, he got to his feet and returned to his seat. She let her head sink back, sighed, closed her eyes and began to concentrate on what she was going to Tripoli to do.

She was furious with herself. After receiving the leg wound at the house in Brentford she had obeyed standing orders and phoned in immediately to the stand-by number operational units always held in their heads. It was the stand-by officer who had suggested she go to Scanlon's place. It was reasonably safe, and it gave her a chance to find out more, on behalf of the general staff, about their newest recruit. In the days, and nights, she had been with him she had deployed every bit of skill she possessed to wheedle information out of him. Every moment of that time had been devoted to finding out as much as she could about the man, what his motives were. She was supposed to be the expert, he was the simple Paddy soldier, the man they were setting up for the most dangerous job the organization had to offer.

With her eyes still closed, she gave a bitter little laugh. She knew she was an attractive woman, young, intelligent and clever. She was supposed to be able to wind people like Mike Scanlon around her little finger, make them give up their closest secrets. Until then, it had always worked, the way it worked with the Trade Attaché. And that bastard Scanlon had turned the tables, and had done it so completely that for a while she had found herself on the brink of falling in love with *him*. She laughed again to herself and bit her lower lip. When they landed at Tripoli she was still smarting at the thought of the way he had manipulated her.

She hung back, waiting until everybody else was off the plane before making her way down the aisle, between seats strewn with wrecked newspapers and scraps of food. She followed the other passengers across the pitted tarmac to the immigration shed. Jeeps roared past with soldiers draped in them, their feet propped on the bodywork in postures they had learned from World War Two movies. Two tanks stood close by the shed. Officers lounged half out of the turrets with berets at an angle and goggles around their necks, smoking. Mary smiled to herself at this show of strength. It could be an outbreak of persecution mania or just a minister arriving home; the outbreak of war or the travel plans of a senior member of the ruling group triggered about the same reaction.

She was the last one to the passport control booth. Already she had aroused a lot of curiosity from the indolent, uniformed men who infested the building. One af-

ter another they had found pretexts to loiter past, staring and sniggering. Some made smirking remarks to
companions in a parody of schoolboy lust. She handed
her passport to the man in the booth. He stared hard at
her, one side of his mouth already drawn up into an odd
grin that was part contempt and part menace. Disdain-
fully, he unfolded the letter that lay enclosed in the passport. The side of his mouth slid back into place. He sat
straighter. Licking his lips, he glanced up at Mary from
under his brows, all trace of disdain gone from his face.
Without a word, his head down, he picked up a telephone and spoke in a series of gutturals. Even without
knowing Arabic Mary felt that he sounded pissed-off.

For several minutes she remained in front of the
booth, smiling gently, while the immigration official fid-
geted with papers on the desk in front of him, out of her
sight, trying to look like a man with urgent things to do.
Things a mere woman could not begin to understand.

"Good morning, Miss. Welcome to The Libyan
People's Jamahiriya."

The speaker was a tall man with a skin almost as
dark as a negro's but with fine, aquiline features. He
shook her hand with a respectful courtesy, took her documents from the man in the booth and led her into an
office. It was furnished with three tubular chairs, a
Formica-topped kitchen table and an angular coat
stand. A sink and worktop stood incongruously along
one wall. Pale patches on the grey paint where pictures
had once been tacked were a reminder that this had for-
merly been an American base. The illustrations that had
been removed would surely not have suited the current
regime's puritan outlook.

The man surprised Mary by holding a chair for her
as she sat down. He took a chair opposite her and studied the letter, looking up at her once or twice. He drew
in his cheeks and chewed at the flesh inside.

"So, I'm to provide you with a gun?"

There was a tinge of desperation there, as though he hoped she would tell him he had misread the letter.

"That's correct. A handgun. Preferably a two-two revolver, but something else would do. An automatic, even." She smiled coolly.

He flinched. His lips moved as though he were about to add something, a plea. His eyes dropped again to the letter. Finally, he shrugged, exhaled through his nose and pulled a phone toward him.

It was mid-afternoon before Mary was driven from the airport in a black, high-mileage Mercedes. In a place as overarmed as Libya, getting hold of a spare firearm was child's play. They had produced the gun in minutes. Then she had sat around for three hours waiting for the right person to show up and sign the paperwork. The weapon that lay in the bag on her lap was not the .22 assassin's weapon she had asked for. It was a big revolver with a cracked horn grip, and looked like something Wyatt Earp might have used. Mary opened her bag and hefted it again, getting the feeling of the enormous grip in her hand.

She sat watching grimly, her face set, as they entered the outskirts of Tripoli. It was the first time she had been to the city, and she was mildly surprised at the neat blocks of flats lining the freshly tarmacked road. Somehow, she had been expecting something different; unfinished, breeze-block shacks and sick dogs, maybe.

They left the low-cost housing behind and entered a district of widely spaced villas. The driver, who had shown no sign of speaking English, grunted and nodded ahead of them. She shifted in her seat, pulled the strap of the bag further up on to her shoulder and slid her hand inside, gripping the gun tightly.

The driver braked in front of a villa where a bored sentry lounged, reading a tattered paperback book. A dusty jeep stood at the curb. The sentry looked up in mild curiosity as Mary climbed from the car. Recognizing the driver, he nodded to Mary and went back to his book. She returned the nod and stood for several seconds looking at the villa. A sudden, violent gust of wind brought a swirl of grit that made her eyes water. She dabbed at them with a fingertip. The dust and the tear-drop made a reddish smear on her finger. She blinked a few more times to clear the tears, pushed her way through the gate, mounted the steps and pressed a bell-push. Her expression was utterly stony. Inside her bag the rough grip of the revolver filled her palm. Her index finger rested on the trigger-guard, ready to slide the last half-inch on to the trigger.

The door opened, and Pat stood in the doorway staring at her. He was red-eyed and dishevelled, still struggling to surface from his siesta. He gaped as she pushed past him into the entrance hall, ignoring his surprised attempt at a greeting. She stared around her, her head cocked, alert for sounds from within the house.

"Where's Scanlon?" she asked in a low, hard-edged voice.

He rubbed at an eye with the knuckle of his index finger. "Uh?"

"Scanlon, you ape," she muttered angrily, jerking her head toward the open door of the lounge. "Where is he? In there?"

Pat took his finger out of his eye and stared stupidly. He shook his head. "He's gone. He left here two hours ago."

It had been shortly before noon that same day, two and a half hours before Mary reached the villa, when a car had drawn up outside. Jack Randall had hurried Mike into it, leaving Pat watching them from the gate, sullen and angry. All morning the big man had been by turns truculent and wheedling, desperate to be involved. He had no more notion than Mike just what the job was going to be, only that it was a big one. Something spectacular, big enough for the two top men in the organization, men who were almost Provo legends, to be involved personally. And he, Pat, was being shut out. Mike and Randall had exchanged half-smiles as Pat had stormed back into the house, slamming the steel gate with a crash as the car drew away.

Since breakfast Mike had patiently borne the brunt of Pat's vituperation. It was not hard to see what was needling the man. As far as he was concerned, Mike was a new boy, a jumped-up interloper who had not been in the movement five minutes and was elbowing his way in front of Pat, with all his years of loyal service. Now, seated in the dusty interior of the Mercedes, Mike put Pat from his mind. The cold rage he was nursing was not aimed at a washed-up dummy like Pat. It was aimed at O'Keefe, and at himself for his failure a few hours earlier to accomplish what he had come to Libya to do.

It had been almost three o'clock in the morning when he and Randall had returned from the meeting with the Colonel. O'Keefe and Pat had been waiting up for them, Pat sullen, O'Keefe edgy and anxious to know the outcome of the meeting. They had gone to their rooms, with O'Keefe still congratulating Mike, at three-thirty.

Mike had not slept. He had taken off his shoes, lain on his bed, and waited. After half an hour he judged it time to move. He swung his legs silently off the bed and sat up. The soft sound of movement along the corridor made him curse under his breath and drop back on to the bed. Somebody was still awake. He waited another forty minutes. The only sound was the occasional noise of a car passing outside. A motor roared close by and then faded. Only Pat's snores, resonating through the thin wall, disturbed the total silence. Rising carefully from the bed, he eased the door open, paused to listen, and walked noiselessly to the kitchen. Still making no sound, he took a hammer from the box of tools among the junk beneath the sink, hefted it, testing its balance, and returned to the lounge. He moved to the open door of the corridor from which all the bedrooms opened, then froze for a moment as the rhythm of Pat's snoring broke into a spluttering cough. He waited for a few seconds until the steady, sawing rasp resumed. Then he reached out, put a hand on the knob of O'Keefe's door and very slowly, squeezing hard to have the feel of the metal, twisted it. The mechanism made no sound. He pushed open the door and slid through the gap into the room.

The curtains were closed, leaving the room in pitch darkness. One of his first moves on arriving at the villa had been to check on the lay-out of the rooms. The bed was four paces diagonally to his left. He measured the four steps. The bedclothes pressed softly against his shin. He raised the hammer high over his right shoulder, and with his left hand he groped for the switch of the bedside lamp. In a single movement, he flicked on the switch, rose on to his toes and swung his shoulders, bringing the hammer swinging downward.

The bed was empty.

Mike sank down and sat with his head in his hands, cursing his luck and almost weeping with frustration. He had taken the faint sounds to be somebody going discreetly to the bathroom. He had paid no attention, either, to the sound of the motor starting up. Plenty of traffic, a lot of it military, plied the streets of Tripoli throughout the night. He stayed slumped on the bed for many minutes, unable at first to believe his ill luck. Gradually, he made himself accept that the bird had flown. He had had his first real opportunity to slay the monster and it had slipped through his fingers. A single blow of the hammer would have dealt with O'Keefe. Randall would have been no harder. And Pat, sleeping as soundly as he did, would have been a pushover. With a Land Rover and a full tank of petrol he could have driven across country and been in Tunisia before any-body was aware what had happened. Now, he would have to rely on Randall to lead him to wherever O'Keefe had gone. At length, with the hammer dangling uselessly in his fingers, he walked, head bowed, into the kitchen and replaced it in the box.

He returned to his room and lay down to wait for the dawn. O'Keefe had had a lot of lucky breaks in his career. Tonight had been the luckiest one of all.

The car took them to the Al-Azziziyah barracks. They were shepherded through the gates without a stop and driven straight to a waiting helicopter. The pilot raised a hand in acknowledgement of a shout from the officer who had escorted them on the drive. A moment later they were airborne.

"Okay, so where are we going?" Mike had to bel-low to make himself heard over the engine's clatter.

Randall grinned. "To load the boat. The deal was that we would only be summoned if the stuff arrived."

"And if it hadn't?"

Randall grinned again, without any mirth at all. "I would have shot you. Or Pat would have done it. He'd most likely have insisted on it."

"Uh-huh. He's been a real pal, ever since I got here. Where are we taking the stuff once it's loaded? Back home?"

Randall shook his head. For the first time since Mike had met him his smile showed a glimmer of good humor.

"No. We're all off on holiday. To sunny Malta."

Captain Andropoulos prepared to leave the bridge. Life was very good. Being skipper of the *Maribella* was prov-ing to be an even better end to his career than he had expected, and the trip was turning out to be a very pleasant one. There had been the usual unruliness for the first day or two, but after that, the sea air and the crowded programme of sports and lectures had ensured that the children were all ready for bed by ten. There had been very little of the night-time cavortings that sometimes meant he had to have crew members policing the corridors until the early hours.

He smiled gently to himself. Most of the cavorting on this particular cruise had been done by him, and some of the crew. In fact, he had been obliged to give a few of them some serious warnings. Even on this trip there were some wild elements among the girls, and many of them were not yet fifteen years old. It was something the company was very strict about, and since it was one of the few things that threatened this very agreeable posting, he was strict about it, too. The job had too many advantages to throw away.

He decided on a turn around the ship before going to his quarters for his afternoon rest. As he strolled the immaculate deck a group of girls passed him, led by a teacher, a woman in her late twenties. The few days of sunshine had put attractive blonde highlights into her light brown hair. He smiled at her. She was one of the advantages he had been thinking about.

Approaching his middle fifties, he was spending increasing amounts of time in front of mirrors. The grey at his temples and behind his ears was spreading almost daily, but his hair still grew as thick on his forehead as when he was a teenager. He felt confident he was still handsome. Nevertheless, it was reassuring to find that young women could still share his view, as that young lady seemed to do. He had danced with her the first night out, at the introductory evening for the staff. She had responded to his murmured invitation by turning up at his cabin that evening, and every night since. A very satisfactory trip, from every point of view.

He cast an eye at the sky. Clouds had piled high overhead, driving northward in great heaving columns.

There was a lot of wind up there. To the south-west the cone of Stromboli stood out against the racing clouds. In a very few hours they would be passing through the Strait. The children would love it; they would line the rail as the ship passed Stromboli. No child he had ever known failed to be fascinated by the sight of a volcano —the very word made their eyes widen.

He turned into an entrance and descended some stairs to a cabin whose door was marked with a red cross. A uniformed nurse sat at a desk. She smiled up at him.

"How's the patient, nurse?"

"Oh, he'll do fine, Captain. There's no concussion. He'll be up and about tomorrow morning."

The captain nodded, making his way across the room. Through an open door he saw a lad sitting up in bed, supported on a wedge of pillows. "Good. So he'll be able to enjoy Valletta," the captain said, loud enough to include the boy. He approached the bed.

The boy looked up at him with his one good eye. The other was hidden behind a thick pad of lint and sticking plaster. Deep purple bruising spread beyond the dressing, over the boy's cheek and across the bridge of his nose to his other eye. Captain Andropoulos flinched at the extent of the bruising and then quickly smiled, a big, encouraging smile.

"So, Jamie, Nurse tells me you're feeling better?"

Jamie nodded and smiled up at him. The effort of smiling made him wince.

"Good. So tomorrow you'll be terrifying the criminals of Malta." He smiled. "There'll be a hero's welcome for you at breakfast in the morning, I'm sure."

Jamie gave a shy laugh. The captain reached down and squeezed his shoulder. "Good lad." He pointed a tobacco-stained index finger at the boy. "It's dinner at my table for you tomorrow night, if you'll be kind enough to honor me." His grin widened. "At least I can bask in some reflected glory."

He left the sick bay, still smiling. Inside, he was seething with anger. The boy was lucky not to have been killed. He had argued with the company for a year, urging them to leave Naples out of the programme. A dozen children had lost purses or wallets to the motorbiking muggers of the city. The boy had tried to stop two of the animals who had snatched his girl-friend's bag. From what the girl had said one of them must have hit him with a knuckleduster or something similar. The captain emerged on to the deck. Valletta would offer a respite from that kind of thing. He liked Malta a lot; it was a gentle, old-fashioned place that the modern world had somehow neglected to spoil. Interesting, though. The children, especially the British kids, always seemed to love it.

A sudden flurry of rain made him curse and quicken his pace toward the shelter of his quarters. He brushed at the sleeve of his tunic, irritated. The raindrops had left orange-red blotches the size of coins on the white fabric. He eyed the sky balefully. He knew what the cloud and the red rain meant—the *ghibli*, blowing from the south. The redness was the dust the wind picked up as it roared across the Sahara, and which the rain brought down. They could be in for a very nasty night. It would make the peace of tomorrow, riding gently in the deep, perfectly protected shelter of Grand Harbour, even more welcome.

CHAPTER

21

Mike strained to see what they were descending on
to. A thick haze made it impossible to make out the
ground at all. As the helicopter dropped lower, he could
feel it sway under the buffeting of the wind. Below them
was a uniform khaki murk. He looked at Randall. From
the moment they had left the villa the man's personality
had changed. After the depression that had set in following the news of the courier's interception he seemed to
have come alive again. Until the last few minutes he had
been humming and whistling to himself, surprising Mike
with a repertoire of hit tunes from the nineteen-fifties.
Only in the last few minutes had he been more subdued.
The turbulent wind outside had been throwing the machine about with sickening unpredictability. He now sat,
pale and sweating, wishing the flight would end soon.
Even the incipient airsickness, though, had not totally
suppressed his new-found good humor. He still managed to shout an occasional remark to Mike, mostly
heavy-handed sarcasm directed at the absent Pat.

When Mike turned again to the window he saw the sea. Or, at least, he saw the thin white line of the surf that told him where in the brown mist the sea lay. As they descended further, he could make out a single short L-shaped pier which projected at an angle to the line of the shore, forming a harbor from a shallow notch in the coast. Two small ships were moored there. Apart from the unnatural straightness of the harborside and the pier there was nothing else in the immediate area, no building or road, to indicate that this was a port.

They flew on for some distance, losing the sea and the pier to view, before putting down on a ruined asphalt landing pad next to a collection of rotting corrugated-iron huts. They stepped out on to the crumbling asphalt. The pilot climbed down beside them. Squinting against the wind, he took Mike by the arm and led them to the edge of the pad. Silently, he pointed to where the remains of a cement track, almost obliterated by sand, snaked between the dunes. Coils of sand eddied and danced around the bare, half-buried patches of cement, whipped up by the fierce wind. The pilot eyed the sky anxiously.

"Follow this. It will lead you to the harbor. It's about a kilometer." He grinned. "If you don't get lost."

He took his hand from Mike's arm and strode toward the helicopter. Mike and Randall watched him scramble back into his seat. Seconds later they reeled back amid a squall of wind, sand and noise as the machine burst into life and seemed to spring from the landing pad. It side-slipped away into the murk. By the time they recovered themselves it was already lost to their sight.

Randall was grinning, too happy to be back on firm ground to notice much else. "Nice feller," he said jovially, jabbing a thumb in the direction of the departed helicopter.

Mike spat grit and looked around him. The sand skittered around their ankles, and visibility was no more than thirty yards. He made a wry face and turned to face Randall.

"Tell me something, Jack. You ever been in a sandstorm before?"

Randall shook his head, keeping his lips tightly closed against the sand.

"I have. And this is the beginning of one. Don't underestimate it. Keep your eyes on the track ahead. Don't look back. This wind'll wipe out our footprints in seconds. And it can get a lot worse than this."

They advanced, scanning the ground ahead for the exposed patches of cement. The sand yielded under them, sucking them in up to their ankles. The whole time Randall was a couple of paces behind Mike. Mike wondered if it was because he saw him as the leader, thanks to his experience of the desert, or because a trace of suspicion still lingered beneath the affable manner and he was just keeping Mike where he could see him. The sand stung their eyes and scoured their faces. They trudged forward with their heads tucked into their chests, spitting grit. They had only an Arab's notoriously optimistic estimate of distance to go on, and the conditions made nonsense even of that.

They had been walking for forty minutes when the shape of a ship loomed ahead of them. A canvas sheet was slung from the stern, slapping and bulging in the wind. It hid the name and port of registration. This may have been the most desolate, God-forsaken spot on earth, but still somebody was taking no chances. It was an accepted fact of life that in the main Libyan ports Mossad spies were everywhere and knew everything. The Libyans themselves were resigned to it. Nothing went on in Tripoli or Benghazi that was not reported the same day to Tel Aviv. It was the Israelis who had tipped off the British years before about the *Claudia*, the cigarette smugglers' vessel that had been caught off the Irish coast trying to run a big shipment of guns. The British had tracked her right from Libya, through the Mediterranean and almost into home waters before they had moved. It seemed that both the Libyans and the Provos had learned from the experience.

They reached the foot of the gangplank. It was a coaster of, Mike guessed, about eight hundred tons. Fifty yards long: a flat deck, wheelhouse and accommodation at the rear, a low forecastle at the bow. And rust everywhere—it seemed to be *built* of rust.

A figure scowled down at them from the top of the gangway, one hand shielding his eyes as he watched them ascend. Mike stepped on to the deck and raised a hand in greeting. He grinned.

"Hi, Harry. How you doing?"

"About time!" O'Keefe said angrily. "Where the hell have you been?" He looked pointedly at his watch. "I saw the helicopter go over three-quarters of an hour ago."

Mike shrugged. "No need to get excited, Harry. We didn't hang around. It's like wading through a foot of fresh shit back there."

O'Keefe grunted. "Yeah. Well, time happens to count." He shoved past them and strode down the gangway on to the quayside. "Come with me. I want you to talk to those bastards over there. The captain's been fucking me around. Pretends he can't speak English. Wouldn't help me get started with transferring the stuff."

Mike looked at his watch and nodded. "Anything you say. Let's go and talk to him." He stood back, gesturing to Randall to precede him down the gangway. As he waited his eyes swept the deck. Nowhere was there anything loose; no wood, no metal, nothing that might make a weapon.

They walked the seventy yards or so to the second boat. It was about the same size and type, but smarter—there were patches that still had paint on. Mike stopped them at the foot of the gangway.

"Got any money?"

They both looked at him strangely for a moment. Then O'Keefe pulled out a handful of crumpled currency and passed it over. Randall shrugged, took out his wallet and held it out. Mike took it, stripped the money out of it and handed it back. He pushed all the cash into his own pocket, and climbed on to the boat with the others at his heels.

There was no sign of life. They entered the wheelhouse. It was deserted. Mike pushed open a door and started down a steep companionway. The gloomy corridor below decks stank of diesel and fish. He shouted and hammered on a door. The other two stood at the foot of the ladder looking wary. At his second shout a door at the end of the narrow corridor swung open, and an Arab with a four-day growth of greying stubble appeared. His eyes were unfocused. He wore crumpled underpants and a stained singlet. One hand pawed absently at his crotch, loosening the cloth.

"Where's the captain?" Mike asked.

The man's mouth gaped in a massive yawn, and at the same time, he slowly planted a finger in the center of his own chest.

Mike smiled. "Captain." He held out a hand. The captain stared blankly at it. Mike took it back, still wearing the smile. "You have the shipment for us, I believe."

The captain looked past Mike at the other two, and rubbed at an eye with the heel of his hand. It was tiring work. He yawned again. Making a special effort, he jerked a thumb over his shoulder.

"You can take it. It's there."

Mike bowed his head. "Captain, there are *three tons* of merchandise there. You don't have a winch."

The captain nodded. He had noticed the same thing himself. He shrugged and made as though to turn back into his cabin. Mike stepped on to the threshold behind him. The cabin had the meaty smell of confined humanity with a cloying overlay of sweetish cologne.

"Captain, your men will help us?"

The man looked at him with an expression of unspeakable disdain. He let go the cloth of his underwear so that he could draw his shoulders back. "My men are seamen. They aren't stevedores."

Mike drew his hand from his pocket. Money sprouted like rockery plants between the fingers of his closed fist, American dollars, English pounds, Dutch guilders, Libyan dinars. He showed it to the captain.

"Could they *learn* to be stevedores?"

The captain wet his lips. His head was slightly on one side, as though he were trying to count the cash. He looked quickly past Mike, checking that none of his crew was witnessing the scene. With a sudden movement, he clasped Mike's fist in both his, as though Mike were a favorite cousin about to emigrate. With his eyes still on the corridor he clawed the money from Mike's palm into his own. "One moment, please." He pushed Mike back across the threshold of the cabin and closed the door in his face. A moment later he reappeared, empty-handed except for a bunch of keys. He had pushed his feet into a pair of plastic flip-flops. He pulled his door to and locked it.

"Crew!" he shouted, at the top of his lungs. "Come on, you idlers! There's a job to be done!"

Mary pushed into the lounge, driving Pat before her by the sheer fury in her eyes.

"He's left? Where's he gone, for Christ's sake? I've *got* to get to him. Where is he?"

Pat shook his head resentfully. "I can't tell you."

"What's that supposed to mean? You don't know, or you're not going to say?"

He flinched under the laser stare. "I can't," he said with a trace of a whine. "O'Keefe's instructions. Nobody's supposed to know where they are. Outside of them and me." He added the last words with a kind of desperate pride, promoting himself to a vital role as an insider. "The job's too important."

Mary went on staring at him. Her anger and exasperation were so strong her face actually stayed blank, as if in shock. With no change of expression, she stepped forward and thrust out the heel of her hand. The blow caught Pat under the sternum. He made a sound like escaping steam and crashed down into a chair. He sat staring up at her, his stubbled jaw agape as his lungs fought for air and his brain for understanding. Mary dragged the gun from her shoulder-bag and jammed it painfully hard under his chin.

"Listen, you fucking slob. I've been sent here to *kill* Scanlon. The bastard's an informer. A grass! D'you understand me? Dublin sent me here to get rid of him." She paused to let the words penetrate the man's tangled wits. "You're right about the job. It's big all right, the biggest in years. And one of our team's a fucking agent for the fucking Brits!" She lowered the gun and stepped a pace back from the cowering Pat. "So where are they?"

Pat straightened in his chair, massaging his neck. His eyes kept flickering from her face to the gun. In her rather delicate hand it looked huge, as if one shot would pulp his head.

"Al-Bahri," he said hoarsely.

"Where the hell's that?"

"Along the coast. East of Tripoli."

"How far?" As she spoke she was already shoving the gun back into her bag.

He watched the bag for a moment after the gun had disappeared into it, as if he thought it might spring back out again. Finally, he let out a long breath and looked up at her. "A hundred kilometers. Perhaps a bit more."

"How were they traveling?"

"They had a helicopter."

"Shit. You'd better get *us* one then." She gestured to the phone. "You've got the contacts. Tell them we need it now, but don't tell them why."

Pat gestured morosely at the window. The light was a murky orange. "They can't. Not in this shit. Even if they were ready to go up, they couldn't get down again." He straightened further, encouraged by knowing something she did not. "You can't see the ground from thirty feet up in this sort of crap."

"So we'll drive. You know the way?" She made no effort to keep the doubt from her voice.

He pulled his shoulders back, nettled at her contemptuous tone. "Know it? Yeah, sure I do." He gave her a superior smirk, scoring another point. "Finding it'll be the problem. This stuff's worse than an old-fashioned London pea-souper. At least in fog the roads are still *there*. In this stuff they can just disappear altogether. The dunes just creep right over them. Wipes 'em out completely."

She shook herself, boiling with angry impatience. "I don't give a toss about that. I've been sent over here by the top people to kill Scanlon, not to listen to the Libyan weather forecast. So, for fuck's sake, come on! Move yourself!"

Pat heaved himself out of the chair. He still held a hand to his chest, sullenly massaging the point where she had hit him. "O'Keefe's the top man," he muttered, sulky and defiant as a child.

"If we don't get there in time, O'Keefe's probably going to be a *dead* man." She held his sulky gaze. "And that'll make two of you!"

Without another word, Pat picked up a jacket and led the way outside. With a wave of dismissal to the driver who had brought Mary from the airport, they climbed into Pat's mudcaked Land Rover.

CHAPTER
22

MIKE EMERGED FROM THE STIFLING HOLD ON TO THE
Libyan vessel's deck. He swore loudly as he caught his
shin on the last rung of the steep iron ladder, stumbling
and almost dropping the stack of brickettes he held
clamped under his right arm. He was naked to the waist.
Red dust clung in his hair and eyebrows. Sweat ran
down his caked chest, darkening the waistband of the
fatigue trousers.

It was proving to be a longer and harder job than
O'Keefe had seemed to be bargaining for. The Semtex
was stored in crates the size of tea chests. With lifting
gear, they could have had the whole lot moved in fifteen
minutes. As it was, Mike, Randall and the four Libyan
crewmen had been laboriously removing it from the
crates and humping it across to the other vessel. It had
already taken more than an hour. It meant carting the
brickettes, slippery and awkward in their polythene
wrapping, up the narrow ladder, down on to the quayside, seventy yards along the quay to their own boat, on
to the deck and down another ladder into the forecastle.

At first, they had tried teamwork, with one group throwing the polythene sacks off the deck down to the quayside for another team to collect and carry to the second ship. The experiment had lasted three minutes. The Czechs made great explosive, but their plastic bags were terrible. After the first half dozen sacks had split and spilled their contents into the harbor they had given up.

Mike moved down the greasy gangplank on to the quayside. The handkerchief tied around his face kept some of the sand out of his mouth, but it still slashed cruelly at his eyes, forcing them into narrow slits that reduced his field of vision to a few yards.

The four Libyans loomed out of the tan fog, slouching and complaining in low voices. They, too, had cloths knotted around the lower halves of their faces. Above the cloths their eyes turned to watch Mike as he passed them. Hostility brimmed in them. The captain had failed to mention the money to his men. Close to the gangway of their own ship he encountered Randall coming toward him at a labored trot. He stopped in front of Mike, one hand on his chest. With the other hand he probed behind the lens of his glasses and picked grit from the corner of an eye. He took several gulping breaths before he was able to speak.

"Jesus, but this is hard work. Is there much more of it left?" Inexplicably, Randall had kept his jacket on. Maybe he was keeping up appearances in front of the natives. Mike shrugged and smiled at the other man's pleading look. Beneath the nice tailoring the man was overweight and out of shape.

"Not too much. Another case or two. Four or five more trips each ought to do it."

"Thank fucking Christ for that. I'm knackered!"

"Yeah." Mike shifted the weight of the stack of Semtex under his arm and nodded toward the ship.

"Why the fuck doesn't Harry give us a hand? He thinks the stuff's going to get up and jump back overboard?"

Randall shook his head. "Ah. That's Harry O'Keefe for you. He's like that. Always has been." Behind the handkerchief Mike thought he detected a movement that might have been a hostile grimace. His eyebrows twitched. It was the first time he had heard Randall speak O'Keefe's name with anything less than total respect. "He's the movement's intellectual dynamo. He thinks the rest of us are there to serve him. Like a fucking queen bee. Especially when there are heavy objects want carrying."

"Yeah, I've known a few people like that." Mike looked behind him. The Libyans had disappeared into the murk. He hitched his load higher. "Better get on with it. We don't want to keep our leader waiting."

He moved on quickly up the gangway, swung himself through the door and went backward down the ladder into the dimly lit forecastle. He carried his load across and added it to the stack. He stood up, massaging the beginning of a twinge in his elbow joint, and looked around. There was no sign of O'Keefe.

"Harry?"

There was no reply. Mike stood, still massaging his elbow and staring curiously at the stack of Semtex. Packing cases piled two high, almost to the ceiling, had been arranged around three sides of a square. On O'Keefe's instructions, they had stacked the Semtex in the space enclosed by the arrangement. Enough additional crates stood nearby to complete the fourth side of a square. Mike looked around, frowning, trying to penetrate the darkest recesses of the low forecastle.

"Harry! You there?"

He called loudly, loud enough for the sound to reverberate, bouncing off the bare metal that enclosed him. There was no response. Stepping quietly in his rubber-soled combat boots, he moved the few paces that took him around behind the stack of crates, the only part of the forecastle he could not see. He was quite alone. Harry O'Keefe's jacket lay meticulously folded on top of a scratched aluminum box with a hinged lid and a handle on top. The box was the size and shape of a woman's vanity case, the type of thing photographers use to protect delicate equipment. Mike paused for a moment, listening intently, and then knelt by the box. Holding O'Keefe's jacket carefully in place with his thumbs, he snapped open the two spring fasteners and lifted the lid. He stared inside. The only thing in the box was what looked like a kind of walkie-talkie. He was reaching for it when hurried footsteps rang on the deck. He closed the lid, snapped the fasteners back into place and strode quickly, without quite breaking into a run, around to the front of the stack.

O'Keefe was half-way down the steps. His back was to Mike. In his right hand he carried another of the aluminum boxes. Mike silently snatched up a bag of Semtex and let it fall heavily on to the stack. O'Keefe looked sharply over his shoulder.

"Ah, it's you." He glanced at Mike's sweat-streaked torso. "Just the man I needed. You can put those muscles to some good use. Here." As he spoke he stepped off the ladder and over to where a half-dozen more crates stood a few feet from the main stack. "The stuff's nearly all here." He tapped one of the crates with two fingers. "I want you to start moving these over here." He indicated the spot. "I want them to fill up the gap, so the stuff's completely enclosed. Okay?" He turned away, glancing irritably at his watch, not waiting for Mike to answer.

Mike put his hands to two corners of the first crate and shoved. It did not budge. He tried again, putting more beef into it. Still it did not move. Blowing, he crouched behind the crate, put his back to the rough wood and heaved. With a harsh grating sound the box moved a few inches. He drew up his legs, took a deep breath and tried again. By four-inch moves, he manhandled the crate into place. Randall and the Libyan sailors came down the ladder more or less together and dropped further loads on to the pile. They turned for the ladder again, with Randall behind the Libyans, trying to hustle more effort from the grumbling men. As he climbed the ladder at their heels he turned and fixed Mike with a resentful stare, plainly convinced that Mike had joined the ranks of the intellectuals and was leaving him to do the graft.

Mike crouched behind another crate and pushed. In the breather before his next effort he called over his shoulder to O'Keefe. "You know, Harry, I hate to tell a man his job, but isn't this a waste of time? There's not a customs officer in the world would fall for it. If anybody at all comes down here the first thing they're going to do is shin up and have a look. It won't take them fifteen seconds to find the stuff."

"Just do as I asked you to and let me worry about the thinking. It's not here to fool anybody, so just shut your mouth and get a move on. That dumb bastard of a captain's cost me enough time as it is."

Mike had been gathering himself for another heave. At O'Keefe's words he frowned and slowly let his body slacken. He pushed himself to his feet and stooped to examine the crate. The rough planks of its lid were firmly nailed into place. He glanced toward O'Keefe. He was crouching, busy with something close by the Semtex, and only the yellow-grey of the crown of his head was visible. Silently, Mike moved to the three remaining cases. On the second one he found what he needed. A nail, carelessly driven, had started to go askew. Whoever had done the nailing had not bothered to remove the nail and start again, but had simply hammered it flat along the surface. Even that had been sloppily done, leaving an eighth of an inch of clearance between the bent shaft of the nail and the wood.

He glanced again in the direction of O'Keefe. The man was completely hidden by the wall of crates. He could hear his constant soft humming, interrupted occasionally by the snick of a tool. Using the pressure of a thumb, Mike pushed the shank of the bent nail around through ninety degrees until the turned-over piece projected beyond the edge of the crate. He hooked a forefinger under it and began twisting and pulling. The metal bit painfully into the flesh of his finger joint. He ignored the pain and kept pulling until the cheap, unseasoned wood loosened its grip. Keeping his eyes toward the spot where O'Keefe crouched, working only by touch, he inserted his fingers under the end of the freed board and raised it a few inches clear of its neighbors. He dropped to his knees and squinted through the gap. Enough light from the dim overhead bulb penetrated around the board for him to see what the crate contained. It was filled to within a foot of the top by a jumble of loose ironmongery; he could make out scaffolding joints, hammer-heads, bolts and screws.

The suspicion that had until then been only forming congealed into icy certainty. For a count of two he knelt motionless, considering the discovery. Then, he got quickly to his feet, crossed the short distance to the wall of cases behind which O'Keefe worked and looked casually around it. He found himself looking directly into O'Keefe's eyes. The tiny sound of his rubber soles had been enough to alert the man. His hand had moved as though by instinct to within six inches of the shoulder holster that hung loosely against his ribs. His other hand held a pair of electrician's pliers.

"What's up?"

"Look," Mike answered, struggling to keep his voice even, "if we're short of time, there's a better way to do this. I'll go and give Randall a hand to finish loading. Then we can be away. He can help me with this once we're under way."

O'Keefe's eyes stayed on his. Mike had the very uncomfortable feeling that the man in front of him with a gun and a taste for using it was reading his mind. O'Keefe let his shoulders rise and fall. "As you like. Get a move on, that's all."

Mike turned and bounded for the ladder. He emerged on to the deck, reeling from what he had just learned as though from a blow. What he had just seen confirmed his suspicion beyond any doubt. On the floor in front of O'Keefe the lid of the second aluminum box was thrown back. Inside it lay a spool of flex, the end trailing from the case. O'Keefe had been working on it, stripping back the insulation. By his knee a half-dozen metal cylinders spilled from a crumpled brown paper bag. Mike had recognized them as detonators.

He ran headlong along the deck and almost threw himself down the gangway to the quay, slithering on the film of sand. Until a few seconds ago he had supposed the Semtex was to be shipped to Ireland, for delivery to the Provo quartermasters. He had been assuming it was to be eked out, kilo by kilo, in a war of attrition, or as five-hundred-gram seed explosives for the oil-drum bombs packed with home-made explosives which they were using with such horrific effect in their latest campaign in Ulster. He had been comfortable in the assumption he would have a voyage of several days in which to act. Now, he knew it was not to be like that. The entire ship was being made into one monstrously lethal bomb. A deadly sheath of metal around a three-thousand-kilo high-explosive payload.

He sprinted head down along the quayside, heading for the Libyan vessel.

Mary urged Pat to drive still faster, lashing him with curses as though he were an animal. He hunched forward like a whipped dog, his big chest almost touching the wheel as he tried for the extra yard of speed. His red-rimmed eyes were narrowed as he strained to see deeper into the haze. It took all the concentration he could muster to keep the Land Rover on the narrow ribbon of road surface. Dust caked the windscreen. The screen washers had long since been emptied, and the frayed wiper blades screeched on the dry filth, tearing narrow, streaked arcs of visibility amid the opaque murk.

The asphalt was almost lost to view, discernible only as a darker shade under the dancing layer of dust. Shimmering fingers of sand leaped from the crests of the dunes and fluttered down to form new, miniature dunes that frequently covered the width of the road. It was as though the desert itself were inching forward toward the sea, consuming the road that insolent men had dared to carve through it. Every few seconds, still cursing through tightly gritted teeth, Mary stole angry, impatient glances at her watch. It was already late in the afternoon and most of the light had gone. Although it was impossible to see even the direction of the sun through the uniform brown opacity, she knew it must be dropping low toward the horizon. Once it fell below it they would be utterly and irretrievably lost. In such conditions the headlights would not penetrate ten yards.

"How much further can it be, for God's sake?"

Pat's narrowed eyes flicked down for a split second to glance at the instruments. He turned his attention back to the road and took a few seconds to calculate. He shrugged. "A few kilometers. A few minutes in normal conditions. In this stuff I don't have a fucking clue." He jerked his chin at the windscreen, indicating the encroaching sand. "It won't need much more of this before we've no bloody road at all. Then we'll really be fucked. Take the asphalt away from this fucking country and the whole fucking place looks the same. Ever since I came here the—"

"Drive, Pat, for Christ's sake, and just concentrate on the road. Keep the reminiscences. When we get the British out of Ulster you can go home and write your memoirs."

He shot her a quick glance. She was surprised to see that his eyes had a momentary moistness to them, as though her words had cut him. When he spoke again there was an odd, almost wistful note in his voice. "Ah, you young people, with your college educations, and all. You think us old fellers are living in the past. You don't think we're worth listening to. Just a bunch of ignorant old buggers. Well, let me tell you, I've been in this place for years. I could tell you things about these people—"

"Drive. Please." Her tone was exasperated but much gentler. As she spoke she opened her shoulder-bag and began carefully checking the gun that lay there, ensuring that no drifting grit had impaired its mechanism.

Pat relapsed into a tight-lipped silence and hunched an inch closer to the windscreen. They drove on for a further few minutes, the bucking of the Land Rover growing wilder as the humps of sand spreading over the road grew bigger. Abruptly, a grunt from Pat jerked Mary's attention back from the gun to the road. She pressed close to the glass.

"What is it?" Her hand had plunged into the open bag.

"The way down to the harbor!" he bellowed triumphantly, already swinging the wheel. They rocked off the road on to the remains of a track formed of intermittent concrete blocks. The very unevenness of the track made it easier to follow than the road had been, the unnatural straightness of the projecting stones contrasting with the soft curves of the sand.

"How much of this is there?"

Pat turned to give her a brief leer. "A couple more minutes. Then we'll have the bastard." The triumph slid abruptly from his face to be replaced by a frown that was full of angry pessimism. "If they've not already left!"

Mike dashed along the quay, not even noticing that the stinging, sand-laden wind had increased in strength. It was blowing something close to a gale, shrieking around the superstructure of the two ships.

He skidded to a stop at the foot of the gangway to the Libyan vessel. Four dark forms materialized above him. He stepped back, panting, to let the four Libyans saunter past, then sprang up the gangway in two strides, ran to the top of the ladder leading down into the hold and stood there listening. Over the wail of the wind he only just heard the sound of Randall starting to climb the ladder. He withdrew a few paces. As Randall's head emerged Mike stepped briskly forward again, toward the ladder. Randall pushed roughly past him.

"About time you decided to give us a hand out here," he said sullenly. "This is about killing me."

Mike grinned, saluted, and swung himself into the hold. He stayed down there only for a few seconds, just time enough to be certain the Libyan skipper was not lurking there, then hauled himself back up the ladder and out on to the deck. Crouching low, keeping his head below the level of the hatch covers, he hurried back along the narrow walkway between the hatches and the ship's side, moving toward the wheelhouse. The light was on inside. Behind the grimed glass he saw the figure of the captain standing at the control console. His head was down as he studied something out of Mike's line of sight. Still crouching low, Mike moved around the side of the wheelhouse, past the adjacent galley, to the crowded stern deck. He stood up, pulled open a narrow door and stepped over the high threshold.

He was in a cramped lobby from which a door led to the galley. Gently, he pulled it open. Across the galley to his right, three paces away, another door stood open, leading to the wheelhouse where the captain was busy. Mike stepped into the galley, his rubber boots silent on the ribbed steel plates of the floor, and let the door swing soundlessly closed behind him. Immediately to his left was another door. It stood open, fastened back on a rocker device that held its lower edge. He stepped silently into the gloomy corridor beyond it and took two quick paces to the companionway leading to the accommodation below deck. He swung himself down it, his feet hardly touching the steps.

At the bottom he paused and listened. There was no sound. He was in the corridor that led to the Captain's cabin. Several other doors opened off it, and he pushed open the first. A glance at the two disheveled bunks told him it was a crewmen's cabin. He turned away, letting the door swing closed, and pushed open the next. He swore under his breath—another cramped cabin, with the slightly fetid smell of unaired bedding.

The next door he tried was locked. He turned the handle and slammed his shoulder against it. It had no effect. He abandoned it and burst into the captain's cabin. The bed was unmade but everything else was neatly arranged, and the smell of cologne hung strongly in the air. Working very fast now, all caution gone, Mike began ripping open the drawers of the cramped desk and dumping the contents on to the bunk. It took him perhaps forty seconds to find out that there were no keys of any kind. With another curse, he turned and ran for the foot of the companionway where a further ladder led down to the engine-room.

The engine-room of a small ship is cramped and close but usually the most orderly place on the vessel. This one was no exception. The layout was similar to many others he had seen, a mass of pipes painted in bright primary colors, and, in a corner near the stairs, a workbench. He stepped over to the bench and began tearing open the drawers beneath it. He reached into the second of them and grabbed a short wrecking-bar.

Four seconds later, he was jamming the flat end of the bar into the jamb of the door of the locked cabin, just above the lock. Gripping it with both hands he yanked with all his weight. The lock gave with a crack and the door swung open, leaving him staggering. He slipped the bar into one of the pockets on the thigh of his fatigue trousers and stepped inside. On the far wall of the tiny cabin was a rack of automatic rifles, their oily surfaces glinting in the light from the doorway. Beneath the rack was a metal cabinet, like an office filing system. He stepped into the cabin and pulled it open. Half a dozen handguns lay on the top shelf, and there were cardboard boxes of bullets on the floor. He snatched up one of the handguns and rifled through the boxes for the right caliber ammunition. Hastily, he tore open the box and began loading the gun.

His informed guess had been right. It was widely rumored that all Libyan vessels and their crews were regarded as quasi-military. In a country where fear of a coup was a constant, and justified, preoccupation, many groups—police, merchant seamen, customs—formed parts of a kind of militia, armed and available to buttress the regime in time of need. Right now Mike's need was greater than the regime's. He pushed the bullets into the gun, handling the unfamiliar weapon awkwardly, snapped the chamber closed at the second attempt, dropped the weapon into another of his copious pockets and buttoned the flap over it.

He looked down at himself. The fatigues were cut for comfort, baggy and loose-fitting. The weight of the gun made them sag a little but as long as he did not crouch, stretching the material tight, there was no tell-tale shape to betray the gun's presence. He ripped a scrap of cardboard from the ammunition carton and left the cabin. Outside, he folded the scrap of card very small, held it against the door-jamb and pulled the door firmly to. To a casual touch the wedge would hold it firmly enough. He strode to the companionway and almost ran up the ladder. At the entrance to the galley he paused to listen. He could hear faint sounds of the captain moving around in the wheelhouse, well away from the door. Placing his feet with the utmost care, he moved through the galley and eased open the door to the stern deck. Wincing at the sudden howl of the wind, he slipped through and out on to the deck. He crouched below the level of the window and cushioned the door's closing with his fingertips, hoping that the rush of wind through the galley would not arouse the man's curiosity. He stayed in a crouch for a few seconds more, recovering himself. His chest was pounding. He judged that he had been below less than two minutes. No sound came from inside the galley. Still doubled over to keep below the level of the windows, he turned and began heading for the hold and another load.

Something hard hit him with tremendous force in the kidneys. He gasped and staggered to his knees.

"Don't move, you fucker!"

23

MIKE LET HIS WEIGHT SAG AGAINST THE GALLEY WALL, one hand clutching at his side. Still gasping, he half-turned to face his attacker. His shock at seeing Pat leering back at him lasted only a fraction of a second—then he started calculating his chances.

Pat's resentment of Mike was making him careless. Instead of standing off a pace, leaving himself room, he was close up against Mike's back, taking satisfaction in grinding the gun barrel hard into his spine. Mike grimaced and straightened a little, shifting his weight, finding his balance. Pat was a big man, tough and beefy. But he was out of shape and would never have been nimble. Moving imperceptibly, Mike readied himself to turn on him. He felt certain he had the speed to get hold of the gun before Pat could react and shoot him. Pat ground the gun harder into his back, urging him on. For just an instant, the pressure of the gun made Mike waver. In that moment another voice sounded, a few feet from him.

"You bastard."

His surprise was almost as strong as his despair, and any notion of tackling Pat evaporated. He slumped back against the wall and turned to his right. Mary had emerged from behind the life-raft that lay lashed to the deck. Randall was at her shoulder; both held weapons aimed at his stomach. Mary spoke again.

"You dirty, treacherous bastard." Her eyes blazed. Her voice was choked with fury. "You grass! You filthy little informer!"

She moved closer, until her face was a foot from his, and spat. It was not a thin spray of droplets but an expert, greasy gob of saliva, the kind of thing a girl can learn on the backstreets of Belfast. It hit Mike below the left eye. He could feel it gather momentum as it began to slide down his cheek.

"Hello, Mary. Nice to see you." He smiled behind the handkerchief, a wry, resigned smile. "What's new?"

Pat drew back the gun and drove it forward again into his back, making him wince. "Don't be fucking smart, mister. Get your hands on your head."

With a sardonic look at Mary, Mike complied. Still holding the gun in his back, Pat leaned around and ran a hand over his thigh. He grunted. Mike felt his breath on his neck. Pat fumbled the button undone and pulled out the gun. The pressure left Mike's back as Pat backed off a pace, holding the weapon high. He grinned sarcastically at Randall. "Where did he get that, for Christ's sake?"

Randall looked as if he were sucking a lemon. "Down below." He jerked his head toward the wheelhouse. It was a gesture that took in most of the country. "They've all got guns. Probably got a whole armory down there. Let's go."

Pat prodded Mike violently. "Move! Follow Jack."

Mary nodded. "Don't say anything in Arabic to the ragheads, okay. But talk to us. Smile. Look natural."

Mike's eyes did not crinkle as he gave her another

short, bright grin. He fell into step three paces behind Randall as he led the way past the wheelhouse and along the deck to the gangway.

On the quayside they encountered the Libyan sailors who, without Randall to harass them, had slowed to a dawdle. Mike saw Randall push his weapon into a pocket as the Libyans detached themselves from the blur, and he guessed that behind him Pat and Mary were doing the same. It was important to them not to advertise their difficulties to the Libyans; they already had enough of a credibility problem without having it reported back to Tripoli that they had started shooting each other.

The figure of O'Keefe loomed up in the haze, standing next to the Land Rover that had brought Pat and Mary. He wore nothing over his face. His expression was blank, as though unaware of the dust which lashed at his eyes and tried to force its way into his ears and mouth. Pat looked quickly around, making sure the Libyans were out of sight. Satisfied he was not being observed, he pulled out the gun he had taken off Mike and brandished it. "I got the fucker just in time. He'd got himself this." He lowered the gun, preening.

O'Keefe nodded without even looking at the weapon. His eyes were on Mike. He stepped forward and punched him in the nose with all his force. Mike staggered back against the vehicle. It was a tremendous blow. His shoulders hunched in a stoop as he clutched at his face, astonished at the strength of the man. His eyes watered, momentarily blinding him. He shook his head, trying to clear the tears. Blood poured from his nose and ran beneath his fingers. Rage flared, taking hold of him. He straightened, snarling, his fists bunched, ready to leap at O'Keefe, who was standing leaning slightly back from the waist. His right arm was extended straight toward Mike, holding a gun. His left hand held his right forearm, steadying his aim. Behind the tinted glasses, his eyes were fixed unblinkingly on a point in the center of Mike's chest. Off to his left he was aware that Pat, too, held a gun at the ready.

Mike felt a flash of surprise at the sheer simplicity of it. He was going to die now. His rage had melted away, leaving only a hollowness, an overwhelming sense of disappointment. He had failed Allix, failed their child. His chance had come and gone back at the villa, and he had wasted it. He dropped his hands to his sides and stood straight, watching O'Keefe's fingers tense.

"Don't do that!" Mary's voice was peremptory, almost a shout.

O'Keefe's eyes flickered to her. "What?"

"Don't shoot him."

O'Keefe turned his eyes back to Mike with a look of patient contempt. "What? He's an informer. A stool-pigeon. We always shoot stoolies," he added, addressing Mike and smiling reasonably at him, as though a man of the world like himself would understand. Mike just looked at him with mute hatred.

"Yeah, I know." Mary glanced around, checking that none of the Libyans had reappeared to witness the scene. They were nowhere in sight, taking their time in the relative shelter of the hold. "Look, Harry, I was sent here with instructions. The people in Dublin *have* to know who the bastard is. They must know what he's been able to pass on." She shot Mike a look of pure venom. "The double-crossing fucker had descriptions, addresses, some damned good sketches. We've got to know if there's more."

"So ask him."

She shook her head and gestured again over her shoulder. They could hear the Libyans moving along the deck with fresh loads. "Not here. There are some huts up there. Pat and I'll take him up."

O'Keefe looked at his watch. "Forget it. I'm the one who gives orders to Dublin, not them to me. If we don't get out of here the whole damn operation's going to blow away from under us."

She shook her head in protest. "Look, Harry, the stuff this bastard had could blow the whole operation out of the water. It could set the entire movement back forty years." A note of pleading entered her voice. "We're the coming generation, Harry. We don't *want* to go back to the way it was when you started out. We want to keep what you fought for, build on all you and Jack and the rest have done, not start all over again." She touched his arm. "You and Jack get on with what you have to do. We won't be gone more than fifteen minutes." She turned and gave Mike an icy smile. "A feller with a bullet in his ankle doesn't keep you hanging around for answers." She smiled again. "Especially not when he knows the next one'll be in his balls." She smiled yet again, a big, wide one with even less mirth in it. The smile switched off abruptly. She nodded at him, then jerked her head toward the Land Rover. "Get in."

Mike hesitated. From where he stood to his left Pat kicked him viciously in the side of the knee. "Move, fuck you." With a look of pure malice over his shoulder at Pat, he climbed slowly into the jeep.

When they reached the huts, Mary descended first, climbing carefully down from the front passenger seat without once letting her weapon waver. Pat swung his legs out of the vehicle, making to jump to the ground to follow her. She put a hand on his thigh.

"No, Pat. I can handle this bastard. Stay here and keep watch. If Jack and Harry let him get a gun, Christ knows what else they're capable of. And those Arabs make me nervous. It's quite likely they saw some of what went on back there—it wouldn't be the first time we've had trouble with innocent Libyan sailors."

The reference was not lost on Pat. A few years earlier a Mossad spy among the crew had betrayed a vessel carrying a shipment of arms for the Provos. The British had sunk it just outside Irish territorial waters with three top Provos aboard. It was as a result of that incident that Pat had been sent out as a permanent link-man. Reluctantly, he dropped back into his seat.

Mary turned to Mike and gestured with the gun. "In there!" She was forced to shout over the whine of the wind around the dilapidated structures.

He opened the door of the hut. A gust of wind tore it from his hand, slamming it back on its corroded hinges. He took a pace inside.

"Keep moving."

She waited until he had gone several more steps before entering the hut and dragging the door shut behind her. After the fury of the wind outside the interior seemed for a moment to be strangely hushed. They stood surveying each other, twelve feet apart. Mike stared at her, weighing the odds, mentally calculating distances. His thoughts made him shuffle his feet a fraction apart, getting set for something he had not yet even formulated.

Mary shook her head. "No, don't. Don't even think about trying it. It only works on television, and on television the bullets aren't real, and the baddies can't shoot straight." She waggled the gun. "These are. And I've had a lot of practice."

He shrugged and gave her a contemptuous smile. "So you're a very dangerous lady. What the fuck did you bring me up here for? You might as well have let Harry shoot me back there. I've got nothing to say."

She ignored his remark. The bright, perfect eyes drilled into his face. "You will have. First, who the hell are you?"

He shrugged and dropped his eyes from hers, ignoring her.

She stepped forward, extending the hand that held the gun until the muzzle was a yard from his groin. "You saw the way O'Keefe was. He's very anxious to get away. We don't have the time to screw around while you play the hero. I wasn't kidding about the fifteen minutes. You'll be talking by then, I guarantee it. Everybody does. Now, one last time, the easy way. Who are you working for?"

He looked up slowly to stare into her face. He remembered the days they had spent together, how he had had to fight against the way he had started to feel about her, how gentle the oval face could seem when she was at ease, framed by the soft, clean brown hair. Abruptly, he smiled and shook his head.

"Come on, Mary," he said hoarsely. "You can't shoot me. Not me."

The extraordinary eyes burned back into his, unblinking. She swallowed hard, just once. Another second passed before she spoke. Her voice was a diamond-edged whisper.

"Try me, Michael."

Something inside him turned to bile, a tiny hope he had not even been sure was there until it died. His smile died with it. It would not make the slightest difference what he said now. Her words to O'Keefe had been the truth. Somehow they had found his files. They knew he had seen too many faces, knew too many places for him to be allowed to live. For her it was simple—she had no choice but to kill him. He might as well tell her what she wanted to hear and let her get it over with.

"M15. I met someone while I was working out in Saudi. A few years ago, now. A man who worked in the embassy. I told him about my dad. When I got back to the UK I had a visitor, a bloke who wanted to know if I'd be interested in helping them. Infiltrating your mob. For Queen and country." He said the last words with a bitter laugh, turning away from her.

A bullet smashed into the timber of the wall inches from his skull. A splinter of wood sliced his cheek. He staggered and clutched at his face, not really hurt, but angry with himself for the shout of surprise and pain which escaped him. Taking advantage of the moment, Mary stepped forward and coolly kicked him in the groin. He staggered and sank back heavily against the wall.

There was a sudden scream of wind as the door flew wide, and they both turned to look. Pat stood wild-eyed on the threshold. The handkerchief had slipped from his face and his pistol was clutched in his huge fist. Mike laughed through his pain at Pat's appearance; they could fight over who got to shoot him. Mary's face filled with dismay.

"Pat!"

He did not respond to her call. His eyes were fixed on Mike. The veined flesh over his cheekbones showed purple. He was trembling with unleashed rage. There was killing in the air and he wanted some of the action.

"The bastard not talking?" He spoke more to himself than to Mary. "I'll get it out of him. Then I'll finish the bastard."

He took a step closer to Mike, who still slumped helplessly against the wall, his hands clasped to his groin, and grinned into his upturned face. The pain he saw there seemed to please him. Mike smiled at him, a smile of utter contempt. With the smile still on his face he swung his right arm in a short arc.

The wrecking-bar caught Pat across the top lip. Blood spurted from the split flesh. He staggered backward, roaring, and almost lost his footing. A grab at the doorframe saved him from falling. He had recovered his balance before Mike was able to do more than force himself upright. Pat took a single step forward and raised the pistol.

The three shots sounded so close that the echoes from the corrugated metal roof ran together into a single roll of noise. Mike was aware of the smell of gunsmoke and the sound of screams, and he felt a searing pain in his ribs. It took a second or two to recover his senses enough to know this was not what death felt like. Screwing up his face with the pain, he looked slowly around him.

Mary crouched in the doorway with her back to him. She fired off two quick shots at something outside the hut. Over the reverberations of the shots and the howl of the wind Mike heard the noise of a motor. Swearing, Mary got to her feet, and with the gun loose at her side she pushed the door shut and walked over to Mike. He sank to his knees. She stopped two feet away and stood looking down at him. The events of the last few moments seemed to have drained her. She looked haggard, and at the same time relieved, like someone who had carried a load for too long and was finally free of it. When she spoke her voice was hardly audible.

"I'll ask you again. Who the hell is it you're working for?"

"I told you. The British. M15." He spoke through gritted teeth.

She shook her head. "Balls, Michael. You're not M15." She crouched down in front of him, the gun dangling between her thighs. One hand cradled her face. She looked very tired.

"What makes you so sure?"

Her voice was a weary mumble behind her hand. "M15 have only *ever* managed to fully infiltrate one person into the Provos." She raised her head and gave him a worn smile. "And that's me."

CHAPTER

24

FOR SEVERAL SECONDS THE ONLY SOUNDS INSIDE THE HUT were the swooping whine of the wind and the hiss of the flying sand on the metal of the roof. Mike had slumped to a position where he sat on his heels with his back supported by the wall. Blood oozed between the fingers of the hand he held clutched against his ribs, low on his left side. He stared dumbly into the face opposite him. Slowly, he began to laugh. The laugh swelled until a searing burst of pain choked it off into a roar.

"Oh, shit," he gasped. "Of course." He shook his head. "You're the one. It *is* coming from the inside. You're the informer."

She nodded. "Was." She gave him a lop-sided smile. "Until you came along and blew it." She shook herself and became brisk again, reaching out and pulling his bloodied hand away from his side. "Quick, let me look at that." She knelt and bent her head, examining the wound. He stifled a scream as she probed with her fingers, making no effort to be gentle. She pulled back and grimaced. "I don't know anything about these things but it looks to me as though the bullet might still be in there." She stooped and picked up her bag, which had slipped to the ground in the scuffle. She delved inside and pulled out a wad of paper tissues. "Here. It's the best I can do."

"Thanks." He pressed the tissues to the wound, trying to staunch the bleeding.

"I'll try and get back."

He looked up abruptly. She was already reaching for the door latch. "Uh? Where the hell are you going?"

"After those bastards. I might still get to them before they can get under way."

"Hold it!" He began to push himself to his feet. "Give me a hand."

"To do what?" She spoke over her shoulder, shouting above the roar of the wind as she opened the door.

He struggled upright without her help. "I'm coming with you. I want those bastards, too. What else do you think I'm doing here?"

She shook her head and gave him a grim smile. "I was planning to ask you that. But not now. And I don't need a cripple's help—those people are pros."

He moved to the door, his face creased in pain, and put a hand gently on her shoulder. "I'm coming, Mary, whether you like it or not. Look, I can walk. I won't slow you down. You're not going to be moving very fast in this storm, anyway."

She hesitated for a moment more, looking him up and down. Then she shrugged and gave him the wryest of smiles. "Uh-huh. You'll do what you want, anyway. Just promise me, if there's any shooting you'll get on the ground and stay there, okay?"

He saluted and grinned. The handkerchief was still knotted around his neck. He pulled it up over his face. "Let's go."

* * *

The light from the sun had almost gone, and what little remained cast a thick reddish gloom that made it impossible to see more than a few yards ahead of them. Cupping hands over their eyes to shield them from the vicious lashing of the grit-laden wind, they moved away from the hut.

They advanced carefully, their eyes on the ground just in front of them and their feet scuffing the sand as they searched, by sight and feel, for the half-buried blocks that marked the track. Around their feet the sand they kicked up eddied and flowed with the shifting force of the wind. Mike was the first to catch sight of the regular angles of one of the blocks, an inch above the surrounding sand. He called to Mary, only five feet from him. The wind whipped his words away so that she did not hear him. He reached out and took her by the hand. Leaning close, he shouted in her ear.

"There! That's it! Let's go and get those bastards."

They turned to their right, northward, and began following the track, picking their way from stone to stone. Many times they thought they had lost it. Then, one of them would stand still while the other circled, staying just within sight. If after a complete circle the track had not been found, the first person would then move around the other. By ensuring the stationary one always faced the same way and by counting the paces, they were able to cover a lot of ground without losing all sense of their departure point.

After one of these maneuvers they found themselves on a stretch of track that had somehow survived more or less intact. They were able to step up the pace, almost running, two feet apart. Mike's ribs hurt with a headsplitting pain. He gritted his teeth and called to Mary.

"Look, if you're M15 there's something I don't understand. The Selfridge's job we did—the bomb. We could have killed dozens of those kids."

She flicked him a mischievous glance before turning

back to keep her eyes on the uneven track. "Could have —but didn't. The place was virtually empty by the time it went off."

He was panting, the pain constricting his chest, leaving him short of breath. He slowed almost to a walk and stared at her in horrified disbelief. He could see her profile. There was a hint of a smile on her face. "Jesus! Does your lot fight *that* dirty? Were your people ready to let you go that far, to keep your cover?" Disgust fought with the pain and disbelief in his eyes. "That Animal Liberation bomb was a stroke of sheer luck. If it hadn't been for those nutters it would've been a fucking massacre in there."

She shot him another glance, a look of amusement and pity. She gave another brief shake of her head. "It wasn't luck at all, Mike."

He stopped short. He let the hand fall from his side, dropping the now useless wad of scarlet-soaked paper to the ground. Above the handkerchief his eyes widened. "It wasn't the Animal Lib people? It was your bunch?"

She had stopped and turned to face him. She smiled, keeping her lips pressed together against the sand. "Yes, it was. And yes, it was." Her smile widened at his perplexity. "That's right. It *was* us. And it *was* the ALF. Ever hear of the ALF doing any real damage? Of them hurting anybody?" She shook her head at him. "Of course not. Except maybe once or twice, when some splinter group of real fanatics has gone off the rails." She turned away, touching his arm. "Come on, we've got to move."

She broke into a run again, and he struggled along behind her. He was having touble keeping his balance. The wound was pumping blood, and the loss was making him lightheaded. He stumbled up beside her.

"How about their other bombs? The incendiaries, all that stuff?"

She shouted her reply, her head cocked. "Come on!

None of that ever does any *damage*. A few grams of phosphorus in the pocket of a mink coat, a bomb going off in a laboratory wastebin at three in the morning. No organization that was really serious could be that incompetent, surely. And what a great way to empty a building we need to get a look at without arousing anyone's suspicions." She laughed. "We run half a dozen groups like that. Remember the 'Angry Brigade'? It was a bit before my time, but they had the press eating out of their hands on that one. They loved it. The Anarchist threat to civilization as we know it."

"Hasn't anybody from the press ever cottoned on to it?"

She laughed outright. "Are you kidding? Half the press practically let us write their stuff for them, anyway. But that's not the point. The groups are genuine. They really exist. We just run them."

Mike's foot caught the edge of a block and he stumbled and sprawled in the sand. The pain of the wound made him bellow. She paused and dragged him roughly to his feet. He stood holding on to her for a moment. The cloth of his trousers was clinging to him, soaked with blood. He was breathing in shallow gasps.

"Can you go on? I'm not waiting."

He stood with bared teeth, a hand clamped to the wound. The wave of pain receded. He pulled back his shoulders and let go of her arm. He teetered for a moment, balancing with the exaggerated care of a drunk. "Let's go," he muttered.

They continued for a while in silence. The track had disappeared again, and they staggered through soft sand. Mike floundered in the yielding surface, scarcely able to lift his feet clear for each new step. Only the fact that Mary was obliged to drop to her knees every few yards to scrabble in the sand to search for traces of the track enabled him to stay with her. Nowhere was there any sign of the Land Rover's passage to guide them. Its tracks, like their own footprints, had been obliterated in seconds, scoured out of existence by the ferocity of the wind. He sank to one knee beside Mary, glad of another chance to rest, as she once again crawled in the sand.

"How about the arrests?"

She shouted over her shoulder, not taking her eyes from the ground, where she probed up to her elbows in the sand. "What arrests?"

"The ALF people. They've caught some of them. Are they bogus, too? And the trials?"

"No. They're genuine. You'd be amazed. Once word gets around, before you know it you're getting *applicants*. Kids, mostly. Loonies falling over themselves to join up. The worst ones we take on. That way we've got somebody to throw to the wolves once in a while, to keep the whole thing credible. Neat, huh?"

"Yeah. Is it legal? The security service provokes them in the first place and then arrests the buggers."

She made a quick, wry face. "We only take on the real nuts. It keeps them off the streets."

He was still looking for an answer when she gave a cry and scrambled to her feet. She glanced behind to where another block was in sight, lining it up with the one she had just uncovered. "This way." She jumped to her feet and set off at a trot.

He struggled up. She was already just a shadow. He glanced at his watch as he ran, and his eyes widened in surprise. It was almost an hour since they had left the hut. He ran on into the haze, his head down, his eyes sweeping the ground in front of him. Mary was lost to sight ahead of him. A sudden shape looming from the mist made him gasp and stagger back a pace. Mary was upon him in a moment, a finger pressed to her lips. She leaned close enough for him to hear her whispered words.

"Idiot. Two more steps and you'd have run into the sea." She pointed to a spot a yard or two ahead of him.

The ground ended abruptly at a sharp masonry edge. Beyond it, several feet below, was the water, the same dun shade as the sand.

The ships had been moored to their left, a little distance west of the spot where the track hit the quay. In total silence, with Mary ahead and slightly to Mike's right, they followed the line of the quayside, straining for a sight of the first vessel. Abruptly, Mary hissed a warning sound and threw herself face down in the sand. Without pausing to look for the danger Mike hurled himself to the ground behind her. He dragged himself along on his belly to come up beside her.

"What's up?"

She put a finger to her lips and pointed ahead of them. Shielding his eyes with a hand, he squinted in the direction of her gesture. A momentary lull in the wind brought a brief lightening of the murk. Ten yards ahead of them Pat lay stretched uncomfortably in the sand, watching them. A gun was clasped loosely in his hand.

They lay confronting each other for several seconds. Then, very warily, Mary got to her feet and advanced on the man. Pat's broad face gaped unblinkingly back along the quay, its expression not changing at her approach. Mike came up behind Mary, and together they reached him.

Mary turned to Mike, her face puckered in disgust. A low drift had already formed along Pat's side, and fingers of sand had begun extending across the small of his back and his neck. His legs were half-buried. It was as though the ground were reclaiming him. Sand stuck thickly to the crimson that colored his collar and hair.

Pat had not died from a lucky shot from Mary as he fled the hut—with such a wound he would not have driven another yard. Even Mike, with no experience of guns, recognized the meaning of the scorch marks on the cloth of Pat's collar. The shot had been fired from point-blank range. A single shot to the base of the skull, at the back. Old Pat had been executed. By a pro.

Without a word, Mary stooped, plucked the gun from Pat's fist and handed it to Mike. Together now, at Mike's pace, they continued moving, edgy and watchful, along the dockside. Despite the covering noise of the wind, they did not speak a word. Both were listening intently for any sound: a foot striking metal, a voice, or the throb of a motor. They heard nothing except the wind and the lapping and sucking of the sea against the concrete of the quay.

They caught their first sight of the ship together, a darker blur that rose above them. Staying two or three yards apart, they drew a few steps closer to the looming shape. Mike swore, softly and distinctly. Through the gloom he had caught sight of the ship's name. It was the Libyan vessel. O'Keefe's had been moored to the east of it, the closer of the two vessels to the track. Their bird had flown.

They paused at the foot of the gangway, listening hard. There was only the howl of the wind around the superstructure. Mary went up first. Mike struggled behind her, supporting himself on the thick wire rail. The gun felt awkward in his hand. His brief spell in the training camp had not been enough to make him at home with firearms. Crouching, Mary led the way, creeping along the narrow walkway at the side of the deck toward the rear of the ship. The glass of the scabbed wheelhouse was spotted with dark stains. Nobody moved behind it. Still at a crouch, she led the way to the door. They paused for a moment, keeping their heads well below the level of the windows. Mary reached out and checked Mike's pistol. Satisfied, she put her hand on the door-handle, leaned close to him and put her lips to his ear.

"I'm going in." She nodded at the gun. "Ever used one of those?" He shook his head. She shrugged. "It's not difficult. If you hear any shooting come in after me and fire at anyone that isn't me, okay?" He nodded. "Well, here goes." She yanked down the handle and threw herself inside.

There were three men in the wheelhouse. All of them displayed the unmistakably awkward postures of the dead. The captain lay in a corner away from the other two, linked to them by a vivid trail of blood, as though he had had enough life left in him after he was shot to crawl that far. Mike and Mary stood shoulder to shoulder looking down at the dead Libyans. Each of them had been shot more than once. The dark stains on the windows were splashes of blood. They stared at the carnage for several seconds. Mike spoke first, and his voice had a new strength and urgency.

"There are two more of them."

Together, they turned and stepped into the cramped galley. A pan of water bubbled on the stove. Putting aside the pain, Mike swung himself on to the companionway that led below. Mary slithered down the steep ladder after him, jumping lightly down the last few steps to land soundlessly beside him. They advanced along the short, dim corridor, cautiously checking the cabins, each with its individual cocktail of smells, made up of bedding, food and toiletries.

They found the first of the men in the cabin next to the armory Mike had broken into earlier. He was reclining on a bunk with his head thrown back on the pillow, his eyes closed. A bottle of aftershave with a half-inch left in the bottom stood on the worn carpet next to the bed. The man's hand trailed slackly next to it. Blood had run in rivulets down the arm, as though the man wore his veins on the outside, and had soaked the carpet and the twisted bed-sheet. There was no sign of a struggle. Mary, her face pinched in disgust, looked from the five-day stubble on the man's throat to the bottle on the floor. She raised her eyebrows, perplexed. Mike shook his head, grimacing, and mimed a drinking gesture.

"Aftershave lotion?" she murmured incredulously.

He nodded. "No alcohol allowed on board, so they wind up drinking that stuff. I doubt if he felt a thing."

"Isn't it poisonous?"

He shrugged. "Have you tried some of those purple drinks they have stacked at the back of hotel bars? Let's go and find the other bozo."

As he spoke the ship shuddered. The pool of blood which had gathered on the plastic-tiled floor by the bottle shivered and broke up into tiny rivulets. They ran for a couple of inches before being absorbed by the frayed edge of the carpet. Mike froze for just an instant, staring at the blood, and then turned and left the cabin. He was at the end of the corridor before Mary appeared at the door.

"Where the hell are you going?"

He did not look round. "The engine room. The damned ship's going down. Go and make sure of the other crewman!" He pushed open a heavy iron door to his right and disappeared.

He put his toes around the outside of the ladder and slid down, the friction of the metal agonizing against his wound. He splashed down into a foot and a half of water. Biting his lip hard and bending to avoid the mass of overhead pipework, he began scrambling across the bright primary-painted pipes and valves. He had knocked around enough small ships and supply vessels while working on offshore rigs to know what he was looking for. Groping and splashing, he fought his way around the crowded space, struggling toward the corner of the engine-room. The water was above his knees, impeding him and concealing obstacles. His foot caught under something, sending him full-length in the water. He struggled upright, cursing. Beneath his feet he felt the ship shudder and settle further.

His shin struck against something hard, but he hardly even noticed the pain, so intent was he on reaching the corner where he could see the greasy water boiling and seething as it flooded in through the open sea-valve. He clambered over a low rail, then paused and inhaled deeply, filling his lungs to the limit before exhaling totally. He repeated the process three times, took a long breath, and disappeared beneath the water.

He found the edges of the hole in the engine-room floor where the covering plate had been removed, and took a firm grip. The inrushing sea threatened to sweep him back up and away from the hole, and the swirling movement of the water made it impossible to see anything. He settled the fingers of one hand closer on the metalwork until satisfied his grip was as secure as it could be, then let go with the other hand. Obliged to strain with all his depleted strength to keep hold, he began groping under the water with his free hand.

Three times he was forced to surface, his lungs bursting for air. At the fourth attempt he found what he was looking for. His fingers closed around the distinctive contours of the "strainer," the component at the heart of the sea-valve which, when removed, allowed the sea to flood unimpeded into the ship. Gulping in another lungful of air, he dragged himself back beneath the swirling water. This time, feeling his strength diminish further as he fought against the surge, he hauled himself through the hole left by the missing plate and into the black cavity beneath the level of the engine-room floor.

In total darkness now, with his back braced against the underside of the steel floor to hold him in place against the pressure of the water, he grappled to fit the strainer back into place. It took him most of a minute before he felt it slide home into its seating. His lungs bursting, he yanked the lever on top, securing it firmly. Already blowing the air from his aching lungs, he pushed himself upward.

He lay for a full minute, half-floating, only his head showing above the still water. At last, as the heaving in his chest subsided, he half swam, half crawled his way to the bright blue-painted motor that operated the pumps. He gave a smile of satisfaction at the first good news for a while—the water was three inches short of swamping the motor. Had he been ten minutes later it would have been unusable. He laughed outright to himself at the second piece of good fortune. They had left the ignition key in the engine. On a well-run ship the key stayed in place the whole time. A really experienced scuttler would have removed it. But then scuttling ships was a field where only a limited number of people had much experience, and the IRA's main business was terrorism, not insurance swindles. He gave the key a half-turn, and with a soft thump the pumps began working.

He found Mary back in the blood-spattered wheel-house. She stared at him in frank amazement as he staggered over the threshold from the galley.

"What the hell happened to you?"

He wiped the water from his face, leaning his weight heavily on the flag locker. "It's such a lovely day I thought I'd cool off with a swim. The other guy dead, too?"

She shook her head. "He's not on board."

He straightened. "What! Did you look all over?"

"Every inch of the thing. He's gone."

"Shit! How about Pat's Land Rover? Did you see it? Is it still down on the dock?"

She shook her head again. "Uh-uh. I had the same idea. I even went down on the quay to look for it. It's gone."

"Damn!" He indicated the dead men on the floor. "If their pal manages to find his way out of this crap and brings the Libyans down on us we're in very deep shit."

"Even if we didn't do it?"

He gave her a disbelieving look and a snort of

laughter. "You really have to be the *British* secret service to think like that! You think the Libyans are going to come back here, find half a dozen of their citizens stretched out dead, reliably reported to have been shot by a bunch of Paddies, find two of the Paddies still handily at the scene, and start reading us our *rights*?" He shook his head. "You M15 people may know a lot about the IRA, but there are some serious gaps in your knowledge of Arabs!" He pointed beyond the window, in the direction of the sea. "I'm serious, Mary. I know these people's mentality. They won't fuck around. You'll find yourself swimming around out there. With those bobbing gently, twenty feet away." He pointed at her breasts.

"So what do we do?"

"Get this thing under way and get after those bastards O'Keefe and Randall." His face lost all trace of its smile. "That's what I came here for."

She looked at him strangely, and then turned to let her gaze travel over the wheelhouse. Close by the sprawled bodies the blackened remains of a fire still smoldered. The drawers of the chart locker were all open and empty. The flags too had been removed from their locker. Scraps of colored cloth and pieces of paper lay around the edges of the fire.

"Aren't you being a little optimistic, Mike? There must be twenty thousand square miles of sea out there for them to get lost in."

He pursed his lips. "No, Mary. They're heading north. In a dead straight line."

She looked startled. "How the hell do you know? Even Pat didn't know what they were cooking up."

"Randall let it slip."

She raised her eyebrows in an expression of admiration. "They really *did* trust you. That pair wouldn't tell a secret to themselves in a mirror. Can we get word to Malta? We have people there." She caught his slight look of surprise. "No need to be surprised. A lot of Libyans use Malta for holidays. Girls are easily available, so is alcohol. We pick up a lot of stuff there."

"Yeah, I bet." While she was speaking, Mike had moved to the VHF radio. The casing had been forced open, and wires spilled from it. He looked at it sourly. "There's no way in the world I can fix this. Even if I could, what would we tell them? We don't even know the name of their vessel. Do your people, or the Maltese, have the manpower to stop and search every ship?"

"So what *can* we do?"

"Like I said, we get after them. From the depth of water down below I doubt if they got under way more than half an hour ago. I know a fair bit about ships. The motor someone's put in this thing looks beefy enough to give us some extra speed. I intend to find them. And I intend to stop the bastards. Permanently."

CHAPTER
25

Mary cast a skeptical look around the cabin. She gestured toward the gutted radio and the dying fire.

"You think we'll be able to get this thing started?"

He followed her gaze. "That won't stop us, anyway. It depends on what they did down below. They thought they'd sunk the thing. Another ten minutes and they would have been right." As he finished speaking a fresh burst of pain made him draw breath sharply. His hand went to his side.

Mary moved quickly toward him. She put a tentative hand on his arm. "Shouldn't I find something to put on that?"

He tried a smile of gratitude, but pain contorted it into a grimace. "M'mm. But later. First let's try and get under way." He looped an arm over her shoulders, leaning his weight on her. "Give me a hand down."

When they reached the foot of the ladder they stood for a moment surveying the engine room. The water had receded but was still up to Mike's knees. A thick film of oil reflected rainbow colors in the light. Mike hitched his arm more firmly over Mary's shoulders. The stink of the diesel was adding to his light headedness. He could feel a stirring of revulsion in his stomach. He breathed deeply, fighting down the urge to be sick.

Pointing, he motioned her forward. "Over there."

The scum of oil had told him what to look for. Awkwardly, with Mary stooped under his weight, they splashed through the filthy water. He swore through gritted teeth—it was exactly as he had feared. A section of fuel pipe had been hacked away, probably with an axe. Diesel still dribbled from the bright copper of the severed ends. He stood with gritted teeth, supporting himself between Mary and the engine casing, trying to muster the energy to think.

The fuel was pumped from big wing tanks into an overhead tank. From there it was gravity fed to the engine through a copper pipe. The one they had cut. Without it the engine was useless. He looked around the room, concentrating on the festoons of pipe and cable.

In the days before helicopters had become the routine means of transport Mike had spent countless days and nights on supply boats in the Gulf and the North Sea, waiting for the weather to improve enough for him to make the transfer to a rig. With nothing more to entertain him than the vessel's library of one-hand magazines and damaged paperbacks, he had usually ended up gravitating to the engine-rooms, killing the boredom in conversations with the engineers. Most of those engine-rooms looked pretty much like this one.

His eye traveled to a corner of the room. "That's it. We've got it," he called hoarsely, turning to look quickly at Mary. He withdrew his arm and indicated the workbench. The metal drawers beneath it still hung open. "Over there. You'll find tools in the drawers. Can you bring me some here? I'm going to need wrenches and a good heavy hammer. The fuel pipe from that generator should do it for us, I hope."

Mary was already hurrying through the water to the bench. She spoke without looking round. "The generator? Don't we *need* that? Doesn't everything else work off it?"

He was making his way laboriously towards the generator. "Off *one* of them. There are two. One's enough to run the vessel. Hurry it up with the gear."

She stooped in front of the bench and delved briefly before straightening and heading for Mike, straining under the weight of a huge tool-box.

Two minutes later Mike was struggling to free the second end of a three-foot length of pipe. On removing the fitting that clamped the first end a stream of oil had run from it, drenching Mike, his tools, and all the metalwork. A viscous film of oil clung to every surface, making it hellishly difficult to get a purchase on the smooth metal. Finally, using a bundle of cotton waste Mary brought him, he managed to grip the pipe firmly, give it a last wrench and pull it free.

Trimming the replacement to size with a hacksaw blade and fitting it in place of the damaged section took him most of an hour. He had directed Mary to set to work the pumps that filled the daily service tank, drawing fuel from the wing tanks, so that by the time he finished the repair it was full, ready to supply the engine. He spent a further few minutes bleeding air from the system and priming the engine. That done, he took a fistful of cotton waste and wiped the worst of the filthy grease from his hands. Mustering what felt like the last of his strength, he took a firm hold of the bar set into the flywheel and swung it. The engine came to life and settled into a low thumping rhythm.

He turned to Mary. She had been frowning and agitated as he swung the flywheel. At the sound of the engine starting up the frown gave way to a huge smile. She shook her head, as if mocking herself for having doubted him.

"I'm impressed."

Mike smiled now. "Yeah. To tell you the truth, so am I." He was leaning heavily on a nearby rail. He raised an arm for her to slide beneath it. She groaned as she took his weight. He continued smiling down into her upturned face for another instant. Then, as abruptly as a light going out, his smile faded. His eyes hardened again to a steely determination. "So, now help me back up there and let's get after those murdering bastards."

O'Keefe scowled through the spray-streaked glass. There was anger and contempt in his face. Randall stood beside him, his hands spread flat on the Formica of the instrument panel to steady himself. His face was deathly pale. O'Keefe spoke without bothering to turn to his companion.

"Just give it a rest, will you? I had no choice. The man was a drunk. A stupid, thick, obstinate drunk. You've watched it happen. He's been getting to be a liability for the last year or more."

Randall moistened his lips. "All right, I know that. But he could have been put out to grass somewhere, out of harm's way. Down in the Republic, maybe. The poor bugger didn't deserve to be killed."

O'Keefe gave an impatient shake of his head. "Nowhere's far enough to be out of harm's way, Jack, not any more. Not for a drunk. We're fighting a war. Booze and our business don't mix. The first one that offered Pat a glass of stout, he'd have been spilling his guts about what an important Republican he was. Within a week he'd have had half the RUC intelligence people sitting up at the bar with microphones under their ties buying him drinks." He looked down through his tinted glasses at the shorter man. Randall kept his eyes on the impenetrable darkness ahead of him. He did not see the utter disdain in O'Keefe's face. "I spent a long time setting this one up, Jack. I wasn't about to have him screwing it up. Nor anybody else."

Something in the tone of the last words made Randall look up sharply. O'Keefe was smiling a shark's smile. Randall pulled at the collar of his shirt. He felt unbearably hot and confined, and somewhere, deep in his stomach, the first stirring of seasickness had begun to churn. He opened his mouth to say something, but before the words came, a sudden flood of saliva made him gulp. O'Keefe spoke again.

"The British have been having it too much their own way, Jack. They're calling us terrorists while they shoot down Irish people in cold blood, either doing it themselves or setting up their UDR stooges to do it for them. Their papers are full of how we killed the three soldiers in York. They don't even bother to mention the lads at Liskeard. For years now, since Birmingham, I've listened to you and the people in Dublin. We've played it by the rules. Military targets. Telephone warnings. Civilians given time to get clear. And where has it got us?" He made an angry chopping motion with his hand. "Nowhere! The British are taking no prisoners. The four Liskeard lads were shot right there in their boat, on the high seas, without a chance to defend themselves. They weren't even armed."

Randall looked up at him. O'Keefe's eyes glinted. His face looked feverish in the semi-darkness. It was as though he were letting himself be borne along on his own anger.

"They *were* our lads, Harry," Randall said, slightly tentatively.

O'Keefe flashed him a look of pure venom. "Okay. I know that. That's no reason to put them down like dogs. And how about the girl in Berne? Was she ours? Of course not! She was nothing to do with us. She'd never been near the movement. Just an Irish girl minding her own business."

"Nobody ever proved it was the British that shot her."

O'Keefe laughed. "Sure! It was the Swiss! You know how the Swiss are. Devils for shooting tourists." He looked derisively at the other man. "Grow up, Jack, for Christ's sake."

"Okay. I still say there was no need to do old Pat in. He was past it, I agree, but he'd been with the movement a long time."

O'Keefe snorted. He snatched off his glasses and wiped his eyes with the back of his hand before fixing them firmly back on his nose. His voice softened.

"Look, don't give me the 'old Pat' stuff. I'm the one recruited him. It was a mistake twenty years ago. It just took me until now to put it right. You know as well as I do, we sent him to Tripoli so he'd have no one to talk to. If Pat'd been in on a job like this he wouldn't have been able to keep his mouth shut for five minutes."

Randall gulped down another mouthful of saliva. "And the Libyans? What in the name of Jesus made you do that?"

O'Keefe laughed outright, as if he thought it a genuinely funny question. "Oh, come on, Jack! Don't *you* start acting like a sentimental prick. You know how it is out here. Any one of them could have been an Israeli, or working for them. They've got half North Africa in their pocket. We'd have been looking great if the moment we left he'd got to his tricky little transmitter, disguised as a can of couscous or something, and told his friends in Tel Aviv about us."

"Yeah, maybe. I still say you didn't have to kill them. You'll have fucked us up with Ghaddafi for good."

O'Keefe laughed again. "Ah, shit. Ghaddafi was going to be pretty pissed off with us either way! I don't know what Scanlon was up to or what crap he shot

Ghaddafi to get him to hand over the stuff, but I bet he'd have had a lot more trouble if he'd told the truth."

Randall spat on the floor and rolled his jaw in a gesture of disgust at the taste in his mouth. "What *is* the truth, Harry?"

Harry O'Keefe grinned wolfishly. He put an arm over Randall's shoulders in a parody of comradely warmth. "I thought you'd never ask. We're going to sink a ship."

"In Malta? What kind of a ship? Does the British Navy still hang out in Malta?"

"Not the Navy, no."

Randall turned to stare at the man next to him. "What the hell kind of . . ." He broke off momentarily, disconcerted by the smirk on O'Keefe's face. "A *civilian* ship?"

O'Keefe nodded. "Better. A school ship. Three hundred or so of their finest young people. The cream of Britain's youth." He spoke in a mocking imitation of a news commentator.

Randall looked at him in silent disbelief for several seconds. "Christ," he said at length, "I knew it was something spectacular you had planned. But three hundred *kids*?" He paused again, adjusting to the news. "Where the hell is this going to leave us with Ghaddafi?" he finally said, limply.

O'Keefe laughed. "In the shit, I expect. Who cares?" His tone was ebullient. His eyes shone. "I wouldn't be surprised if the British didn't bomb the shit out of him, like the Americans," he said happily. He slapped Randall on the back. "Come on, Jack, cheer up. We don't need the flaky bastards any more, you know that. Christ, you're the one that gets the credit for setting it up. We'll soon be able to get all the plastic we want from our friends over the water. It's all in hand. Guns, too. The boys in Boston are seeing to all that. We won't have to be going down on our knees to a bunch of bloody Arabs any more. Not for Czech and Bulgarian rubbish, either. From now on it'll be American, Belgian, Israeli-made stuff, from the mail order catalogues over there. It's all set up. Our lads and girls won't have to put up with their fucking guns jamming on them any more. No more standing there like clowns, clutching jammed weapons, while a British soldier reads 'em the yellow card and then takes his time about shooting them."

Randall looked at him dully. The increasing hold of the seasickness had drained him of his power to react. He had known Harry O'Keefe for more than twenty years. O'Keefe was a man who had been planning killings all his life. They were as far away from achieving their goals now as when he had started, and yet, it still fired him. His determination, his sheer, undiminished *enthusiasm* for it all were as strong now as when he'd been a young man. The only time the man would talk to you, behave like a normal person, was when he was going to kill people.

"Look, Harry, what *exactly* is the plan?" Randall tried to smile. He felt too bad to do it successfully. It was the lifeless rictus of a skull. "Or are you still worried about security?"

O'Keefe laughed. "I never have been with you, Jack. As a matter of fact, you're about the only one. Just with all that's been going on I didn't trust the *walls* back there in the villa. Some of the stuff they've got for bugging places nowadays, it's unbelievable. Microphones no bigger than fly turds they stick on windows! That's without us having a fucking infiltrator like Scanlon along." His face blackened in a sudden squall of recrimination. "Jesus, but that was fucking stupid! I just hope Pat was right. I hope he did something useful for once and killed the bastard. I wouldn't count on it, though."

Randall stared gloomily ahead. "And the girl. What do we make of that?"

O'Keefe shrugged. "Oh, shit, Jack, who knows?

She shouldn't have been sent up to the guy's hotel. The two of them lonely, stuck in a room together for days on end. They're a nice-looking pair. It's not surprising if they fell for each other. Anyone but the idiots in London would have expected something like that to happen."

"So you think she was okay? Up to then?"

"I haven't even thought about it yet. But I'll tell you what. If she ever shows up back home, then first chance we get, we'll put a Black and Decker through her knee-cap and ask her." He grinned unpleasantly, in case Randall thought he was joking. In another abrupt change of mood he slapped Randall matily on the back again. Randall retched. "We're off to Malta, like I told you. And when we get there we're going to put this tub alongside the British boat and blow the fucking thing out of the water." He looked delighted with himself.

Randall frowned, trying to care about something other than his sickness. "But, Harry, kids? You want to start killing kids?"

O'Keefe looked at him impatiently. "Sure. I told you. There's three hundred of the little bastards. And a few dozen Greeks. Crew." He mentioned the Greeks as though they were ballast. Abruptly, his expression clouded and he looked at his watch. "If we get there in time. We were already late. The sodding around with Scanlon made it worse."

Randall nodded toward the window. "This weather won't help. I thought the Mediterranean was supposed to be calm," he added disconsolately.

"Yeah. Well, it is, most of the time." O'Keefe seemed to notice Randall's pallor for the first time. "You don't look too well, Jack. D'you want to get below and try and get a couple of hours' sleep? I can take care of things here for a few hours. I'm going to be busy later on."

Randall looked up, his face a waxy mask, but did

not immediately respond. He was sick and getting worse. His stomach was a churning cocktail of bitter juices. He could hardly think straight. A lie-down was what he wanted more than anything else, but a residual shrewdness that had survived the sickness made him suspicious of something indefinable in O'Keefe's affable manner. There was a note of falseness. A tiny, prickling suspicion at the very back of his mind suggested that it was just possible O'Keefe no longer entirely trusted him, that if he went to sleep around O'Keefe he just might not wake up again.

"Thanks, Harry. The stink of diesel below'll only make me worse. I'll stay up here where I can make myself useful."

A gust of sand-laden wind almost hurled Mary back into the wheelhouse. Her knuckles were bleeding. Mike glanced up from where he was stooped over the blank radar screen.

"Okay?"

She nodded, looking ruefully at her raw knuckles. "Fine. Both lines are cast off."

As Mary spoke, the ship swayed and shuddered, responding to the wind's buffeting. The stern struck the quayside with a force that almost shook Mike off his feet. Supporting himself on the chipped instrument panel he shuffled the couple of steps to the wheel. His weakness and the unfamiliarity of the controls made him clumsy. In the now almost total darkness he could not see the quay. The stern struck twice more with a resounding grinding noise and then they were clear. He pulled the ship around, heading at what he judged to be an angle of about forty degrees to the quay. Somewhere ahead of them lay the stone pier. They moved forward very slowly. The entrance was narrow; if he misjudged the position of the pier in the blind conditions he wanted stay afloat for a second try.

The ship reared suddenly, as though struck by a tremendous blow. Immediately, the bow plunged again and spray slapped loudly against the window. Next to him, Mary staggered and grabbed at his arm, scrambling to regain her balance as the ship rolled wildly to the side. She clung to him, cursing and laughing at once.

"What the hell's that?"

Mike let his breath out in a long moan of relief, touched her hand and smiled. "The weather. That's it—we're clear. We're in the open sea." As he spoke he began hauling the ship around on to a northerly heading.

She gave him a lop-sided smile. "Great. So we're on our way. But on our way where?" She made a sweeping gesture with her arm. "There's an awful lot of sea out there."

"They're heading for Malta. So will we."

"You think they'd still go there? Knowing you know about it?"

He rammed the lever forward, opening up the engine to its fullest speed, and shrugged. "What else can we do? Whatever it is O'Keefe's got set up, it's damned important to him, so important he was in too much of a hurry to do a proper job on this ship. Okay, he tried to sink it. But he could have *really* crippled it, if he'd given himself the time. He's not a sloppy operator, Mary. It's as if he had an appointment to keep. He didn't strike me as a man to miss a meeting. Especially not if there's going to be a chance to hurt someone."

She nodded. "I'll go along with that. I've only met him a couple of times but I've never known anyone so cut out for cruelty."

"Yeah. Also, don't forget, they don't think they have to worry. Pat very likely told them he'd shot me, and they think they scuttled the ship. As far as they know we're sitting on the dockside back there. In the middle of nowhere, with no transport and no radio, in a sandstorm with night coming on. What do they have to worry about?"

She smiled up at him. "You almost convince me. Except for one little thing." She grimaced at the bodies that still lay sprawled on the floor. "The crewman that escaped. If he got back to Tripoli, or even to a phone somewhere, he's going to have reported what went on. The Libyans aren't going to like it."

"For sure. But I wouldn't worry too much about pursuit."

She stared at him. "Oh, sure. Maybe you haven't been keeping up. They took delivery of half a dozen patrol boats from the French eight or nine months ago. If they come after us with those things we'd have as much chance of outrunning them aboard a rubber duck as in this thing."

He nodded. A wave of fatigue swept him, almost putting him to sleep where he stood. He fought it off with a shake of his head. "Look, I've been around the Third World quite a bit. I've seen them with their fancy hardware. Everyone's eager to sell them their latest technological wizardry. But buying it's less than half the story. The trick's in knowing how to keep it running. By the time they've had the stuff six months none of it works, unless they've got the supplier's technicians operating it for them. And, I'm delighted to remind you, the Libyans refuse outside help. They spurn it, in the name of 'Libyanization.' Same thing they did in the oilfields a few years ago. Until the oil stopped flowing and they had to ask the Canadians to come in and get them out of the shit."

"But they've got *six* of the things."

He shook his head, exhausted. "Mary, the *British* navy can hardly muster half its boats at any one time. And that's with four hundred years of trying." He reached out and pulled her closer to the wheel. "Can you take over? Just watch the compass there. Keep us heading just west of north, like that. Unless you need me earlier wake me in an hour, will you?"

Before she had a chance to reply, he sank to the floor. He was asleep immediately, his shoulders propped against the control panel and his chin on his chest.

CHAPTER
26

RANDALL STOOD WITH HIS FEET SPREAD WIDE, GRIPPING THE wheel hard. His face was immobile, his complexion had taken on a strange, off-white tint. Sweat stood out on his forehead and under his eyes. His shirt, still carefully buttoned at the wrists, clung wetly to him. Great dark arcs showed beneath each armpit. A pool of fluid eddied around his shoes, spreading wider each time the violent pitching of the ship sent the floor lurching to impossible angles. He had fastened the door back to its fullest extent. The vile stink of the liquid still filled the wheelhouse and permeated his nostrils, making him feel still sicker. A scrap of dry bread slid around the panel in front of him. Every once in a while he bit off a piece and chewed tentatively at it, grimacing as though it were cardboard.

It had been O'Keefe's idea. It would take more than a sandstorm and a force nine gale to stop O'Keefe giving advice. Putting something into his stomach was supposed to alleviate the cramps. It was not working. He groaned as another contraction sent a pain shooting through his diaphragm, as though someone had taken a handful of his guts and squeezed. He swore miserably and spat foamy saliva onto the floor.

In the bow of the ship, in the cramped and heaving space below the foredeck, O'Keefe worked with the contented unconcern of a man who knows it's payday. The bow was taking the worst of the effects of the tremendous seas, rearing and crashing back into the troughs with sickening impact. O'Keefe whistled a tune to himself. He was crouched by the stack of explosive, in the remaining gap in the wall of packing cases. He worked rapidly and methodically, with no appearance of haste. With a pair of pliers he was cutting lengths of thin flex from a spool at his side. When he had a sufficient number he put down the pliers and began picking up detonators from the paper bag. After wiring each detonator he sat back on his haunches and studied the stack of Semtex, like a sculptor admiring his own progress, before reaching forward and pushing it into its chosen place.

He laughed to himself, a soft snuffle of amusement. The biggest bomb he had ever made up to then had been no more than five hundred pounds. It had been enough virtually to destroy a heavily fortified police post in a village down near Newry. One of the reasons he had been interested when word of Scanlon's recruitment had been reported to him was that the man knew about explosives. He had hoped for some advice. He laughed again. He would just have to do his humble best without help from the security service, or whatever the bastard had been. He resumed his whistling, pushing detonators deep into the stack. He appeared quite oblivious to the oven-like heat, the movement, the dingy light, or the oppressive stink of diesel that pervaded the ship. Like other men of his age tending their gardens, he was a simple man utterly absorbed in a simple pleasure.

When the last of the detonators was satisfactorily in

place, he gathered the ends of the wires that trailed from them and began connecting them to a set of terminals fixed to a square of plywood. That done, he bared the ends of the flex that remained on the spool and fixed it to a second set of terminals. With all the wires secure, he held the board against one of the packing cases, took up a hammer and drove home the two nails that protruded from it. Clutching the spool, he clambered laboriously to his feet. He arched his back and sighed deeply, massaging his kidneys with his free hand. "Must be getting old," he murmured to himself, with the arch lack of conviction of an in-law fishing for a compliment. He took a short step backward and stood for a few seconds with his lips pursed and his head on one side, contemplating the job he had done. He made a satisfied clicking noise with his tongue and set the spool down carefully on the greasy floor, taking care to loop the cable high over the packing cases, out of harm's way. With another deep, ironic sigh, he crouched, set his back against a crate and began heaving it into place, closing off the last gap in the wall. The Semtex now lay completely enclosed in the cases of loose metal.

Feeding cable off the spool, he made his way up the ladder and out on to the deck. Keeping his head down against the spray and the wind, he closed the door gently, taking great care not to crimp the cable. He took off the tinted glasses and pushed them into an inside pocket of his jacket. He retreated a few yards along the deck, keeping close to the rail, before pulling a short length of stiff wire from a pocket and securing the cable tightly to the rail. He continued in this way for the length of the deck, lashing the cable to the rail every two or three yards.

It was hard and dangerous. Several times, he had to throw an arm around the rail and hang on for his life as the full weight of a wave crashed on to him, almost tearing him overboard. The mixture of grease and sea water made the deck as treacherous as ice. The unsure footing and the constant, random danger from the waves obliged him to shuffle along in a deep and painful crouch. By the time he reached the wheelhouse his thighs were burning and cramped. He was soaked to the skin, with water still cascading from his clothes, and his knuckles ran with blood. He stepped backward into the wheelhouse, still whistling. Tucking the trailing cable into a corner of the threshold, he dragged the door closed. Immediately, his face crinkled in disgust. He whirled to look at Randall, fumbling his glasses back on. His eyes went from Randall's unmoving profile to the shifting, rancid pool of vomit on the floor. His lips clamped into a narrow line. He made no comment.

Randall heard the door close. He glanced around with lifeless eyes. Although O'Keefe had not uttered a word, he could feel the man's contempt like a lash. For Harry O'Keefe seasickness was just another failing, a lack of will, something he was doomed to having to put up with in people weaker than himself. Randall lurched under the impact of another contraction and spat in-expertly on to the floor. A trickle of saliva clung to his chin.

"Okay?"

As O'Keefe spoke he moved to Randall's shoulder and checked the compass for himself. He nodded, shot a fleeting glance at Randall that was almost surprise, as though he had been expecting them to be off course, and moved across to the radar. He twisted a knob. A second later the screen brightened, and the wash of the scanner beam began sweeping monotonously around it. O'Keefe stood watching intently. At each sweep of the beam the whole of the fluorescent screen glittered with a swarm of white flecks. He continued staring down, trying to dis-tinguish the one persistent spot among the mass of "clutter" that would signify pursuit.

For several minutes he remained hunched silently

over the screen. Finally, with a single curse, he reached down and flipped the apparatus off. The screen darkened.

"Nothing there?" Randall asked lifelessly.

O'Keefe grimaced. "Fuck knows. It's impossible to tell in this filth." He turned to pick up the spool of cable from where he had set it down by the door. "Just keep us on course and flat out. Do you think you can do that?"

Randall stiffened at the other man's patronizing tone. He glanced once at him over his shoulder, swallowed hard and said nothing.

Behind him, O'Keefe measured off a few yards of the cable and cut it from the spool, which he then tossed aside. He pulled out the pliers and bared the ends of the wires, then crossed to the chart locker, pulled out a drawer and produced a roll of insulating tape. Still working with the same methodical speed he had shown earlier, he taped off the bared wires and then ran the cable across the floor from the door, taping it firmly in place as he went. The last two yards he ran up on to the instrument console. He slapped a two-inch length of tape over the end to hold it there.

Returning to the chart locker, he plunged an arm in up to the elbow and ferreted for a moment beneath a stack of charts. When he turned away he held in his hand a set of nylon ropes, each fitted with a toggle arrangement, as on the guy-rope of a tent, enabling its length to be adjusted. Randall had turned his head and was watching him. With a quick smile to him that might have been encouragement and might have been mockery, O'Keefe began securing the ends of the ropes to eyehooks that had been previously set into the woodwork of the wheelhouse.

Captain Andropoulos reached for his coffee cup. He exaggerated the movement so that his cuff rode up clear of his watch, enabling him to check the time discreetly. He sighed inwardly with relief. It was approaching ten o'clock. In another few minutes he would be able to leave them to their sterile argument.

The evening had severely strained the captain's innate courtesy. It had started simply enough, with somebody asking him for a progress report on the injured boy, Jamie Pike. He had conveyed the opinion of the ship's doctor and of the nurse, to the effect that he was progressing well and would be going ashore with the rest of the children for their tour of Malta the next morning. An acid-tongued woman on his right, a lecturer in Italian history who would have preferred to conduct her entire life in Latin, had seized the opportunity to deplore the state of affairs in which it was no longer safe to walk the streets of Naples. In no time at all the conversation had somehow veered to the dilapidation of Athens. The woman and another diner, a classics master at an obscure public school who had worn the same seedy jacket to dinner every evening, had soon been competing to denigrate successive Greek governments, lamenting their failure as custodians of Greece's past, a job they seemed to feel they would have handled many times better themselves.

The captain had maintained a diplomatic silence throughout the exchanges. They had plenty of opinions of their own. The last thing either of them seemed to want to hear was the opinion of a Greek. The worst of it was, they touched a nerve; Athens was undoubtedly a mess. But he could not help wondering if they had travelled on the London Underground recently.

With an inclination of his head and a smile for the whole table, he rose to his feet. "If you will be kind enough to excuse me. I shall need to be on duty early for our arrival in Valletta. Goodnight." With another dip of his head, he turned and left the dining-room. In the corridor he paused, considering whether to pay another visit to the boy. After an instant's reflection he shrugged and turned toward his cabin. The lad was probably asleep, and the welcome the company's agent in Valletta had planned for the boy would be recognition enough for him. He reached his own cabin and let himself in silently. Smiling, he stood just inside the door and began unbuttoning his uniform jacket. Beyond the open door of the bedroom he could see the shape of the light-haired young woman's legs beneath the bedclothes, and her hands holding a book. He cast off the rest of his clothes and stood for a moment looking down at his body. It was tanned and still hard-looking, thicker in the waist than twenty years ago but without being noticeably fat. He stood a little straighter, pulling another centimeter off his stomach, and walked to the door of the bedroom.

The young woman looked up at his soft tread in the doorway. She smiled and put aside the book. Captain Andropoulos glanced at his watch and returned her smile. He would not be needed again until the pilot boat met them outside Valletta harbor, early the next morning. Apart from the unpleasantness in Naples, and the irritations of his dinner obligations, the voyage was proving perfect. Just the kind of thing he had dreamed of to see his career to a peaceful conclusion.

Mary shot anxious glances down at Mike. He had been asleep for more than an hour, and in all that time he had not moved. His face and chest glistened. Stooping, keeping one hand on the wheel, she pressed her palm to his forehead; it was burning. She hesitated another moment and then left the wheel and ran into the galley. It took her a few seconds to find a cloth and run water into an aluminum bowl. She hurried back into the wheelhouse. She was still a step from the wheel when the ship gave a tremendous sideways lurch. The entire vessel shuddered as a huge wave broke over her. Mary felt her footing going. Sprawling, she snatched at the wheel with her free hand, just saving herself from being hurled across the precipitous slope of the floor. Mike pitched to one side and rolled among the ashes of the burnt-out fire. Mary dragged herself back to her feet. A glance at the compass told her what had happened. The few moments she had been away from the wheel had been long enough for the wind to turn the ship around so that it was broadside to the huge swell. She hauled on the wheel. Twice more the ship plunged and shook under the weight of water before she managed to pull her back on course so that the waves, driven by the southerly wind, were again at their back.

Mary waited a moment, until the ship was steady on its course again, before running across to Mike. She grabbed him roughly by one wrist and, taking advantage of another roll of the ship, dragged him bodily back to where she could reach both the wheel and him. Steering with one hand and keeping her eyes on the compass, she wet the cloth and began wiping him clean. Awkwardly, she rubbed the oil and grime from his face and chest, rinsed the cloth and began dabbing at the wound. An abrupt movement of the ship made her stumble. Her weight pressed on to the injury. Mike opened his eyes, bellowing with pain. She pulled herself upright. He was staring angrily up at her, his expression empty, as though he did not know who she was. For a moment her eyes moistened. Then, gulping back the tears, she shrugged.

"You asked me to wake you."

He sat looking up at her for a moment and then broke into a laugh. She laughed with him. When he spoke, his voice grated.

"You okay?"

She nodded. "I'm still here, and I'm not seasick, if that's what you mean."

"That'll do."

He reached for the wheel and pulled himself first to

his knees and then to his feet, grimacing with the pain. His knees flexed and nearly gave way. He leaned hard against the instrument panel, breathing heavily.

She looked anxiously at him. "You going to be okay?"

He thought about it for a while. "I don't know. Give me the wheel a moment." She stepped back and let him take her place. "Right now I feel like hell. Do me a favor, will you?" She nodded. "Go and look in the cabinet over there, next to the flag locker. It's the first-aid chest. See if you can find a flat tin with some tablets in. Bring it over here."

She ran to scrabble in the chest. "There are four tins like that."

"Bring them all."

She placed the tins on the panel in front of him. They bore labels stuck over them, hand-written in Arabic. Mike's vocabulary was not sufficiently up to scratch to practice pharmacy. He prised open the tins and bent forward to examine the contents. He selected the one he wanted, took two of the six capsules that lay there and pushed them into his mouth. He swallowed and grinned at her. "They'll make a new man of me."

She was watching his face. "What the hell are they?"

"Speed."

"Amphetamine? They carry that in the *first-aid* kit?"

"That's right. Most ships used to carry them at one time. The British stopped it, made it illegal. Maybe the Libyans did, too, for all I know. But an awful lot of skippers on wrecks like this aren't that particular about that sort of thing. Fortunately." He stepped away from the wheel, indicating to her to take over. "Grab this. I'm going to try to work on the radar."

* * *

Mike emerged a second time from the engine-room carrying tools. The first time he had almost passed out on the ladder. This time the drug was in his bloodstream. He loped the few steps into the wheelhouse and resumed work on the radar. The attempt to disable it had been crude; they had just ripped away the two leads, one from the scanner, the other from the power supply. Mike had needed only to remove the housing in order to get at the terminals and reattach the leads. He selected a tiny electrical screwdriver from among the batch of tools he had just retrieved and set to work again.

"So, now why don't you tell me who you *really* are." Mary was looking across at him, smiling wryly.

He glanced up at her and then immediately back to his work. He laughed through his nose. "Yeah, why not? My name really is Mike Scanlon."

"And was Patsy Scanlon really your dad?"

He laughed again. "Uh-huh. He sure was. The old bastard."

"And all the stuff about the police killing him. Was it true, or did you make it all up?"

He looked at her from under his brows. "Are you kidding? The Birmingham police may have pulled a few stunts dealing with Republican sympathizers but killing my dad wasn't one of them. It's true that at the time a few people tried to make a big sixties thing of it, a civil rights case. Solicitors with pony tails, out to show the world that there was no difference between Birmingham, England, and Birmingham, Alabama." He shook his head, frowning, as he reached for an awkwardly placed screw. "They were a bunch of self-serving dickheads. It was all balls. Dad died the way he deserved to. Drowned in his own vomit."

She shuddered. "Yuk." She paused, concentrating on the compass as she righted the ship, which had strayed a little from their course. "Okay. So your name really is Mike Scanlon. That doesn't really answer my question." She smiled across at him. "Do you want to tell me what made you get involved in all this? Or are you a member of some kind of brotherhood, sworn to take your secret to the grave?" she asked mischievously.

He paused and looked across at her. "Are you asking as you, or as a member of M15?" His face was absolutely grave.

Her own smile faded. She kept her eyes on his for some time. "Just as me," she said, finally, in a voice not much above a whisper.

He pursed his lips, still holding her gaze. At length, he nodded, letting out his breath with a hiss. "Okay, Mary, yeah. I *will* tell you. I'd like to." There was a moment of dead silence between them as he paused, assembling his thoughts. "You remember the shoot-out last autumn? The football ground?"

She nodded, her eyes fixed on his. She still did not speak.

"They killed a woman, remember?" She nodded, almost imperceptibly. "She was mine, Mary. We were going to get married." Momentarily he turned his attention back to the radar, pulled out the screw he had been fiddling with and laid it on the floor. He turned back to her and went on speaking, his eyes again on hers. "And she was pregnant. The child was mine." She bit her lip, still not speaking. Her eyes had widened. "I decided to get back at the people who did it. That's why." He turned away and began fiddling with a wire. She was still staring at him, wide-eyed. Her face had gone quite pale, making her eyes seem unnaturally bright in the pallor. Stooped over the damaged radar, he had not seen the color drain from her face. "How about you? How does somebody from MI5 get so far into their organization?"

She was so long in answering he glanced up, preparing to repeat his question. He raised his eyebrows at the sight of her face. "Don't tell me if you don't want to.

I'm not that interested in cloak-and-dagger stuff, to tell you the truth."

She shook her head. Her voice had a faint tremor in it as she tried to laugh. "You're asking me? You got closer to the top in a few weeks than I managed to do in years."

"I was different. My background held up—and they needed an Arabic speaker. How many recruits out of the back-streets can do that? I was a gift to them. But how the hell do you get to impersonate a girl from the Catholic slums when they all know each other?"

"I wasn't impersonating one. I *am* one. I'm from Belfast. And I was born and brought up on the Falls Road."

He stared at her in genuine amazement. "What would make a Catholic girl take that kind of risk?"

She shrugged and made a face. "The truth is, I *was* IRA *before* I was MI5."

"Christ! You were a member and you changed sides? You really were taking a chance. Whatever made you do that?"

"What turned my stomach was when the killing started up again. The mainland campaigns. It was when O'Keefe started to call the tune. Up till then I'd gone along, I could see the point of it. Once O'Keefe was in control it all became senseless. Killing for its own sake. The man's mad."

"Yeah, I noticed. Why didn't you just drop out? That's what most people would have done."

She made a wry face. Her voice dropped even lower than before. "That was what I intended to do, Mike. Then I did something silly." She made a self-deprecating little gesture. "I tried to stop a killing. They were going to do a feller in, a Protestant. He was a part-timer in the UDR. I knew his daughter. She was a *friend* of mine. I managed to let him know what was going on, just enough so he could arrange things so he wouldn't be there when they hit."

"And did he?"

She shrugged and gave a bitter little laugh. "Sure. They arranged it very nicely. The Provo squad went to his house at five in the morning looking for him. He'd been called away in the middle of the night, to his mother, in the hospital. He really did have a sick mother, ninety-two years old. As the squad was piling back into their car an army patrol happened to come round the corner. They wiped out the entire squad. Three men. It was lovely. Nobody would have suspected a thing, the way they organized it."

"So, why didn't you just fade out after that?"

She gave him a long, penetrating look. "Because the British wouldn't let me, of course. Right after this happened, the same morning, they picked me up off the street. They had the UDR man in the car with them, to identify me. They took me to a house somewhere, sat me down with a cup of tea, and told me the score. Either I stayed in the movement and worked for them, or they'd put it around that I was an informer."

He stared at her for a moment and then gave a low whistle. "Oh, shit! How long ago was this?"

She shrugged. "Three years. A bit over."

He shook his head. "It must have been killing you."

She nodded. "I've been pretty scared. But, you know, I *wanted* to do it. Somebody had to stop O'Keefe. Most of the time you get used to it. The worst thing is wondering if the MI5 people will do something stupid and give you away."

"That I can believe!" As he spoke he tightened a last screw and dropped the screwdriver. He straightened. "Here goes." He turned a flat knob on the radar. The screen filled with light. He smiled his satisfaction and hunched over the glass. He watched in silence for a minute as the beam flipped around, trying to make sense of the dots that filled every inch of the screen.

A radar antenna is mounted high on a ship's superstructure. In calm weather, when the vessel is stable, it will give a picture of the surroundings so clear it can pick up a tin can floating on the water at a range of three miles. When a ship is pitching in the kind of wild weather they were going through the antenna was as likely to be looking down at the ocean floor or at the moon as at the horizon. This made it a very unreliable instrument. A sandstorm made it worse. The sand showed up like rain, an impenetrable mass of blips that masked almost anything else. Nevertheless, Mike persisted, staring at the luminescent screen. Among the clutter, at the very outer limit of the range, one dot seemed to persist, to remain on the same bearing. He watched the scanner beam through three more turns. Twice he did not pick up the dot. The third time it was back. With a curse, he flipped off the set.

Mary looked around sharply, alarmed by his cry. "What's the matter?"

"You remember what I said about their patrol boats?"

"Yes."

"I take it all back. I think one of them's after us."

"Jesus! Now what do we do?"

"Stop."

"Are you kidding?"

"No." He moved toward her as he spoke. "We stop." Under her disbelieving gaze he reached out and pulled back the lever that controlled their speed.

CHAPTER

27

RANDALL WOULD NOT HAVE BELIEVED IT WAS POSSIBLE TO feel worse than he had an hour before. Now, the constant retching and the fluid loss had left him hardly able to stand. Only his grip on the wheel kept him on his feet. The taste of bile was in his mouth the whole time, making him spit continually in the effort to free himself of it. His jowls were slack with exhaustion. Long ago, he remembered hearing tales of men pressed into service at sea who remained seasick for weeks until finally, driven mad by it, they threw themselves overboard. He had never believed the stories. He did now. He was scarcely aware of what O'Keefe was doing. He knew that he was working around him, and that he never stopped his damned whistling. Randall found the energy to resent it. O'Keefe's total calm, his imperviousness to anything except the job in hand, only heightened Randall's sense of his own inadequacy.

He moaned as another spasm racked him. It was really painful now, as if his stomach, with nothing left to get rid of, was trying to expel its own lining. He tried to spit again, only blowing saliva feebly on to his chin. It dripped down to his chest. He did not care. All his last shreds of determination were focused on one thing, to hold out for the few remaining hours until it would be over.

O'Keefe finished attaching the last of the cords to its metal eyehook and stood up. He stretched, and massaged his back. Maybe he really *was* getting too old for the game. He looked around him, appraising his work. Satisfied, he ambled across to where Randall clung to the wheel.

"How's it going, Jack? Feeling any better?"

Randall did not speak. Even in his far-gone state, he could detect the mockery in the other man's voice. He felt O'Keefe's fingers squeeze his shoulder.

"Good. You're doing great. Think you can stay awake?"

Randall nodded. O'Keefe gave his shoulder another squeeze, digging his fingers unnecessarily hard into the flesh. Randall watched out of the corner of his eye as O'Keefe moved across to the radar screen. He looked on as O'Keefe flipped the switch and stood staring down at the screen. He remained stooped over the screen for no more than thirty seconds, then swore to himself and switched it off again. Randall wondered vacantly why he did not leave it on. He did not care enough to ask.

O'Keefe turned to him, the irritation in his face giving way to a grin. "Well, nothing should be happening for a few hours. If you're okay here I think I'll get my head down for a while." With a cheerful nod to Randall he disappeared into the galley.

Mary was still staring incredulously at Mike as he ransacked the wheelhouse, searching for something.

"But what the hell have we stopped for? Aren't they coming for us?"

"I imagine so. But we can't lose them, so let's try

and confuse them." As he finished speaking he pulled a skein of thin nylon rope from a recess of the flag locker. "Got it." He pushed the rope into a pocket and lifted the rubber-clad flashlight from its wooden rack next to the wheel. He grabbed two more of the amphetamine capsules and tossed them into his mouth. He gulped them down and took Mary by the arm. "Come on."

She gave him a long look that said she suspected he had completely lost his senses, and allowed herself to be dragged to the door.

They inched their way along the deck, clinging to the rail. As the ship lost its forward momentum it was completely at the mercy of the sea and wind. The deck bucked and slewed beneath their feet. Spray and wind slashed at them. A wave smashed broadside into the helpless ship, sending it rolling through forty degrees. The rail dipped below the surface of the sea. Mary screamed as she felt herself afloat. Abruptly, the vessel righted itself, leaving her sprawling, both arms clinging tightly around the rail. Mike took a fistful of her sweater and hauled her upright.

"Come on. It's a few more feet. To the lifeboat."

They worked feverishly to release the boat, in constant danger of being swept overboard. It took them several minutes before the boat lurched free of its restraints. Mike grabbed Mary to him. Holding hard to the rail with his free hand, he shouted instructions into her ear. She watched in sheer dumb amazement as he took the nylon cord from his pocket and, wedging himself against the rail, began fumbling with a knot. It was many years since Mike had taken pride in being able to tie knots one-handed, and it took a dozen abortive tries before he got it right. With an exclamation, he got to his feet and looped the line over Mary's head. He settled it close under her armpits and drew it tight through the running bowline he had made. He pulled hard on the line to test the knot.

"Ah!" She yelped in pain. "That hurts!"

"Not as much as drowning," he laughed. "Shut up and get in the boat!"

Smiling, she jabbed her middle finger upward at him in an obscene gesture and allowed him to bundle her into the crazily swinging lifeboat. He lashed the free end of the line to the rail and began lowering the boat. It struck the water with a sickening jolt. Mary lay for an instant in the bottom, recovering her breath, her arms wound tightly around a seat. Above her, the ship's side rose in a sheer, black mass, shifting and wallowing and threatening at any second to crush the tiny lifeboat. The beam of the flashlight slashed through the darkness. She pulled herself to her knees and set to work, moving with the desperate efficiency of terror. Following Mike's instructions, she raised the short aluminum mast. Satisfied it was firmly in its footing, she crawled to the stern and started the motor. Hauling on the nylon cord and pushing with her feet, she maneuvered the boat so that its bow pointed at an angle, away from the hull of the ship. With a deep intake of breath, she engaged the motor. The lifeboat jerked forward, heading clear of the ship. Clinging tightly to the cord, Mary let herself trail over the stern and into the sea.

Mike saw the boat slide away. He craned over the rail in panic, forgetting the danger, as Mary's head disappeared momentarily beneath the black water. It surfaced again not more than a foot from the plunging side of the ship. Jamming the lamp into a pocket, he dropped to his knees so that the rail was jammed under his armpits and began hauling on the rope.

The cord bit into Mary's flesh. Above her the line was too thin to offer any real purchase to her wet hands. At one moment she was half out of the sea, with her weight dragging the rope taut, the next she was back in over her head as the ship wallowed and dipped. Each time she fell back into the water she felt the line tighten as Mike used the chance to reel in the slack.

The ship rolled to starboard, dragging her clear of the sea. She found herself almost lying on her back against the rough metal of the hull. As the ship continued its dizzying roll, she writhed on to her face. The cord cut deep clefts in her fingers as she worked herself into a kneeling position. With a single enormous effort, she pushed herself to her feet. She was standing on the ship's side, leaning at an angle of forty-five degrees over the boiling sea. With Mike taking most of her weight, she began walking up the side. She was only four steps from the top when, with sickening suddenness, the ship plunged back into a trough. Her stomach churned as the hull beneath her twisted through ninety degrees, swinging the ship hard over on to its port side. Her feet fell away from the metal. She dangled in mid-air, clinging desperately to the cord above her head, spinning like a corpse on a gibbet.

Above her, Mike clung with all his remaining strength to the cord, hardly able to hold the dead weight of her. With another sickening rush, the ship fell back under the impact of the following wave, slamming Mary back against the steel side. She took the force of the impact on the soles of her feet and her shoulders, like a wrestler hitting the mat. Flipping herself over on to her knees, she scrambled up the last two feet. Mike's arms closed around her and dragged her bodily back aboard.

They fell to the deck and lay there, gasping for breath. Blood ran from a cut on her left hand where the cord had sawn through the skin. Her knuckles were bloodied and skinned. Mike recovered first, pushed himself to his knees and began unfastening the end of the cord from the rail. He stood up and grinned down at the panting Mary.

"Come on."

She lay with her face upturned, staring at him. In

the darkness she could not see the grin. Only something in his voice alerted her.

"Come on *where*?"

"To do the second boat."

She dragged herself back over the rail and dropped, spent, to sit on the deck beside Mike. Her hands and the whole left side of her face were flayed from the friction of the corroded metal of the hull. She slumped against Mike, soaked and trembling. The sound of the second boat's motor was already lost on the wind.

"How did I do?"

He tightened his arm around her shoulders, pulling her head to his chest. "Great." He smiled into her up-turned face. "We make a terrific team."

She let her head fall back against his skin. "M'mm. What does the team do next?"

"Get back in the dry."

They crawled back to the shelter of the wheelhouse. Mike made immediately for the controls, opened the engine up fully and pulled the ship back once again on to its heading. "Let's hope it works."

"Now I'm back alive, what exactly was it all supposed to do?" Mary asked.

He turned to answer her. She was naked but for a pair of soaked white briefs. Her jeans and a brassiere lay at her feet. She was intent on wringing water from her sweater. The grace of her movement caught at his throat, silencing him. He watched the minute flexings of her thighs, the tightening of the ridges of muscle that formed a channel up her spine, and felt himself touched by a sudden stillness, an unutterable tenderness, that drove all thought of their situation momentarily from his mind.

His continuing silence made her look up at him. As her eyes fell on his, the query that had been in her face fell slowly away. Her hands were stilled in mid-gesture, her elbows still cocked in the act of wringing out the sweater. They remained like that for a further second, silent and immobile. Mike swallowed and spoke. His voice was husky.

"Do you know anything about radar?"

Her eyes remained on him, her expression at first unchanged. Then, very gradually, a smile seemed to flower on her face. She slowly shook her head. "Uh-uh. From the Falls Road, remember?"

He laughed and nodded, still disconcerted. "Right. Well, first of all, it's an over-rated invention. If that was a Libyan patrol boat they might well not have seen us. In this weather it's a stroke of pure luck to find anything our size over a distance of more than about three miles. We probably only picked *them* up because they've got so much height on their superstructure."

She made a face. "I still don't see the point of launching the lifeboats. Not unless we'd got into one."

"No? Look, at the top of each of those masts you just almost drowned putting up is a radar reflector. If they did get a trace of us and come this way then there's a good chance they'll start picking up the lifeboats. That'll give them three options instead of just one."

"Does it make a difference, with the speed of a patrol boat?"

"A lot, believe me. The geometry of it's working for us. By the time they check out our two decoys we'll be so far out of Libyan waters I don't think they'd dare chase us. They'd be too nervous of running into trouble with the American fleet."

"I hope you're right. Now what do we do about finding O'Keefe and Randall? Or Malta, for that matter."

"If we find Malta we find them. And finding Malta's easy."

"Without charts?"

"Uh-huh. We've been heading seven degrees west of

north since we left the coast. We know Malta's about a
hundred and fifty miles almost due north of Tripoli."

"We do?"

"We do! I do, anyway. Our top speed in this
weather's about eleven knots. Say, twelve and a half
miles an hour. So after, let's say, ten hours we turn east
for an hour or so. Then north again. Then east, and so
on."

She was smiling at him in disbelief. "Are you making this up?"

"No. It's the Chichester technique. Or my version
of it."

"The what?"

"The Chichester technique. Francis Chichester. Remember him? He used it to sail single-handed to Hawaii
or some other God-forsaken pin-point in the Pacific
without navigation aids."

"Did he get there?"

"Right on time."

"He must have been nuts."

"A complete fruitcake! But don't knock it. He's going to find O'Keefe for us."

Twenty miles to the south-west a tall, slender young
man stood on the bridge of the narrow, camouflage-
painted patrol boat. He spoke excitedly in Arabic into a
telephone. He had fine, smooth features and thick, wiry
black hair that welled exuberantly around the peaked
uniform cap that sat pushed far back on his head. He
wore a sharply pressed short-sleeved khaki shirt with the
shoulder flashes of a lieutenant. He finished speaking
and listened for thirty seconds, then with a final acknowledgement he replaced the radio-telephone. His
eyes glittered as he turned to the two men who stood by
him.

"That was Major Jalloud. The Colonel is returning
to Tripoli. He will speak to us himself very shortly. It

seems that the Colonel is very anxious that we should succeed, whatever the cost. Those were Major Jalloud's exact words. He was quoting the Colonel." He looked at each of the men in turn. The excitement that shone in their faces reflected his own. "Don't let us fail them, gentlemen."

One of the men moved away to lean over a chart laid out on a table against one wall of the bridge. He stabbed a finger at a line drawn on the chart in transparent yellow marker. The line ran from their own position to a point to the north-east of them. The man looked up at the captain.

"The transmission was from somewhere on this axis, Captain."

The captain nodded, moving closer to the chart table. "At what distance?"

The man looked embarrassed. "Impossible to say, sir. It was only there for a very short time, too brief to allow me to get a fix. And very near the limit of the range."

The captain frowned. Doubt flickered in his eyes. "But you're absolutely *sure* it was a radar emission? With the Colonel taking such a close personal interest it would not be admissible that we make any mistake. H'mm?"

The officer shook his head vigorously. "No, there's no mistake, sir. Of course, we have no way of knowing whether the vessel is one of those we are looking for."

"But they used the radar for only a few seconds. They aren't transmitting now?"

"That's correct, sir. Or, at least, we are not in contact."

The captain turned to stare through the big window. His legs were set wide against the exaggerated movement of the tall bridge. Below him the sleek bow threw fluorescent plumes aside as it carved through the heaving sea. Spray flew against the window as a wave crashed against the torpedo housings on the foredeck.

"So, whoever it is, they're afraid of pursuit. It's somebody who knows that their own radar transmissions can be picked up by our scanner." He looked around at his two officers. Very slowly, he smiled. *"Ya'aala."* Smiling coolly, he repeated himself in English. "Let's go."

CHAPTER
28

MARY HELD THE WHEEL TIGHTLY. WIND DROVE SAND IN swirls around the wheelhouse, and her eyes were sore and bloodshot from the lashing of the grit and from fatigue. She did not care—the door stayed propped wide open. She preferred the wind to being shut in with the stink of the dead sailors who had soiled themselves in death. It was after midnight, and it had been a very long day. She looked down at Mike. He lay with his shoulders propped against the flag locker. His eyes were closed. Blood smeared his naked torso. She glanced at the dressing on his ribs. It was clean. The blood was from the floor, the blood of the murdered crewmen.

With a frisson, she forced herself to look across at the corpses. They still lay in the same grotesque tangle. She shivered again. In the years since she had first become involved with the Provos she had often been present when killings were planned. On the insistence of her MI5 superiors she had more than once been the driver for what the Provos jokingly referred to, always in a mock-British accent, as a "shooting party" in which the targets were off-duty policemen or officials. Orders or not, she had always contrived not to be in at the kill, and until that afternoon she had never seen a corpse. The most upsetting thing was the sheer ordinariness of it. They did not die spread-eagled in dramatic, biblical poses. They lay awkwardly, with limbs twisted at graceless, uncomfortable angles. Their faces, devoid of expression, were no longer handsome or ugly, but simply uninteresting. She looked away with another shiver. It was so ugly and cheap and pointless.

"Penny for your thoughts."

She turned sharply. Mike was smiling softly up at her. She returned the smile, slowly, taking time to return from contemplation of the deaths. Her face was pallid. "I thought you were asleep."

He got to his feet, and moving to her side he laughed and shook his head. "Sleep? After these?" He took up the tin with its remaining pills from where it lay in front of her and rattled it. "I was just resting. And trying to figure out what we do next."

"I thought you always knew."

He responded with a mock sour grimace. "I'm going below to see if there's anything in the armory we could use."

"Against a patrol boat?"

He glanced at the watch on his wrist. "Look, if my reckoning's right we're closer to the Maltese or the Tunisian coast than the Libyan. With the possibility of the Americans in the area I just can't see a Libyan warship coming any further."

"And if they don't agree with your analysis?"

"We're screwed. If that was a patrol boat and they find us there won't be a thing we can do. I'm trying to not even think about it. But maybe there's something that might stop O'Keefe, if we can get near enough."

He made his way carefully down the ladder. The amphetamine was keeping him in a false state of alertness. He had to fight to counter it, to remember how close to collapse he really was. Making himself move slowly, he advanced to the tiny cabin that housed the armory.

He examined the rack of rifles. To him, they all looked the same; short, easily carried, infantry weapons. Weapons for the soldiers of rich countries, designed to throw huge amounts of metal in the general direction of targets you could not even see. There was no sign of anything with the telescopic sight that might have given someone with no expertise, like himself, some chance of picking off a target at a distance.

He turned his attention to a steel chest that lay in a corner. It was fixed to the wall with sturdy metal brackets and fastened with a heavy padlock. He thought for a moment before snatching one of the rifles from the rack. He stooped and found a box of ammunition in the place he had previously found the pistol bullets. He loaded the rifle quickly, grateful for having learned at least that during his few hours in the training camp. When he had pushed a handful of shells into the magazine he turned to the chest and dropped to one knee. He aligned the gun so that the barrel pointed parallel to the front of the chest, its muzzle an inch from the heavy padlock. With his teeth clenched, he settled the gun closer against his shoulder, pulled the trigger and held it until it stopped firing.

The noise in the confined metal-walled space was more than he could have imagined. His head rang for several seconds. When it cleared, he lowered the gun and looked at the chest. Where the hasp had been was a mess of bright-edged grooves and ripped metal. The smashed lock lay on the floor three feet away. He threw down the gun and raised the lid. He snatched away the layers of oiled kraft paper that lay on the top, and revealed a layer of carefully packed rockets, each gleaming darkly under its film of oil. He laid the rockets on the floor, delved further, and pulled out two heavy objects, three feet long and swathed in canvas. He ripped off the canvas from one of them, disclosing the unmistakable tubular shape of a rocket launcher. He wedged three of the rockets tail-down into the waistband of his fatigue trousers. Bending awkwardly, he gathered the launcher and the rifle under his arm, slipped the remainder of the carton of bullets into his pocket and headed for the ladder.

The captain of the patrol boat cursed the weather aloud. Here, so far from the coast, the sandstorm, and the wind on which it was carried, had begun to abate. The sea had not. Even with them both at their back the patrol boat wallowed and rolled atrociously, bucking and writhing like a maddened animal. The boat was built for speed in calm coastal waters; it had never been conceived as a warship for duty on the open seas. The bridge, set high above the narrow deck, swayed and trembled with a crazed unpredictability that forced the men on it to keep a grip of something solid or be thrown to the floor. The window in front of the captain was opaque with spray. A shout from one of the crew made his head jerk around.

"What?"

"Something there, Captain." The man was hunched low over his screen, squinting. In his excitement he did not look up at the captain, but simply jabbed a finger repeatedly at the screen, as though that were indication enough.

"What? On what bearing?" the captain snapped.

There was a short silence. "North, twenty-three degrees west." The voice paused again. "But I'm not sure. Damn! It's gone! It was there. I'm sure. It's so difficult."

"Imbecile! Here!" The captain motioned to another young uniformed man to take the wheel. He pushed the operator at the radar screen roughly aside. "Show me!"

The man prodded at the screen again. The area he indicated showed as a dense cloud of white spots which flickered to life as the beam passed over them. The captain stared at the fading after-images. The beam passed again. Again the cloud gleamed briefly. He watched for another dozen sweeps, never taking his eyes from the screen, never blinking.

"There!" He pointed to a spot in the top left part of the screen. He kept his finger there. For several more sweeps the two men watched in silence. The other man reacted first.

"That's it! There is something out there, Captain."

The captain was already hauling himself back to take the wheel. "Give me the bearing! Quickly!" As he spoke he eased the two throttle levers forward, piling on as much extra speed as he dared. The bow of the patrol boat reared under the extra thrust and the vessel surged forward, leaping the vast troughs.

The captain stared anxiously down at the deck. Armed sailors lined the bow, secured by harnesses clipped to a line that ran around the rail. A battery of powerful searchlights swept the sea around the patrol boat, which was moving very slowly now, twisting and thrashing among the waves. The troughs were deep enough to conceal a house. He saw an officer on the deck below him raise a walkie-talkie to his lips. The voice squawked from a receiver at the captain's elbow. He squinted out into the illuminated area of sea, following the direction in which the man was pointing. It was several seconds before he caught the brief flash of metal above the wave-tops. He swung the wheel, bringing the ship around. With a word to the officer at his side, the captain pulled on an oilskin cape and hurried from the bridge.

He made his way sure-footedly along the deck to join the man with the radio. Together, they leaned on the rail, straining for a further sighting. The patrol boat rose on a wave and hung there for an instant. Below them a lifeboat sat in the trough. It was wallowing, full almost to the gunwales with sea water. It was moving, pushing laboriously through the swell, leaving hardly any wake on the rolling sea. The captain took the walkie-talkie and spoke into it. They closed on the lifeboat. The sailors, at a command from the officer, readied their weapons. They came alongside. The captain looked down into the tiny boat. Objects floated between the seats; otherwise it was quite empty. He swore fiercely, whirled around and strode back toward the bridge.

Mike re-entered the wheelhouse and dumped the firearms on to the floor. His breath was coming in short gasps. He squatted beside the weapons, with Mary looking anxiously down at him, and waited until his chest stopped heaving. Moving slowly, he loaded the rifle, filling the magazine with as many bullets as it would hold. That done, he took up the rocket launcher, and examined it, trying to work out how to use it. He had often seen them on the news in years past, in film from Afghanistan or Beirut, but he had never been remotely close to one. But if Afghan guerrillas could do it, then it was not likely to be beyond him. It took him twenty seconds to figure it out. Satisfied, he stood up and carried the weapons to the empty chart locker. He pulled out a drawer, laid them carefully inside and closed it. In the drawer they were handy but safe from being tossed around by the ship's movement. He walked over to join Mary.

"You okay?"

She kneaded an eye with the backs of her fingers and yawned. "M'mm. Oh, God, yeah. Dog-tired but okay. But what I still don't understand is how we're going to *find* those bastards. Surely, they could be anywhere at all out there."

His face clouded. He was looking somewhere beyond Mary. "They could be," he said, hardly moving his lips. "But I hope they aren't. Not after I've come this far for them." He caught her looking at him. There was a moistness around her eyes that had nothing to do with the strain or the fatigue. He laid a hand very gently on the back of her neck, touching the damp, dust-coated hair. He made a wry face. "Sorry, Mary, I was somewhere else for a moment there. Why don't you let me do this for a while? Try and get a little sleep."

O'Keefe jerked upright, suddenly wide awake. He sat immobile for a moment, listening, in the habit formed over half a lifetime, for the sound of trouble. Hearing nothing but the vibration of the engine, he relaxed. He got up and moved to the sink, splashed water on his face and ran wet hands over his hair. He filled a grimy glass with water from a jug in the refrigerator, drank it off, and walked into the wheelhouse to rejoin Randall. He flinched at the stink. Randall still stood motionless, exactly as he had left him almost two hours earlier.

O'Keefe yawned extravagantly. "M'mmm. I needed that. You ought to do the same."

Randall stayed silent. O'Keefe shrugged, half-smiling at Randall's surliness; it was like working with a fucking zombie. But he was getting used to it. He walked over to the radar screen, moving with a new bounce since his sleep, put a hand flat on each side of the console and spread his feet. He peered down at the screen. There was a lot less interference. Come to think of it, the sea seemed to have lost some of its violence. He glanced over at Randall.

"Hey, Jack, you're in luck. I think it's calming down." Randall turned his head and gave him a look of unutterable misery. O'Keefe laughed and turned back to the screen. He stiffened. His head sank two inches closer to the bright circle of glass and he stared at it for some time. He shot Randall a strange look. Then he turned away from the screen and walked back into the galley. He stood there, chewing his lip and swearing softly, until he had counted off fifteen minutes on his watch. He returned to the radar screen. "Fuck it!" He looked once at Randall and then turned immediately back to the screen. "Fuck it! Fuck it! Fuck it! Fuck it! Fuck it!" His voice had risen to a shout.

The strength of his anger penetrated even Randall's torpor. He looked around from beneath sagging eyelids. "What?" he asked, tonelessly.

O'Keefe shot him a look of pure venom. In the rush to get away he had sent Randall to cripple the other ship. He swore again. For the first time in years he had abandoned the principle that had done so much to keep him a free man for so long. He had entrusted somebody else with a job he should have taken care of himself. He looked again at Randall. He let all the rage, disdain, and finally, utter hatred which he felt, fill his face. Randall flinched under the impact, drawing his head back into his shoulders.

In the fifteen minutes O'Keefe had let pass, fretting in the galley, the spot on the screen had drawn closer by what he judged to be about a mile. A patrol boat would have been overhauling them much faster. There was no doubt in his mind. There was hardly any traffic between that part of North Africa and Malta. It was Scanlon and that poisonous little bitch of a woman!

"You fucking idiot," he articulated, hardly above a whisper. "You utter fucking, vain little prick!" Randall's only response was to blink stupidly. O'Keefe jabbed a finger at the screen. "It's them, you useless, brainless git. They're coming after us."

The captain of the patrol boat cursed Ireland. He cursed all the people of Ireland. He cursed the ancestors of the Irish. And he cursed their unborn children. The second lifeboat had been empty, too. He stood with the radio-telephone in his hand, drumming his other fist against his thigh. He had been waiting like that for twenty minutes. A voice sounded in the receiver, harsh and angry. The captain stiffened and cupped his free hand around the instrument, as though trying to contain the other man's words, to limit their effect.

"Do you hear me, cousin?"

The captain nodded vigorously. "Yes, Colonel. Yes, I hear you very well."

"Answer me then, if you aren't dumb! Have you found the treacherous dogs?"

The captain shot a worried glance at his radar officer. The man looked away. The captain wet his lips. "No cousin, Colonel. Not yet."

"What! Jalloud told me, assured me, you were tracking them. Was it not so?"

The captain grimaced. "We hoped it was so, Colonel. What we found were decoys. They had put out their lifeboats. I'm afraid we have lost them, Colonel."

The room from which the Colonel spoke was a sparsely furnished room in an air force barracks in Benghazi. The only furniture in the room was a desk and a chair. A piece of telex paper with six inches of text on it lay on the desk. The Colonel was alone. He paced from end to end of the room as he spoke, his brown woolen robe swirling as he turned. In one hand he held the telephone, in the other a photograph, the one Mike had handed him in the desert, the portrait of the girl O'Keefe and the Turks had kidnapped in Hamburg. Tears ran down the Colonel's face. His voice was hoarse with grief and rage.

"Lost them? You tell me you have lost them? You are my cousin. My own family. My own flesh. You are supposed to be the best officer we have, not a whimpering fool. Our people make sacrifices. We buy the finest equipment, the latest boats for our navy. And the fools, the imbeciles, who wish to call themselves crew, cannot catch a thirty-year-old coaster in an empty sea? These are not common thieves we have sent you to find, cousin. They are enemies of our people. Enemies of our flesh. They have taken our trust and betrayed it. We must have them. Do you not have some idea where they are headed? Are you, too, going to betray the people's trust, my dear cousin?"

The threat of the last words was so blatant the captain gulped audibly. "No, Colonel, of course not. They must have been heading north. They could be trying for Italy. Sicily, perhaps. Or maybe Malta."

"Then that is where you must look, cousin. You know how to do these things. Or were your years in Bremerhaven spent *only* with girls?"

The heavy sarcasm stung the captain. "No, cousin. I studied hard, and the Germans taught me and the others well. But, with respect, cousin, we are far to the north already. There are American warships on exercises in the area."

"Woman! Have you encountered American ships?"

"No, Colonel. We have seen nothing. But it is quite possible they have seen us. It is quite possible they have watched us since we left port. They may very well be listening to us now. Who knows what they might do if we disobey the warning they gave."

"I do not want to hear about their warning. Are you listening, Americans?" The Colonel had raised his voice until he was shouting into the phone. He spoke English, almost without accent. "I care nothing for your warnings!"

The captain was surprised to hear a hint of a catch in the Colonel's voice, like a choked-off sob. He started as the Colonel again began addressing him, his voice high with anger. "These people *must* be caught. Do you understand me? You are an officer. You must do whatever is necessary. Anything, do you understand me?"

His voice lowered suddenly, became totally matter-of-fact. "If not you will be shot."

In the empty office the Colonel threw the phone down on to the desk. With anguish in his face, he took up the telex message and read it through again. The flow of tears increased as he read. Finally, he let the message flutter out of his hand to the floor. He raised the photograph and stared at it again. The poor girl was dead. The German police had traced the kidnappers' camper. They had found it at a campsite near the Dutch border. There had been gunfire. Two Turkish immigrants had died. And the girl. He sank slowly to the floor and sat cross-legged. His face contorted, he put the photograph to his lips. He began to cry aloud; huge, retching sobs.

The captain continued holding the phone to his ear for several seconds. The men on the bridge were all being careful to avoid his eyes. At length, he thrust the phone at a young officer. "Give me all the speed you can. We will begin with a box fifty kilometers north and twenty east of here."

It was almost three hours since they had launched the lifeboats, and in that time the weather had improved dramatically. Mike had the wheel. Mary emerged from the galley, carrying two glasses filled with thick black coffee. She handed one to Mike, standing at his elbow.

"What's happening?"

He sipped at the coffee. She had sugared it heavily, Arab style. Normally, the taste of sugar made him grimace. Now, he was glad of the energy. He nodded at the compass. "We're heading east. Another ten minutes and we should turn north again."

"Chichester style?" she asked, mischievously.

"Right. Don't knock it."

"Who's knocking? What happens after we change course?"

"We'll just keep heading north."

"Shouldn't we try the radar? See if we can pick up O'Keefe and Randall?"

He shook his head. "Not yet. The Libyans might still be close enough to pick up the signal. We'll give it another hour."

"And in the meanwhile?"

Something in her tone made him look sharply around at her. She was smiling mischievously. She was still naked except for the white cotton pants.

"Hell, Mary," he said, smiling and shaking his head in disbelief. "There are people out there trying to *kill* us."

She shrugged and gave a theatrical pout of disappointment, then broke into a sly smile.

"Precisely. If these are my final moments, shouldn't you help me make the most of them?"

CHAPTER

29

"**D**AMN THE BITCH! DAMN SCANLON! DAMN THOSE witless bastards in Dublin!" O'Keefe turned away from the screen and strode restlessly to the door. He beat futilely on the glass with the side of his fist. "I should have done the whole thing myself. I should have known! As soon as I let those stupid fuckers over there in on the thing they screw it up. Damn them all!" He was speaking to himself, not to Randall, spitting the words in a barely audible stream, his face inches from the glass of the window.

"Come on, Harry. Is it that bad? We'll be at Valletta in under three hours now the weather's improved."

O'Keefe looked around quickly at Randall. It was the first real sentence he had put together for several hours. "The weather's not the only thing that seems to have improved!" O'Keefe looked at his watch. He had been looking at it constantly for the last half an hour, since their pursuers had turned north. "Yeah, it is that bad. And worse than that. They turned north a while ago. They must have picked us up. Since then they've been closing on us."

"How's that? I thought you told me this ship had an up-rated motor. We're supposed to be able to out-run an ancient tub like that, you said."

"Thanks for reminding me—so we should. Except half the ships in this area have been converted for the cigarette-smuggling racket. If the Libyans have been earning pin money on the Spanish cigarette run then they can probably get fifteen knots out of that thing. Of course, if it had been scuttled properly, the way it was supposed to have been, they wouldn't be getting *any- thing* out of it, would they?"

Randall flinched. "Oh Christ, Harry, that's right. Everything's my fault." There was a whine in his voice. "It wasn't me that asked to have the Brit bastard, Scan- lon, sent over to help, though, was it?"

O'Keefe made as though to answer and then gave up the idea and made do with a look of purest con- tempt. He turned back to study the screen, stared down and for the fiftieth time calculated their chances. It was not quite as bad as he was telling Jack Randall. In an- other hour and a half they would be around the eastern- most extremity of Malta, Delimara Point. Once behind that they would be able to stay close to the curve of the coast, virtually invisible to their pursuers. Half an hour more would bring them to the entrance to Valletta har- bor. The way it looked, they would be only minutes early for their rendezvous. Scanlon and the girl did not know the name of the ship. Even if they found some way of alerting the Maltese authorities, without knowing that, or what their intentions were, that few minutes would be all he needed.

Once they struck, the confusion would make it easy enough for them to get ashore, pick up the car and drive the few miles to Saint Paul's Bay. There, they would board the rented launch that lay ready. By noon they would be in Sicily. Come evening, they would be back home in their anonymous, suburban Dutch flats, watching what they had done on the television news. By tomorrow morning the Provos' struggle would once again be front-page news. And not just in Britain, but all over the world.

Never again would the British dare to cut down Nationalists in cold blood. After today, their own public opinion would never stand for it. The complacent British public, with their mortgages and their fitted kitchen units and their winter evenings spent hunched over their holiday brochures, would find out that their children, too, were vulnerable; as vulnerable as the three Ulster schoolgirls shot down by the SAS in Irvinestown last Christmas. By mistake! Thinking the girls were an active service unit. They had enlisted the entire British media establishment to persuade the public that the girls had been shot in a Nationalist feud. The publicity machine had really rolled for them. And it had worked—everyone in England had swallowed it. And everyone in Ireland knew the truth. He grinned to himself, still facing the window. This time the publicity machine would be rolling the other way.

Still grinning, he turned to Randall. "Glad you're feeling better. You must be looking forward to a nice boat trip to Sicily."

Randall gave him a brief, malevolent stare and remained silent.

The steward placed the tray on the low table with a carefully calculated clatter. Alongside the coffee jug stood two cups. The steward had worked for the captain for a long time. They knew each other's habits. He glanced through the half-open door to the bed beyond. At the sound of the tray being put down, the captain's big, squarish head rose from among the deep pillows and turned toward the steward. He gave the man a lazy grin and a slow wink. The steward returned the grin and padded out of the room.

The captain slipped from the bed and walked naked across to the table. He filled two cups, returned to the bedroom and sat down on the edge of the bed. The woman stirred softly and opened her eyes, squinting in the light of the bedside lamp. Groaning jokily, she put a hand around the captain's waist and pulled herself upright. She took the cup of coffee he offered, drank some off gratefully, and turned to look at the clock on the bedside locker.

"Five o'clock!" Her voice was a mock croak of horror.

He knew what she meant. They had made love until long into the night. It had been after three when they had finally gone to sleep, and at his age two hours sleep was just not enough.

"You're not getting up? I thought we weren't supposed to dock for ages yet."

He looked down at her over his coffee cup. The flesh around his eyes crinkled in a laugh. "Another two hours. But there are a few things I have to do before that. I'm needed on the bridge."

She put down her cup and sank back luxuriantly into the pillows. She reached up and twined her hands around the back of his neck. "Up there you have officers to do things for you. Down here there are things to do that only you are required for, Captain." As she spoke she hung her weight around his neck and arched an eyebrow mischievously.

He looked down into the laughing face. It was his custom to give himself plenty of time in the mornings, and by now he knew that she knew it. They were still quite a way off Valletta. His people knew the approach like the backs of their hands. It was deep water all the way, without an obstacle. The first mate had the bridge. He was an excellent man, and he knew the captain from way back. He made allowances for the weaknesses of late middle age. The captain had already promised himself that his day in Grand Harbor would be a lazy one. The children would be off the boat early and not back until late, spending the entire day visiting the island. He was going to have to put in an appearance at the welcome for the boy. Apart from that, he would have the day to himself, free to spend it in his cabin, if he wished, catching up on the sleep he had missed. The woman's weight on his neck increased as she arched herself playfully upward. His smile brightened. He let his empty cup drop to the carpet and fell gently on to her.

"Fifteen kilometers, Captain. Less than thirty minutes."

The Libyan captain nodded. "Excellent. Lieutenant Jarmila will prepare his men."

The officer, three or four years older than his captain, saluted and spoke excitedly into a microphone.

The boat sliced through the swell, heading northwest. They had been patrolling for two hours, sailing first directly north, then east, south again for ten kilometers, back west again, and then once again northward. Almost an hour ago they had made their first definite radar contact. Out at the very limit of the range of their apparatus, over forty miles away, a vessel was sailing north. The blip that showed on their radar, together with the dotted trace of its radar emission, showed a slow-moving vessel heading directly toward Malta. They were overhauling it at better than thirty kilometers an hour.

The captain did not move from his position. He stood staring through the toughened, smoky glass at the luminescent white flecks on the sea ahead, listening as the officer, perched on the padded edge of the high stool, with his head bowed over the radar, called the bearing and distance of the target. At ten kilometers the captain got his first sight of their quarry, a momentary glimpse of a light above the waves.

Somebody on the ship must have become aware of them, too. The radar operator called out excitedly. It had changed course and had begun sailing west. The captain twitched the wheel, bringing the patrol boat swinging to close with their target.

"Sir?" A young man, no more than nineteen years old, was looking at him. He nodded, giving permission to speak. "We will not approach close to them?"

The captain frowned at the note of anxiety in the young man's voice. "Of course we shall. Why do you ask such a foolish question, Jamil?"

The young man picked at a fingernail. "Sir, the ship is one of our own merchant ships. The people on it have had many hours to examine it. They will surely have found the armory. They will have weapons, sir. They will have the rockets."

The captain had been about to sneer at the young man. His expression altered abruptly. He stared ahead, pensive. Not a man on the ship had ever been involved in any hostile action. Their experience amounted to patrolling the waters off Tripoli and Benghazi, familiarization with the ship's systems and target practice on hulks. Nobody had ever been on the hulks to fire back. The patrol boats were fast, heavily armed and dangerous, effective against the lightly armed smugglers they were intended to combat. But their thin aluminum hulls would be extremely vulnerable to weaponry designed to penetrate tank armor. Without looking again at the young man, the captain gave an order.

They were seven kilometers from the target when he spoke again. A second later he watched as two puffs of white smoke issued prettily from two batteries of tubes mounted on the foredeck. The two French-made missiles, each the size of a man's leg, seemed to hang for a moment in the glow of the floodlights that lit the deck, before accelerating away to become bright specks in the darkness.

The two quick orange flashes of the exploding missiles flared and died, to be replaced by a duller, steadier glow. The brightness grew as fire took hold. At a word from the captain, the patrol boat advanced on the burning ship, trapping it in a blaze of searchlights. It was listing heavily to port, its deck already partly awash. Men scrambled down the sloping side of the vessel toward a lifeboat that hung half out of the water. The stern of the vessel was in full view, illuminated by the powerful lights, and the name of the vessel was visible, written in Roman script. Its port of registration, clearly legible beneath the name, was Tunis.

The captain made a sound that was almost a whimper. It was not the Libyan vessel they had been seeking. On his orders they had just crippled an innocent cargo ship trading out of neighboring Tunisia. The captain chewed noisily at a thumbnail. There was already a lot of friction between the two countries, arising from their long-running territorial disputes. He stared at the sinking ship, watching the men scrabbling toward the tossing lifeboat. He could see their faces clearly as they stared toward his vessel. One of the men raised a fist and appeared to shout at them. They could not hear his words, only see the anger in the face. The captain stopped chewing his nail and muttered something. One of the officers looked around at him unbelievingly.

"Sir?"

"You heard me. Proceed."

Still staring incredulously at the captain, the man spoke into his hand-held radio. Down on the deck the officer supervising the men turned to look up at the bridge. The man with the radio spoke again. Below them, the officer shouted an order. The sailors lining the rail opened fire. A minute later there was no more movement on the wreck. One body lay half out of the lifeboat. The others had disappeared, swept away by the waves. Another prolonged burst of fire sent splinters flying from the lifeboat. The corpse jerked foolishly. Finally, the lifeboat slid beneath the surface, leaving the riddled body floating, a pale stain on the black sea.

The captain turned away. Tears ran down his cheeks. He was shaking. "We shall go north. Directly to Valletta. My cousin has commanded it." His voice was quavering. "We must do as the Revolution calls us to do."

O'Keefe had recovered his calm. The mass of Malta filled the left-hand half of the screen ahead of them. Delimara Point was thirty minutes away. Already, other vessels dotted the screen. Once around the Point, there would be nothing that the girl and Scanlon could do to stop them. The five miles that separated them might as well have been fifty miles.

He smiled to himself. From Delimara Point he had timed the run a dozen times. He knew to the second how long it would take from rounding the headland to slipping into the entrance to Grand Harbour. The pursuing ship would be no more than an inconvenience. They would have a few minutes to wait. In ideal circumstances he would have wanted to spend them outside the harbor. Now they would have to lurk inside, which might attract the attention of the Maltese harbor authorities. It did not really matter. By the time they got around to investigating, in their easy-going way, the whole operation would be over.

Mike craned forward, straining to penetrate the darkness ahead of him. He was muttering to himself, willing the ship to greater speed. Frustration and anger boiled in him. To the east, the black of the sky was tinged with grey. It was a quarter of an hour since he had seen the first clustered pin-points of light ahead of him that signaled the scattered settlements of Malta. He turned toward the galley door.

"Mary!"

She emerged a few moments later, shaking off sleep, holding a blanket, foraged from the crew cabins, wrapped around her shoulders. She walked across to Mike and stood close, leaning lightly against him, her head against his shoulder. "What's up?"

He took her hand and slapped it on to the wheel. "Grab this. It's time to take another look for those bastards behind us."

With a gentle pressure on her hand he moved to the radar set, gasping as he went. The last Benzedrine tablet had gone long before. Its effect was wearing off, leaving him in the grip of the pain. It was over an hour since he had last dared to use the set. In the improved conditions he had only needed to leave it on for a matter of seconds to get a fix on O'Keefe's ship. He had immediately turned it off again, not expecting, but not daring to ignore, the possibility of the Libyans tracking them down. Now, only a few kilometers off the coast, moving into the safety of Maltese waters, he discounted the possibility of any further pursuit. He turned the switch and bent over the screen.

CHAPTER

30

"**W**HY DON'T YOU SIT OUT FOR A WHILE?**" AS HE
spoke, O'Keefe took Randall by the arm and pulled him
roughly away from the wheel. "Get some fresh air if you
like. I'll take over here." He released his grip on Randall, already dismissing him. Without a word, Randall
crossed to the door, threw it wide open and sat down
heavily on the threshold with his head in his hands, totally oblivious to the gorgeous sunrise that was beginning to unfold in front of him.

O'Keefe stared ahead. It was light enough now for
him to be able to see clearly the reddish cliffs ahead and
to the left of the bow. He swung the wheel, aiming to
cut as close as possible to the rocky shore. He kept the
ship to its limit, not slowing at all as he closed in on the
rocks. He had prepared well for this moment, studying
charts and making trial runs until he knew every outcrop of the coast by heart. Nevertheless, he was grateful
it was the Mediterranean, with no tides to complicate
matters.

There were only the crews of two or three brightly

painted fishing boats to witness the streaked and flaking ship's headlong rush across the wide mouth of Marsaxlokk Bay toward the white line of surf that boiled around the foot of the cliffs. They lined the sides of their own boats to watch in wonder at the surprising turn of speed the decrepit vessel was showing in its apparently suicidal run at the shore.

O'Keefe watched the rocks approach, his expression absolutely cool. There was just a hint of the flutter in his stomach, the flutter that for thirty years he had felt in the moments before a job came to its climax. The cliffs loomed above them. Randall had turned to watch them. He sat in helpless, grey-faced horror as they seemed about to smash into the luminous red stone. Abruptly, O'Keefe gave a shout of triumph and punched the air in front of his chest. The wall of rock was rushing past feet from the port rail. They had made it! For the last seven or eight miles into Grand Harbour they would hug the rocky, indented coastline, staying so near to it they would be effectively hidden from any pursuers.

Around them fishing boats bobbed, some still at rest, some already making for port. In fifteen minutes more they would be in sight of the cargo ships lying at anchor off the harbor, awaiting berths. It would further confuse any hunters.

Mike swore. The dot disappeared from the screen, absorbed into the white mass that was the outline of Malta. He smashed a fist on the panel beside him, furious and bitter.

"What's wrong?" Mary's voice was thick with anxiety. She was afraid they had lost O'Keefe. Above all, she was afraid for Mike. He was deathly white. Twice in the last few minutes his legs had buckled, dropping him to his knees.

"We've lost them. They're behind the island." He

spoke without looking at her, still staring fixedly at the screen.

"Won't we pick them up again when we get around the point?"

He shrugged. "I don't know. I doubt it. They'll stay close to the shore. Once they get into the traffic around the harbor entrance it'll be a bastard of a job to find them. It's a hell of a big harbor and we don't have a notion what they're up to. They'll gain a lot of time while we check . . ." His voice trailed off for a moment and then came again as a barely audible murmur. "Shit!"

Mary looked around at him. He stood, clutching at the radar bracket for support, his head bowed over the screen. "Mike? What's wrong? Are you okay?"

He turned to look at her. His eyes had a hazy, unfocused look in them. He pointed at the screen. "The damned Libyans! They're coming for us."

He had barely finished speaking when his legs buckled under him. He slid to the floor and lay still. Leaving the wheel, Mary rushed across to where he lay, fell to her knees and shook him. His head fell to one side and he groaned softly. Satisfied he was not dead, she scrambled to her feet and bent over the screen. A vessel was on a course straight for them. It grew closer as she watched. Mike had to be right. Even with the little knowledge of radar she had picked up in the last few hours it was apparent that the other boat was closing on them fast, much faster than any merchant vessel. With an anxious glance down at Mike, she ran back to the wheel.

There was no need to consider what to do next; events were making her choices for her. She had to make a run for the harbor. If they were going to find O'Keefe, that was the place to look. And once inside the Libyans would surely not dare to follow them and attack a foreign ship. The hell with it! Even if they did, at least they would have a chance of getting ashore and *running* away! If they were caught while at sea they were dead.

Abandoning the compass, she steered toward the extremity of the point ahead. The danger from behind made her reckless. She took the ship slicing among the rebounding, leaping breakers, shaving the point almost as closely as O'Keefe had done minutes before. She relaxed just a little as she veered to port, steering for the next promontory, a couple of miles ahead, comforted by the idea that for the moment, at least, the Libyan boat would have lost her trace. It was going to be a game of cat and mouse. According to the rough sketch Mike had tried to draw for her earlier in the night, done from memory of sailing holidays there many years ago, it was probably about eight or ten miles to Valletta. They could most likely sink her with missiles from well beyond that distance. Except that, having once lost track of her, even people lusting for revenge would want to come close enough to be sure that they were sinking the right ship.

O'Keefe grinned, the grin of a man completely happy and at ease with himself. When he called to Randall, his tone had lost its earlier bullying note; he was a man at peace with the world.

"Hey, Jack! Look at that."

Almost beyond making the effort, sick and exhausted, Randall pulled himself to his feet and turned his head to follow the direction of O'Keefe's gesture. The two of them stared into the distance. Three miles ahead of them a liner, its lights still on but made pale by the dawn, its white paint glowing rose-pink, was sliding into the harbor entrance.

Captain Andropoulos watched as the sandstone bastions that guarded the approach to the harbor drew closer. Beyond them, the buildings, of the same red stone, seemed to send back the pale sunlight, as though lit from within. He had entered this harbor hundreds of times, yet it never failed to take his breath away. The rocks beyond the city seemed to be made of flame. The low domes of the dozens of churches shimmered in the light. He murmured something to the pilot and pointed, smiling, at the deck below.

The rail was lined three deep with children, all of them craning to admire the view. It was a rare sight at such an hour; children at sea sleep soundly and long, and their teachers had done wonders in getting them on deck so early. The threat of missing the ferry would have helped. There would be only one, at seven-thirty. Anyone missing that would be confined on board until they sailed again in the evening.

The ship slipped past the massive fortifications and on into the tranquil waters of the huge harbor. The graceful bulk of the liner towered over the many smaller vessels that crowded the vast anchorage: rust-scabbed cargo ships, yachts and flashy cabin cruisers. Gaudy *luzzus,* the gondola-like fishing boats of Malta, hurried across the liner's bow, missing by feet as their owners waved to the cheering children, steering one-handed with casual precision.

There was another brief exchange between the captain and the pilot. The ship slowed further, and a moment later, an anchor dropped from the stern, splashing heavily into their wake. The liner continued to make headway as, behind it, the anchor chain ran out with a roar. The captain and pilot conferred again. The water around the stern boiled as the engines surged into reverse, and the ship shuddered and stopped. The bow anchor plunged into the sea. At another command from the bridge, the rear anchor cable tautened and shook. Slowly, as the powerful winch wound in the cable, the ship was dragged backward. The front cable tightened now as the giant anchor bit into the seabed. A last word from the bridge and the ship was still, pinioned by the two straining chains amid the busy throng of smaller boats.

Mary's face ran with tears and spray. She was crying with anger and frustration. Ahead of her, she could clearly make out the ships plying in and out of the harbor. A short way offshore several more rode at anchor. To her unschooled eye almost any one of them could have been O'Keefe's. With another frightened glance down at Mike, she left the wheel and ran through the galley and out on to the stern deck. The angular shape of the patrol boat was cleaving directly through the swell toward her, hurling aside a pair of deck-high plumes of white water as it came.

She had watched the vessel for some minutes. Three times it had altered course, looping close to other craft before swinging back toward her. The detours were no doubt to check the identities of the other vessels before deciding once again that the ship making flat out for the harbor mouth was the best bet. The gap was shrinking fast now. She knew there would be no more than seconds in it if they were to reach the safety of Valletta harbor before being overhauled. She turned on her heel, ran back inside, grabbed the wheel and brought the bow back the few degrees toward their destination. On the floor beside her Mike shifted his position an inch and moaned softly. She called his name. He did not stir. She called again, bellowing so loud her voice reverberated among the steel surfaces of the bridge. His chin lifted off the floor. His lips worked but no sound came from them.

She bit hard on her lower lip and then, abruptly, drew back her leg and kicked him hard in the side of the thigh. "Sorry, Mike," she murmured, and kicked him a second time, brutally hard. He rolled on to his back and opened his eyes. He lay staring blankly up at her, apparently oblivious to what had woken him.

"The Libyans!" She jabbed him again with her toe and jerked a thumb toward the stern. "They're right there."

Gradually, as though he were coming out of a trance, understanding seeped into his face. Taking the hand she reached down to him, he pulled himself first to one knee and then on to his feet. He shook his head and blinked at her, slowly forcing his eyes back into focus. "What are you talking about?"

She jerked her head over her shoulder. "Remember those unusable patrol boats you were telling me about?" One cheek twitched in a sardonic little smile. "There's one of them back there, about to blow us out of the water."

He stared at her for a moment, as if he still hoped she might be kidding, and then snatched the battered binoculars from their wooden housing close by the wheel. He turned and hurried to the galley, dragging one leg and clutching a hand to his wounded side.

He emerged on to the deck. Supporting his back against the galley wall, he trained the binoculars on the sleek craft that bore down on them. He could see men crowded at the bow and the spiky silhouette of the weapons they held. High on each side of the boat, just behind the bow, he could see that there was a number painted in white on the grey and green of the camouflage. He was unable to make out enough detail to see what it was. It was a crumb of comfort. The Libyans probably could not yet read the name of their quarry. He turned and looked ahead, past the wheelhouse to the fortifications of the port entrance, trying to judge distance. He looped the lanyard over his head and let the binoculars fall against his chest. With his lips drawn back in a grin of pain, he turned and hobbled back to the bridge. Mary was staring grimly ahead of her, her face pale and strained. He put an arm around her shoulders, standing very close to her.

"How about O'Keefe? What's happening with those bastards?"

She shook her head. Frustration made her voice almost a sob. "I don't know. We lost them when they rounded the point." She swept a hand in front of her in a helpless gesture. "They could be anywhere out there."

He nodded. With his free hand he dashed sweat from his eyes. "Yeah, they could. But they're not. They've got big trouble planned. That bomb they're sailing in's big enough to sink an aircraft carrier. They're not planning to waste it among the junk out here." He gestured to the ships that lay at anchor around them. "They'll be in the harbor, I'm certain of it. That's where we need to be, too."

She turned her head to look at him. Their faces were inches apart. "And you think we'll make it?"

He held her eyes for a second, then shot a glance behind him. He turned back to her, his face solemn. Gently, he bent his head and kissed her hair. "I doubt it, Mary."

He bent and picked up the rocket launcher.

The captain slammed down the binoculars and spun to face the older officer. "Have you got him?"

The older man flinched. "Not yet, sir. I have Major Jalloud. They are looking for the Colonel. They think—"

"Idiot!" The captain snatched the radio-telephone. "Jalloud? Is this true? My cousin cannot be *found*?" His voice rose in contemptuous incredulity. He listened for a moment, his eyes glistening with rage, as Colonel Ghaddafi's right-hand man replied. "Then you must give me authority yourself." He listened again. His lips moved as he mouthed silent curses. "What? Yes. Well, no. That is, we are completely certain but we are not yet able to read the name. In five minutes we shall know. In six they will be in the port. Eh? Of course we are within their wa-

ters." He listened again. "And what if I *am* mistaken?
Are we women now? It is better that we act and are
mistaken than that *I* am right and you do *not* give your
authority. One last time, Major. Do you agree that I
proceed?" He paused, breathing heavily, his face contemptuous and impatient as the Major spoke. "Well,
find the Colonel!"

He almost screamed the last words, then thrust the
telephone back into the hands of the officer, who
clamped it to his ear and began jabbering into it.

The captain turned angrily away and began pacing
the bridge, drumming a fist into the open palm of his
other hand. He was still pacing when a cry from one of
the others on the bridge made him pivot toward the
front. He snatched up the binoculars again, and drew
breath sharply. For the first time, he was able to read
clearly the name across the stern of the vessel. It was the
one on which his fellow seamen had died. He swung the
binoculars higher, examining the deck of the ship. He
swore bitterly. A man, naked to the waist, stepped from
the galley. He gulped. There was no mistaking the purpose of the dull-painted tube the man held under his
arm. As the captain watched the man raised a pair of
binoculars, and for an instant the captain had the uneasy impression they were looking into each other's
eyes. The captain dropped his binoculars and in the
same movement turned to his gunnery officer. He
shouted a single word of command.

O'Keefe's icy calm had completely returned. He was
whistling again as he made meticulous last-minute ad-
justments to the web of cords that stretched around the
wheelhouse. Through the wide-open door the sound of
young voices reached him, a sound that had been growing in volume and excitement for several minutes. Smiling, but with his eyes oddly fixed behind the dark lenses,
he looked up at the doorway. Randall stood outside,

scanning the water and the quayside around them with
dull but watchful eyes. A loaded rifle stood just inside
the door, within his easy reach. His face had the texture
of putty. Beyond Randall, a quarter of a mile away, the
bow of the liner showed beyond the headland that
shielded the deep inlet, where O'Keefe had chosen to lie
up and wait, from the main harbor. O'Keefe's smile
broadened. A new sound had reached him over the
other noises of the awakening port; he had heard it
many times during his careful reconnaissance trips to the
island. It was the engine of the ferry approaching the
liner. His smile turned to a frown as yet another sound
reached him, mingling with the chugging of the ferry. It
was music, the discordant clamor of a band heard from
a distance in the open air. Dismissing this with a shake
of his head he bent to check again the cable that ran
from the doorway and across the instrument panel in
front of him. With his foot, he pushed the aluminum
box, which had never been out of his reach since the
Semtex had been loaded, closer into the angle of the
floor and the console. He glanced down to check its
position, seeing that it was handy but out of harm's
way. He pushed his glasses back more firmly on to his
nose and called to Randall. His tone was almost gentle.

"Ready, Jack. You can let go that line."

Randall ran, stumbling, to the stern and unfastened
the single line that held them to the quayside, letting the
end drop into the water. The ship began to ease out into
the center of the inlet. Even behind the tinted glasses
Randall's eyes squeezed into a squint against the brightness of the water. He could see the whole length of the
liner now. Mid-way along its side a gangway, covered
with a brightly striped awning, led down to the gently
lapping water. Children thronged the rail around it.

CHAPTER

31

As the captain of the patrol boat watched him, Mike stepped over the threshold from the galley and out on to the deck. He held the rocket launcher cradled in the crook of one arm. The swollen, brown-painted snout of a rocket protruded from it. A bout of dizziness swept over him, making him sag against the wall, fighting to keep his feet. The dizziness passed. He straightened and raised the binoculars, and began screaming at Mary, not even knowing if she heard, urging her to get more speed from the ship somehow.

The Libyan boat was close enough for him to see the faces of the men on it craning toward him, eager and excited as the faces of racegoers. He dropped the binoculars. It was beyond him why they had not already blown them out of the water—a boat like that carried missiles enough to have sunk them ten times over. He did not waste time looking for explanations. With a shake of his head to clear the last of the dizziness and the sheer disbelief, he began to raise the rocket launcher to his shoulder.

At the moment he moved the men broke from the rail and ran, leaving the foredeck of the patrol boat empty. He did not need the glasses to see the reason. His and Mary's luck had run right out. The covers protecting the batteries of missile tubes had been removed, leaving him gazing into their gaping black muzzles. Dry-mouthed, he pulled the rocket launcher hard against his shoulder, rested his cheek on the metal, and fired. ·

He watched the tail of flame, bright even against the sunrise, flash toward their hunter. It struck the on-coming boat on the bow, just below the anchor. He was still staring, dumb-struck, a couple of seconds later, when the sound reached him; not an explosion, but a metallic booming noise. The rocket had bounced off the sharply angled metal. A spume of water flew up as the rocket exploded harmlessly in the sea forty yards from the boat. Fear clutched at his stomach. At any instant he expected the missile tubes to spit flame. Murmuring to himself, he snatched another rocket from his waistband and began fumbling it into the tube, made awkward by haste and panic. Before he had finished reloading the ship swung sharply under him, throwing him to his knees.

He dragged himself back upright, swearing hard at the sheet of pain that had enfolded him. His heart pounded as he braced himself for the impact of the missiles. He was struggling to raise the weapon again when he broke off with a shout of surprise. He could no longer see the patrol boat. The point of land that sheltered the harbor to the south-east was rushing past only yards from him. He looked quickly to his left. Nearly half a mile away, on the opposite side of the harbor mouth, the unmistakable sand-red bulk of Fort Saint Elmo was sliding astern. All the pain fell away. He drove a clenched fist at the air above his head and gave a single long whoop of victory. They were into the shelter of Grand Harbour.

Moments later, the patrol boat sped into view. It rushed straight on across the mouth of the harbor for three or four hundred yards before turning out to sea in a sweeping arc. Dragging the rocket tube with him, Mike turned and ran to rejoin Mary.

O'Keefe was alone in the wheelhouse. He teased the controls, easing the vessel out into the middle of the inlet. He, too, had a full view of the liner now. Children had begun moving down the gangway. Across the intervening water he could hear somebody shouting instructions, and the mysterious music had grown louder. Automatically, he looked at his watch. It must be the years of British domination; Malta was one place in the Mediterranean where things happened on time. The flat-decked ferry, with the yellow and blue canopy that made it look like a floating marquee, rounded the stern and edged up to the gangway.

O'Keefe's smile faded to a look of mild puzzlement. Under the canopy, on a raised platform in a corner of the ferry's deck, a five-piece brass band was playing. The children, instead of spilling down on to the deck of the ferry in the usual free-for-all, descended in an orderly fashion, responding to shouted instructions from a red-coated steward. With another steward organizing them, they formed rows on the deck, leaving a space at the foot of the gangway. More children stayed on the gangway, lining it on each side to form an avenue. A uniformed man had appeared at the top of the gangway. O'Keefe judged from the uniform that he was the captain. His arm rested over the shoulders of a boy next to him, whose face was partly hidden by a bandage. O'Keefe grinned—they were having some kind of ceremony. He would be providing them with some unexpected fireworks.

Randall stood by on the stern deck, his hand on the release catch of the inflated Zodiac. He was breathing deeply, partly from tension and partly from relief at the relative steadiness of the deck beneath his feet. He was staring at the packed ferry and gangway. O'Keefe's shouted words reached him from inside the wheelhouse.

"All right, Jack. Here we go."

O'Keefe's voice was boyish, vibrant with excitement. Randall's own expression did not change. He went on staring blankly at the liner.

Mary still had the wheel. Mike stood close by her, a hand on the panel in front of him and the other arm across Mary's shoulders. She gazed hopelessly at the harbor spread in front of them. A few seconds ago she had been crying with relief; now, her tears turned once again to tears of frustration.

"Oh, my God," she sobbed, "it's so damned *huge*. I had no idea. I thought it would be, I don't know, like a little *bay*." She threw out a hand, shaking her head. "This just goes on forever."

He nodded, scanning the scene around them through narrowed eyes. The harbor was two miles long, and inlets almost a mile deep cut into its sides. He did not look at her as he spoke, hardly moving his lips. "Yeah, right. Why do you think the British hung on to it for so long?"

"But, Mike, it'll take us hours to search. There must be dozens of ships like theirs in here."

He shrugged. The movement made him gasp. "Well, we'd better start somewhere. Head over there." He pointed to the first of the inlets immediately to their left. Grimacing at the pain the movement brought, he took his arm from Mary's shoulders, raised the binoculars and began scanning the moored vessels.

The Libyan captain's eyes blazed. "But I could have *destroyed* them! If *you* had not delayed us with your womanish hesitations, Major, I could have crushed them like insects. I would have *done* it, even without your authority. But I was too late. Too late because of *your* girlish scruples." The captain's anger had brought tears to the corners of his eyes. "My cousin will have your head for it, Major."

The man at the other end of the line replied in a very low, weary voice. "He's my cousin, too, Lieutenant. He was not available. He had gone out into the desert, for one of his walks. So he could not authorize you to do as you wanted. So you did not do it. That is all. There will be no reproaches. You did your best."

"My best? I could have done so much better, Major. I could have done as the Colonel instructed me. If *you* had not been such a coward, had not prevented me."

The other man sighed heavily. "Look, Lieutenant, I personally admire your devotion. But this is a delicate matter. The Maltese are our friends." A sardonic note crept into his tone. "I hardly have to remind you that we do not have very many of those. Come home, Lieutenant."

The line went dead. For some seconds the captain stood quite still, staring at the handset. It was several seconds before he spoke again, an unbroken flood of insults.

Following Mike's instructions, Mary maneuvered the ship around. They raced back out of the inlet, their wash rocking the small boats that lined the quay as they travelled much too fast for the conditions. Nothing in there had resembled O'Keefe's vessel.

They turned into the next, deeper one. There, too, they drew a blank. They re-emerged, following a long finger of land that protruded far into the main harbor. They reached the end of the promontory and swung to their left. Mike's attention was attracted to the gleaming white outline of a liner riding at anchor, a half-mile further into the harbor. A gaudily canopied ferry boat was passing beneath the stern. It turned as he watched and came to a stop alongside the liner, dwarfed by its towering bulk. He watched the press of people, dark against the white paintwork, that crowded the liner's deck and began to funnel down the companionway. The thought struck him with horrifying force.

"Quickly, Mary! Over there! The liner! Head for it."

Her head jerked back as she was hit by the same realization as Mike. She swung the wheel hard.

"Come on, Mary! Faster! Get this damned thing opened up, for Christ's sake!" He began moving toward the door.

She rammed the lever to full ahead. The ship shuddered and gathered its last few knots of speed. Behind them, men shouted and gesticulated angrily as the tiny, garishly painted *luzzus* reeled in their churning wake. Three hundred yards to the right of the liner, coming from the town side of the harbor, a launch made its way toward it. They could see figures crowding the rail. Nothing remotely resembled O'Keefe's rust-heap. The liner's passengers began to spill on to the flat, open deck of the ferry. A cry from Mary drew Mike's attention from the liner.

"Look! Over there!"

He followed the direction of her outflung arm. The scabbed bow of a ship was easing out from behind a headland. He snatched up the powerful binoculars just as the vessel moved into full view. He swung the glasses, gauging the distances. With a choking sound he let them drop to his chest, fighting down the urge to vomit. They would never close the gap in time.

O'Keefe's calm had snapped completely now. He was almost screaming instructions at the blank-faced Randall. Stumbling and muttering to himself, Randall moved to comply, struggling to manhandle the inflated Zodiac over the stern. He managed to rest it on the rail, untangled the last rope that impeded him, and shoved it over into the sea. A single thin line held it fast to the ship. Moving with a zombie-like languor, he climbed stiffly on to the rail and lowered himself down into the dinghy.

In the wheelhouse O'Keefe sweated and cursed. His actions had taken on a feverish quality. The ship crept forward. At the same time as holding it on course toward the stationary ferry he manipulated the cords, taking up the last tiny margins of slack. All the while, he was looking anxiously at his watch. They were no more than four hundred yards from the liner as he adjusted the last of the cords. Finally happy with it, he glanced quickly around to check the others. He nodded and murmured something to himself. Smiling, calm again now the last of his preparations was completed, he bent and picked up the metal box from its place at his feet. He looked once more at his watch, clicked his tongue in satisfaction, and pulled back on the lever in front of him, slowing the ship to walking pace. He looked ahead, checking for one last time that the vessel was headed for its target.

"Bastards!"

He screamed the word, his face contorted into a gargoyle mask of fury. A launch, its rail crowded with people, had rounded the stern of the liner and stopped directly between him and his target. Spitting curses, his newly restored calm swept away in the fresh storm of frustration and fury, he began fighting the cords, slackening them enough to be able to alter his course.

Captain Andropoulos stood at the head of the gangway, his arm lightly over Jamie's shoulders. His smile beamed, but his eyes were bored. This was the damned oil company's idea. They wanted the thing blown up into a full-scale hero's welcome. A little knot of people waited on the deck at the foot of the gangway, the men overdressed in dark suits and the women with gloves up to their elbows—the party of local English and Maltese worthies that Chieftain had cajoled into forming a reception committee.

Still smiling, he scanned the harbor. There was no sign of the launch. He had to stay there, grinning like an idiot, until the photographers arrived. As he watched, a rusted tramp emerged from an inlet opposite and began nosing out into the main harbor. He made a faint moue of contempt at the rundown state of the ship and went on looking for the photographers' boat.

He glanced down briefly at the boy, who was grinning from ear to ear and shifting from foot to foot, proud and embarrassed. Captain Andropoulos gave his shoulder a squeeze. At the same moment a launch emerged from under the stern of the ship, a knot of men in shirtsleeves or lightweight jackets pressed to the rail. All of them were hung with the paraphernalia of their trade, and were already busy taking pictures. The captain's smile broadened with relief; he could go ahead now and get the thing over with. Automatically, his gaze flicked back to the rusty ship. A tinge of consternation mingled with the smile.

The scabbed tramp had drawn nearer. His eyes narrowed; the vessel seemed to be heading dangerously close to his ship. He stared at it, the smile still stuck on his face like a mask. His arm fell from Jamie's shoulders. He was about to turn to shout for a megaphone when he suddenly relaxed again. The filthy old tub had altered course, as though whoever was on the bridge had just seen them. He let out a long breath and began ushering Jamie on to the gangway ahead of him.

Mike stood on the open deck gripping the frame of the wheelhouse door. His voice was cracking as he screamed at Mary for more speed, knowing within himself that it was useless. Eight hundred yards ahead of them, beyond the effective range of Mike's weapon, the dilapidated ship had emerged completely from behind the headland and was steaming toward the liner. It was moving quite slowly but directly toward the spot where the ferry was filling with children. Mike screamed louder, interspersing his exhortations to Mary with bitter curses aimed at himself. Already consumed with frustrated rage, he was now choking down an overwhelming sickness. Only in the last few seconds had he been able to see the faces of the passengers. Only now did he understand the full horror of what was unfolding ahead—O'Keefe's victims were children.

His stomach heaved. He spat bile on to the deck. There was enough Semtex stacked in the forepeak of O'Keefe's hulk to blow the liner and all the children into a million pieces. Those laughing faces, hundreds of them, were about to be violently shattered. Ripped into bloodied scraps.

And he was the one who had made it possible.

Colonel Ghaddafi would never have agreed to supply the Semtex if he had known O'Keefe's purpose. He had not wanted to supply it at all. He had *refused*, outright. It had been Mike, in his blind search for revenge, who had managed to change the Colonel's mind. By letting O'Keefe talk him into taking part in blackmailing the Colonel, preying on the man's love for his sick daughter, he had ensured the massacre of these unsuspecting children whose laughter floated to him across the narrow stretch of water.

Ahead of him the floating bomb had closed to no more than four hundred yards from the *Maribella*. As he gazed helplessly, a launch cut close under the stern of the liner and drew near to the waiting ferry. He heard the strains of a new tune waft over the harbor as the musicians struck up again with fresh vigor.

He stiffened, his breath coming in a gasp. The ship had stopped. As he stared in mute disbelief, the bow of the vessel swung until it was heading almost straight toward him. He gave a shout of excitement as he understood what had happened. The launch was blocking O'Keefe's run at the ferry. He was changing course to get around it. For a short distance O'Keefe was obliged to close the gap with Mike and Mary's ship. Shouting to Mary to keep her course, he hitched the rocket launcher under his arm and began struggling toward the bow.

Captain Andropoulos shepherded Jamie slowly down the steps between the rows of applauding children. Below them the reception committee had been smiling up at them for nearly a minute. They were beginning to show the strain. The three gaunt women that Chieftain had mustered for the purpose looked like death's-heads. The men were scarlet-faced. One of them looked as though he were going to be seasick. The captain's grin widened. As he smiled he kept half an eye on the tub that had been approaching them. His smile dissolved into a shrewder look. It was moving on a safer course now but had suddenly picked up speed. As he watched, it slowed again and the bow began slewing around.

The captain stopped, letting Jamie move on ahead of him. He threw a puzzled glance back up the gangway toward his own bridge and then turned quickly back to face the ship. He wondered if the man at the wheel were drunk; it happened more often than anybody realized.

Abruptly, he stopped wondering anything at all and gave a shout of alarm. The vessel was pointing straight at them, and it was gathering speed.

O'Keefe hauled the wheel around. His face was flushed and damp with sweat, his clothes were plastered to his back. He had been swearing without interruption for a full minute. Haste made him clumsy as he struggled again with the cords. As he worked he constantly cocked his wrist, counting the seconds. The second hand swept past the twelve and began ticking off the last minute to the half-hour. His tongue flicked over his lips. He had set his watch exactly by the Greenwich time signal half an hour earlier. There was no room for approximations. He made one last frantic effort to tighten the cords and then, with a cry of disgust, tore them free of the wheel.

"Fuck it," he said aloud to himself. "We're close enough."

Holding the ship on course with one hand he reached with his left for the radio set mounted on the panel between two windows. The front casing of the radio had been removed. A metal box with a switch on it was taped next to it, connected to the set by a length of flex. The cable that he had laid from the forecastle ran up the wall to the box. He paused for just another second, one finger resting on the switch. His glance flicked across the forecastle with its deadly cargo and on to the liner, now no more than three hundred yards away. The voices and the music drifted to him through the open door. As he watched he saw a sudden flurry of movement on the ferry and the gangway, and the pale faces turned in unison toward him. He saw the children begin milling around, shoving and grappling as they crowded to the foot of the ladder. A few jumped overboard and began swimming.

He laughed aloud. "Too late, you little British bastards!"

He flipped the switch. Spinning on his heel, he snatched the metal box from its place on the floor and sprinted out of the wheelhouse to the stern. He paused for just an instant, glancing back, and then threw himself over the rail. He slithered down the rope and fell heavily into the Zodiac.

* * *

Crippled and weakened by his wound, Mike was only halfway to the bow when he saw the water boil and seethe around O'Keefe's ship. It slowed and slewed to port, and for a moment it presented its entire orange-streaked length to Mike. Gritting his teeth, shutting out the pain and fatigue, he hauled himself upright and wedged himself into a position where he was half-sitting on the hatch cover. In his exhausted haste, he caught the rocket launcher clumsily against the edge of the cover. It clattered back to the deck. Summoning his last shreds of will power, he stooped and retrieved it. The best of his opportunity had passed. The other ship had already completed its turn and was at an oblique angle to him, steaming toward the ferry. The screams of the panicking children carried with absolute clarity over the water.

Still battling nausea, he snatched a rocket from his trouser waistband and loaded the launcher. As he did so, the figure of O'Keefe, unmistakable with his silver-grey hair picking up the low sun, burst from the wheel-house and sprinted to the stern. Mike noticed with a dream-like vagueness that O'Keefe was carrying something. The sun struck it. It was the metal box, the one he had kept at his side during the stacking of the Semtex. He finished loading the weapon as O'Keefe threw himself over the stern and dropped into the inflatable that bobbed behind the ship. A figure that he supposed was Randall sat at the back of the craft. The line attaching it to the ship snaked away and Mike saw O'Keefe's head turn as though to give an order to Randall. He groaned in sick anguish. In another ninety seconds the bomb-ship would be striking its helpless target. Trembling, hardly able to support the weight of it, he tried shakily to line up the weapon on the vessel ahead.

The Libyan captain paced the bridge. In the minutes since their quarry had slipped into the refuge of the harbor, all the time he had been speaking to Jalloud, they had been circling no more than five hundred yards off the harbor entrance. He was kneading his lips nervously with one hand, biting the flesh of the inside of his mouth so hard it bled.

Jalloud was a woman. He had been in power too long. It had made him soft. He saw danger everywhere. He was afraid of his own shadow. Afraid even of the Maltese! Among the old guard only the Colonel himself maintained the pure spirit of the Revolution. Only the Colonel prized the lives of the Libyan people, all Libyan people, as they deserved to be prized. The Colonel would understand. Vengeance was not a luxury, to be taken only when it was convenient. It was necessary, in order to live like a man. It was the natural order.

Abruptly, the captain stopped pacing. His hand dropped from his lips to his side as he stood straighter, bringing his shoulders back. The other officers on the bridge exchanged glances. With an exclamation, the captain spun on his heel. Roughly, he pushed aside the man at the wheel and took it himself. With a call for more speed he swung the sleek boat hard to port, and they swept into the mouth of the harbor. His face immobile, he surveyed the expanse of water. He gave a short cry of triumph. One-handed, he grabbed the field glasses that lay against his chest and held them to his eyes. Straight ahead, not more than twelve hundred meters distant, their quarry was sailing directly away from them, toward another tramp vessel and a white liner. He let go the glasses and spoke a terse command.

Mike had dropped to his knees; seated on the hatch cover he had been too weak to support the weapon firmly. He leaned hard against the rail and laid the tube of the launcher along it. He gave a single quick glance back at Mary and settled his cheek hard on the metal. The bomb-ship was two hundred yards from the liner. He would not have a second chance. He squinted along the tube. He needed to hit close to the bow. Anything less would not cripple the ship enough to prevent its own way from carrying it on to its target. He adjusted his aim, sighting at deck height to allow for the dropping trajectory.

He was still preparing to fire when the patrol boat's missiles slammed in a cluster into their stern. The deck bucked wildly under the impact of the explosions, throwing Mike sprawling into the walkway alongside the rail. By the time he dragged himself to his feet, the stern was already deep in the water. The bow pointed crazily upward. Mike looked around frantically for the weapon, oblivious of anything except the need to sink the bomb-ship. The launcher had gone, slipped into the sea. With a deep-throated cry of anguish, he turned and staggered along the sloping deck toward the wheelhouse. As he approached Mary reeled from the open doorway on to the deck, bleeding profusely from a cut on her head. She collapsed into the angle between the deck and the wheelhouse wall.

Leaving her where she lay, Mike turned away and scrambled across the deck in front of the wheelhouse to the pod that housed the life-raft. A fresh burst of adrenaline gave him a new reserve of strength. With desperate speed, he freed the cover and threw it clear. Half falling and half running, he dragged the raft to the rail and pushed it over. It hit the water already partly inflated.

Mike moved to Mary and hooked his arms under hers. Using the last ounce of his meager new store of strength, he dragged her over the rail and on to the steeply angled side. They rolled and fell, skinning their flesh on the rough metal, hitting the water in a tangle. Holding her by a fistful of clothing, he dragged her to the raft. Waiting only to ensure that she was conscious enough to cling to the line looped around the inflatable, he turned to watch in stark, helpless horror as O'Keefe's ship closed in on the doomed children.

* * *

O'Keefe fell into the Zodiac and unsnapped the ring which held the line fast. He spun to face Randall. "That's it! Let's get going! Quick!"

Randall knelt by the powerful outboard. He was quite still, staring at the crowd of children less than three hundred yards away. He seemed paralyzed.

"Come on, fuck you! Get moving!" O'Keefe was choking with anxious rage.

Randall turned his eyes from the children to stare at O'Keefe. "They're just a bunch of kids, Harry," he said in a thin, dead voice.

O'Keefe stared back at the other man in sheer disbelief. A look of contemptuous understanding washed over his face. "Oh, Jesus, no." He was shouting. "Not now. No conscience now. Let's just fuck off, out of it." As he spoke, he moved toward Randall and grabbed a handful of lapel, trying to drag him aside. With a moan of protest Randall lashed a backhand blow at O'Keefe's head. Laughing through his nose, O'Keefe leaned away from the blow and jabbed an elbow into the other man's cheekbone. Randall's hands flew to his face. O'Keefe sank stiffened fingers into his unguarded stomach. Randall's breath hissed out of him. He fell forward, still trying to hinder O'Keefe by clutching his arms ineptly around his legs. O'Keefe leant back from the waist, picked his spot, and cracked his fist into the side of Randall's head. He grunted and fell sideways. O'Keefe dragged him aside and grabbed the tiller. The inflatable bucked and began to speed in a wide curve away from the ship.

From more than a quarter of a mile away, Mike was screaming at the top of his lungs with a futile, desperate notion of warning the children. His words were lost on the water. The children were screaming and struggling, clawing at each other as they tried to gain a place on the gangway or reach the rail. The water around the ferry was thick with their bobbing heads, swimming just clear of the ferry, imagining that the impact of the collision was all they had to fear. Mike could see the faces of the swimmers turned toward him as they looked back, riveted by what was happening; the ship bearing down on the ferry, the stricken vessel sliding below the surface, the camouflage-painted warship which had appeared so fleetingly, opened fire and then sped off beyond the point, and now the survivors clinging to a tiny raft as small boats hurried from all sides to help.

Mike had seen the end of the scuffle in the Zodiac. For an instant he had allowed himself to hope that it meant something had happened that would thwart O'Keefe's plan. When he saw the nose of the boat lift and turn away, he knew it was all over. O'Keefe's mad, pathetic determination had won.

He fell silent. Randall's head had appeared once again above the side of the inflatable. In a jerky movement, he lunged forward, appearing to grab something. He raised a pale object, as though to throw it overboard; it was the metal box. Before he could bring down his arm, O'Keefe dived on him, smothering the movement. His bellow of rage carried clearly over the sounds of screaming. The two men wrestled to the floor of the Zodiac, disappearing from Mike's sight. A second later O'Keefe sat up, clutching the box close to his chest.

An idea struck Mike with absolute, blinding clarity. He looked at his watch. It was almost a minute past seven-thirty. With a shout, he began pulling himself into the life-raft. Mary looked on helplessly as Mike scrambled in, disappearing beneath the black fabric of the canopy. Too dazed to speak or cry out, she watched in blank dismay as the ship edged closer toward the frightened children. She heard confused voices and saw some heads turn toward the ship. A voice rang out, amplified by an electric megaphone, in a belated, hopeless effort to warn the vessel off. Even through the distortion of the megaphone she could hear the stammering alarm in the voice as the ship continued on its course.

On the Zodiac O'Keefe rose to his knees and heaved something over the side. He began scrambling back to the tiller, fumbling with the metal box as he went. In the struggle, with nobody steering, the Zodiac had traveled in a semi-circle, veering back close to the ship. As O'Keefe settled and again took control, its nose reared from the water and it began accelerating away once more.

Inside the canopy Mike was on all fours. He looked wildly around the interior, straining to see in the semi-darkness. His eyes alighted on what he sought. He snatched the orange plastic-clad radio distress beacon from its housing, his fingers almost numb with panic. He could not see what was happening outside. With a murmured word, he slid open the transparent plastic shutter and pressed the switch beneath it that set the beacon transmitting.

Mary's eyes widened in amazement. Still a hundred and fifty yards from the liner, the streaked, rusting ship simply disappeared in a blinding eruption of yellow flame. The flame condensed into a hemisphere of boiling black smoke. Mike's head appeared from under the canopy. It seemed a long time before the wind of the explosion rocked the raft.

They stared in silent horror at the scene. Slowly, the pall of smoke drifted upward. The front two thirds of the ship had gone completely, leaving only a sawn-off section of the stern surmounted by the bridge. As they watched, that section tilted and slid beneath the surface. The Zodiac had gone, vaporized in the blast.

The ferry and the liner were intact. The screams that carried across the water, breaking the dead silence of the seconds following the explosion, were the sounds of shock and relief, not the keening, uninhibited sounds of true agony. Mike looked around at a choking sound from Mary. She was being sick. His own eyes closed. As the first rescue boat closed in he fell back, unconscious, into the raft.

EPILOGUE

THE TWO MEN FLANKED MARY AS THEY STRODE THROUGH the deserted corridor. The one on her right was in his middle thirties, the other close to sixty. The older man wore dark, expensive clothes. The sober effect was offset by big gold cufflinks, a silk pocket handkerchief and a silk tie. It was the slightly dandified anonymity of the upper-echelon civil servant. The younger man wore a no-nonsense grey suit and a maroon knitted tie. His shoes were rubber-soled, with a tread on them that would outlast their owner. He had owned them long enough for them to be molded to every contour of his splayed feet. Neither of the men spoke or smiled.

Between them Mary stared straight ahead of her. Her forehead above her left eye was covered with a three-inch square of lint. She was still breathing hard from recent argument. The tense set of her face expressed all the anger she felt.

The older man stepped aside to allow a nurse to hurry by in the other direction, bowing slightly in acknowledgement. He remained in his stooped posture, watching with a half-smile until she had disappeared and the muffled sound of her footsteps had receded. He straightened, dropping the ironic smile, and led them around a corner.

Two men confronted them, standing alertly in front of a door with a round window set in it. A piece of curtain obscured the view through the glass. One of the men wore the uniform of the Maltese police and carried a short machine-gun, the other wore slacks and a polo shirt. Over the shirt he wore the kind of light cotton windcheater that plainclothes policemen in warm countries find useful to conceal guns. Both the men were dark and below average height. The one in the windcheater had a neck that seemed to start sloping outward from the level of his ears, and was so thick-chested his arms hung at an angle from his sides. On seeing the newcomers he hurried forward with a brisk, springy step and held up a dark-furred paw, stopping them while they were still out of earshot of the uniformed policeman.

He spoke to Mary and the two men in a low voice. The older man nodded several times, then thanked the man and dismissed him with a supercilious nod. He turned to Mary and the man in the grey suit.

"Well, you'd better get on with it." His voice was a deep and leisurely public-school drawl, and he smirked at Mary as he spoke. The overall effect was of pure condescension. At a nod from him, the younger man took Mary by the elbow and steered her toward the door. The uniformed policeman opened it for them and stood to one side.

Mike lay half upright against the pillows, his eyes closed. He wore a green hospital gown. A greying stubble sprouted riotously at his throat and jaw. The visitors were three steps into the room before he opened his eyes. At the sight of Mary his dazed, empty eyes filled with animation and his whole face lit up in a smile. He held out a hand with the fingers extended. After a moment's hesitation she reached out for it. Without a word, he drew her close and kissed her with leisurely, gentle insistence. When he had finished he released her hand, letting her straighten. She was looking down at him, with surprise in her face—and something else. The something else was making her bite her lip hard. Holding her gaze, his lips curving in the faintest of smiles, Mike raised an eyebrow and inclined his head toward the man.

"Don't tell me. He's one of your mob?"

She nodded, her mouth twisting in a wry smile. She gestured to the man. "David. A colleague. This is Mike Scanlon." As she said the last words she looked down at Mike with a hint of proprietorial mischief in her smile. David nodded and gave Mike's extended hand a perfunctory shake. Mike's lips twitched in amusement. Returning the man's nod with an almost imperceptible one of his own, he let his head fall back against the pillows.

"So, what's the score, Mary?" he asked, ignoring the man. "First, were any of the kids hurt?"

She shook her head. "Nothing too terrible. A bloody miracle really." She reached down and touched his shoulder. "Thanks to you. A couple got caught by flying ironmongery. One of them has a nasty head wound, but he'll be okay. A girl broke a leg falling down the gangway."

He let out a long breath, settling his head and shoulders deeper into the pillows. "Thank God!" He lay with his eyes closed, letting himself relish the news. It was several seconds before he opened his eyes and looked up at her again. "And O'Keefe? Randall? Did we nail those bastards?" His voice was a whisper.

As Mike had been lying with his eyes closed David had silently picked up one of the chairs that stood close to the bed and set it down behind Mike's head, near the bedside table where a glass of water and a bowl of oranges stood. He sat down, out of Mike's line of vision, and began toying with the water glass. Now, at Mike's words, his hand was stilled. He leaned forward, listening intently, his eyes on Mike's face. Mike glanced round at him once, mildly curious, and then lost interest. He turned to Mary, raising his weight on to his elbows.

"So, did we get them or not?"

She gave him a smile, thin and tense. "*You* got them. Both of them. The Maltese police are still fishing out the pieces of O'Keefe. It's not clear yet exactly what happened to Randall. He had no shrapnel wounds. But then if it was him I saw O'Keefe heave out of the Zodiac he would have been at water level, out of the direct line. Maybe he was dead before O'Keefe threw him overboard. Anyway, however it was, he's in the morgue now."

Mike's head fell back again on to the pillow. His eyes slid shut. He let out a long, slow sigh. "That's good." He spoke very softly, almost to himself. Mary dropped to her knees beside him.

Sitting forward in his chair, David leaned close, intent on Mike's words. His hand remained resting on the bedside table, close to the water glass. His fingers were lightly curled into his palm.

"They deserved it, Mary. They earned it, for what they did to Allix. And to the baby." Mike's voice had weakened, growing hoarser and fainter. "They weren't part of O'Keefe's war, Mary."

Her eyes moistened. She gulped and tightened her grip on his hand. As she did so David made a soft grunting sound and rose brusquely to his feet. In a casual movement, he slid his closed hand into his pocket, and with a nod to Mary, he sauntered out of the room, his thick soles squeaking on the plastic tiles.

Mary watched him go, her lips tightly pursed. She gulped hard and spoke, leaning close to Mike's ear. "Look, Mike, can you hear me? I'm going to have to leave you for a while." He opened his eyes. Smiling, he increased the pressure on her fingers. "No, I have to, really. But look, tell me one more thing, just so that I know. However did you *know*? How did you know how he was going to trigger it?"

He looked at her from deep among the pillows. "The *time*, Mary," he whispered. "O'Keefe waited. He could have gone for it earlier, before the launch came along and screwed it up for him. But he waited until after seven-thirty. After the half-hour."

She looked perplexed. "So what?"

"He had to wait till then. Until the three-minute radio silence began."

"Uh?"

"On the hour and the half-hour, there's a three-minute radio silence at sea. It's supposed to leave the airwaves clear to allow people to pick up distress signals. He *had* to wait for that silence. Any earlier and some other call might have sent it up, with him still on board! For three minutes from seven-thirty he could be pretty sure of having the airwaves to himself."

The effort of so much explanation seemed to tire him. His eyelids drooped again. Gently, she disengaged her hand from his and rose to her feet. She stood for a moment looking down at the stubbled, battered face, then rubbed a knuckle under her eyes, sniffed once, and tiptoed from the room.

David was waiting for her outside the door, talking in a murmur to the plainclothes man, his weight balanced on the outsides of his feet. At Mary's appearance he nodded to the policeman and turned away to fall into step beside her. Together they walked around the corner and twenty yards down the corridor to where the older man waited. He gave Mary a quick, half-mocking look before turning to David and raising his eyebrows in a studied look of interrogation.

"Well?"

David pushed out his lower lip and nodded. "It's as

she said—there's no problem. He thinks it was an IRA bullet that killed his woman."

He shot a glance at Mary as he said the last words, sharing a cool smile with the older man as they caught her almost imperceptible shudder. The other man smiled and nodded slowly.

"M'mm. Good." He turned to Mary and patted her patronizingly on the arm. "We'll leave things that way, won't we, Mary. We don't want to let our emotions interfere with our work, eh." Mary stared back at him without responding. Contempt blazed in her face. He shrugged, unease breaking through the cool exterior. "Yes, ah, well . . ." He turned to David and held out a hand. "Better give me back that stuff. I signed a chitty for it."

David pulled his fist from his pocket. He opened his hand and tipped an ampoule of thin glass filled with a clear liquid into the other man's palm. One end of the ampoule was drawn into a thin point, making it easy to break off cleanly. The older man took a flat metal tin from a pocket and prised it open. It was lined with cotton wool. He slipped the ampoule carefully inside, pressing it snugly among the cotton wool, and put it away, patting his pocket. He smiled down at Mary. She was staring into his face. Her contempt had given way to horrified anger.

"You fucking bastard!"

The man drew in his chin in mock shock. "I beg your pardon, my dear," he said urbanely. "Is something wrong?" His eyes went to David's. Mary followed his look. The younger man was smirking.

Mary moved closer to the speaker until she stood a few inches from him. He stared down at her from his foot of extra height, prevented by the wall behind him from retreating. She looked up into his sneer.

"I said, you fucking bastard! What was that stuff? You never told me about any of that!" She spun to face the grinning David and shoved him in the chest, making him stagger. He recovered himself and for a moment made as though to strike her. A look from the other man stopped him. "And you!" Mary spat. "You were going to give it to him, weren't you?" Her voice fell to a whisper. "You'd have—"

"Keep your voice down." The older man's voice was like ice.

She dropped her voice to a whisper, glancing around the empty corridor. "You'd have killed him! He achieved more in a few months than you've been able to in twenty years and you were prepared to knock him off. If he—"

"Shut up, now!" The older man grabbed her by the biceps, digging his fingers deep into her flesh. He shook her, looking into her eyes, facing the fury that was there. "Yes," he said, speaking softly and very distinctly. "We *were* prepared to. It's a war, remember. You've heard the Paddies say it often enough." His accent made the disparaging words sound oddly dissonant. "People get hurt in wars." He released her arms and straightened, recovering his languid posture. "If the truth came out it would only serve the Paddies' purpose. So we'll make sure it doesn't. Won't we?" The last two words were weighted with an unequivocal threat. He paused. Without taking his eyes from Mary's he tapped the pocket where the flat tin lay. "Because we still *are* prepared to, my dear. If we need to."

She looked from one to the other, silently considering them. Contempt gathered again in her face. "Bastards!" she said, conversationally, almost as though talking to herself. "A bunch of mad, self-righteous, irresponsible bastards." Without another word, she turned and began running back down the corridor.

David moved as if to intervene. The older man gestured to him to be still. "Remember, Mary, we still are."

The policeman looked up in surprise as she burst

around the corner. The plainclothes man glanced briefly at the corridor behind her, as though hoping for some superior authority to materialize and endorse his action, but made no attempt to stop her entering the room. She threw open the door and halted in the doorway. Mike lay as she had left him, his head on one side. He was breathing deeply and regularly, at a volume just below a snore. She closed the door, much more gently than she had opened it, and crossed silently to the bed.

She had been standing motionless for almost a minute before he began to waken. He blinked several times, looking empty-eyed into the expanse of pillow. Then, very gradually, the flesh around his eyes gathered as laughter seeped into them. He turned his head to look up at Mary. She had been crying soundlessly. At the sight of his smile the silent weeping gave way to huge, choking sobs. A stray tear splattered on to his face, making him laugh aloud. Her own laughter mixed with her crying, causing her to clutch a hand to her heaving chest.

With an effort, he pushed himself half upright. Grimacing and laughing at the same time, he wormed his way from the center of the bed toward the edge. He threw back the blanket and patted the space he had made. She hesitated, looking around at the door. Then, with a laugh, she brushed away her tears with her palm and swung herself on to the bed. Wincing and laughing, he turned and folded her in his arms.

They kissed for a long time. When they finally emerged from the kiss they lay side by side, their faces inches from one another's. Mary's lashes were still webbed with tears. He raised a hand and stroked, very tenderly, at the skin of her forehead around the dressing.

"They offered me a new identity."

She smiled and sniffed. "I know."

Grinning, he took a handful of her hair and gently drew her head back, the better to see into her eyes. "So do you have any ideas for our new name?"

BRIAN MORRISON is the author of two previous novels, *State of Resurrection* and *Blood Brother*. He has spent many years in Paris, but now lives with his wife and two daughters in Devon, England.

AMPBELL ARMSTRONG

ents of Darkness

spended from the LAPD, Charlie Galloway decides his
 has no meaning. But when his Filipino housekeeper is
rdered, Charlie finds a new purpose in tracking the
er. He never expects, though, to be drawn into a
nspiracy that reaches from the Filipino jungles to the
ite House.

azurka

 Frank Pagan of Scotland Yard, it begins with the
rder of a Russian at crowded Waverly Station, Edinburgh. From that moment
 Pagan's life becomes an ever-darkening nightmare as he finds himself
pped in a complex web of intrigue, treachery, and murder.

ambo

per-terrorist Gunther Ruhr has been captured. Scotland Yard's Frank Pagan
st escort him to a maximum security prison, but with blinding swiftness and
utality, Ruhr escapes. Once again, Pagan must stalk Ruhr, this time into an
rth-shattering secret conspiracy.

ainfire

nerican John Rayner is a man on fire with grief and anger over the death of his
werful brother. Some
y it was suicide, but
yner suspects
mething more
ister. His suspicions
ove correct as he
comes trapped in a
viet-made maze of
trayal and terror.

sterisk Destiny

terisk is America's
ost fragile and chilling
cret. It waits some-
ere in the Arizona
sert to pave the way
 world domination...or
mnation. Two men,
hite House aide John
orne and CIA agent
d Hollander, race
 crack the wall of
ence surrounding
sterisk and tell
e world of their
rrifying discovery.

If you would like to receive a HarperPaperbacks catalog, please send your name and address plus $1.00 postage/handling to:

HarperPaperbacks Catalog Request
10 East 53rd St.
New York, NY 10022